BOOKS BY THOMAS ROGERS

AT THE SHORES
THE CONFESSION OF A CHILD OF THE CENTURY

AT THE

SHORES

Thomas Rogers

SIMON AND SCHUSTER
NEW YORK

Copyright © 1980 by Thomas Rogers
All rights reserved
including the right of reproduction
in whole or in part in any form
Published by Simon and Schuster
A Division of Gulf & Western Corporation
Simon & Schuster Building
Rockefeller Center
1230 Avenue of the Americas
New York, New York 10020
SIMON AND SCHUSTER and colophon are trademarks of
Simon & Schuster
Designed by Jeanne Joudry
Manufactured in the United States of America
1 2 3 4 5 6 7 8 9 10
Library of Congress Cataloging in Publication Data

Rogers, Thomas, date.
    At the shores.

    I. Title.
PZ4.R728At   [PS3568.O456]   813'.54   80-36839

ISBN 0-671-24969-X

To Mary Louise Munts, Sister, Solon,
   and (grand)parent of her own Jeremy

Since Love is the son of Plenty and Poverty he gets his fortunes from them. First, having his mother's nature he is always poor; and far from being tender and beautiful as most people think, he is hard and rough and unshod and homeless, lying always on the ground without bedding, sleeping by the doors and in the streets in the open air, always dwelling in want. But from his father he has designs upon beautiful and good things, being brave and go-ahead, and high strung, a mighty hunter always weaving devices, and a successful coveter of widom, a philosopher all his days, a great wizard and sorcerer and sophist. He was born neither mortal nor immortal, but on the same day he is sometimes blooming and alive, sometimes dying, and what he procures in plenty always trickles away so that Love is neither wealthy nor poor nor wise nor ignorant.

—Plato, *The Symposium*

Prologue

To COME out of the lake after a long swim and to fling himself onto the hot sand, that was a pleasure. To feel the sand warming his chest and the sun warming his back, that was a pleasure. And then to sail his Dolphin on a bright summer day, sheet in one hand, tiller in the other, his brown legs braced against the combing as he leaned out to windward using his own weight as leverage to counteract the press of wind against his sail—all that was a pleasure too. It was even a pleasure on windy days to feel the boat tremble, to feel it slip in the water before it went over. And then, grinning in the wave-torn lake, it was somehow a pleasure to watch Phil Forson sail by in his own Dolphin, making the derisory sign at him because he, Engels, had gone over again. Or if the lake were getting rough, instead of giving him the finger, Phil might call out, "You okay, Jerry?"

He always was. One could easily right those Dolphins. Minutes after going over he would be back aboard, dripping from his immersion. Then, with the wet sail flapping in the wind, the wind chilling his wet body, he would collect the boat almost as one collected a horse, pushing down the dagger board with his foot, resetting the tiller, gathering in the sheet, and getting underway again. All that was a great pleasure, but was it greater than to run along the beach either alone or with Forson?

In those days there was nothing but high dune, grass covered, tree crowned for miles to the west. After storms when the beach was wet and hard, he could run for miles seeing nothing but dune and lake, except off to the northwest, where, especially when north winds had cleared the sky, he could see the towers of Chicago thirty miles away across the water. To run, just to run was a very great pleasure . . . the gulls that rested on the empty beach beyond all the houses would start to move as he approached. First they rose to their feet, a dozen at a time. They would begin to walk away from him, and then, if he were coming fast, their wings would open as they too began to run, and he would see white wings, gull wings, arched for flight as they ran and then flapped upward into the air before tucking in their legs and settling into a gull flight that might take them in a wide circle out over the lake and back in to land behind him on the deserted beach where only his footprints disturbed the wave marks on the sand. He liked to run alone.

He swam in the lake, sailed on it, and ran along its shore as if he loved the lake more than he loved Rosalind. And perhaps he did. One could love a lake. Certainly he loved that lake, Lake Michigan, that inland ocean of fresh water. "Michigan" *meant* fresh water, and there it lay, stretched out to the northern horizon, the faintest pale blue on summer mornings as he sat with his arms around his knees beside the pine tree on top of the ridge, waiting for Phil to join him for their morning swim. Phil would come down the path from his house, a beach towel over one shoulder, and then they would go down the dune together, sometimes without even saying "Good morning." Why should they? It was obviously a good morning, with the sun just up and the lake awaiting them. Pale blue in the calm mornings, cloud darkened in the afternoons, wind roughened and white-capped during storms, the lake was always awaiting him. He could not remember a summer day when he had not wanted to be in the lake. He had swum in the rain and in the wind, when wind-driven waves crashed like ocean surf and ran up the beach undercutting the low beach dunes. Those were almost the best swimming days, though he couldn't swim in such waves. He rode them, dove through them, fought with them as the sandbars underfoot developed unexpected pockets. One minute he was waist deep, the next he was up to his armpits with a wave coming down over his head. They could catch you if you didn't catch them. Trying to ride waves into the beach he had gone over the top, had waves break on him, hold him down, and drag him along the fine sand bottom until he was out of breath. And that was almost as good as catching a wave just right and coming into the shallows headfirst in a sea of foam. That was perfect. But it was almost as perfect to be tumbled by a wave, to be dragged on the bottom, even to have one's skin scraped a little. Why not? It was part of the whole experience. The lake could be rough. So, let it be rough with you, because—finally—it would never really hurt you. That was what he had always felt about the lake even before he was a good swimmer, when he was simply a little boy playing in the water betwen beach and sandbar while his mother and Mrs. Forson and Mrs. Hyatt sat a few yards away under their beach umbrellas, keeping watch as he and Anne and Phil and Shirley paddled and splashed. Inner tubes and water wings were their toys then, not Dolphins.

Later they had a raft, a square framework of two-by-fours planked over and kept afloat by oil drums that boomed hollowly when you banged on them. For years the raft had been their chief toy, and how many times had they rushed to the beach to save it when a summer storm blew up and the lake, calm as a millpond at noon, came alive with waves threatening to drag the raft from its mooring, tip it over, and spill its oil drums, scattering them for miles along the beach? How often had they *not* gotten to the beach in time and then had to walk miles, first to collect their drums and then to float them back to their part of the beach, there to reassemble the raft and re-anchor it? They had taken the raft ashore at the end of every day, but how often, at night, after dark, when the roar of the lake grew louder, had they not gone down to drag it higher up the beach away from the encroaching waves? The raft was like a character out of some movie serial, frequently imperiled, frequently beset by dangers, and yet wonderfully durable. For years they had dived from it and played on and around it.

They had thrown golf balls from the raft, white golf balls that sank slowly through the clear water until, just before they settled to the bottom, you caught them, then kicked upward, the golf ball held in the fingers of your outstretched hand so that the others on the raft would see it, the golf ball, emerge first, and then your hand, and so know that you caught the ball before it settled. And gradually, as the summers passed you could throw the ball farther and farther from the raft and still get to it. Jerry even learned to run along the bottom of the lake, his head down near the sand, his feet digging in, his arms back along his sides working like fins as he moved parallel to the bottom faster than anyone could swim underwater. He ran with his eyes open, watching the rippled bottom beneath him, looking up for the descending golf ball, and feeling more like a fish than a boy, though no fish ever surfaced periodically to look at its mother sitting placidly on the beach. No fish ever drew its mother's attention to how far out it had swum. "Hey look!" he shouted to his mother, "flat-footed!" Then, throwing up his arms, he would sink through seven or eight feet of water until he was standing flat-footed on the cold bottom, not realizing his mother had no idea how far below the surface he was actually sinking. "Flat-footed," he and Phil would shout time after time until one day they noticed they were not getting any attention. "We were way out over our heads and you weren't paying attention," Phil said. "What could you have done if I'd started to drown?" Jerry asked, looking down at his soft-bodied, unathletic mother who could swim only a hundred yards. Mrs. Engels had shaken her head. "Not very much, I'm afraid," she'd said, and Jerry had wandered off, awed by the idea that, without having realized it, he'd been on his own in the water and that he and Phil were actually better life-guards for each other than their mothers had ever been.

That was how it went. Often he discovered he was bigger and stronger than he thought and could do things he hadn't believed he could do—as on the day he and Phil swam out to the fishnets for the first time. Swimming to the nets of the Horton Fish Company, a good half-mile from shore, had been a remote ambition for years. Jerry had felt that when he was big and grown-up he would be able to swim out to the fishnets, but one summer afternoon his sister Anne had said, "Jerry," you're really a very good swimmer now. You and Phil are both very good swimmers. I bet you could make it to the fishnets," and with this encouragement he and Phil had set out, Anne alongside in the rowboat encouraging them. And when they made it, rather easily, she egged them to swim out and back without hanging onto the boat. Jerry could still remember the leaden feeling in his arms as he had flogged his way shoreward, Phil far ahead of him by then, Anne still alongside saying urgently, "It's not much farther, Jerry. You can make it. I know you can make it Jerry. You're almost there." He had gone slower, and slower and slower until he seemed barely to be moving through the water. He felt all that was keeping him afloat was Anne's voice. When suddenly there was sand underfoot and he rose and staggered toward the beach with Anne's voice like a paean in his ears crying out to the mothers and the little kids, "They made it! They both made it! Out and back! Jerry made it, too!" None of his victories for the U-High swimming team, those merely professional triumphs, had brought him half the satisfaction he felt then, and yet he could no longer even remember which summer it was that he and Phil first swam out to the nets.

They merged, season into season, the linked summers of youth, until Jerry was clear back in his childhood with bucket and spade making sand castles and drip castles and digging down to water a few feet from the lake. In those days he could hardly get through the waves to the sandbar or stand up on the bar against the force of the waves. If it was at all rough, he had to hang onto someone's hand to keep from being swept off his feet and washed back to the beach. They formed human chains, with Mr. Hyatt, Mr. Forson, or Jerry's own father standing out where the waves broke, anchoring a whole line of kids whose light bodies were getting washed around in the broken waves. But even in those days when a one-foot wave could knock him down, he still felt the lake could never really hurt him. There was nothing there to be alarmed about, no rocks, no icky seaweed, no crabs or flounders, nothing but fresh water and clean sand and silver minnows inshore between bar and beach. He could remember floating face down, eyes open, mouth open, doing the dead man's float while beneath him a school of minnows moved slowly through the clear water. Or again, years later, when they had the heavy cypress rowboat that was so hard to get into the water and so hard to pull up again on the beach, he could remember rowing in it thirty yards offshore and looking down to the sunlit bottom where a turtle was slowly walking out toward deep water. It was the only turtle he had ever seen in all the summers, and it was not even a snapper, so how could you feel afraid of a sunlit lake that had only minnows and silver perch and a single solemn turtle trudging north? How could you fear a lake like that, even if it was a lake 300 miles long?

Imagine! A lake so big that Jerry Engels, who had grown up at its southern tip, had never even seen the Straits of Mackinac where Huron and Michigan meet, and did not even know how to pronounce "Mackinac" until he heard Rosalind say it correctly one day when she was describing a cruise she was going to take with her grandparents. He was a child of the shallows and the sandbars. When he sat on the ridge looking north, he had no real idea of what was up there. On August afternoons when the cry "The boats are coming" was raised, and everyone rushed to the porch to look north to where the blue water, normally empty, was now flecked with white sails as the big yachts appeared one after another, he thought he was seeing part of the Chicago to Mackinac Race. And as the boats drew nearer, heading for the harbor at Michigan City twelve miles to the east, he would see spinnakers set and bellied hard in the wind, and think that those yachts had come booming all the way down the lake from fabled Mackinac, though actually he was watching only the middle leg of the Tri-City Race. Still, this was a lake on which you *could* have a 600-mile race in big boats, a lake on which violent storms far to the north *could* break up the lumber barges and ore freighters and cause waves to pound ashore hundreds of miles to the south where there might be no wind at all. Those, in fact, were the best waves for riding because they were heavier and more regular than the wind-whipped waves of local storms.

Ships sank and people did drown in this lake. How could you have a body of water that large in which no one had ever drowned? But this was a lake, not the sea, and though it might take lives it never tortured men with thirst. One could drink the water in which one drowned. Death would come quickly or not at all, for though it was a big lake one could not float for days or weeks, helpless on a raft or a bit of wreckage, suffering from sun and thirst. Such fates took place elsewhere, out on the wide oceans of the world. Here, on this great inland lake, one either drowned or froze to death at once, or else one survived. Storms here never reached the intensity of hurricanes or typhoons. They came quickly, and though they might last through three-day blows, they went away again, having swept the southern beaches clean, washing the flotsam and jetsam high up against the beach dunes, leaving the beach itself firm and hard and clean so that Jerry Engels could run along the beach, knowing that his footprints, his naked footprints, were the only ones on the beach between Indiana Shores and Burns Ditch six miles to the west. . . . Years later when he was in college, his roommate Carlos once said, "Your Indiana Shores is like the seacoast of Bohemia," and it was. His lake, his shore, his dunes, and woods, and swamps were as wonderful and improbable as the Bohemian coast, for there, in sight of the towers of Chicago across the water, with the open hearth furnaces of Gary only sixteen miles to the west, he had shuffled along the beach through singing sand, seen flocks of bluebirds resting on the telephone wires, and walked through fields of bottle gentians. He had stood at the crest of the live dune and looked down on oak woods and lupine-filled meadows that were going to be buried as the dune shifted southeast. On windy days he had even felt the dune moving as he stood there, the wind-driven sand stinging his bare legs while wild grasses bent and tossed and traced feathery patterns on the wind-rippled dune. . . . He just had to laugh when he told people he had grown up in Indiana and saw they were thinking of cows and corn and silos, for what he was thinking of was a log cabin on a wooded ridge with a large cottonwood in front of it and a clump of junipers nearby in which a pair of cardinals lived. A wren built her nest every spring just above the cabin door, and from the porch every summer evening one could hear the whippoorwills cry from behind the live dune. He had found a hummingbird one morning hanging by its beak from the porch screen and held it in his hand thinking its neck was broken, only to feel it revive on his palm, move, sit up, and then dart away in hummingbird flight. That was his Indiana, a place of birds and wild flowers and animals, and to get there one left the Indiana most people thought about and drove north a mile across a swamp where red-winged blackbirds sat on the cattails, where beavers dammed the slowly moving water, and where blue flag and turk's cap lilies grew in the ditches along the road, which was the only road into town. If you could call it a town where there were no stores and in those days only thirty houses. In his earliest memories the mail was not even brought into town. It was delivered to a communal mailbox out on Route 12, and walking for the mail was a real expedition for the kids as they picked their way barefoot along the sandy ruts of the unpaved roads, stopping to eat blueberries, stopping to chew sassafras leaves, and stopping—once—to watch in wonder as a mother skunk led her five kittens across the road in front of them.

It was a wild place then, a place that had never quite developed into the country club community which had been planned in the 1920s, for the Depression had cast its spell on Indiana Shores. The Club House and the Guest House, large log buildings atop the highest dune in town, were seldom used now, the golf course had reverted to peat bog and oak wood, and the planned yacht harbor had never been dredged. Even now when the war was over and new houses were going up, even now there were no community tennis courts. That and that alone struck Jerry as an imperfection. There should be courts. Otherwise, the Shores was a perfect place to have grown up, his family the perfect family, their cabin the perfect summer home, and his girlfriend Rosalind the perfect girl.

The Boy Who
Liked Girls

FOR AS far back in his consciousness as he could go there had always been three women in his life: his mother, his sister, and his girl. The difference was that Mother and Sister were always the same women, whereas the role of girl had been filled by what seemed like a cast of thousands.

He treated his first girl, a disheveled doll, with apache roughness, dragging her around by an arm or a leg. Yet he loved her. He refused to go to sleep unless she was beside him, and he could still vaguely recall the strange feeling—it might have been pathos—when he observed her one day hanging by her head between the slats of his crib. Probably by then his affections were already moving onward to a certain Louise, the girl next door. He had played with her under the spirea bushes on Davis Avenue in Whiting, Indiana, and he associated her with the lilies of the valley that grew under the spireas and with the patch of bare dirt where they had made mud pies. Then Louise's parents moved and she began to fade from his consciousness until now she was simply a sweet blur with a pink ribbon tucked into the farthest recesses of his memory. Most of his earliest loves were like that. He could not even remember the name of the girl in first grade who sat next to him on the rug while Miss Miller read stories. One morning during story time she vomited almost into his lap, and he was astounded to see she had had carrots in her stomach. No one he knew ate carrots for breakfast. It made that girl even more fascinating, and for days thereafter he watched her closely, wondering if she were going to vomit again. She never did, and gradually he lost interest in her. His tendency then and for many years thereafter was toward fickleness and promiscuity.

He loved the girls in his class, the girls on the block, the maid at home, his sister's friends, some of his mother's friends, and all his teachers except Miss Miller who wore a red wig and scared him. He even loved girls he just happened to see out the window of the car. The Engels family was driving out to the Shores one weekend when he fell in love with a girl he saw standing on the bank of the industrial canal in Whiting. Traffic was stopped along Indianapolis Boulevard to allow a tanker to make its way into the Sinclair Refinery. For several minutes Jerry looked at the girl. Two little boys were wrestling with each other almost at her feet. Behind her there was a shack and a line of washing strung between two cottonwoods. He could not understand why a pretty girl like that was watching those boys struggle with each other in the cindery dirt of the canal bank. Then, just as traffic started to move again, it came to him that she lived there. That shack was her house, and those boys were her brothers, and their mother (who had done the washing he could see) was too busy to watch her children herself so the girl had to see that her brothers did not roll down the bank and drown in the oil-scummed water of the canal. This insight (or guess) heightened the beauty the girl held for him and connected her in his mind with his own sister, Anne.

It was impossible for him to sort out all that Anne meant

to him. Anne knew him better than anyone else, even his mother. Anne knew, for instance, that he was a coward, and that he would go to extraordinary lengths to avoid a fight with other boys. He could hide his cowardice from his parents, and from his friends, and even from the very boys who were inclined to pick on him. He treated such boys with a special, assumed friendliness as though he were totally unaware they considered him a sissy because he liked to play with girls. Sometimes he fooled them, but he never fooled Anne who always knew which boys worried and frightened him. "Jerry," she would say, "you don't have to be afraid of Alan. I was looking at him on the playground. He's no stronger than you are. I was looking at his arms. They're no bigger than yours. Look at your arm. Look what a muscle you can make. You could beat up Alan. I know you could." And thus encouraged he had eventually fought with the various Alans and Jeromes and Patricks who plagued his boyhood. And as he scuffled with and hit at them in back-yards and alleys he could generally hear his sister's voice on the sidelines urging him on and offering tactical advice. "Bite him, Jerry!" Anne would yell. "He bit you, you can bite him."

Anne not only helped him preserve his honor as a boy, she helped him with girls. He would describe to her some third grade beauty he admired. "Tell her you love her," Anne always said. Anne was a dynamic, do-it-now sister. Sometimes she was frighteningly dynamic. "Or I'll tell her if you want me to," she might add, and Jerry would experience a moment of exquisite terror. "Oh no!" he would cry, half wanting Anne to go ahead anyway. Often she did go ahead, cornering the girl during recess and saying, bluntly, "My brother likes you." Then, his secret in the open, Jerry would watch anxiously for the girl's reaction. If she stuck out her tongue at him, his heart would break, but if she refused to look at him, or if she looked away when she caught him staring at her from his desk in Miss Shepherd's homeroom, then he would take heart, and during the next recess he might try to talk to her or to hold her hand during a game of Red Rover.

He got used to his reputation for liking girls and learned how to behave when boys came up to him and said challengingly, "Do you like Mary Catherine Sobieski?" or "Did you hold hands with Ellen Kluzik?" "Who told you that?" he would say with amazement if this looked like a protective older brother. There was, after all, no shame involved in trying to avoid a fight with a bigger boy. But if the question were put by someone his own size, a rival or, more likely, one of those boys who thought it sissified to hang around girls, Jerry would say, as confidently as possible, "Yes, we held hands," or "Yes, I like her." He had learned that the more boldly he admitted he liked girls, the less trouble he was going to have from his contemporaries.

His boldness, however, could collapse in an instant, as on Valentine's Day in fourth grade. He had sent a valentine to every girl in class, only he addressed them upside down: *Jerry Engels to Elizabeth Ann Palmer*. When Mrs. Tyson opened the box they had all been stuffing valentines into, she kept reading out Jerry's name. He would go up in front of class to get his valentine, excited to know who was sending him one, only to find it was one of his own which he would have to hand back to Mrs. Tyson or else deliver personally to the girl for whom it was intended. The class caught on and began to laugh at him. At first he laughed at himself as he delivered his own valentines. Yet even while he was laughing, his cheeks had begun to burn, and when all the valentines were delivered and class was over he fled home to throw himself into his mother's arms.

There he found peace. His mother was beautiful. She was calm. She was comforting and helpful. In the morning he went into the big bedroom where his parents slept and where his crib had stood against the wall where his mother's vanity table was now placed. Long after he could really tie his own shoelaces, he pretended that he needed his mother's help. He would sit on the blue linen carpet in a patch of sunlight in which he could see motes of dust dancing and raise first one foot and then the other. He did not watch how his mother tied his laces; he concentrated on her face bending toward him through the dusty sunshine. Then, his laces tied, he set off for school in high spirits. At lunchtime he raced home— they lived just across the street from school—and his mother was there to sit with him while he ate even if she were going off later to a luncheon of her own. Then again, after school, he would feel her presence even if she were not at home. The maid—Julia for many years, then Helen—would welcome him and feed him and give him a message from his mother. Finally, at night his mother always came into his bedroom to stand beside his bed for a moment, to touch the sheet that covered him, to touch his cheek, and then to turn out the light and close his bedroom door.

She liked flowers and dogs and the country. At the Shores in early spring she took him walking in the woods to look for trailing arbutus. It sometimes bloomed while there were still patches of snow on the ground, and he could remember crouching to smell the arbutus and inhaling not just the fragrance of these tiny white flowers but a deeper, broader smell of cold earth and wet leaves, which somehow, along with the arbutus, became associated in his mind with his mother. From her he learned the names of flowers and trees and birds. She let him keep rabbits in a hutch in the back-yard in Whiting. Later, when they lived in an apartment in Chicago, she let him raise a pair of Easter ducklings. He swam them in the bathtub and actually kept his promise to her that he would clean up after them. Over the years she let him have turtles and cats and a brief-lived owl. He had a tank of fish and a chameleon, and his mother saw to it that there were always rotten bananas in the house to provide the fruit flies on which the chameleon lived. But she never let him have the monkey he yearned for. There was always that final reservation. At Christmas time every year when he pleaded

27

with her to give him a monkey, when he vowed passionately that if only he had a monkey he would never ask for anything else, he knew even as he worked himself up almost to tears that he was not going to get what he was asking for. There was a limit to her love, a beautiful reserve which he could never penetrate. When he crept out of his bed at night it was never in order to climb into bed with his mother and father. Instead he tiptoed down the hall to Anne's room.

She welcomed him into her bed where they played Orphans, a game of her invention that involved pulling the bedclothes over their heads and pretending they were all alone in a storm, or drifting together in a boat, or huddled on an ice floe somewhere in the North. When Anne whispered to him at night, "Jerry, you sneak into my room when the lights are out," he always gave a quick, emphatic nod. And on those nights when he knew he was going to sneak into Anne's room, he felt a special tenderness toward his mother when she came to tuck him in. It was the tenderness you felt when you knew you were going to disappoint someone who loved you. His mother did not like him to sneak into Anne's room at night. He knew that. He had been told not to do it, and so when he knew he was going to do it he felt particularly touched by his mother's kind, trusting, loving goodnights. She was so good to him, and she didn't realize . . .

Sometimes, of course, she did realize. He and Anne would play too long, and he would fall asleep in Anne's bed where his mother would find him the next morning. "Now Jerry," she would say, "you promised me you wouldn't do this," and then he would remember that he *had* promised, and he would feel even sorrier that he had disappointed her again. She expected him to be good, and he wasn't always as good as he wanted to be. "I won't do it anymore," he would say, and she would nod, apparently satisfied, apparently believing him, though after he had been caught in Anne's bed, his mother usually reminded him for several nights running that he was to stay in his own bed at night. "You have your bear," she would say, reminding him of the teddy bear that had replaced the doll he had outgrown. "You have your bear, and if you're thirsty here's a glass of water beside your bed." He sometimes tried to pretend he had woken up thirsty and gone to the bathroom for a drink and wandered sleepily into Anne's room by mistake. No one really believed this, but his mother showed respect even for his lies by putting a glass of water beside his bed. It added to his love for her and made him feel quite sure he would never disappoint her again. Only, of course, he did. How could he resist, especially when Anne encouraged it? "Jerry, you come into my room tonight," she would whisper, and at once all his promises and his sorrow at disappointing his mother would be forgotten.

When he was ten his family moved from Whiting to Chicago so that Anne, who was three years older than Jerry and four years ahead of him in school, could start ninth grade at the University of Chicago High School. Jerry was put into the fifth grade of the University Laboratory School.

He was not happy that year. The only person he knew at school was Rosalind Ingleside whose family owned a summer place in Indiana Shores. He had seen Rosalind in the summer, but her family lived more than a mile down the beach, and mostly he played at his end of the Shores. He was not confident of his relationship with Rosalind, who seemed to be one of the most popular girls in fifth grade. Also, in Chicago he could see how much richer her family was than his own. After school she was sometimes picked up by a big black limousine with a chauffeur at the wheel. It was her grandmother's limousine. He had no grandmother like that. It seemed to him he had nothing like what other kids at the Lab School had. One girl got five dollars a week for her allowance; he got twenty-five cents. One boy had free passes to half the movie houses in Chicago because his family owned the chain. Jerry's family didn't own anything except their summer cabin, though Jerry's father was now Associate Director of Research of the Standard Oil Company. Yet in Chicago even the Standard Oil Company seemed to dwindle in importance. Whiting was a company town, Chicago was not; and one boy at school told Jerry that the Standard Oil Company of Indiana was not even the largest oil company in the country. Jerry knew this was false because for years he had been seeing a billboard at the edge of Whiting which read: *Entering Whiting, Home of Standard Oil, Site of the World's Largest Complete Oil Refinery*. He complained to his father that John Williams had said Standard wasn't the largest oil company in the country. "It is, isn't it?" he said, but his father shook his head. Texaco and Standard of New Jersey were larger, he said. The billboard only meant that at Whiting, Standard of Indiana produced a wider range of petroleum products from candles to asphalt than was produced at any comparable refinery. This was terrible news to Jerry. He had staked his reputation at school on the size of Standard Oil. He felt deceived. He felt his father had let him down. His father dwindled along with the size of the company.

And classes were terrible. French slayed Jerry. Everyone else had already had a year of French so he was behind to begin with and fell further behind every day. What was it all about? What was this *pas de, pas de, pas de* everyone shouted when Monsieur Coppée waved his warty forefinger at the class? *Pas de, pas de, pas de* they all yelled, Jerry along with them, though on his painfully done homework he was careful to write, *je n'ai pas des pommes*, having at least learned that *de* was singular and *des* was plural; so if you were saying (in French) that you didn't have any apples you would use *des*. M. Coppée blew up when he came across Jerry's *pas des pommes*. "You pay no attention," he said angrily. "You're stupid. We have rehearsed it a thousand times and still you write *pas des pommes*. Out!" And the warty forefinger motioned Jerry from the room. Jerry left, crushed. He had never been called stupid and thrown out of class before. Schoolwork was not his strong point, but until he started going to the Lab School he had never considered he was dumb.

And then the whole business of being a sissy came back to haunt him all over again. Because Rosalind Ingleside was the only person in class he already knew, and because she also happened to be the prettiest girl in class, and because she was really a nice, friendly girl, he got to know her. When they left Miss Hozier's homeroom to walk to Music or to Art or to French he walked with Rosalind. Through her he began to know Anne de Lancey and Carolyn Webster and Rachel Fein. This was good. They were obviously the girls you would most want to know, and he was soon beginning to feel half in love with all of them. Rachel lived in his direction and he tried walking her home after school. But the better he got to know the girls, the worse his situation became with the boys. They could not decide whether he was just a plain sissy or whether he was one of those natty little beaus, a premature spark starting early on his career as a lady's man. Neither type of boy is everyone's favorite, though the spark is at least tolerable. The trouble was that Jerry seemed to be neither the one nor the other. He didn't dress like a beau or talk and behave like a spark. He could hardly dance at all, and he felt terribly embarrassed by his clumsiness during Social Dancing periods at Sunny Gym, periods that were almost as terrible to him as French itself. Nor did he seem to be the normal sort of sissy. He liked soccer. He was a pretty good swimmer. He could run. What was he then?

If he had known what he was he would have been glad to give the other boys some help in categorizing him, but he didn't know. He had no ideas about himself. "Are you Jewish?" Jimmy Kaplan asked him one day. "What's Jewish?" Jerry asked, thinking this might be the answer to what he was. "You're not Jewish," Kaplan said, giving him a shove in the chest. So he was not that either. "What are we?" he asked his mother when he came home that day. He was feeling particularly discouraged. His mother, when she understood the question, explained to him that they were Congregationalists who were not sure if God really existed. It didn't seem to help. He felt mired in ignominy. The only boy at school who wanted to play with him was Bernard Pear, a fat boy, one of the class oddballs. This was not the sort of friend Jerry was used to having. In Whiting he had palled around with the top boys in his class. Phil Forson was his best friend. "Couldn't we go back to Whiting?" he asked his mother.

They took long walks together in Jackson Park. While Jip chased after squirrels and sniffed around the edges of the lagoons, he and his mother talked everything over. "Maybe if you had a party for some of the boys and girls you like . . ." his mother suggested. "They wouldn't come," said Jerry. "I'm sure Rosalind Ingleside would come," Mrs. Engels said. "You know Rosalind from the Shores." "Mother," he cried, "Rosalind is the most popular girl in class. She's only being nice to me." That was what hurt the most, his feeling that even the girls he'd gotten to know were only being nice. He couldn't have said why, but that seemed to him the ultimate degradation—for girls to be nice. "Rosalind wouldn't come. I won't ask her," he said, and he began to behave badly.

He threw a rock through a window of a house on Dorchester and ran away before he was caught. At school he stole candy from the school shop and was detected and punished. Then he punched Jimmy Kaplan without any warning—in passing more or less—and shouted, "You're Jewish, you're Jewish!" He had learned what Jewish was. Worst of all, he began to be rude to the very girls he liked most. At Social Dancing one afternoon it was Girls' Choice. Jerry was sitting by himself on the boys' side of the gym floor. He saw Rosalind coming toward him. He looked away. When she stopped just in front of his outstretched feet he refused to look up. He had never felt so miserable in all his life. She asked him to dance. Mulishly he shook his head. That night he cried himself to sleep.

His life became a burden to him. There was no way out. Anne tried to buck him up. "Jerry," she said, "you'll make friends. I know you'll make friends. Look at all the friends you had in Whiting. People always like you." He shook his head. Life had changed. He was not what he once was. He would never make friends again. Now he had only his family, Jip, and his turtles, one of which was dying.

Then one afternoon Gloria Offenbach kissed him.

"Come here," she said, beckoning to him from a little cloakroom off the main corridor of Blaine Hall. Listlessly Jerry obeyed. "Come here," she said again, receding still farther into the cloakroom. Faintly curious, Jerry followed. Then she threw her arms around him and kissed his lips. "Sssh!" she said, as if the noise in his soul were audible to her ears. "Don't tell anyone," she added, shoving him away with some strength. It was the beginning of what he thereafter considered the first great affair of his life.

Gloria liked him for his badness. She was a nice girl, but she wanted to be bad herself. So, as Jerry's reputation as a bad boy grew, she grew more and more interested in him until finally she threw herself at him that afternoon in the cloakroom. He understood this. She told him in fact that she hoped he'd hit Jimmy Kaplan again, and to please her he did. If he'd known how, he would have robbed a bank for her. As it was, he did everything he could to recommend himself to her. He began to fight with other boys, thereby paying off some grudges he himself felt for their earlier treatment of him. To his pleasure he discovered that fighting at the Lab School was easier and less painful than fighting at George Rogers Clark School in Whiting where the boys tended to stand up and really hit at each other. At the Lab School boys argued, then insulted each other, and finally worked themselves up to pushing, shoving, and ultimately wrestling. They tended not to use their fists, which was fine with Jerry. He liked wrestling better than hitting. He provoked quarrels. In the locker room of Sunny Gym he would grab a boy's gym clothes and toss them on top of the lockers. He snapped his towel at unoffending rear ends. He behaved very badly, and the quarrels he provoked in the locker room spilled out onto the gym field and into the courtyard of Blaine Hall. He was particularly cruel to Bernard Pear, persecuting him at school and chasing him all the way home one day.

His reward for all this was another surreptitious kiss from Gloria, flashing looks as they passed in the hall, and an occasional squeeze of the hand when no one was looking. Their love began in secrecy and remained a secret. Just as Anne had never acknowledged her role in encouraging Jerry to come to her room at night, so Gloria never publicly allied herself with Jerry. He could and did choose her as his partner in Social Dancing, and he showed great ingenuity in managing to be near her without seeming to single her out, but he accepted her terms. He did not insist on trying to walk her home, though he did learn where she lived and frequently walked Jip past her apartment house on Dorchester. He loved her, and the thought that she really loved him was enough to console him for the isolation and the daily warfare of his life at school.

But then, oddly enough, that isolation showed signs of ending. The boys in his class started to like him. They didn't understand it, but this Jerry Engels, who had at first seemed like such a softy and a sissy, was proving himself to be not exactly a tough guy but at least a scrappy one. He did not win all his fights, in fact he lost most of them, but he fought. And because he was happy once more, there was no particular bitterness in his fighting. It semed more like rowdy enthusiasm than anything else, and indeed Jerry himself began to feel that some of the boys he was regularly scuffling with were actually his friends. One day, coming out of Blaine Hall after school, he encountered Jimmy Kaplan and Ernie Hill with their arms on each other's shoulders, hanging together the way boys did when they were feeling good and looking for something to do. Jerry stiffened, thinking that if a fight didn't break out there would at least be an exchange of ritual insults. The three of them eyed each other. Then Kaplan said, "Hey, Engels, want to go up to Stineway's with us for a sundae?" Jerry nodded. Kaplan and Hill separated, and suddenly Jerry found himself between them, their arms on his shoulders, his arms on theirs. He wondered if he was letting Gloria down by reverting to his normal pacific behavior, but this reconciliation with Kaplan took place too late in the school year for its effects to be known, and then in sixth grade everything was different.

Gloria herself had changed. She was now intensely social. She moved through the corridors of Blaine Hall surrounded by a bevy of best friends, all of whom looked at Jerry significantly whenever they saw him. Gloria had told them something, though Jerry could never be sure exactly what. "What does she say about me?" he asked Gloria's friends, who would only laugh and roll their eyes. When he asked Gloria herself, she grew lofty and remote. "What do you mean?" she said, as if there had never been anything between them worth talking about. "You know," he said, referring to that first kiss in the cloakroom and to the other kiss he had earned by his fighting. "I don't know anything," she said, as if they were perfect strangers, but the next time she passed him in company with her friends Jerry felt all eyes were upon him, and then from behind his back he heard half-smothered giggles. He was wild with curiosity. He knew he was supposed to have Done Something. Furthermore there seemed to be notes he was supposed to have written Gloria. He sometimes saw her and her friends looking at pieces of paper they hid when they saw him coming. If these were really love letters, then Gloria must have written them to herself, but she would not admit that either. She teased and mystified him unmercifully, and because of her behavior he was acquiring a new reputation at school. This new reputation was that of a Lady Killer. He was supposed to be a dangerous boy where girls were concerned.

Though undeserved, this reputation was not in Jerry's

opinion a harmful one. Nice girls like Rosalind and Rachel and Anne de Lancey did not shun him because of it, and some boys actually admired him for it. His reputation with the boys had stabilized now. The Forsons had moved to Chicago and Phil was a classmate, which further solidified Jerry's position at the Lab school. Phil was his greatest friend, and in any group of boys Phil was bound to be generally admired. He was strong. He was good at all sports. Letter grades were not given at the Lab School, but Phil was clearly at the top of the class academically. With a friend like Phil at his side, Jerry finally assumed his natural position in the class hierarchy. He was not a leader, rather he was the close friend of the class leaders. When they balloted in the spring of that year for the next year's seventh grade offices, John Williams was elected Class President, Phil was elected one of the Representatives to the Student Council, Stan Wengrowitz and Ernie Hill were Boys' Club Representatives, and Jerry was rewarded with the position of Treasurer, a position in which he was destined to be a dismal failure, though no one foresaw that at the time. He was happy. He had arrived. He thought no more of returning to Whiting. His main desire was simply to straighten out his reputation with the girls, particularly with Gloria.

She was a bewildering girl. Sometimes he thought she actually disliked him. Other times she seemed glad to receive the attention he now openly paid her. At a Colony Club party in the spring they roller skated together at the White City all one afternoon, and afterward he felt that at last things were on a simple and natural footing. She would be his girlfriend and he would be her boyfriend and henceforth things would go swimmingly, but before the year ended she had become mysterious once more, and then in seventh grade she changed again, this time physically. She was now taller than he was by an inch or so, and she had developed one of the most noticeable busts in class. When they ate fudge sundaes together at Stineway's she would lean across him to get another napkin, thus pressing her soft breast against his chest, reminding them both that she was getting to be a big girl. She dressed up, too, and when they went to the movies together she began appearing in heels that lifted her a good three or four inches above his level. He seemed to be losing ground with her, sinking almost, a sensation that deepened during the sudden clinches she sometimes initiated as they sat together at the back of the Piccadilly Theater or when he walked her home after a party at Carolyn Webster's house.

Carolyn gave a party every Friday night to which virtually the same group of kids came week after week. These were not exactly formal parties. They were gatherings at which the kids played games, Kick-It in particular. There were Cokes and potato chips. In good weather they might do something outdoors in the backyard of the Webster house on Harper Avenue with the Illinois Central trains periodically roaring along almost overhead. But on Sadie Hawkins' Day every year there was a real party during which the girls chased the boys, and on Sadie Hawkins' Day in seventh grade Jerry had the sensation of being physically overwhelmed by Gloria.

He had let her see which direction he was heading so she would be able to catch him when the girls started out in pursuit of the boys. Yet when she did catch him in the Utleys' yard, just across from International House, he got more than he had bargained for. He thought when she caught him that they would hug, perhaps even kiss, but instead she came running straight at him, knocked him to the ground, and fell on top of him. He had never been hit that hard even in soccer. He was winded. Her weight pinned him to the ground, her face was just above his, she was breathing heavily from the chase. He wanted to say, "Get off me," but he couldn't. They lay face to face. Time seemed to stretch out. He could feel her breasts pressed between them even through the thickness of the overcoats they were both wearing. She looked down at him, her expression inscrutable in the darkness. He knew he should kiss her, but she had hurt him when she knocked him down, and now he didn't feel like kissing her. He wanted to get her off him. Neither of them said anything. Then at last, when they seemed to have been lying together for an age, he felt her stir. She was going to get up, and at that moment he felt a return of love. "Don't," he said, putting his arms around her, his pains forgotten. She hesitated. "Don't get up," he said again, tightening his grip on her, and this time she made up her mind. She seemed to press down on him more heavily than ever. Their lips met, and he received what was really his first passionate kiss.

It was also almost the last kiss he ever got from Gloria. By spring, when he called her to suggest they see a movie together, she would put him off on the grounds that she knew the movie wasn't any good. Then one evening when he had called her just to chat, she ended the conversation after fifteen minutes by saying she had to hang up because she was expecting another call. He knew then that he had lost her, that is, if he had ever had her in the first place, which wasn't entirely clear. It saddened him because she was a likeable girl aside from being exciting. She kept white mice which bred all the time, and in sixth grade she had sometimes invited him up to her apartment to look at nests of tiny baby mice, still pink all over. And in the seventh grade she began to write poems which she gave him to read. He could still remember one about rain that fell down, down, down, down. He missed her, though he kept seeing her every school day for another year until she disappeared from his life at the beginning of ninth grade. Yet, by the end of seventh he had lost the sense that there was something intimate between them. It evaporated after that first passionate kiss for which he was not ready.

His sadness over the loss of Gloria was mitigated by the fact that already, late in seventh grade, he was falling in love with Anne de Lancey. He was by then in deep trouble over his accounts as Class Treasurer. He seemed to have misappropriated, or perhaps just lost, thirteen dollars and sixty-seven cents. Anne was Class Secretary and knew about the shortage. Finally Jerry made up the deficit by cashing in one of his War Savings Bonds. It made him feel unpatriotic to do so, but there was no other way out. He announced that the money had been there all along in a different cash box from the one which had patently not contained the missing funds. He even bought a second cash box and scuffed it up to make it look used. "I forgot there were two boxes," he told Anne, not sure she believed any of this. Nevertheless he avoided public disgrace. At the end of the year he bequeathed to the next seventh grade class two cash boxes and an even balance.

Throughout most of eighth grade he thought of Anne de Lancey as his girlfriend. He tried to impress her with his seriousness and trustworthiness. She was Class Vice-President that year, and Jerry's pals had made him Class Secretary, a position he accepted feeling it could not cost him more than the Treasurership had and might give him an opportunity to show Anne his true worth. At meetings he kept trying to come up with good ideas about how the eighth grade could aid the war effort. The war dominated things that year. It was 1944. Gas was rationed. Sugar was rationed. Tires were hard to get. One was supposed to save toothpaste tubes and tinfoil and collect scrap iron. Jerry conceived the idea that everyone in eighth grade should pledge fifty percent of his or her allowance to buy War Savings Stamps, but this was rejected as unrealistic. He had another idea. He proposed that U-High boys should volunteer for sentry duty in front of those university buildings, such as Sunny Gym, which had been requisitioned by the Navy, thus freeing Navy sentries for higher purposes. He rather liked the idea of himself standing on the steps of Sunny with a rifle in his hands. This idea, too, was rejected as unrealistic. It was too bad, he thought. He was trying to do his best. He wanted Anne to know he was heart and soul in the war effort.

That being so, why did he start to fool around with the map in the Language Corridor of Belfield Hall? The Student

Council had put up a world map over which the battle lines were traced on a sheet of clear plastic. The idea was to give U-High students a bird's-eye view of where our armies were in Europe and Asia. It was a good idea. Jerry had favored the map when it was first hung. But armies move so slowly that one day Jerry and Ernie Hill got the bright idea of speeding things up. Surreptitiously they traced a large American salient into the heart of Germany. They captured Berlin overnight. This gave ideas to other kids, and soon the map became a local battleground between Jerry and Ernie, who were all for winning the war instantly, and Bernard Pear and Christian Falks, who kept staging fearful Axis counteroffensives. Jerry would glance at the map Monday morning and discover the Germans were in Moscow and the Japanese in Honolulu. Then he and Ernie would have to find some quiet moment to alter these positions. Finally a third group of kids, whose identity Jerry never discovered, joined the fray. Switzerland entered the war and began to conquer all of Central Europe, and at that point the map was taken down. Editorials appeared in the *U-High Midway* and the Principal even referred to the scandal at a school assembly during which he also announced that David Ingleside had been killed during the Battle of the Bulge. The war was no joke.

Why then had he done it, Jerry wondered. Why had he risked being exposed as a jokester when he really wanted to do his best so that Anne would admire him? She liked him, but he wanted more than that. It was not enough just to take her to the movies and to Colony Club parties and to chat with her on the telephone at night. He wanted her to think of him as a serious person, and he was not sure that was how she saw him. His reputation in school was that of a lightweight, a potential goof-up. When he rose at Class Assemblies to read the minutes of the preceding meeting, pals of his like Ernie and Jimmy Kaplan booed him in advance, and there was often a ripple of laughter. He felt a pang of regret at this treatment. No one made fun of John Williams, who had repeated as Class President. No one laughed at Phil, who was the first eighth grader ever to be elected Boys' Club Vice-President. But he was not like them. Somehow he did not command respect. He lacked dignity. Yet, since he remained popular with both girls and boys, maybe it didn't make any difference?

He *was* popular. He could see it in the way people looked at him, and feel it in the way he was welcome wherever he went. He had something that people liked, even if they didn't admire him. But what was it? He didn't know. He had never understood himself. He had always thought he was ordinary. In fact he knew he was ordinary, and yet people reacted in a special way to him. Even teachers reacted specially. Miss Collins, for instance, who taught Latin, treated him differently from her other poor students, maybe because she remembered his sister who had been her best Latin student in twenty years. Whatever the reason, he could feel and even be embarrassed by the difference between Miss Collins' treatment of him and of Marjorie McConkey, for instance. Miss Collins would say sharply to Marjorie, "Have you studied? Did you do your homework?" to which Marjorie would respond with a toss of her head. "I did what you told us to do, I just didn't understand it." "I'm not surprised," Miss Collins would say. To Jerry's failures, however, she showed a milder side of her personality. "I didn't finish this passage," he would confess, and she would say, more in sorrow than anger, "You've got to buckle down, Jerry."

It was unfair. He felt the unfairness in the way Miss Collins indulged him and snapped at Marjorie. Often after class he would join Marjorie in the Language Corridor. "I hate her! I hate her! I hate her!" Marjorie would say, clutching her zipper notebook to her chest and beating on it with her fist. Jerry nodded sympathetically, though in fact he rather liked Miss Collins. Was that it? Did Miss Collins know who liked her and who didn't, and did that account for the differences in her treatment of students? But how could she know? Jerry

41

had never said or done anything to show Miss Collins he liked her. He smiled at her, of course, but then he smiled at everyone.

He wondered sometimes if the indulgence that people, especially women, showed him was due to the fact that he was getting to be good-looking. He was thirteen now, and he could see he looked nicer than most of the other boys. He had no spots. He was neither thin nor fat. He was beginning to grow. Probably that was one reason why a girl like Anne de Lancey liked him. Among the girls she was the equivalent of John Williams and Phil Forson and Stan Wengrowitz among the boys. She got all As, she was a leader, she was good at girls' sports, and by rights her boyfriend should be one of the top boys in the class, but maybe she preferred him, Jerry thought, just because he was better looking than Phil or Stan. But would such a consideration apply to a woman like Miss Collins who was fifty? What difference could it make to her what a thirteen-year-old boy looked like? And yet it made some difference to him that she had very fine, slender ankles and that under the fuddy-duddy clothes she wore, you could see she had a real bosom. In Latin class he often found himself just looking at Miss Collins' ankles, or at her bosom. (It was one of the reasons he did so poorly in Latin.) So if he cared about her looks, maybe she cared about his. It was something to think about, anyway.

There was a lot to think about, though unfortunately the things he thought about most were never taught in class. He thought about people, particularly girls. He was growing promiscuous again. The years of his involvement with Gloria had given him the feeling that he should always have a single main girlfriend, but toward the end of eighth grade he found himself feeling a trifle confined, even a little bored with Anne de Lancey. She was very intelligent and good-looking, of course, but Rosalind Ingleside was even better looking, and (in a different style) so were Rachel Fein and Sandra Wertenbaker and Marylynn Morris. . . . Actually he took Carolyn

Webster to the last Colony Club party of the year. He felt he probably had more in common with her than with anyone else. He had never sensed that she cared passionately about the war, which was ending anyway, and besides they were both of them inclined to be flirtatious. They had a very nice time together at a picnic in Palos Park.

Dating, real dating with an almost sure goodnight kiss at the end, began in ninth grade, and he plunged into it with enthusiasm. He dated widely, spending most of each week considering which girl he would ask to the movies or to a party that weekend. There were more parties than ever now that the war was over and everything was getting back to normal, which was how he liked things. The war had been sort of interesting while it was going on, but he realized it had imposed a strain on him. It made him feel he ought to be doing something he wasn't doing, which was not a sensation he liked. Now he felt he was doing exactly what he ought to do—leading a normal life.

There were new girls in class that year, among them Shirley Hyatt. In Whiting her family lived two blocks from where his had lived. In the summer they occupied a house on the same ridge in Indiana Shores, so Shirley was not a new girl to Jerry. But she had a new look, and as she quickly became popular at U-High, Jerry had his first experience of frustration and sexual jealousy. Shirley was really his girl, he felt. He (and Phil) had known her longer than any of the other boys in class. He had actually gone to playschool with her. Now here she was at U-High making a big hit with the boys and becoming best friends with girls like Carolyn and Marylynn and Rosalind. "The Lins" they called themselves. Shirley joined them, and for a while she was called Sherlin, then Shelin, and finally, for some obscure reason, Eyore.

He watched the four of them parading through Belfield Hall with their arms around each other's waists, their pleated skirts swinging in unison, their angora sweaters matching, their hair combed down across their foreheads in the Veronica

Lake peekaboo style. He envied their intimacy, and he wondered if Shirley were telling U-High girls things about him,
such as that he used to play with dolls. Once in playschool
he had actually fought with Shirley over possession of one of
her own dolls. It would not have bothered him now for such
facts to become known. He was just curious. What did bother
him was Shirley's popularity with the boys.

She began going out with half a dozen different boys, most
of them Jerry's good friends. He wondered if she let them
kiss her. He didn't quite like the idea of Ernie Hill kissing
Shirley. He knew Ernie. Ernie was a member of Jerry's
particular circle of friends, that group of boys who had eaten
lunch together outdoors in Scammons Gardens ever since
seventh grade. Jerry thought of them as the "Hard Core."
They ate in the wind and the rain. They ate in blizzards and
howling gales. Like musk-oxen they turned their backs to
the winter storms and fed from their lunchboxes, holding
their sandwiches in mittened hands and sometimes virtually
disappearing into clouds of steam when they opened their
thermoses of hot cocoa. In fair weather they were joined in
the garden by fair-weather friends, but only he and Ernie and
Phil and John Williams and Stan Wengrowitz and Jimmy
Kaplan and Bill Murphy had never missed a day in Scammons
Gardens. They stood around an abandoned sandbox, sometimes teetering on the edge of the sandbox, and while they
ate they talked things over.

In seventh and eighth grades they talked about the facts of
life. Murphy, whose father was a doctor, brought books to
school, and not just medical textbooks. One day he turned up
with Mantegazza's *Human Sexual Customs,* from which he
read them choice passages about exotic initiation rituals in
Africa and Asia. In ninth grade they were more grown-up,
of course, though still there was a lot of joking and talking
about sex. They speculated one day about the possible effects
of administering Spanish Fly to Miss Collins, a conversation that both disturbed and fascinated Jerry, who listened

44

avidly but contributed little. Often he was relieved when such conversations were stopped by Phil, or more usually by John Williams, who said from time to time, "You guys are *sick*." Often the talk was sick, though fascinating, and the point was that Ernie Hill had more to say along these lines than anyone except Bill Murphy himself. The thought of Ernie alone with Shirley was distinctly worrisome, although at the same time Jerry felt that Ernie was a great guy. Next to Phil Forson, Ernie was probably his best friend.

He was glad in a way that Shirley's social life was hampered by the fact that she had to commute from Whiting where her family still lived. There was an old Standard Oil Company rule that one of the senior men at the refinery had to be in town at all times in case of fires or explosions. Thus Mr. Hyatt, who was Superintendent, could not live in Chicago like Jerry's father or Mr. Forson, both of whom were in the Research Department. This made it difficult for Shirley to date frequently, but then, late in the fall, Mrs. Hyatt and Mrs. Engels reached an understanding and Shirley began to use Anne Engels' bedroom during the school week. Anne had gone off to Swarthmore that year, and there was her bedroom and bath going unused. Shirley moved in and filled Anne's drawers with her sweaters, each neatly folded and slipped into a plastic bag to keep the wool from getting matted. On weekends when Shirley went back to Whiting Jerry would sometimes slip into her room to open her drawers and stare at the clothes she had left behind.

His mother thought it would be an advantage to Jerry to have Shirley around. She was such a good student that her example was bound to stimulate Jerry. Perhaps they could even study together. Anne Engels, who had been a superb student, was too far ahead of Jerry to be anything more than a myth of excellence filtered down to him by still-admiring teachers like Miss Collins. Jerry and Shirley were actually in some of the same classes. Surely that would act as a spur?

It did, but not in the direction Mrs. Engels hoped. Jerry

threw himself even more completely into extracurricular activities. The swimming season began. Usually it was dark before he left Sunny Gym, his hair still damp from the showers, to trot home to dinner. After dinner he got on the telephone right away to talk to the girl he was currently dating. Like ships that pass in the night, he and Shirley saw each other at meals and in class at school. Once, coming home from one of his own dates, he got out of the elevator and found Shirley and Ernie in the lobby in front of his door. They looked flushed. They were together on a padded bench where no one ever sat, nor did either of them rise when Jerry unlocked the front door of the apartment and stood aside to let Shirley enter first. "Goodnight, *Engels*," Ernie said with a meaningful, even gloating tone in his voice. Jerry went in alone.

He studied less than ever, and when Christmas came and Shirley went back to Whiting for two weeks, he felt a huge wave of relief. Anne came home. Her room reverted to normal. Those neatly folded sweaters in their slipcases disappeared and in their place was the explosive welter of Anne's clothes, some still cascading from her suitcases even after she had been home for a week. Jerry could now stroll into the room when he felt like it and throw himself onto Anne's bed to have heart-to-heart conversations with Anne about (among other things) how impossible it was to live with Shirley right next to him. "I feel like she's my sister, but I'd like to date her," he explained to Anne. "It's driving me crazy, and I know she goes out to the 55th Street Promontory with Ernie Hill." The 55th Street Promontory was becoming the spot where you took girls when you were hoping to do more than kiss them.

Anne listened to all this with the usual keen interest she took in anything that concerned Jerry's emotional life. "Do you take girls to the Promontory?" she asked. Jerry nodded. "It's too cold now, though," he added. "But what do you do there?" Anne asked. "Nothing much," he admitted. "But what?" Anne wanted to know. Such details interested her. "Well, I feel them," Jerry said. "Jerry!" said Anne, her eyes alight with curiosity. "Just their breasts," he hastened to explain, "and usually I don't even get my hand under their sweaters." "They let you do that?" Anne asked. "Some of them do," said Jerry. "Not all, though." "Which girls?" Anne asked.

He became a little uncomfortable when conversations with his sister took this turn. He felt Anne should understand what went on at the Promontory and shouldn't really ask him which girls he necked with. He didn't even tell boys that kind of thing. But then Anne was different, he reflected. She was above all this. Out of it. She was a college girl now. And maybe she really didn't know what went on at the Promontory because after all she hadn't dated much in U-High. She had been too busy at girls' sports and winning all the school prizes. She had been the first girl in U-High history to win the John Crerar Shop Prize. He saw her name on half a dozen of the plaques that lined Belfield Hall. She was an exceptional person. So when she kept probing he finally named names. "I've done it with Marylynn," he said, "and Sandra, and Carolyn. I even undid Carolyn's bra." Undoing a bra was considered a real accomplishment. "Why Jerry!" said Anne.

They were lying face to face on her unmade bed. In addition to the usual chaos of clothes in her room there were Christmas wrappings all over the place. Jerry began to feel the comfortable, unbuttoned sense of intimacy he often felt in his sister's presence. He went on voluntarily. "She hasn't got big breasts," he said, "but she's very sensitive." Anne nodded. Their faces were close together. He was feeling now as close and as intimate as he had felt in the old days when he snuck into her room to play Orphans. "I don't love Carolyn, though," he said, "I don't love anyone now." "Why not?" Anne asked. "I don't know," he said reflectively. "I think if I could date Shirley I'd fall in love with her, but how can I?

We're living together!" It came back to that. "It's driving me crazy," he added. Anne was sympathetic. "Have you told the parents any of this?" she asked. "Oh no!" he exclaimed, "and don't you tell them either. They'd die if they knew it all."

Anne told them something, however, for when Christmas vacation ended Shirley did not return to the Engels' apartment on 56th Street. Jerry felt guilty about depriving her of a Chicago base of operations, but he was profoundly relieved all the same.

He did not blame Anne for divulging some of his secrets to the parents. She had done it for the best, and anyway he was in the habit of accepting anything Anne did. In the old days when he was blamed for getting into bed with her, it had never even occurred to him to wonder why she didn't own up to her part in the proceedings. What Anne did was right. She was his sister who had shepherded him through his childhood, getting him to fight the boys he had to fight, and telling on him when he stole candy from Whalen's Drugstore. When he was too shy to tell girls he loved them, she had even done that for him. No one else he knew had a sister like Anne. He felt he owed her almost everything. In fact if there was someone he really loved more deeply than he had ever loved any girl, it was probably Anne. He missed her when she went back to Swarthmore and wondered what her life there was like. Somehow he never knew as much about Anne's life as she knew about his. It made him feel selfish that they talked all the time about his affairs rather than hers, and he began the New Year with a resolution that from now on he would write Anne regularly and really keep in touch.

Shirley was not long without a room in Chicago. That winter Mrs. Yngling, the mother of Mrs. Forson, died. Her room in the Forson house became vacant, and after a decent interval Shirley began to use it without, so far as Jerry could tell, disturbing Phil. Of course Phil's room was on the third floor at the front, whereas Shirley's was on the second floor at the back. Phil and Shirley weren't right next to each other as Jerry and Shirley had been. Still, Jerry had to admire Phil's composure.

He could now contemplate asking Shirley for a date, but when he visualized himself going to the Forsons to pick her up and saying "Hello" at the same time to Phil's parents, whom he called Uncle Walter and Aunt Beth, his heart sank. It would be like calling to take out Linda Forson, who was ten. And could he kiss Shirley on the Forsons' doorstep when he brought her home? And what if Phil bumped into them the way he had bumped into Shirley and Ernie Hill? The more he thought about it, the more impossible it seemed, so he resigned himself to the fact that Shirley was out of bounds as far as he was concerned.

It was a pity, though, because he was almost sure he could have fallen in love with her. She was the kind of bright, aggressive, pretty girl he always liked. She was similar to Anne de Lancey, only sexier. He would have loved to study with Shirley if only they could become sweethearts. That was the sort of stimulus he needed. He was not competitive, he was amative. Even in sports what stimulated him was not the desire to win but his love of his teammates and his love of running and swimming.

When he told his sister he was not in love with anyone it was the simple truth, though at the same time he felt there was more love in him than ever before just looking for an outlet. He spent his days and nights feeling vaguely excited and half in love with everything and everyone: girls at school, his pals in the Hard Core, his teammates, U-High itself, the city streets, even the city smells. On winter mornings there was sometimes a close, acidy smell in the air which he would draw into his lungs in deep breaths, feeling *this is Chicago*. He had grown to love the city as much as he had loved Whiting. On his way to school in the morning he often forgot the half-finished or hastily done homework zipped into the notebook he carried on his hip. He would lose himself in the sights and sounds and smells of the city. The bare trees along Kimbark poked up into the low winter sky. Darkening snow lay on the ground. A milkwagon would be making its slow way along the curb, the horse steaming in the cold air, milk bottles clinking in their wooden cases as the driver swung on and off. He walked the same blocks every morning, never tiring of what he saw. These were the blocks he knew best in all the city. He had soaped many of these windows and stuck pins into many of these doorbells on Halloween eves. He loved these blocks. Marjorie McConkey lived at the corner of Kimbark and 57th. Gloria had lived halfway down the next block. Where he crossed the street he had once nearly been run down by Mrs. Richardson at the tiller of her noiseless electric car. Marylynn Morris lived in the pillared apartment house between 57th and 58th. He would take her out Friday night. And then he was at the corner of 58th and Kimbark and there was Scammons Gardens behind its iron railings which had almost been donated to the scrap drive during the war. He would eat his lunch there with his best friends. And beyond Scammons he could see the gray bulk of Belfield Hall where in a few minutes he would have to explain to Mr. Whiting why he had done only half the assigned algebra problems.

Caught between nostalgia and anticipation, he walked the tightrope of the now until his parents gently shook the rope, disturbing his smooth passage from home to school, from Algebra to Art, from lunch to Study Hall where, one day, he sat looking at Carl Becker's *Modern Democracy* while across the table from him Carolyn Webster drew a whimsical sketch of a young man hanging by one arm from the limb of a tree, eating a banana with his free hand while with his prehensile feet he held an open book up to his bare behind. "Is that me?" Jerry whispered. Carolyn smiled provokingly. "Let me see it," Jerry said, and a discreet scuffling broke out across and under the table, in the midst of which he remembered his father saying, only the night before, that he would have to improve his grades at school.

His whole future depended on his education. His family had no money. Their Chicago apartment, their summer cottage, his tuition at U-High and Anne's at Swarthmore all came out of what Mr. Engels earned at Standard Oil. If Jerry wanted his own children to enjoy private schools and summer homes and long car trips to New England and to the West Coast and to the Florida Everglades he would have to earn a good salary, which meant studying hard not just in high school but in college, and not just in college but in graduate school. Mr. Engels had a Ph.D. in Chemistry from Johns Hopkins. Did Jerry think he was going to get into a college like Swarthmore or a graduate school like Hopkins without studying? And if he didn't get into such schools what would he do, what would become of him? To belong to the educated upper-middle class you had to be educated, and to get an education you had to study. It was axiomatic. And as that axiom came home to him Jerry abandoned his struggle to get possession of Carolyn's drawing. "Okay, I'm not interested," he told her, and he looked some more at *Modern Democracy* until he saw Carolyn had relaxed her guard. Then, swift as lightning, he snatched her drawing away from her and read the title she had given it: "Jerry on a Limb." "I'll get you for this," he promised, crumpling it up and tossing it back at her.

Insofar as he had a single girl in ninth grade it was Carolyn. He went further with her than with anyone else, and felt closer to her, though there was now a sharp dividing line between himself and the girls he dated, an edge like a sword blade. He had lost the sense he often had with his earlier girls that they were linked in some sort of secret and perfect union. Now he could no longer just feel close to a girl, he had to feel her, and that led to struggles and sparring around in the dark and a sense on his part that they were really very separate and cut off from each other. He felt he

51

had lost something without having gained anything new, because though he was involved these days in sex play, there was no sex. He was not even sure he wanted to go that far with a girl.

His father had been talking to him about sex as well as about the future. They took walks together on Sunday mornings through the park, past the Museum of Science and Industry, and over the humpbacked bridge onto the island where they sometimes sat for a while—it was spring now—on a bench in front of the Japanese Tea Pavilion. Mr. Engels explained sex to his son. It was a fine experience between married couples. Jerry was given to understand, in a discreet way, that his father and his mother enjoyed sleeping together. It was to be hoped that Jerry would be as happy with his future wife as Mr. Engels had always been with Jerry's mother. Married love was a wonderful thing to look forward to, and Mr. Engels even gave Jerry a copy of Marie Stopes' *Married Love* so he could read about what was ahead of him. The real point of these talks, however, was that married love lay in the future, the rather distant future, and meanwhile such sexual experiences as Jerry was likely to have as an adolescent boy would be neither fine, nor happy, nor wonderful.

Mr. Engels avoided details at this stage of his argument. He was a clearheaded, lucid, scientifically trained man quite capable of helping Jerry with his algebra and his Latin and his English grammar and his biology, but he allowed a certain cloudiness to envelop the whole question of what was wrong with adolescent sex. Nevertheless there was no loss of meaning in what he had to say. He used words like "dangerous" and "unhealthy" which in Jerry's mind translated easily into the grand old story aired in a thousand locker-room conversations and passed on faithfully from generation to generation of schoolboys. Jerry knew his father was talking about premature ejaculation and early impotence induced by self-abuse, and of clap and syphilis picked up from bad women. That led to paresis and madness. Or alternately you could knock up a nice girl, which led to scandal, outraged fathers and brokenhearted mothers, shotgun weddings, marital unhappiness, and divorce. Or if you did not face the music and stand by the girl you'd gotten in trouble, there was another sequence of miserable events which involved the girl's killing herself with an amateur abortion while you ended up in a gutter somewhere, dead drunk from trying to forget it all. It was perfectly clear, and Mr. Engels' warnings about sex led to a conclusion as axiomatic as his warnings about grades. To provide his family with the same kind of good life he himself had enjoyed, Jerry would have to be well educated. To have the kind of married love his parents enjoyed, Jerry would have to control himself sexually for the next eight or ten years. "You do understand?" his father would ask him, and Jerry would nod, impressed by the reasonableness of it all.

Only . . .

Only on Halloween in tenth grade Paul Friedlander got hold of some blue movies which he showed in a basement room of his apartment building on Blackstone Avenue. Practically all the guys in class attended, even John Williams. Jerry went, of course, and watched in horrified fascination while two women licked and kissed each other. The picture danced and shifted on the cement wall of the basement room. Specks of dirt in the projector shifted around, covering first one part of the women's bodies and then another. Jerry was aroused despite himself, though when the second picture began he felt like shouting in protest when it showed two men and a single woman doing things he would not have believed possible. It was all so ugly. He was repelled. He felt close to tears, and yet when all three films had been shown (there were three in all) and Friedlander asked if anyone wanted to see them again, Jerry heard his voice, among others, saying, "Yeah, show them again." But he closed his eyes at crucial points during the second showing when he knew they were coming to scenes he just could not bear to look at again. Now was that reasonable?

Or was it reasonable what they did afterward? They poured

out of the basement of Friedlander's apartment building and went on a rampage through the streets of Hyde Park, breaking street lights, overturning a little foreign car, twisting street signs out of shape, and smashing basement windows. They had never done so much damage on Halloween Eve. They smashed the glass globes in front of the apartment building where Gloria Offenbach had lived, and only the sound of a police siren in the distance stopped them from throwing bricks through the plate glass windows of Stineway's, their favorite hangout.

That siren scared them into breaking up and running. "Everyone scatter," some clear thinker yelled. Jerry fled down Kenwood, past Scammons Gardens, past Belfield and Blaine. Steps pounded along behind him most of the way. He thought he and Phil were running off together, but when he was out on the grass of the Midway and slowed down to let Phil catch up, he found he was alone. He ran on, pursued now by the Furies, by outraged nature, by something-or-other, but not by the Chicago Police Department. He knew the police weren't going to catch him. He was too fleet.

In Jackson Park he slowed down to a walk that took him out to the lakeshore, and up the shore to the Promontory. He stood for a long time on the rocks at the tip of the Promontory, listening to the lake slap against the stones. He climbed down until he could feel spray from the breaking waves. He would have liked to swim, but it was too cold. He let the spray wet his hair, his face, his overcoat. With his hands he rubbed the moisture on his cheeks until his cheeks felt warm and glowing. He rubbed and rubbed, beginning now to feel good again. He touched his wet hair. It reminded him of swimming practice, of coming out of Sunny Gym when the street lamps were already lit, and of finding Phil and Ernie and John Williams and the other guys from the basketball team still standing on the steps talking to each other. At that moment, after practice, at the end of the school day, there was something soft and peaceful in their companionship. Frequently they prolonged those final moments, going off together to Stineway's where they crowded six into a booth for four. They ordered hot fudge sundaes, which they downed before splitting up to go their separate ways to the dinners their mothers had planned for them. Those sundaes after practice and before dinner were sweet occasions when everyone felt good and happy and relaxed. *We're good.* Jerry thought. He and his friends were good guys, so why had they watched those movies and broken so much glass? He sighed. He wished he understood life.

That Christmas when Anne came home she was full of fresh insights into the Engels family. She had been taking a psychology course. "I treated you so terribly," she told Jerry, "I don't know why you like me now." He felt puzzled. "What do you mean?" he asked. "Well, do you remember my telling the parents when you stole candy from Whalen's?" He nodded. It was not an event he was likely to forget. "Well, did you know that I was stealing candy?" *"You* were?" he said. That *was* news. "All the time," said Anne, "and no one ever caught me at it. I felt so guilty that when I found out you were doing it I just had to tell the parents about you. Getting you punished sort of made me feel better about what I was doing." "I don't see why," he said. "It should have made you feel worse." But Anne just went right on with her insights, none of which quite clicked for Jerry. "And those fights I used to get you into," she said. "I really treated you terribly!" "But it was good for me to fight!" Jerry protested. Anne brushed that aside. "I really liked to watch you fight with other boys. I used to get excited." "But why not?" he asked. Fights *were* exciting. "Don't you see how I was manipulating you?" Anne said. "Well, you used to encourage me to fight and to get in bed with you, but I don't see that as manipulation," he said. "Well, it just was," Anne told him, a little annoyed that he was not following her intellectual lead. "Why was it?" he asked. "Well, you used to get scolded for fighting, didn't you, and I never took any of the blame." He nodded, remembering now that he had been blamed for fighting, as well as for getting in bed with Anne. "But I was the one who did it," he pointed out. "Why should the parents blame you?" "Well, it's a miracle you still like me," Anne said, "after all I did."

They were lying on her bed, as they usually did during their confidential talks. He felt vaguely flattered by the importance she now attributed to insignificant childhood events and by her assumption that his role in their childhood was more innocent and somehow nobler than he remembered it as being. "Of course I like you," he told her. "I think I love you," he added, and that started her off on a new track. "We're a very Oedipal family," she told him. "Daddy has always been closer to me than to you, and you've always been closer to Mother than I've been." He nodded, waiting for the point, which—after a moment—he realized she had already made. "That's Oedipal?" he said. "Very," said Anne. He nodded again, waiting for more. "Don't you see how I always did the things Daddy approved of, the things *you* ought to have done? I used to earn money shoveling snow off the walks in Whiting." "Well, you were bigger," he said. "I was only seven or eight then." "But it went on," said Anne. "I won the Shop Prize at U-High. I got all As. Those are things Daddy appreciates." That was true, certainly. He thought about it. "Well, you're smarter than I am," he said, "and anyway I never liked Shop very much." "Jerry!" said Anne, "you're not dumb. You have a very good mind. You're probably a lot more original than I am, but I got the encouragement to be a good student." "Listen!" said Jerry. "You should hear him encourage me to do better." "That's not the same, though," she said. "Does he appreciate the things you are good at? Does he go to watch your swimming meets? Is he happy about how popular you are with girls?" "Unh-unh," said Jerry feelingly. "You see?" Anne said. "He appreciates the things I'm good at, but he doesn't appreciate the things you're good at." "Because you're good at better things," Jerry said. "Jerry!" Anne exclaimed. "You don't see it at all." "Well, explain it," he said. "Look at all you've accomplished," Anne told him. "You're captain of the swimming team this year, and you're one of the most popular boys in your class. I was never popular. Nobody liked me. I had maybe three friends." "You're making friends now," he told her. "You were telling about them." "All right," said Anne, "but we're talking about high school. Your friends are the best kids in U-High, and you're a good athlete. Look what a good athlete you've become. You're on the cross country team, you're captain of the swimming team, you're on the tennis team." "I like swimming and tennis and running," he said. "But don't you see? Most fathers would be proud if their sons were doing as well as you're doing, but all he does is worry about your grades." "And about sex," Jerry added. "Well, there again," Anne said, "a lot of fathers encourage their boys to become men." Jerry laughed. "You think he should *encourage* me to go ahead with girls?" "Well, why not?" Anne said. "Why not!" he exclaimed. "Yes, why not?"

They stared at each other. "You mean that?" he asked her at last. "Yes!" she said. "You really think Daddy should encourage me to get *more* involved with girls?" She met his eyes without answering. He rolled away from her until he was staring up at the ceiling. "Boy, Anne," he said, "you don't have any idea . . ." "What do you mean?" she asked. "Are you mixed up with a girl now?" He shook his head. "No, but I'd sure like to be." "Who are you seeing most of?" she asked him. "Oh, nobody in particular," he said. "I think if I started going steady with anyone I couldn't keep it under control." "Well, why should you?" she asked. He rolled back toward her. "You don't know what you're talking about!" he told her. "You shouldn't be encouraging me. I need help the other way." "You're practically grown," Anne pointed out. "I'm fifteen," he said. "Well, look at you," she said. "You're already bigger than you were this summer. Your voice has changed. You could be sixteen or seventeen the way you look." "Oh come on!" he said, "There are guys in class ahead of me. Phil is, and John, and Stan." Anne shrugged. "The same's true for them, then." "You think we all ought to go out and have an experience?" he asked her challengingly. "Well, . . ." She wouldn't quite say *yes*. What she did say was, "It wouldn't be so terrible if it happened." "I'm not so sure," he told her. "I'm not even so sure if I want it. I mean, I *say* I want it, but I'm not so sure I'd really like it. I saw a movie about it," and he told her of his experience in Paul Friedlander's basement. "It was disgusting," he said. Anne shook her head impatiently. "It doesn't have to be like that," she said. "How do you know?" he asked her. "Have you . . . ?" "We're talking about you," Anne said.

It was an important conversation. He dismissed much of what Anne had said. She had certainly not been terrible to him, and thinking things over he decided his father treated him all right, maybe better than he deserved. But in the last part of the conversation Anne might have been right. She'd always been right before when she told him to tell girls he loved them, and to kiss girls, and to call them up. So maybe she was right that he should try for more. But with whom? With Carolyn? She and Ernie Hill were dating a lot these days. Jerry wasn't sure but what they had decided to go steady. He couldn't horn in there. So who should it be? He considered the girls in his class. Rachel Fein? Anne de Lancey? But they were serious girls. He couldn't do that to them without being in love with them, and he felt he couldn't fall back in love with either of them just to do *that*. Sandra Wertenbaker then? They had been very friendly at times, and she was not as serious as Rachel or Anne, though on the other hand, like Carolyn, she was now more or less preempted by a steady boyfriend. That was the trouble. By dating so widely he had let girls slip through his fingers, so to speak, and now the really attractive ones, the ones he could most easily imagine doing it with, were beginning to be serious about other boys, while the serious girls seemed out of the running for the purposes he had in mind.

He dug deeper into the echelons of U-High womanhood and came up with the name of Marjorie McConkey. What about that, he asked himself. There was something spirited and attractive about Marjorie. He liked the way she clenched her fists after Latin and beat on her notebook. And though no beauty, her figure was pretty good. He fell into a gentle daydream in which he and Marjorie, tightly clutching each other's hands, walked out on the Promontory while waves crashed against the rocks. Then the crashing waves reminded him of something. Marjorie liked music. She played the cello. She was very musical. He should take her to an opera. What would opera tickets cost, he wondered. He checked *The Daily News* and was a little discouraged by the prices listed there, but in February he went ahead with his plan, purchasing two tickets for *Il Trovatore* at the Chicago Opera Company and calling for Marjorie one Friday evening.

He had felt she was flattered when he asked her for a date, also a little surprised when he suggested they go to the opera. Now, picking her up, he felt like a real heel, because he could see she had bought a new dress for the occasion, a long brown watery-silk job that he couldn't really say he liked. She had a ribbon in her hair, which also seemed wrong to him, and she was carrying a beaded purse that looked like it belonged to her mother. Moreover she kept letting it swing on its metal chain. It beat time against his hip as they walked to the 57th Street IC station. "I didn't know you like music," she said. "I like some music," Jerry said cautiously. "I like *Il Trovatore*," he added. He had waited for something like *Il Trovatore* because he could remember the "Anvil Chorus" which he had learned to identify in Mr. Labby's eighth grade Music class.

He was not at ease. Usually, going out with girls was the easiest thing in the world for him, but this evening nothing

seemed quite right. At the Randolph Street station he insisted they take a cab to the Opera House, although Marjorie
assured him there was plenty of time for them to walk.
"You can't walk in those shoes," he told her. Among other
things she was wearing shoes that inched her up to the point
where she was just a trifle taller than he was. But that wasn't
the reason he didn't want to walk across the Loop with her.
He felt that a taxicab, despite the cost, was more or less
what she was owed after she'd bought that brown dress to
make herself look nice for a guy who had been thinking
about her the way he had.

They arrived at the Opera House half an hour before
curtain time. At first vast stretches of empty seats surrounded
them. They were on the main floor, toward the back of the
hall. It seemed like a city block from the stage, although the
tickets had cost Jerry three dollars and seventy-five cents
apiece. When they'd settled themselves and looked at the
program, they started to talk about common U-High con-
cerns. "Have you seen the Virgil we're supposed to do this
weekend?" Marjorie asked him. Latin class was their strong-
est U-High bond.

It seemed rather awful to Jerry that they should sit in the
Opera House talking about their Latin homework, but he
fell in with the conversation and while the seats around them
filled up, they deplored the number of lines Miss Collins
thought fit to assign every day and gave free expression to
their total lack of interest in *The Aeneid*. "I don't see why
anyone needs to know Latin anyway," Marjorie said. "No one
speaks it anymore." "It's supposed to be good for grammar,"
said Jerry, near despair in various ways. He had just realized
that even when all the seats filled up and the lights dimmed
he couldn't behave as if he were at a movie. He couldn't get
his arm around Marjorie and maybe touch her knee. They
would just have to sit side by side and listen to the opera. By
the time the orchestra had tuned up and the conductor had
bowed to the audience he was wishing he had decided on a

movie after all. Then the curtain rose, people applauded for some reason, and the opera began.

"I didn't remember much of that," he said to Marjorie at the first intermission. He hadn't even heard the "Anvil Chorus." Had it been taken out of the opera, or had he been mistaken that it was there in the first place? Moreover, what was happening on stage? Marjorie explained some points of the plot to him, and he felt a little better. Evidently she understood something of what was going on, and so far as he could see she was enjoying herself. She sat very upright watching the stage, breathing deeply and regularly, her rather full bosom rising and falling in a noticeable way, or at least in a way he noticed. Then when the "Anvil Chorus" began after the intermission, he felt much better about things and even took Marjorie's hand and held it until the next intermission.

They had been sitting a long time by then, so they got up and went out into the lobby where Jerry offered to buy Marjorie a glass of orangeade. They drank orangeade among the operagoers, and Marjorie showed a trace of the spirit he admired in her by saying loudly that she hated people who clapped at the end of arias. He felt on the whole that though it was not his kind of evening, she was happy. But what was it that made people like music, he wondered, and want to sit for hours on end listening to operas? He twisted in his seat and fidgeted through the rest of the performance. When he saw a shiny look in Marjorie's face at the end, and heard her clap as loudly as anyone, he had trouble believing her feelings were genuine.

But they were. She was jubilant on the way home, saying again and again as they walked to the Randolph Street station that it had been *great*, that Zinka Milanov was wonderful, that Warren had a great voice, that the whole thing was just great. She strode along through the crowds on Randolph Street, talking and gesturing with her hands, obviously buoyed up by the whole experience, her bead bag swinging like a bolo as she made her points. Her enthusiasm got to

Jerry who began to feel that he, too, had enjoyed himself. By the time they were riding south on the IC, he had a happy, elated feeling which he knew came mainly from her but which seemed fairly real nevertheless.

Then she invited him up to her apartment, saying that her parents were probably already in bed. When she let him in with her key, he saw her cello leaning against a chair in front of a music stand in the sun porch that opened off the living room. She went down the hall to tell her parents she was home. They were evidently lying low. Jerry waited in the living room, looking around the place. He knew the layout of the whole apartment, though this was the first time he had been inside. But it was like a million other Chicago apartments: living room and sun porch in front, a bedroom, probably Marjorie's, next to it, another bedroom beyond that, with a bath between them, and in the back the dining room and kitchen. He had been in this kind of apartment a hundred times.

When she came back to the living room she had gotten rid of her coat. She asked him if he wanted coffee, but he didn't drink coffee and was surprised she did. She gave him a root beer instead and they sat on the couch. He was not sure she expected him to kiss her, but he did right away and savored the coffee taste on her lips. She began to breathe strenuously as he got his arms around her. He felt she was responding well, but when he touched the watery silk above her breast she suddenly burst free and moved to a chair. Their eyes met. "I'm sorry," he said. "That's all right," she said, but she made no move to rejoin him on the couch. He drank some more of his root beer and wondered what to do now. She sat upright, her half-drunk cup of coffee abandoned on a table at the end of the couch. He handed it to her, and she sipped some coffee. After a moment he said, "Would you like to go out again?" "With you?" she said. "Yes, with me," he said. "For what?" she asked. "Well, for anything." "I don't know," she said. "Do you want to ask me?" "Well, sure," he said, "I *was* asking you." "For when?" she asked.

"Well, do your parents let you go out on weeknights?" "I guess so," she said. "Would you like to see a movie Tuesday night?" "All right," she agreed.

So he began dating her, rushing her in fact. He even timed things so that he walked her to school in the morning. One weekend night she invited him up again, this time to meet her parents who were evidently becoming curious about him. On that occasion Marjorie played a cello piece, which solved the problem of conversation.

He realized almost from the start that the whole thing was a mistake. Even if he'd known how to seduce a girl, Marjorie was the wrong girl for him to try to seduce. And not because she wasn't passionate. She was very passionate. Too passionate, in fact. One touch of his hand above her breast always set her off like a bomb, the explosion of which usually threw him aside. She leaped from couches, she bolted upright in movie seats, she rocketed up from the grass like a flushed pheasant. He couldn't handle her. It was like Gloria all over again, only at a higher level. He realized that though she was not a serious girl like Rachel or Anne de Lancey, she was serious in another way, about music, about feelings, about nature. She had a terrific chest, really, and in the spring when things began to bloom in the park and they took evening walks through the misty air, he would hear her inhaling like a swimmer before a race, practically hyperventilating. What had gone wrong, he realized, was that her status as a poor and slightly troublesome student had misled him into thinking that if he could get her away from Latin he would find she was his sort of girl, or what he thought of as his sort of girl: someone sort of lighthearted, and happy, and sexy. Someone who enjoyed things. But though she enjoyed things a lot, she was far more serious than he was. She was not lighthearted. She was falling more in love with him than he was with her, which was a situation he was not used to. It put him in a false position, and periodically made him feel uncomfortable.

He liked being loved, it was not that, but since he had first started to date her with the idea that maybe he could eventually make love to her, he found himself feeling like a heel to have aroused all this passion in her that now he'd be ashamed to satisfy even if she'd let him, which he didn't think she ever would. Though passionate, she was also curiously rigid. On the one or two occasions when he'd almost gotten her to neck with him, she tended to go stiff in his arms as if she were holding herself together by some effort of will. He avoided her breasts on those occasions, knowing what that led to, but even when he got her to open her mouth a little while they kissed, he had the feeling of holding onto a statue or a piece of wood like Charlie McCarthy, with a hinged mouth but nothing else that was movable.

He liked her a great deal, however, and was taken up with her through most of the second half of tenth grade even though she was out of his usual social set. He knew that kids in school were wondering why he was dating Marjorie so much. He even had an ugly little encounter with Bud Hollander who came right out and said, "Hey, Engels, is McConkey putting out for you?" Hollander was the sort of guy who liked to collect the names of girls who put out.

What did you say to such guys, Jerry wondered. It was like the old problem in grade school in Whiting when boys had asked if he liked so-and-so or held hands with such-and-such a girl. In those days he'd solved the problem by telling the truth. Now it didn't seem right to say anything. If he told Hollander the truth and said "No," he would seem to imply that Hollander had the right to ask such a question, which he didn't. It would also imply that Jerry was dating Marjorie only in order to get her to come across, which was no longer true. Puzzling over what answer he should have made, Jerry realized he probably ought to have socked Hollander for asking the question. But socking guys was just not his style. Actually he'd smiled and said, "Wouldn't you like to know?" and then hated himself for the rest of the day because it seemed to imply he was really doing something with Marjorie.

He felt protective toward her. When he caught glimpses of her in the music room sawing away at her cello, he felt maybe he really loved her. In class when a teacher loaded some new assignment on them and Marjorie raised her head indignantly and gave an angry toss to her long hair, he had the feeling again. But when he was alone with her he knew he didn't love her. He was sorry about it, but he just could not love her, and this was not because she had a rather big, plain face. He knew she was nicer and more interesting than much prettier girls, but he was embarrassed by the fact that she loved him so much, and he was handicapped because sex was so much on his mind. Though he was not trying to seduce her anymore, sex lay between them like some heavily mined territory through which, he felt, it would be dangerous for him to advance. Sex divided them, and he couldn't love a girl he felt divided from.

In eleventh grade he began going out for long walks at night. Jip was his pretext. He was taking Jip for a walk, he told his parents, but Jip was an old dog now and not nearly as interested as Jerry in exploring Hyde Park at night. Indeed, Jerry felt at times that he was wearing Jip out, yet night after night he took Jip on long walks. Sometimes he even crossed the Midway and ventured down to 63rd Street, where, one night, Jerry was sure he had seen a prostitute standing beside a pillar of the El tracks. He walked by her slowly. She looked at him, but said nothing. He turned up Maryland Avenue and stopped to count his money. There was a dollar bill in his wallet and some change in his pocket. He didn't know what prostitutes charged, but he was sure that was not enough. Then Jip tugged at the leash, interested in a smell up ahead. Jerry allowed himself to be led away from 63rd Street.

The whole neighborhood became erotically charged for him. At night when he sallied forth with Jip, he felt he was going out to meet some woman. She would be standing by a lamppost; she would be framed in a lighted window; she would be coming out of a house as he passed. He looked up at lighted windows, trying to imagine the life that went on inside each apartment. When he saw potted or hanging plants in a window, he sometimes lingered in the street, hoping to see a woman's figure appear to water her plants or pinch off a withered bloom. Plants meant women, parks meant women. But in the parks he met men he knew were interested in him, so he avoided the parks and walked Jip up and down the city streets.

Amalgams from scenes in all the Katharine Hepburn and Constance Bennett movies he loved would come back to enrich his walks. He would pass a mansion on Woodlawn Avenue and see a party going on inside. Through lighted windows he could see men and women standing around with glasses and cigarettes in their hands. He would linger, and then in his imagination the front door would open, letting out a burst of light and laughter. A radiantly beautiful woman would half run, half stumble down the steps, diamonds in her hair, a fur coat thrown loosely around her bare shoulders. At the doorway a man in a tuxedo with a glass in his hand would call after her, "Are you all right, Mimi?" She would pause to wave a gloved hand, call out, "Wonderful party, Hugh," and then come weaving gracefully out onto the sidewalk where she would pause to peer a little stupidly into her tiny purse. She would see Jerry. "Who are you?" she would ask, as if he were intruding on her. "I'm Jeremy Engels," he would reply in a polite voice. Then she would put out her gloved hand and take him by the chin to turn his face toward the street light so she could see him more clearly. "Well, Jeremy Engels," she would say, "can you drive?" "I've just got my driver's license," he would answer. This was true. He was sixteen now, and he could drive. "Well then," the lady would say, dropping her car keys into his hand, "you're going to have to drive me home."

She would sit beside him in her Bugatti, high and happy as he drove. Sometimes she would sing. He would concentrate on his driving, handling the unfamiliar gearshift beautifully.

Usually she had passed out by the time he drew up in front of her house. He would carry her in his arms to the front door, extending his index finger to push the doorbell. She would snuggle, half conscious, against his chest. Then a frail old butler would open the door and take in the situation at a glance. He would stand aside, saying, "You had better take her upstairs." And Jerry would then climb a wide, curving staircase, the lovely lady murmuring to herself in his arms. When he deposited her gently on her bed, she would come to and look up at him. "Who are you?" she would ask with surprise. "I'm Jeremy Engels," he would remind her. "I drove you home from the party." "Oh!" she would say, "but how did I get here?" "You couldn't walk," he would explain, "so I carried you." "You?" she would say, "but you're just a boy." "I may be a boy," he would answer, "but would you like to see my body?"

He was Jeremy in some fantasies, Jer in others. He was the adolescent lover of an older woman who lived in the Windermere Hotel. He thought of her as Lady Windermere, though she was not English. She was more foreign than that. She was Norwegian, or Russian, or Hungarian. She had been scarred somehow. Communists or Nazis had done something to her. She had lost her husband and her son. She had only Jerry, whom she called Jer, and to whom she sent urgent notes. *I must see you before five o'clock*, the note would read. It would be signed *A*. These notes came to him rather mysteriously. During Social Studies, while Mr. Gewarth was explaining fascism, Jerry would put his hand into his pocket and feel a piece of paper there. A note from Lady Windermere, he would think. Sometimes these notes were wafted into his hand while he was actually running with the cross country team through Jackson Park. *I must see you before five o'clock*, the note would read. *Do not fail me. A.* He would drop behind the pack of runners and slip away across the park to the Windermere.

Then he was in her suite in his running clothes. "I came,"

he would say, his body glowing from his run, the cupped excitement between his legs swelling as she rose to greet him. "Thank God!" she said, "I was afraid . . ." and she would get the curious, haunted look that was the result of her unfortunate European past. "Never mind," she would say, not wanting to explain her fears. "All that matters is that you're here." Then they would go to bed.

He wanted to regularize their union by spending the night with her, but she always pushed him out of bed in time for him to get home to dinner at six-thirty. "Your parents must not know," she said mysteriously, and off he would go, not quite satisfied by the experience. So he acquired another older woman. Her name was Monica Kipling, and she worked in some undefined capacity in the bursar's office. She had been married, but her husband, as she explained, had gotten so adventurous in bed that sometimes she couldn't even tell where he was or what he was trying to do. "So I kicked him out," she told Jerry. Since then she had relied on young lovers who were content to do the same thing over and over and over. Jerry got her name from Bud Hollander, whom he displaced in her affections. She was furious with Bud for having passed out her telephone number to his U-High buddies. Jerry assured her he would never do such a thing. He wanted her too much for himself.

They were happy in bed, though she was sometimes high when he visited her at night, accompanied by Jip. "Hi, doggie," she would say, offering Jip a sardine. Sometimes she carommed around her apartment eating cheese and crackers and drinking bourbon before she took Jerry with her into her bedroom. When they kissed he could taste the bourbon and the cheese and the smoky taste of her cigarettes. They had rollicking good times that often sent Jip into a frenzy of barking outside the closed bedroom door. "Poor doggie," Monica would say. She was a generous, slightly disorganized woman. Jerry thought of her most frequently when he was in Math class listening to Mr. Pauling talk about delta functions.

68

But even she did not satisfy him, and by winter Jerry was already searching around in his imagination for some third or fourth woman to teach him all the arts of love. By comparison with what was going on in his head, real life had become almost banal. He dated Marjorie and various other girls, but he felt his position at U-High was becoming less enviable than it had been. He, who for years had been able to get dates with almost any girl he wanted, was now being cut out as more and more girls started to go steady. As each new girl disappeared from general circulation, he felt a little pang go through him. He was not competitive in general, but where girls were concerned he did feel a kind of rivalry with other boys. He had liked the feeling in ninth grade that all girls were potentially his. Now it was not so. He could not pick and choose as widely as before, and it hurt him to see girls he still liked very much dancing cheek to cheek with their boyfriends at Colony Club dances. Even when those boyfriends were his own best friends. When Phil started to go steady with Rachel Fein, Jerry went through a kind of crisis.

He was losing out, not just sexually but in every way. When his class started high school, U-High began in seventh grade and ended in tenth, after which the class would go into the College of the University of Chicago. It was President Hutchins' Chicago experiment, and for Jerry and his friends it had meant glory in tenth grade when they were presidents of all the school organizations, and editors of all the school publications, and captains of all the school teams. Then the experiment ended. They had been seniors in tenth grade, now they were juniors in eleventh, shorn of their offices. Some of them, like Phil and Stan and John Williams, would be back on top in twelfth grade. John Williams would probably become the first U-Higher to be President of the Student Council in tenth grade and again in twelfth grade. He was the best student, the best athlete, and in fact the best-looking boy in class. Phil might repeat as Boys' Club President, unless he and Stan decided to switch roles, Stan running for the Boys' Club and Phil running for the Presidency of the Senior Class. But Jerry could not hope for any high office in twelfth. The girls were tired of voting for him, and even the boys no longer thought that because he was likable he was automatically fit for some minor position. He was not even sure he could repeat as captain of the swimming team. There was a new boy in school who had displaced Jerry as the star of the team.

A sense of failure, or at least of future failure, gripped him. He could see now, without any parental urging, that his his Cs in U-High were going to hurt him. Could he even get into the College now? And if he didn't go to the College of the University of Chicago, where would he go? Not Swarthmore. Not Haverford, which Phil was considering. He supposed he could get into a Big Ten school, but that would not be the same as Chicago or the kind of Eastern school that some of his classmates were considering. Anne de Lancey was going to apply to Vassar. So was Rosalind Ingleside, whose mother had gone there. Stan was determined to go to M.I.T. Jerry knew he had no chance of making it into that kind of school, though he did try to buckle down and improve his grades. He knew he was not really dumb. He could understand things when they were clearly explained, but he was just not interested in Social Studies, or German (a new trial), or English, or Calculus, or Art, or even Chemistry, which he had always thought would interest him when he got to it because, after all, both his mother and father had specialized in Chemistry when they were in college. But Chemistry seemed to him as uninteresting as other subjects. He couldn't understand what his parents had seen in it.

Nor what his friends saw in it.

In Scammons Gardens during the winter of 1947–48 the members of the Hard Core had begun to talk about things they were learning in class. It depressed Jerry to see how

70

much more his friends were getting out of their education than he was getting out of his. He was further depressed when he heard them talk about things they were reading in the newspapers or in books they picked up just for fun. John Williams read physics books for pleasure. He seemed to understand what made an atom bomb work. He and Stan Wengrowitz argued about cosmology. Phil and Ernie Hill argued about the Truman Doctrine. Admiring, but dismayed, Jerry regretted the good old conversations about human sexual customs. More and more he retreated into daydreams of the perfect woman who would enter his life and transform it.

Her name was Katya. She was a student in the College whom he met one day in the Classics building where U-High Art classes were now held. They no longer made things out of clay or cut-up colored paper. They were being taught Art History, which was terrible, but one day while he was looking at the engravings that hung in the stairwell of the Classics building, Jerry noticed a dark, intense-looking girl on the steps near him. She was the first one to speak. "Do you like these engravings?" she asked. They were pictures of Roman ruins and of some strange prisonlike places. "I like this one," said Jerry, pointing to one of the prison scenes that had staircases winding up and around a great central pillar. "It's interesting," he said. Katya nodded. "What are you going to be?" she asked him. "I don't know," he said. "You have the hands of an artist, or a great surgeon," she told him. "Do you really think so?" Jerry said. "Or you could be a leader," she said. "You have the eyes of a master." "I do?" he said. "Come with me," she replied, taking him to her book-lined room where she began to undress at once. "But before you can do anything," she said, "you must learn love. That is what I will teach you."

Learning love from Katya was more satisfying than anything he could imagine with Lady Windermere or Monica Kipling or the various Mimis and Dotties who passed out in his arms during his midnight walks. The only trouble was

71

that Katya was as unreal as all his other women. What he needed, he thought, was a real woman to teach him real love and tell him the real truth about what he should do. Barring her advent, the best he could look forward to was Anne's arrival for Christmas vacation. Maybe Anne would have some ideas about his future.

For once, though, Anne was so preoccupied with her own affairs that she did not show her usual curiosity about his. She was engaged. "How would you like to have a brother?" she asked Jerry on the first night she was home. They were in the kitchen doing dishes, since it was the maid's day off. He didn't understand her. He thought at first Anne was telling him she was going to have a baby. He glanced at her waist. "His name is Michael," Anne said, and then Jerry understood.

He tried to pretend he was glad about it and interested in Michael, a Swarthmore student, but in truth he felt terrible. He did not need a brother, or rather a brother-in-law. Phil was brother enough for him, and the idea of Anne's being more interested in Michael than in himself was galling beyond belief, particularly when he needed Anne's attention more than ever. He listened to her description of Michael's brilliance, his sense of humor, his wonderful taste in literature, and his serious political convictions, and decided Michael was a phony. He did not even like Michael's looks when Anne showed him a picture of the guy. Michael looked ordinary to Jerry. And he was too old. He was twenty-four. He had spent years in the Army. "Very nice," Jerry said, handing back the photo. "Do the parents know?" The senior Engels had had to go out that evening to a long-standing engagement. "I've written them," Anne said, adding to Jerry's disillusionment with the whole business. He hadn't even been told. He'd been kept in the dark.

"I want you to meet him," Anne said. "I'm sure you'll like each other." Jerry nodded. "I've told him about you," said Anne. "He has a younger brother himself. They have a very close relationship. It's a family like ours." Jerry nodded some more. "When are you marrying him?" he asked. "Not until spring," said Anne. "He graduates then. He's a year ahead of me." "And what about you?" Jerry asked. "I'll drop out of Swarthmore," Anne said brightly. "Michael's going to law school. I'll get my B.A. wherever he goes." "The parents won't like that," Jerry predicted. "They'll just have to accept it," Anne said. "We're very much in love," she added in a tone that made Jerry wonder if they had already made love.

That whole Christmas vacation was dominated by discussions of Anne's engagement and of the parents' opinion that Anne should wait a year and finish at Swarthmore before marrying. Jerry, who sided with the parents on this issue, pointed out to Anne that she would barely be twenty in June. "That's pretty young to be married," he said to her, his own marriage being firmly fixed in his mind as impossible before the age of twenty-five or twenty-six. "I don't think it's too young at all," said Anne. "You let the parents influence you too much," she added. She was very down on the parents that vacation, not just because they were opposing her marriage in June but because they were so middle-class and tied to the capitalist system. From the moment of her arrival at the 63rd Street Illinois Central station, she and her father had been at odds. Anne had descended from the train rather pleased with the fact that she'd made the trip with only forty cents. She'd rented a pillow for a quarter, dined on a ten-cent apple, and had a nickel left. "Why didn't you write me for more money?" Mr. Engels exclaimed. It pained him to think of Anne traveling like that. "I didn't need it," she said. "Oh my God!" Mr. Engels exclaimed.

At dinners there were real outbursts as Anne described how monopoly capitalism throttled useful inventions and weakened the value of others. "Nylon stockings used to last forever, and now they're gone after you've worn them twice. They put acid into the formula to weaken the fiber." "That is ridiculous!" Mr. Engels exclaimed in a rare outburst of anger. "I know Dr. Rose at Dupont, and I *know* he is not weakening his fiber." "How do you know?" Anne demanded. "And anyway, he's a scientist. He has no control over manufacturing." "He is in charge of quality control for Dupont," said Mr. Engels firmly. "Scientists don't control policy," Anne said. "Look at Standard Oil. Do you even know what goes on in refining and marketing?" Mr. Engels took a deep breath. His latest promotion had made him Director of Research. There was now just one management level between him and a position on the Board of Directors. In a few more years he could look forward to being moved downtown to 610 Michigan Avenue. Already the Engels had the privilege of using Red Crown Lodge in Wisconsin, the executive retreat on Trout Lake. "I know a good deal," said Mr. Engels, "and Charlie Hale is a scientist himself. He has a Ph.D. from M.I.T." Mr. Hale was Chairman of the Board. "It's been a long time since *he* was in a laboratory," Anne replied.

She did not give up her position. She also argued with her father about national and international issues. Mr. Engels, who had been raised in Kentucky, had always voted Democratic. In 1932 he had even voted for Norman Thomas, the Socialist candidate, but by 1947 he had grown more conservative. He let it be known he was prepared to vote Republican. It was time for a change, he thought. "You'd vote for Dewey!" Anne cried. "If he is renominated," Mr. Engels said. "Think of the people around him," Anne said. "Look at the people around Truman," Mr. Engels replied. Then he named a few Truman cabinet members he particularly disliked, ending with the name of Henry Wallace. "Wallace had *no* influence," Anne said. She *knew* that Communists, and party-liners, and plain simpletons like Wallace were being eased out of all the positions of importance in Washington. Michael had told her, and Michael knew because his father had been something in the New Deal and was still active in government work.

These conflicts between Anne and her father disturbed

Jerry and undermined his sense that the Engels were an unusually united, loving, mutually admiring family. Privately he tried to tone down Anne's criticisms. "Gee," he said, "Daddy's really a liberal." "He used to be," said Anne darkly, "but look at the things he's saying now." Mr. Engels was not enthusiastic about the FEPC or even about the Truman Doctrine. As Anne saw things, Mr. Engels was heading straight into the quagmire of Republican ignorance and isolationist obscurantism. "Well, I don't know," Jerry said, and then stopped because he really didn't know. He was so ignorant politically that he had no way of defending his father's position. Anne looked at him a little coldly. "And you ought to pay more attention to politics," she said.

Only toward the end of her vacation did Anne begin to show the kind of interest in him for which Jerry hungered. He went into her bedroom one day before New Year's and found her sprawled inelegantly on her bed rereading a letter from Michael. One knee was drawn up and he glimpsed her underpants. She often lay around carelessly like that, particularly when she was feeling good. Michael's letter evidently made her feel good, for when Jerry appeared she reached out a hand. "How's my little brother?" she asked tenderly. In her voice he heard the sentimental and slightly greedy tone that was often the prelude to their best talks. He shook his head in answer to her question. "What's the matter?" she asked. He threw himself across the bottom of her bed and began to tell her about his various problems. "You know what I've been doing?" he said at last. "I've been going in to talk to Mr. Poliakov." Mr. Poliakov was the School Psychologist whose office on the Language Corridor was a popular haunt with some U-High kids. Bernard Pear was in and out all the time, and even popular girls like Carolyn Webster had a friendly, half-flirtatious relationship with Mr. Poliakov. When Jerry learned that Ernie Hill was talking to the psychologist, he began going himself.

Anne was amazed. "Jerry!" she said, "you don't need psychological help. You're probably the most normal, well-adjusted person in U-High. There's nothing wrong with you." He shook his head. "Well, what's wrong?" she asked. "I mean, nothing you've told me sounds unusual. All boys worry about whether they're going to succeed as much as their fathers." "Succeed?" said Jerry. "I don't even have any idea of what I'm going to do. I may not even get into college." "That's ridiculous," said Anne. "You'll get in somewhere. You don't have to go to Chicago or Haverford. I wouldn't even advise you to go to Haverford." "Phil thinks it's the place to go," said Jerry. "Well, don't let yourself be so influenced by others," said Anne. "Michael could have gone to Haverford, or even Harvard, but he didn't like the atmosphere at either place." She considered the matter. "You should probably go to North Carolina," she decided. "It's a very good school. Frank Graham is President. He's very liberal. He might even run for President."

Jerry nodded, feeling that this wasn't entirely relevant. "But it isn't just school," he said, "It's my whole life. You know, I don't even have a real girlfriend anymore." "Who are you taking out New Year's Eve?" Anne asked. "Rosalind," Jerry said. "Rosalind Ingleside?" Anne asked. He nodded. "Well, what are you complaining about? You've always told me you think Rosalind is the best-looking girl in school." "She is," said Jerry, "but she's not my girlfriend. We're just going out together, that's all." "Well, I think that's pretty good," said Anne. "I only asked her because I can't ask half the girls I used to go out with. They're going steady now." "Well, why don't you go steady with Rosalind?" Anne said. "She doesn't go steady," said Jerry. "She never has." "You could be the first she's gone steady with," Anne suggested. "No," said Jerry. "Why not?" "You know why, Anne. Look at her family."

Anne sat up straighter. "Jerry!" she said, "you just don't realize how nice and attractive you are. You're perfectly good enough for Rosalind even if her family is rich. You come from a good family. Daddy's successful. You don't have to feel inferior to anyone." "Even the Inglesides?" Jerry asked. "Mr. Ingleside is just a professor," Anne said. "He probably makes a lot less money than Daddy does. I know he makes less." "Oh, Anne!" said Jerry. "Well, it's true," Anne said. "Rosalind's grandparents are rich, but Mr. Ingleside is no more successful than Daddy, probably less successful." "Look at their house at the Shores," Jerry said, "and where they live in town." "That's Mrs. Ingleside's money," said Anne, "and anyway, look at yourself. Look how handsome you are. If I were a girl I'd want to go out with you." "You are a girl," Jerry said. "You know what I mean," said Anne.

He came away from this conversation feeling better. True, Michael was still there in the background. Anne insisted to her parents that she was going to marry Michael and that after a brief honeymoon they would go to Campobello Island to a youth conference sponsored by Mrs. Roosevelt. Mr. and Mrs. Engels had not yet approved, but even if it happened, Jerry felt reassured by his talk with Anne. Anne still loved him, and when he thought about it he realized that she would eventually have to marry someone. He felt possessive toward Anne, but he was not unreasonable. He wanted her to marry sometime, so why not now? Tentatively Jerry began to feel well disposed toward Michael.

Anne also made him feel better about his forthcoming date with Rosalind. Over the years he had seen a lot of Rosalind, but from that day in fifth grade when he refused to dance with her, he had thought of her as beyond him, even when they were both regularly going to those parties at Carolyn Webster's. He realized then that Rosalind thought of him as a good friend, yet he never dated her. He danced with her at parties, he had gone to a few parties at her house, he saw her regularly during the summer when she came down to his end of the Shores to spend the evening with Shirley, but he had never felt really close to her.

It was perhaps because she was so beautiful. She really was

more beautiful than any girl he had ever seen. Her beauty, plus her family's money, plus their social position in Chicago, made Rosalind seem to him exceptional and unlike any other girl, even though he could see she dressed like other girls and went to the same parties and sat in the same classes and in general behaved as if she were like everyone else. This simply gave her a further touch of romance as far as he was concerned. Rosalind seemed to him like the female equivalent of those princes or caliphs in fairy tales who put on ordinary clothes in order to mingle with their subjects. He was actually quite surprised she had accepted so readily his invitation to escort her to the Colony Club New Year's Eve dance. It was almost like inviting Carolyn or Anne de Lancey or Marylynn or Sandra or Rachel or any of the other girls he'd escorted in the past.

And at first the party itself seemed like other Colony Club affairs. Jerry was even involved in the same joke he and his friends had frequently pulled in the past. The party was at the Shoreland Hotel, and he and Ernie Hill had told the hotel management that it was Bernard Pears' birthday. Bernard was Jerry's friend now, though he was the sort of friend you were always cruel to. Bernard had acne like no one else and he was still fat. Yet now everyone liked him, even the girls. He was a sort of class favorite, and at parties Jerry and his pals always pretended it was Bernard's birthday. At U-High parties this simply involved singing "Happy Birthday to You," but at Colony Club parties, particularly hotel parties, they could usually hoodwink the management into providing elaborate, hotel-type birthday cakes. All hotels seemed to have such cakes in reserve. When you told the manager, even at the last moment, that it was someone's birthday, the manager could generally come up with a cake.

The joke worked again that New Year's Eve. There was a break in the dancing. The bandleader raised his baton and the band played "Happy Birthday" while a waiter appeared, carrying a large three-tiered cake. Everyone laughed because everyone knew the cake was going to be for Bernard. The waiter looked a little surprised, but he advanced toward a table where Bernard was sitting. Ernie stood there, waving to the waiter and pointing down at Bernard's head. Bernard turned beet red, as he always did on these occasions, and everyone joined in the joke by singing, "Happy birthday dear Bernard, happy birthday to you." Through the noise and the laughter you could hear Bernard shouting hoarsely, "It's not my birthday, it's not my birthday, it's not my birthday." He had grown tired of the joke. He shook his head at the waiter. He refused to blow out the candles or to cut the cake. He looked exasperated.

Jerry and Rosalind watched it all from an alcove across the ballroom. "We should stop doing that," Rosalind said, turning away from the scene. Jerry caught her point and felt a little ashamed of his part in the proceedings. It seemed to him typically nice of Rosalind to have used the pronoun *we*. He turned away himself. Now they were facing a tall, many-paned window in which he could see Rosalind reflected. She was wearing an orange strapless evening dress with the tiny salmon-colored roses Jerry had given her fixed to a band on her wrist. As he watched he saw her put out her hand to rest her warm palm against the window. When she removed her hand he could see her palmprint on the cold glass. The print began to contract. Without thinking he bent his head and kissed her palmprint before it vanished. When he looked up at her there was an expression on her face he had never seen before. What was it? Where had he seen such a look? It seemed both familiar and unfamiliar. Their eyes met. His lips, still registering the coldness of the windowpane, began to feel full and heavy. He knew that sensation. It meant he wanted to kiss, and then it came to him that what he was seeing on Rosalind's face was the desire to be kissed.

He drove her home that night still thinking of the look he had seen on her face there in the ballroom with the chaperones looking on. He had not kissed her then, but now he was alone in his family's Oldsmobile, and beside him sat the most beautiful girl in U-High with her evening coat around her bare shoulders. The radio was playing. They were listening to the New Year's celebrations at the Beverly Wilshire Hotel in Los Angeles where it was not yet midnight. Harry James' band was playing, Helen Forrest was singing. He parked on Woodlawn Avenue, a few yards from the driveway that led into the huge yard of Rosalind's house. When he turned to kiss her, she put a bare arm around his neck. Her roses were still attached to her wrist and he could feel them brushing the back of his neck. When they had kissed for a while, she drew back. "Thank you, Jerry," she said, "I had a wonderful time." Then they got out of the car and walked up the driveway to her house. A light was shining in the porte cochere. Her parents had only recently come home from a party of their own. Through a window he could see her father, tall and elegant-looking in a tuxedo with silk lapels and a deep red cummerbund. He opened the door for them. Then—and this really dazed Jerry—after greeting her father, Rosalind turned back to him. With a mischievous look she gave him a final goodnight kiss while Mr. Ingleside stood right behind her. "Goodnight, Jerry," she said. He went home feeling that something really important had happened to him.

He called her at noon the next day. Again she told him she had enjoyed herself the night before. "It was a good party," he agreed, and then he asked if she'd like to do anything that afternoon. "Would you like to go ice-skating?" he asked. "That sounds like fun," she said.

He called for her with his skates slung over his shoulder, and they walked together the whole long way from her house in the 49th Street block of Woodlawn down to the ice-skating area on the Midway. He did not have the car that afternoon, but he was glad for the walk which gave them time to say things to each other. A great deal to say seemed to have accumulated overnight. He hardly noticed the distance or the curious, subdued New Year's Day atmosphere along the city streets.

He was a good skater and so, he was pleased to discover, was Rosalind. "My parents used to flood our side yard in Whiting," he told her, "and I learned to skate holding onto a kitchen chair that I pushed ahead of me." He realized there was a lot about his life she didn't know, though while they were skating he had little opportunity to tell her. They skated in tandem, holding hands across their bodies. Then he would release one of her hands and spin her out until she was facing him, skating backward. Then he would pull her to his side again.

When they had skated for an hour, he began to feel hungry. "Let's go up to the Tropical Hut and get something to eat," he suggested. "Will it be open today?" Rosalind asked. "Let's go see," he said. "If it isn't, we can get something at Stineway's or Gordon's. Something on 57th Street will be open."

The Tropical Hut was open. It was the chic place then for U-Highers to take girls. You went to Stineway's with your buddies, but you took girls to the Tropical Hut, which was dark inside. They got a booth for four. He slid in next to her and immediately took hold of her hand. While they waited for their hamburgers, he told her about winter weekends at Indiana Shores when he and Anne tobogganed on the Live Dune and climbed on the ice that built up along the shoreline. "At this time of year there are real icebergs," he told her. "We never go out to the Shores in the winter," Rosalind said. "You should use your house out there more than you do," he told her. "You don't even use it much in the summer." "I know," she said, "but Mother's so allergic she really has to go to New Mexico in June, and she likes me to go with her, and Daddy doesn't want to be out there alone." He nodded. "What do you do in New Mexico?" he asked. "Ride mainly," said Rosalind. "I can't ride very well," Jerry said. "I spent part of a summer once at a camp in Colorado where all we did was ride, but I never went back. I liked the

Shores too much to want to be at camp in the summer." "I know," said Rosalind. "It's the best place there is for the summer," said Jerry. "Why go to camp when you have Lake Michigan right there at home?" "I know," she said. "Lake Michigan is actually the best place to swim in the entire world," he said. "I mean, in the winter you have to use pools, and anyway swimming meets are based on pools, but I'd much rather swim in the lake than in any pool." "So would I," said Rosalind. "In a pool you just do laps," Jerry said. "I mean, swimming practice is really dull. I mean, I love it, but I'm just doing hundreds of laps. In the lake I'm really free. This summer Phil and I are going to swim out to the nets every day. We're going to start in June as soon as we move out and we're going to do it every morning the lake is calm enough. . . . When will you be at the Shores?" "I'm not sure," said Rosalind. He looked inquiringly at her. "Well, Mother and I will be in New Mexico, and then I think my grandparents will want me with them on a cruise." "But you'll be there by the Fourth of July, won't you?" "I don't know," she said. "You always open your house by the Fourth," Jerry reminded her. "We may not this year," she said. "They may want to go clear up to Mackinac." He noticed she pronounced it *Mackinaw*, like the raincoat. "I've never seen Mackinac," he said, adopting her pronunciation. "My grandmother likes it," said Rosalind. She smiled at him, "But I know I'll be at the Shores early in July. I just may not be there for the Fourth." "The Fourth is ruined anyway," said Jerry. "Without your own fireworks it's no fun. I don't like these town displays, do you? It was better when everyone had his own fireworks, and you could watch the Farr girls with their roman candles and the Trains shooting off skyrockets. It's just not the same anymore." Rosalind agreed, and he felt they really saw eye to eye on lots of things: swimming in the lake, fireworks, and the undesirability of summer camps.

"What's happened to the Farr girls?" Rosalind wondered aloud. "I don't know," he said. "I haven't heard of them since they sold their place. It's been sold again, you know. My family even looked at it, but we like our cabin too much." His eyes came to rest on her lips as she licked away a crumb from her hamburger bun. "Do you want ketchup?" he asked. "No thank you," she said. She took another small bite and he watched in silence as she chewed. Then she said, "Guess who I saw the other day. Nancy Train." "Where?" he asked immediately. "I never see her in town." His U-High, Hyde Park, Colony Club world never intersected with her Francis Parker, near North Side, Junior League World. "I never see any Francis Parker kids." "I do," she said. "Where?" he asked. "At parties," she said, "downtown."

He fell silent thinking of Rosalind's downtown social life. "What's Nancy like in town?" he asked after a while. "The same," said Rosalind. "She's going to Wheaton, she says, or maybe Europe if she can get her father to agree." "Europe?" said Jerry. "You know, Paris . . . London. She and a friend would like to live in Paris and take art classes or something."

Rosalind had finished her hamburger. Now she wiped her fingers. "Aren't you going to eat yours?" she asked. Jerry looked down and saw his own untouched hamburger cooling on the plate in front of him. He wolfed it down and then looked around the restaurant. "Do you want something else?" he asked. "I don't think so," said Rosalind. "Thank you." "Do you want to do anything else?" he asked. "Well, we could skate some more," said Rosalind. "Great!" he said, and as they walked back to the Midway he slipped his arm around her waist. She didn't seem to mind this proprietary behavior, which increased his sense of happiness. While they were talking in the T-Hut he had realized how much their lives were intertwined, how much shared experience they had: U-High, the Lab school, the Shores, memories of the Farr girls, friendship with Nancy Train. Rosalind was not so remote. And she had kissed him the night before as if it were the most natural thing in the world, and here she was, walking with his arm around her waist, right past Belfield and Blaine halls. She could be his girl, he thought. Maybe she was already thinking the same thing herself.

Dusk came early and Rosalind said she had to be home by dark. He walked her, but now the walk which they had hardly noticed before began to seem long. "I'll carry your skates," he told her. "That's all right," she said. "Are you tired?" "No. I walk this a lot," she said. But he knew she was also driven a lot. He could remember her as a little girl climbing into the back of her grandmother's black limousine. More recently he had seen her picked up by Mr. Moxon, a colored man. Mr. and Mrs. Moxon worked for and lived with the Inglesides, and their son had practically grown up with Rosalind's dead brother. And as Jerry thought of David Ingleside and of the Moxons, a sense of the difference between Rosalind's life and his own swept over him. "Here," he said, "you carry the skates and I'll carry you." "Don't be silly," she said, but he scooped her up and carried her half a block. When he put her down as they waited for the light to change at Woodlawn and 51st, she laughed at him. "You didn't have to do that," she said. "I know, but I wanted to." She laughed at him again.

As they approached her house he was wondering if he could ask her to do something with him the next day, which would be Friday. When she spoke it was as if she'd been reading his mind. "It's too bad," she said, "my grandparents are leaving for Florida Saturday and we'll be spending most of the day with them tomorrow." Apparently she assumed that otherwise it would be natural for them to do something together. The thought excited him. To do something together three days in a row was practically going steady. Well, no, not going steady. They had not even talked about that. Still, to have seen each other three days in a row would have been something exceptional. He walked home thinking that Rosalind was certainly behaving as if she were interested in him. Then his mind roved back through the years to that terrible moment in fifth grade when she'd asked him to dance with her. Maybe she'd always been interested in him and he had just been too dumb to realize it. Maybe it was destined, he thought.

Destiny was much on his mind as he became Rosalind's boyfriend that winter. He thought of it that way, not the other way around. He was hers, she was not his. He was her escort. He escorted her to all the U-High dances and to Colony Club parties. Not only that, she invited him to escort her to real balls at downtown hotels, coming-out parties of girls she knew from the Saddle and Racquet Club that her family belonged to. At one such party he actually met Nancy Train for the first time in Chicago. "Jerry!" Nancy exclaimed, "What are you doing here? Are you with Rosalind?" He smiled his answer. Then Nancy introduced him to her escort, a huge young man in the dress uniform of Culver Military Academy. "This is Kevin O'Brien," she said. "His family lives in Ogden Dunes." O'Brien held out a hand and tried to crush Jerry's bones while Nancy went prattling on. Then they danced off.

Jerry knew practically no one at these downtown parties that he escorted Rosalind to, yet he was excited and happy just to be there with her and to be wearing his new tuxedo, the first he had ever owned. His only regret was that his tux did not have a cummerbund, which he felt was *de rigueur*. "You look very nice that way," his mother had told him, and he knew he did. Still, when he saw men with cummerbunds, he wished his parents had been more lavish when he bought his tux. Yet he couldn't complain. Rosalind seemed to be falling in love with him, and even her family accepted him. At one ball he actually danced with Mrs. Ingleside. "Now let's see," she said, "your father is with Standard Oil, isn't he?" In Mrs. Ingleside's world men didn't work for companies, they were with them almost in the same way they were with their wives. They had steady, almost proprietary relationships with their corporations. They did not philander around trying to improve themselves. "Yes," Jerry said, in answer to Mrs. Ingleside's question. "My father is Director of Research." Then he explained that the Director was below the Manager of Research, and that his father still worked at Whiting, not at 610 Michigan Avenue. He wanted things to be clear. "That's very good," Mrs. Ingleside said.

He found her delightful. When he called for Rosalind, Mrs. Ingleside was always welcoming and charming. "What lovely flowers," she would say when he brought Rosalind a corsage. "How nice you look," she told him when he turned up in his new spring suit. "Have a good gallop," she said, as Jerry and Rosalind went off for a ride in the park—during which Jerry nearly fell off his horse. He saw Rosalind taking an English saddle, so he asked for one himself and then sorely missed having a good Western pommel to hang onto at difficult moments.

Mr. Ingleside was less delightful than Mrs. Ingleside. Jerry tried to treat him the way he treated senior Standard Oil Company executives, but Mr. Ingleside wasn't having any of that. He brushed aside Jerry's politeness. When Jerry started to turn up regularly at the house, almost the first thing Mr. Ingleside said was, "So you're after my daughter?" "Now, Jack!" said Mrs. Ingleside, but Mr. Ingleside went right ahead. "This is a dangerous young man," he said, looking Jerry up and down. "I want to put the fear of God into him." Jerry didn't know what to say. Mrs. Ingleside patted his shoulder. "I think you're sweet, Jerry." That added to his embarrassment.

"Doesn't your father like me?" he asked Rosalind. "He pretends not to like any boys," Rosalind said. "Don't worry about it," she added, and soon Jerry did stop worrying because he could see Mr. Ingleside really did like him in a curious sort of way. Mr. Ingleside continued to say terrifying things, things other fathers probably thought but didn't put into words; yet at the same time Mr. Ingleside was clearly more interested in Jerry than other fathers had been. In fact he showed more interest in Jerry's athletic prowess than Mr.

Engels ever had. Jerry was basically a freestyle racer. His best event was the 100-yard freestyle, but he swam the medley as well and had sometimes thought of really working on his breaststroke and competing in breaststroke events. Mr. Ingleside found out about all this and would shoot questions at Jerry about his time in various events. He seemed to have a pretty good idea of what a good time was for a high school swimmer. Jerry wondered if he actually consulted the record books. But even when Mr. Ingleside was most friendly, he still said disconcerting things. He would stroll into the hall where Jerry was waiting for Rosalind to come downstairs and say genially, "Well, how's our breaststroker this evening?" Jerry was glad Rosalind didn't hear that one.

When swimming season ended and Jerry began to play tennis, Mr. Ingleside said, "I'll have to try you out this summer," which gave Jerry a chance to bring up a subject that had been on his mind for several years. Ever since the war the Inglesides had neglected their court at the Shores. It was a clay court which didn't stand up well under the sort of casual maintenance it had been getting. There was sand in the clay, the posts needed to be reset, and even the net was bad. Jerry and Phil had been doing most of the maintenance in recent years, clearing out dead leaves around the backstops, and weeding and rolling and marking the court. Early in June they worked like dogs getting it ready for play because it was the only court at Indiana Shores. The Town Board was planning to build public courts, but so far the nature lovers and the penny pinchers had combined to reject each site that had been chosen. The nature lovers didn't want any trees cut down or blueberry bushes uprooted, and the penny pinchers sided with them because they didn't want any money spent. The result was that tennis at the Shores depended entirely on Mr. Ingleside's deteriorating court. When Mr. Ingleside suggested that he and Jerry should play tennis together during the coming summer, Jerry finally had a chance to speak his mind.

"I think you should put down an all-weather surface," he told Mr. Ingleside. "It would be a lot less trouble to maintain." "The old court seemed good enough to me last summer," Mr. Ingleside said. "That's because Phil Forson and I worked on it so much in June," said Jerry. "Well, work on it even harder this June," said Mr. Ingleside. "Eric Anderson will let you have the key to the rolling shed." Eric Anderson was the town guard who looked after the summer homes during the off-season. "I know he'll let us have the key," Jerry said. "He's been giving us the key, but . . ." He looked up into Mr. Ingleside's smiling face. "But you want me to buy you a good all-weather surface so you won't have to work so hard on the clay," said Mr. Ingleside. Jerry blushed. "You need a new net, too," he said. "And what about floodlights so you can play at night?" Mr. Ingleside asked. "That isn't fair, Jack," said Mrs. Ingleside. She looked at Jerry. "We're really very grateful to you and Phil for the work you do on our court." "*I* haven't said I'm grateful," said Mr. Ingleside. "After all, they use the court more than we do." "And I'm glad someone is using it," said Mrs. Ingleside, with an edge in her voice that ended the conversation.

Jerry decided the Inglesides' funny attitude about their court stemmed from the death of David who had been a keen player before he was killed in the Battle of the Bulge. He didn't bring up the subject again, but it stayed on his mind. He began to feel Mr. Ingleside associated him with David, who had been a good athlete. Jerry could dimly remember seeing David in the locker room at Sunny Gym during his first miserable winter in the Lab School. David must have been sixteen or seventeen then and already developed. To Jerry the big guys like David Ingleside had seemed like full-grown men, but now he realized he himself was as full grown as David had been in those years. That could explain Mr. Ingleside's odd but not really unfriendly attitude. Jerry reminded him of his own son.

Or sons. There had been two Ingleside boys, both older

than Rosalind. David died during the war, and Eric had been killed even earlier in a freak sledding accident when he was just a boy. It happened before the Engels moved to Chicago. It happened, Jerry realized, at the Shores. No wonder the family didn't go out anymore in the winter. And as he thought about that, he felt bad that he had told Rosalind about those winter weekends his family spent at the Shores. He'd probably reminded her, without realizing it, of her dead brother. Though thinking it over, he could not remember her growing silent or pensive as they sat together in that booth in the T-Hut. Maybe she didn't think of her brothers anymore. They were intimate enough for him to ask her about it now.

"I think of them a lot," she said. Then she went on to explain that she thought of Eric even more than she thought of David, even though Eric had died earlier. He had been closer to her in age, and when she passed the age at which Eric had died it was as if she had lost him all over again. "I'm growing away from him now," she said, "but I'm still growing toward David." She looked at him as she said this, and it seemed to him she had never been more beautiful than when talking of her dead brothers.

By spring they were going steady. He avoided Majorie McConkey's eyes when he passed her in the hall, and he felt bad that she was obviously hurt that he no longer dated her. But he had never said he loved her. He had never prostrated himself with her as he liked to do when he was romancing girls, taking their hands as he lay beside them in the grass of the Promontory and kissing all their fingers and murmuring into their palms, "I love you, I love you, I love you." It didn't always mean he did love them, but he hadn't even done that much with Marjorie. Still, he could see she had a case against him, and he felt guilty about her, though not guilty enough to spoil his happiness with Rosalind.

Everyone at U-High now knew they were going steady. The feelings he'd had in the winter that he was being passed up by other guys and on the verge of failure in life were completely gone. He felt affectionate and generous toward everyone, even Marjorie (though he could not meet her eyes). Even Michael, whom he had never seen. Now, however, he was all for Anne's marriage, which had been pushed into July because Michael's father had to be out of the country in June on some government business. Anne would be married at the Shores in early July, and then she and Michael would go straight to Campobello without any intervening honeymoon. The elder Engels had somewhat reluctantly accepted these plans. Jerry blessed them. And he felt nothing but good will for such U-High romances as he saw going on around him. Let Phil and Rachel Fein be happy together. Let Ernie and Carolyn Webster make out, as he suspected they were doing. Let Stan and Anne de Lancey have serious and soulful conversations in every corner of every dance floor. He was only sorry there was not more love going around. He hoped someone would soon take his place with Marjorie and really fall in love with her. She deserved it. Everyone deserved to be in love. He grieved when John Williams and Marylynn Morris broke up, and he searched his mind for the boy who would be really right for Shirley. He felt Shirley's love life was not prospering. She kept rejecting the boys who were most attracted to her, Bernard Pear for one, and while you could see why she rejected them in most cases, Jerry felt Shirley ought to be falling in love with someone. Everyone should fall in love. Everyone should be as happy as he was. To be the boyfriend, the publicly acknowledged boyfriend of Rosalind Ingleside was . . . and he would pause to think what it was. Then, dipping into his scanty Latin, he decided it was the *summum bonum*.

Everything about her surprised and delighted him. She was so good-looking, so glamorous-looking even, that he had always been a little afraid of her. It was one reason he'd never tried to date her before this year, but now that he was really getting to know her he discovered that she wasn't really glamorous at all. Or if she had glamor it was around her, outside her, located in her looks, in the way her family lived, and in all the money she would eventually inherit. Because her brothers were dead and her Uncle David Elbridge a confirmed bachelor, Rosalind would eventually inherit the whole Elbridge fortune, which was really enormous, Jerry realized. Rosalind never talked about it, but she said little things that staggered his imagination. She mentioned one day that her grandparents had given up their apartment in the Drake Hotel to take a smaller apartment at the Blackstone in order to save money. To Jerry the idea of people saving money by moving from the Drake to the Blackstone simply emphasized how rich they had to be in the first place, especially when you considered that they used their Chicago apartment less than half the year. She said, too, that her grandmother did not like to use public transportation. That was why she went to the trouble of keeping a limousine and employing a chauffeur when she was in Chicago. That way she did not have to use taxicabs. And one reason she spent so much of the summer aboard the Elbridge yacht was that she could travel around using her own transportation without even relying on the public highways. She was looking forward to the opening of the St. Lawrence Seaway because then she and her husband could take the *Calypso* down to Florida every winter and use it there as well as on the Great Lakes. It all seemed utterly remote and magical to Jerry, but the glamor of this background did not seem to affect Rosalind's feelings.

Her feelings were really very simple and uncomplicated. She was affectionate. She enjoyed his kisses and she kissed him back, but he felt in her none of the complexity or even passion that he had felt with other girls, most recently with Marjorie. He wondered if for really rich girls like Rosalind love became different from what it was for a middle-class girl like Marjorie. Rosalind already possessed so much that maybe, for her, falling in love meant that you did not reach out for more, you simply welcomed another person into your own rich world, the way Mrs. Ingleside seemed always to be welcoming him into her home.

It was a beautiful house. On the ground floor at the back there was what they called the Garden Room, a wide living room that opened onto a lawn which, in the spring, was bordered by masses of daffodils and tulips and hyacinths. But the soft green grass outside, and the red tulips and the yellow daffodils and the blue hyacinths seemed almost garish compared to the old Persian carpet that covered the floor of the Garden Room. The carpet was so old it looked worn in spots, but when the sun struck it, it seemed to release a silky rose color that filled the room. There were also faded pale blues in the rug. Looking at them, Jerry would be reminded of the old blue rug in his parents' bedroom in Whiting. Where was that rug now, he wondered?

It had been disposed of, along with many of the things which had seemed to him at one time both beautiful and remarkable. When he was unhappy during his first winter in Chicago he had solaced himself at night by mentally reconstructing each room of his old home in Whiting, visualizing every picture and every piece of furniture in its exact place. Now, much of that furniture was gone along with the blue rug. He supposed the rug and the missing furniture had not been much good in the first place and his mother had gotten better things as his father earned more money. Yet those departed furnishings of his childhood stood as little gaps in his consciousness, gaps that Rosalind would never know. Everything her family had ever owned was the best you could get, and when things in the Ingleside house grew old and worn like the Persian carpet, they became, if anything, more beautiful than when they were new.

He would come home from the Inglesides and look around his family's apartment, trying to decide which things they owned were really good, and which might eventually disappear if his father were promoted again and the family

92

moved, as they sometimes talked of doing, into an apartment with a view of the lake. Would his mother get rid of that couch, Jerry wondered? Or would she move it out to their cabin at the Shores to replace the even older couch, in whose cavernous recesses he and Anne used to find treasure troves of jelly beans on Easter morning. Then what would happen to the really old couch, the one now at the cabin, the one that had once been in their living room in Whiting? Would it be given away as junk? He would miss it. And he would visualize it as it stood now in the living room at the cabin, those recesses that used to be stuffed with jelly beans now hidden by a slipcover, new a few summers ago but already faded by the sun.

"What are you looking at?" his mother asked him one day when he was standing in the living room staring at a picture on the wall. "Where did we get that?" he asked her, gesturing at the picture. It was an oil painting of a Japanese woman. It was a dark picture with lots of deep green and an almost purply blue color in the woman's robe. He had seen the picture all his life. He could remember it had hung in the dining room at Whiting where it went with the silky, blue-green draperies which his mother pulled every evening before they sat down to dinner, even when it was still light outside. "Why are you shutting out the light?" his father would ask. "We always pulled the curtains in my house," his mother replied. "Do you think there's something wrong with people outside seeing us sitting at the table eating?" his father asked. "I was just brought up this way," his mother would say, firmly closing the curtains, and Mr. Engels would good-humoredly shrug his shoulders and adjust himself to the way things had been done in the Winterhalter family.

"That picture?" his mother said. "It's one of Helen's." Helen was her sister, a painter in California, an unmarried woman who sold few of her pictures and even fewer of the novels and stories she also wrote. Mr. Engels really supported her, adjusting to this necessity as patiently as he adjusted to the closing of the curtains. He loved his wife too much to make a fuss over such things. "Why?" his mother asked Jerry, who was still looking at his Aunt Helen's painting of the Japanese woman. "I don't know," he said, "I just wondered." He looked around the room at all the familiar things in it. Where had they all come from? Were they any good? Was his Aunt Helen a good painter? Was that desk a good desk? "Where did we get that?" he asked, pointing at the desk. "Your father and I bought it from an antique dealer in Delaware when we were first married," his mother said. "Why are you so interested in this all of a sudden?" "I don't know," he said, looking now at a piece of Chinese embroidery framed under glass. His mother had once told him it was made with a knot so tiny and intricate it put out the eyes of embroiderers who worked at it too long. The Emperor of China had finally forbidden this kind of embroidery. You couldn't get it anymore. "We have some good things, don't we?" he said. "Some," said his mother, looking alert, amused, and affectionate.

He was feeling closer to her than he had felt in recent years. This was partly because he felt closer to everyone now that he was in love with Rosalind and partly because he was waking up to the fact that for many women, for women like his mother, the home they put together was a reflection of themselves, and to know the woman you had to know and understand the home she lived in. But did he understand his own home, he wondered? Did he understand his mother?

She loved colors and fabrics as well as flowers and dogs. Jip had just died and she was sadder about his death than anyone else in the family. It was for her, really, that they were getting a new wire-haired terrier. He could do without a dog now. He had completely lost his old passion for pets, but his mother wanted a dog in the house. Why? Out of the blue he asked her, "Did you always have a dog as a child?" She smiled at him. "I always wanted one, but we never had one." He nodded. "What is it, Jerry?" she said, putting her arms around him. "I don't know," he answered. "Do you want to tell me?" she said. "You're in love, aren't you?" He felt himself nodding as he squeezed her. She said, "I hope it's a happy experience for you. I remember the first time I was in love with a boy. It was the year I was lame. I was home all the time, and I used to sit at the window and watch him mowing his family's yard. His family lived right next to us in Portland. I knew his sisters. I used to play with them, but I didn't know him at all. He was older. He was Jeremy's friend, really. I don't think he ever knew I was in love with him."

For some reason Jerry began to cry. Perhaps it was his mother's reference to her brother, for whom Jerry had been named. He had never known his uncle, who had died in his twenties of tuberculosis. Like Rosalind, his mother had lost her brother. As that connection struck him, he wept even more. His mother began patting him. "I don't know why I'm crying," he said. "I'm really happy."

They backed off and looked at each other. Through the tears in his eyes he could see his mother's face softened with sympathy and understanding. And something else. There was a sweet though sorrowful smile on her lips. Maybe he didn't want to look at that smile, but anyway he threw his arms around his mother again and said, "I love her so much, Mother." "She's a very nice girl," said Mrs. Engels. "She is," Jerry agreed. His mother hesitated. "Jerry," she said at last, "I hope you can stand to be disappointed." Her words conveyed no particular meaning to him. Mrs. Engels said, "She's very nice, and I'm glad you're having this experience of being in love, but . . ." "You mean we can't get married?" He watched something change in his mother's face. "Well, yes," she said, but it was not what she had meant.

Thinking it over, he decided she meant one of two things, or perhaps both. She meant he would not be in love with Rosalind forever, or she meant Rosalind would not go on loving him forever. She meant, really, that this love would not last, but she had seen how he felt, so when he interpreted her reservation, her *but*, as meaning that he and Rosalind could not get married right away, she had decided to keep the truth to herself. Only was it the truth? Would his love end? He shook his head at the thought. Parents believed their children's loves were temporary because they had seen those loves change so often. That was particularly true in his case, because he'd been in love so frequently. He couldn't blame his mother for thinking his love for Rosalind was like all his old loves. She'd seen him in love with Anne de Lancey, and with Gloria, and half in love with Carolyn and Rachel and Marylynn and other U-High girls. She could remember all his girls clear back through grade school to kindergarten when he had come home one day with a hair ribbon he'd forcefully pulled out of Elizabeth Ann Palmer's hair. "Where did you get that, Jerry?" she had asked him when he showed it to her. "I got it from Elizabeth Ann," he said. "I'm going to keep it." "Did she give it to you?" his mother asked. He shook his head. "She wouldn't give it to me when I asked her." "But you can't just take things from girls," his mother explained. "You'll have to give it back to her." He shook his head again. "I want to keep it," he said, but she had made him give it back, even driving him to the Palmers' house where he had been forced to hand over the stolen ribbon and apologize for having snatched it out of Elizabeth Ann's hair.

His mother could remember all that, as well as his passion to have a monkey, and his frantic promises that if only she would let him have a monkey he would be contented forever and never ask for anything else. And she could see how indifferent he now was to monkeys, or even hair ribbons, and so she assumed his love for Rosalind was like every other love in his life, only it wasn't. Parents didn't realize that their children changed, that they could grow up to the point that, like Anne, they insisted on being married. Though he didn't insist upon marrying Rosalind. He was a realist. They were too young. They were still in high school. They couldn't be married. He would not be so foolish as to insist on that. What he did insist upon (though not to his mother or to his father, and not even to Rosalind, herself), what he insisted upon in the recesses of his own soul was that the love he now felt could never end. He would love Rosalind all his life, whether or not they ever married. When he was old he would still love her, and though his love might change and become worn and used like that Persian carpet, it would be as beautiful then as it was now.

"I love you," he told Rosalind on their last date of the spring. As on their first date he had parked on the street beyond the Inglesides' driveway. He had the family car again, though he had had to argue for it this time, since his parents wanted to start packing it that evening for their annual move to the Shores. "I love you," he said again, toying with a lock of her hair. She smiled at him and moved closer, fitting herself under his arm. "We'll see each other in July," she reminded him. "I know." He had the radio on despite his father's constant reminders not to play the radio while the car was parked. It ran down the battery. He reached out to turn up the volume, the better to hear Frank Sinatra. "Do you want to write?" he asked. The thought of corresponding with Rosalind had a mixed appeal. It would be nice to correspond, but what would he say to her in his letters? "Will *you* write?" she asked him. "I will if you will," he promised. "We'll see," she said. "I bet you don't answer." "I will," he assured her, knowing, however, that his letter would be a disappointment to them both. He just couldn't put what he felt into words.

They listened for a while to the radio. Then he said, "I hope you'll be at the Shores for the wedding. Anne's wedding." "What day is it?" Rosalind said. "They've decided to have it on the Fourth," Jerry said, "the Fourth of July." "That's funny," said Rosalind. "I don't know, I think it's kind of appropriate—skyrockets, firecrackers, Roman candles . . ." he said. He had been genuinely intrigued by Anne's and Michael's choice of the Fourth to get married. "I don't think of weddings like that," Rosalind said. "They should be quiet." "Quiet?" he said. "Well, fireworks don't seem appropriate to me," she said. "Maybe music, but not skyrockets."

He saw her point, though skyrockets still fitted better than music with his idea of a wedding night. "What music?" he asked her. "Oh, I don't know," said Rosalind, snuggling a little against him. "Something dreamy, I suppose. Something like that," and she gestured at the radio from which they could hear the strains of "Moonlight Becomes You." "It's nice," he agreed, putting his cheek against hers. They sighed together.

He knew she was happy this way, cuddling as he thought of it. Her conception of love was a more lulling, peaceful conception than his own, but when the mood was on him, as it now was, he could feel the attraction of being together in a gentle, harmonious way. And since it was what Rosalind liked best, he was glad he was feeling in this mood on their last night together rather than in the mood which caused her to draw back and say, "That's enough, Jerry." He did not want to spoil the evening.

"What time is it?" she asked. He held his wrist in front of her face for her to read the time. "Midnight," she said. "Do you have to go in?" he asked her. Her head moved against his shoulder. "Just curious," she said. "You have to, though," she reminded him. He had promised to be in by midnight in order to be up early the next morning to pack the car for the move to the Shores. Actually he had become the expert car packer in the family, fitting together like a jigsaw puzzle all the different household items the Engels still found necessary to transport back and forth between their cabin and their apartment in town. They thought they had two of everything, but when the time came to move they invariably found quantities of things in town which they would need in the country. The result was that by noon tomorrow when he and his mother started for the Shores, they would look like

Okies setting off for California with the back of the Olds packed solid, leaving only a niche for Jill, their new dog, to sit in.

"I should take you in," said Jerry, surrendering entirely to a relaxed parting mood. He turned to her for a final kiss, a warm, hugging, goodbye-for-a-while kiss. It was all he wanted, or anyway all he expected to get. Yet, as soon as it began he felt it was not enough. They could not part this way. He could not let her go now, and when he felt her begin to resist him and to withdraw from their kiss, he sighed out her name. His arms were still tight around her. She was smiling at him and trying to keep him in line at the same time. "Rosalind," he murmured imploringly.

Then her smile departed as the beam of a flashlight suddenly hit her face. Jerry swung his head around. A figure stood at the car window just beside him, shining a flashlight on Rosalind. "What are you doing here? Get out! Get away!" Jerry cried. He was sure this was some sick figure of the night, a creeper, a peeper, who had slipped up unnoticed while he and Rosalind were kissing. "Get away from us!" Jerry yelled. Anger was a rare emotion with him, but he was angry that a man like this one should be shining his flashlight on Rosalind's face. "Get away! Turn that off!" he said. When the man did neither, Jerry hopped out of the car.

The man backed off, shining his flashlight on Jerry now. "What are you doing here?" the man said. "What are *you* doing here?" Jerry asked, his eyes dazzled by the light. "I've been watching you," the man said. "You can't bring your girls here and do that. This is a private neighborhood." It was a guard, a member of the private security force employed by homeowners in Kenwood to supplement the public protection they got from the Chicago Police Force. "You get out of here," the guard said to Jerry, waving his flashlight. "I've had enough of guys like you coming here and parking on these streets." "These are public streets," Jerry said. "Anyway, she lives here." And he gestured toward the car. The guard turned his flashlight back on Rosalind, still sitting on the front seat, the smile wiped off her lips. This fresh invasion of Rosalind's privacy so infuriated Jerry that he grabbed the flashlight. "Hey!" the guard said, startled. He leaped back, and ducked as if Jerry were about to shoot him, and as Jerry directed the beam of light on the man he could see it was a gray-haired fellow in some sort of uniform. Crouching and looking at Jerry, the guard drew his pistol. "All right, give me that," he said, straightening up and pointing his pistol at Jerry. "Not until you go away," said Jerry, a little illogically. From inside the car Rosalind said, "I'm going in now."

She opened the door on her side and got out. Jerry turned toward her. Now he was directing the flashlight beam on her. "Wait!" he said. He moved to follow her. "You!" the guard yelled at Jerry. "Get your hands up! I've got you covered." He was behaving like a maniac, Jerry thought. Rosalind spoke up. "It's all right," she said. "I'm going into the house now." She headed for the driveway. Jerry moved after her. "You've got my flashlight," the guard yelled at Jerry. For the moment he seemed to be more afraid of losing his flashlight than of anything else. Jerry turned and threw the flashlight at the guard. It hit him in the chest and fell to the street, where it shattered. "All right, you're under arrest," the guard said. "My father will pay you for that in the morning," said Rosalind. "Don't move, either of you," the guard said. "I've got you covered."

Why did men like Mr. Ingleside pay a lunatic like this to protect their property? Jerry wondered as the guard marched him and Rosalind up the driveway to the side entrance. He refused to raise his hands over his head, though the guard kept ordering him to do so. "All right, ring the bell," the guard said when they were under the porte cochere. "And don't try anything," he added. Rosalind took her key out of her purse and unlocked the door. "I live here," she said to the guard, standing in the open door. "Come in, Jerry," she added. "Just a minute," the guard said. "He doesn't live here. He broke my flashlight." His tone was still threatening, though he had lowered his pistol at last.

Then Mr. Moxon appeared in the hall. The guard appealed to him. "I caught these kids necking in a car on the street," he said. "This one attacked me and broke my flashlight." He gestured with his pistol at Jerry. "Will you pay him for the flashlight?" Rosalind said to Mr. Moxon. Then she went into the living room to get away from it all. Jerry followed her into the house, leaving Mr. Moxon to deal with the lunatic guard. "Gee, I'm sorry about that," he said to Rosalind. "It wasn't your fault," she told him. He wanted to touch her, to console her. Their parting had been spoiled and he wanted to make it up to her, but he was not sure she wanted him to touch her. This was the kind of event that made her simply withdraw. Violence, anger, craziness, ugliness just had nothing to do with her. Her instinct was to walk away from it, to go into her own home until it was over. "Gee, I'm sorry," he said again. She shook her head. In the hall they could hear Mr. Moxon and the guard talking to each other. "Wait until he's gone," said Rosalind to Jerry.

The living room was lit by a single lamp beside a couch. On the coffee table in front of the couch Jerry could see a copy of *The New Yorker*. A dowager in an ermine cape stood on the steps of her brownstone house while her chinless maid in an extravagant black-and-white maid's uniform blew a police whistle to summon a taxicab. Beside *The New Yorker* there was a bowl of jonquils. Beyond the couch and the coffee table, the room stretched out into the dimness of polished furniture and a faintly gleaming mirror. "I'm sorry," Jerry said again. He felt responsible for having exposed Rosalind to the guard. "We weren't even necking," he said. Rosalind didn't want to talk about it. She stood near the coffee table waiting for Mr. Moxon to settle matters with the guard. At last Jerry could hear the front door close. Mr. Moxon appeared in the entrance arch of the living room. "He seemed to be satisfied," Mr. Moxon said. Then he went away and Jerry looked hopefully at Rosalind. Would she invite him to stay a little longer? She smiled at him. "It's all right, Jerry," she said. "We had a nice evening anyway." She was moving him toward the front door. "I'll call you," he told her. "'I'll come in town to see you off for New Mexico." "You don't have to," she said. "I want to," he told her. In the hall he kissed her cheek and then left. Outside he could smell lilacs in bloom. On the street he found the guard kneeling behind the Oldsmobile recording the license number on a piece of paper. "I don't want to see you here again," the guard told Jerry, straightening up. "I *never* want to see you," said Jerry, getting into his father's car and starting off with a squeal of rubber on asphalt.

Coming of Age in Indiana Shores

ON STILL afternoons when not a leaf stirred in the big cottonwood and the only sound was the faint call of a mourning dove going, chluuuu-cwooo-coo,cwoooooo-coo, Jerry would lie on the cabin porch and daydream of women. He would invent a whole frieze of nameless and almost faceless girls, bending and stretching and dancing across the background of his mind. Then he danced them offstage and allowed a single girl to emerge: Rosalind, Rosalind Ingleside, the star of his show. She was his girl, he was her guy, and it was terrific—except that Rosalind was in New Mexico. Even in fantasy all she did was to smile at her adolescent impresario. Jerry smiled back. Then Rosalind looked at him out of the corner of her eye, and he would feel his heart quiver. He would heave a tender and languishing sigh, and Verlene would stick her head out the kitchen door to ask if he had said something. "No," Jerry would reply, thinking what a very plain maid Verlene was. Why did his mother never hire cute girls to work for them in the summer? That might be something! "I'll make ya lemonade," Verlene would suggest.

103

She was a willing worker, eager to please. Why couldn't she be beautiful as well? Though if this went on, if things didn't shape up soon, Verlene might begin to look good. Sighing again, less languishingly, Jerry would rise and leave the porch to wander down the ridge past the clump of junipers to see what was going on at the Hyatts or at the Forsons.

The Hyatts lived closer, fifty yards down the ridge in a stone house. He would climb the steps, push open the screen door of their porch, and walk in to find Shirley reclining on a lounge chair, in halter and shorts, a bottle of Coke by her side, a John Dickson Carr mystery story in her hands. "Hi," they said to each other without animation. Then Jerry would drop onto another lounge chair to stare somewhat resentfully at Shirley's slim, brown, and very attractive legs. Rosalind's legs were better, but Rosalind's weren't around to be stared at, and meanwhile there were Shirley's right in front of him, demanding more attention than he really wanted to pay, considering that, to all intents and purposes, those were sisterly legs. At least Anne didn't have legs like Shirley's, which seemed to be another point in Anne's favor at this stage of the game.

"What are you doing?" he would ask Shirley, after examining her legs in silence.

"I'm reading a book," Shirley would reply.

On occasions like this it sometimes occurred to him that maybe Shirley had her own version of his problem. Maybe the sight of his legs annoyed her as much as the sight of her legs annoyed him, and at that thought he would stretch his legs to look at them, and perhaps work his thigh muscles, watching them bunch and unbunch. "Stop doing that. You're always doing that," Shirley would say, which seemed to confirm his suspicion that she noticed his legs, which were good legs, incidentally. In fact his legs were probably his best part, he would think, flexing a biceps and feeling to see how *it* was coming along. "You're always feeling yourself," Shirley complained.

Well, he was the only one who seemed to want to do it, not that he was unwilling to be felt by some sympathetic woman who would like his arms and his legs and his torso as much as he liked them. And at the thought of some nameless woman admiring his body, he would tense the muscles of his abdomen and try to make them ripple, drawing another rebuke from Shirley, who was evidently as conscious of what lay beneath his T-shirt as he was of what lay within her halter. "Can't you just sit?" she would ask. "Do you want to do something?" he replied. "I'm *reading* a mystery," she would remind him, blocking out her view of him with the Pocket Book in her hand. "Give me a drink of that Coke," he would say. "Go get your own," she would reply, and at that he might rise and lounge into the Hyatts' kitchen to open the refrigerator and see what was there.

There was never a maid in the Hyatts' kitchen because all summer long they kept their townhouse open. They left their maid in town to cook for Mr. Hyatt, who had to sleep in Whiting three or four times a week because of that old Standard Oil rule that one of the senior men at the refinery had to be on the spot at all times in case of emergencies. Mr. Hyatt shared the chore with Mr. Musgrove and never complained of having to baby-sit the refinery, but it was a dumb rule in Jerry's opinion. What was Shirley's father supposed to do if the whole place exploded and caught fire some night? He was the Superintendent, not a fireman.

Back on the porch, with a bunch of grapes in his hand, Jerry would drop onto the lounge again and look at Shirley and at the sexy cover of the mystery story she was reading. "Let's do something," he would say, experimenting to see if he could toss a grape in the air and catch it in his mouth. "I *am* doing something," Shirley always answered. Jerry, picking the grape off the floor and wiping sand from it, would lean forward, "I'll take you for a sail," he would say, at which point Shirley would remind him that there was no wind. So, having struck out there and eaten all the grapes, Jerry would move on to the Forsons to see what Phil and Linda felt like doing.

These summer afternoons seemed endless. They began with the quiet spell after lunch, the daydreaming period, when he lay on his back and listened to the doves and to the far-off, diminishing hoot of freight trains hauling steel from Gary or oil from Whiting along the New York Central or the Pennsy or the Baltimore and Ohio tracks that snaked through the farmland to the south. Then, moved by the desire to do something and to see someone, he would begin the slow process of getting things started for the afternoon, dropping in on Shirley, dropping in on Phil, and then dropping back in on Shirley to tell her the plans. "We're going to go play on the Inglesides' court," he would tell her. So John Dickson Carr would have had his hour. Shirley, roused at last, would get up to find her tennis racquet and her tennis shoes, and then they would face the problem of how to get to the Inglesides' house. It was a mile by the beach and a mile and a half by the winding roads, and who wanted to carry tennis racquets along the beach or to walk anywhere on a day like this? One could run for miles, yes; one could play tennis for hours, yes; one could swim or sail, yes indeed; but one could not walk. So a car became necessary, but Mr. Engels and Mr. Forson had driven to Whiting that morning in the Engels' car, and Mrs. Hyatt and Mrs. Forson were shopping in Chesterton in the Hyatts' car, and Mrs. Engels and Anne were using the Forsons' car to go for a fitting at the dressmaker's. So that left Nancy Train and her car to be roped in. Nancy was probably wondering what to do with herself anyway. "Call Nancy," he would say to Shirley when the transportation problem had been thoroughly canvassed.

From where he stood on the Hyatts' porch he could see the Train house on the opposite ridge, standing out big and square and unshaded, and if he lingered long enough he would see Nancy emerge, clad in a white blouse and tennis shorts, switching her racquet from side to side as she walked down the drive to climb into her ancient Packard, which had to be parked on a slope to give it a running start. Valiant Foo would then begin to roll silently down the driveway before it coughed and choked into life as it reached the road. And at that point Jerry would leave the Hyatts' porch to get his own racquet and tennis shoes. He would even be moving fairly fast by the time he reached the cabin, pausing only to tell Verlene that if his mother asked where he was when she came home, tell her he'd gone to play tennis. Then he would be off down the steps to the road where soon he'd hear the roar of Valiant Foo's old engine, only eight or nine of whose twelve cylinders still seemed to function.

Linda Forson liked to sit on one of the jump seats, and Phil did not mind sprawling out in solitary grandeur on the back seat. Shirley always sat up front next to Nancy. And Jerry? Well, he liked to slide in next to the girls where he could fling out his left arm along the back of the seat and feel Nancy's soft hair brushing his wrist. "Do you have to crowd so?" Shirley asked, pinned there between Jerry and Nancy. "Who's crowding?" he said. "You," Shirley answered, and at that point he would tap Nancy decisively on the shoulder. "You and me against Phil and Shirley," he would say, whereupon Linda would remind everyone that she hadn't come along just to chase balls.

They let her play. Indeed, Jerry liked to sit out while Phil and Linda played against Nancy and Shirley. Then he could rest on the worn green bench and watch the girls and listen to the score mount from fifteen/love to thirty/love as Shirley and Nancy struggled with Phil's booming serve. And when Jerry was surfeited by the sight of Shirley's legs flashing in the sun and the heave of Nancy's bosom, he could always look upward across the untended lawn to the closed house. His eyes would come to rest on the drawn blinds of Rosalind's windows. *I love you,* he would think, writing his next letter in his head. *When we're playing on your court, I look up at your windows and think of you.* Then a dispute about whether a ball was in or out would draw his attention back to the game in progress, and he would find himself realizing that Linda Forson had begun to look pretty good for a thirteen-year-old. That recognition would make him sigh, then a yawn would develop, and finally he would inflate his chest to its maximum, as if he were caught in some deep internal crisis which could only be mastered by some calming breath work. He looked the picture of health and relaxation with his legs stretched out in front of him and his elbows hooked over the back of the bench, but frequently he was breathing like a spent swimmer.

"What *is* the matter with you?" his mother sometimes asked as he sighed and stretched and yawned around the cabin. His mother was nervous these days. The wedding was getting to her. "Are you ill?" she asked one afternoon. "It's love," said Anne, who apparently felt she understood the symptoms. "Jerry's in love." He closed his eyes as if in pain. Then Verlene chimed in. "Jerry's got growing pains." Not liking to hear himself discussed this way by a chorus of women, Jerry would say, "I'm going out to work." Then he was outdoors, stripped to the waist, the muscles of his chest and shoulders straining as he wheeled a barrow load of sand along the wooden gangplank he had constructed for it.

His role in the wedding preparations was to widen the lawn where Anne was to be married. This involved digging out masses of stubbornly rooted sweet sumac and then cutting into the side of a hill. When he had the area cleared and leveled (it would be sodded later) he was going to build a dry stone wall along the edge. Already a load of limestone lay in the road below the cabin, and as his bright shovel blade cut into the sand, his mind grappled with the problem of how to transport all that stone uphill. Should he build a sledge and haul it up? He rather liked the idea. Then, his barrow full once more, he would wheel it to the side of the yard to tip it. There was now a long tongue of freshly dug sand stretching down the ridge. Honey locust trees screened the sand from the yard and from the cabin, and as Jerry paused after tipping each load, he could smell the locust blossoms and hear the hum of bees overhead.

Working half-naked in the hot June sun, he felt himself transformed into a brawny manual laborer. Though he had been physically active all his life, he had done very little real work. This was probably the hardest work he had ever done, and his muscles, built up by running and swimming and tennis, ached pleasantly at night. He was really developing himself, he would think, massaging his own shoulder. Then the question would occur to him: developing himself for what? Why did he need to be better developed than he already was? What was the point of it all?

Sometimes, while Jerry worked, Phil would turn up to watch and occasionally lend a hand. One day Phil stripped off his own shirt as he shoveled sand. Jerry studied Phil's muscles, which were even better developed than his own, and then shook his head almost sadly. They were strong enough now. They were men. They had both begun to shave. They were men in everything but name. Men, except for one thing that neither of them had ever done. One thing.

He and Phil discussed that one thing from time to time, generally when they were away from their homes, hiking through the woods or walking along the old Golf Course Road. There, out of sight, enveloped by the heavy midwestern heat, Jerry could feel and even say things that would be inappropriate elsewhere. He could, for instance, pause to slap a mosquito on his bare forearm, and then look up from the spot of blood and feel a surge of desire heavier than anything he experienced on the beach or out on the lake when, sailing with his feet braced against the combing, he felt the sun between his spread legs stoking with its solar rays his own internal warmth. Deeply erotic as that could be, it was just not like the feeling that came over him along the Golf Course Road where it felt somehow natural to pause, to smash a mosquito or two, to feel the beaded sweat on his body, and then to say, drawing the words up as if they came from the bottom of his being, "Jesus, I need a woman."

They did not *talk* about sex. These discussions were more like sounds than speech. They were like the sighing of the wind in the treetops or the thud of their feet along the beaten track to which the road had reverted now that the golf course was out of use. These were pulse-beat conversations. "Jesus, I need a woman," Jerry might say, to which Phil would respond in his own way by saying, "Take a shower!" But how could he shower out there in the deep woods, and where was the lake he could always dump himself into if the feeling got too strong as he sailed? There, along the Golf Course Road, the only patches of water were the dark pools that collected in the peaty ground when one of the big tamaracks blew down, its roots ripping a hole where they had vainly sought to grip the soil. There were tamaracks in all stages of declension: three-quarters upright, their weight resting against a neighboring tree; half down, crushing some younger, smaller growth; and finally flat on the earth, a semicircle of spreading roots, still earth clogged, fanned out above the circular pools that formed where the trunks had once stood upright. Those stagnant pools, fringed by marsh marigolds and skunk cabbage, were fine breeding grounds for the mosquitoes that pestered Jerry and Phil and kept them on the move until they had come out onto the golf course. There they usually sought open ground near what had been the third tee where they could sit for a while to look out across the ruined fairway. And there Jerry would revert to the preoccupation of his seventeenth summer.

"Maybe we should go to Michigan City," he would say.

It was known—they at least had heard—that there was a house in Michigan City, a cathouse where there were women (or cats) whom one could visit. A friend of theirs from Horton's Dock, the summer community next to Indiana Shores, had told them about the house. He had visited it, he said. The question was, should *they* go? "What do you think?" Jerry asked. He was genuinely curious to have Forson's honest opinion on the subject. Should they go? He felt Forson might have sounder, wiser views than his own. His own views were chaotic. He was in love. Anne had said so, and he believed it was true. Yet he was also in rut. There were moments when it seemed to him insane that he and Phil had delayed going to Michigan City for a day, much less for the weeks that had already passed of this summer when it just had to happen. What were they waiting for? They were grown. They were men. Hell, Forson was even more of a man than Jerry felt himself to be, so what was his honest opinion on this vital question? *Should they go?*

"Do you want to go?" Phil asked Jerry one afternoon.

He shook off the question. He wanted answers. "Why shouldn't we go?" he asked. "I mean, they're whores," he said, relishing the word. "Whores!" It was their business. That was how they made a living. By not going to them, he and Phil almost seemed to be denying them their fair share of the wealth of Indiana Shores. It could be restraint of trade, maybe indictable under some clause in Truman's Fair Employment Practices Code. Whores had to make a living like everyone else. Only what a living! "You think we shouldn't go?" he asked. "I don't know," said Phil.

Leadership was what they needed, Jerry realized. They were getting nowhere on their own. What they needed was for some determined fellow to take charge—Alec Walker, for instance, from Horton's Dock. Walker had already been there. He knew the address. What they needed was for Walker to say one night, "Okay, we're going. You game, Engels? You game, Forson?" They would nod. They were game. They would get into Walker's jalopy, and he would drive them to the house and tell them what you did when you went in and how much you paid and all that. He had done it, he said. Only maybe he hadn't. Maybe he was bluffing. And anyway, he was not a leader. He was more a lone-wolf type. If he had gone (and he probably had) he had

111

gone alone, so it would be just a little humiliating for them to have Walker as their leader for their first experience. He would patronize them, and they didn't need that. What they needed was for some older, wiser person to take the lead. What should happen, Jerry felt, was that Mr. Forson should take his son, along with Jerry, for a drive some night in the Forsons' Buick. They might go to a movie first, and then afterward Mr. Forson would say, "Okay, boys, it's time," and he would drive them to the house and wait outside for half an hour (because it would be wrong for him to go in), and afterward he'd say something matter-of-fact like, "Have a good time?" or "Now you know the way."

Jerry always imagined Mr. Forson taking this initiative, not his own father. Mr. Forson had been brought up in Baltimore with a businessman as a parent, whereas Mr. Engels had been brought up in Mount Sterling, Kentucky, by his widowed mother and unmarried aunt. It made a difference. More worldly standards prevailed in the Forson family. Jerry had been told he must do nothing until he was married; all Phil had been told was to do nothing until he was damn sure he knew what he was doing. "We know," Jerry pointed out. "We're ready." "We don't know so much," Phil said. "Well, how are we going to find out if we don't go," Jerry asked. "But do you want to do it with one of them?"

It was a difficult question to answer. Sitting with his back against an oak tree, idly knocking apart a fern with a stick he held, Jerry would consider the matter. Did he want to do it with one of *them*? Did he want it to happen with a woman in a cathouse, a catwoman? That could be a little scary sounding. It sounded almost like going to the zoo in Michigan City and getting into a smelly cage with one of the big cats and getting eaten up or torn apart for his money. Some fun. Yet as he thought of a woman pacing restlessly in her room, maybe brushing her hair between visitors, the muscles of her shoulders and arms moving under the light negligee

112

she'd be wearing, he could feel it *might* be fun with her. It would certainly be exciting, though it would still be just a little alarming. "You think we shouldn't go, hunh?" he asked Phil. Phil said, "I think we should get the hell off this subject."

That was easier said than done. Generally they were back on the subject no later than the following morning when they swam out to the nets where they liked to pause to survey their world from the State Park in the east through the tacky beachfront houses of Horton's Dock to the unspoiled dunes of Indiana Shores. With his body and mind rested by eight hours of sleep, with his system invigorated by the half-mile swim, Jerry felt in peak mental and physical form to tackle afresh the burning question of the summer. Should they go to Michigan City?

In the morning he was sensitive to the social and ethical nuances of this situation. They had their families to think of, plus their girlfriends, plus their own consciences, to say nothing of the various legal codes which prohibited the sort of thing they were thinking about doing. All that had to be taken into account and approached, if possible, in a dispassionate, theoretical way. There was a moral issue here, an issue which Jerry finally boiled down to the following question: did Phil think that nice young men—a bit like themselves, for instance—with nice families and nice girlfriends they were serious about, did Phil think such young men who, incidentally, were mature physically, who had begun to shave, who were practically grown up, and—you know—fully developed . . . did Phil think that hypothetical characters such as these would be making a big mistake to visit a cathouse? Little mistakes were all right, but (if possible) Jerry wanted to avoid making a big mistake. "What do you think?" he asked. "You beginning this all over again?" Phil asked. "Well, I mean, do you think it's really wrong?" Jerry asked. Phil, his broad shoulders rising and falling as he treaded water, shrugged slightly. "If you want to go so much, go." Jerry felt forsaken. It was not the response he wanted. "Don't *you* want to go?" he asked. "Not now," Phil said. "I didn't mean *now*," said Jerry, beginning to wonder if Phil had a real grip on the situation.

He could not quite fathom Phil's reluctance to commit himself. Phil had a strong character, of course, but he had a strong body, too. In Jerry's view the two things should cancel each other out and make Phil as much a prey to desire as Jerry himself. So what was wrong, he wondered. Why was *he* the one who always had to bring up the subject? It almost looked as if he was trying to wear Phil down, corrupt him, and Jerry didn't want to corrupt anybody, not even himself.

"Listen," he said one morning, "don't you think we practically have to do it? I mean they probably expect us to go." *They* were their fathers; *they* were their families. "How do you figure that?" Phil asked. "Well, I mean they want us to be grown-up. They want us to be men." Phil agreed. "So?" said Jerry. "So?" said Phil. They rose and fell in the water as they looked at each other. "So, they don't want us to be the sort of guys who think about it all the time, and talk it up, but never do anything. They don't want us to be like Murphy." Murphy was the most foulmouthed, sexually obsessed virgin in the Hard Core. "I mean, we're not like him," said Jerry. "So then, let's stop talking about it all the time," said Phil, reaching a conclusion that had escaped Jerry's attention. There at dawn in the fresh waters of the lake, going to Michigan City had begun to seem almost like a solemn duty. A guy practically owed it to himself, if not to his family, to get laid if only to distinguish himself from Murphy. Having a woman would be a sort of purification, a purging of the blood, a cleansing of the mind. And now Phil had spoiled it all. "You really think we should just stop talking about it?" Jerry asked. "At least before breakfast," Phil said. There was something to that. Even Jerry was beginning to yearn for pancakes and sausages more than for grappling with catwomen.

But by early afternoon his thoughts would be back in their old groove. He would be lying on the porch, listening to the wind and to the sounds of Verlene doing the lunch dishes and his mother ordering meat from Aaronson's Market in Chesterton. "All right, then," his mother said, "I'll have the roast." She never bought anything. She *had* roasts, and *took* legs of lamb, and asked the butcher to *add* a pound of bacon to her order. And as Jerry reflected on his mother's way of ordering meat, a simple, practical, completely unsordid argument occurred to him. "Okay," he would say to Phil, "we've got a problem, right? We're horny. All right, what do you do when you have a problem? You take it to the expert who deals with that kind of problem. You want your teeth straightened? You go to an orthodontist. You want yourself unstraightened down below, you go to a whore." It was just plain common sense. Doctors, dentists, oculists, prostitutes, garage mechanics all existed to take care of particular problems you had with your body or your car. It was foolish not to consult them. They were experts. But then, as he thought about the expert solution he could expect to get in Michigan City, Jerry found his problem actually growing. "Unnnnh!" he groaned, and his mother, fresh from her talk with the butcher, with dozens of ordinary household details on her mind plus the overriding and multitudinous questions to be decided about the wedding, paused for a moment to stare at this son of hers lying on the porch daybed, apparently in pain, wracked by the final throes of adolescence.

She asked, "Is something the matter, Jerry?" He looked up at her and moved his head slightly. Mrs. Engels approached the daybed. "You were groaning." "I'm all right," he said. She smiled down at him. Their eyes met, and the tenderness that had reawakened between them in the spring when he confessed his love for Rosalind swept over both of them. Mrs. Engels sat down on the edge of the daybed, her wedding anxieties temporarily shelved. "You miss Rosalind, don't you?" He nodded and looked away from her. She

reached out to straighten a lock of hair on his damp forehead. "She'll be here soon." "I know," he replied. His
mother smiled encouragingly. He could feel her hip against
his, her hand lingering on his forehead, her whole motherly
presence bending over him as when she used to tuck him in
at night. "Is there anything else?" "No," he said. "You're
not upset about anything? You and Phil haven't quarreled?"
"Oh no!" Again a sweet smile appeared on her face. "You're
working very hard out there," she said, nodding toward the
lawn. "Ummhum." "We're very proud of all you've done,"
she said. And at that point he felt like throwing himself
into her arms and sobbing out, "Oh, Mom, I'm so horny."
Instead of which he said, "I guess I better go work."

Only how could he concentrate on the job he was doing
when he was excited by the play of his own muscles, by the
hum of bees in the locusts, and by the hum of a sewing
machine in the cabin where his mother was making a new
slipcover for the couch? Verlene sang as she mixed up a
batch of brownies. Then she came out and began to hang up
the wash. When she raised her arms he saw dark crescents
under the sleeves of her cotton dress. When she went back
into the cabin he could see blouses, skirts, slips, and even
a few pairs of his own jockey shorts billowing in the wind
that caressed his bare shoulders. Then Anne would appear.
"You're really making progress," she would say. "Oh, Jerry,
it's going to look so nice," and in her enthusiasm she would
hug him. She was in a very emotional mood these days.

And if, under all this stimulus, he decided to dash down
to the beach for a quick dip in the lake, chances were he
would come over the dune and down onto the beach parking
lot just as Mrs. Kincaid was getting out of her car, her arms
full of beach things. "Here, let me help you," he always said,
taking the umbrella out of her hands. Then her little boys
would run ahead, rolling their inner tubes like hoops, and
her little girls would tag along behind, dragging their towels
and dropping their toys, while he strolled with Mrs. Kincaid,

116

conscious of her two-piece bathing suit and conscious also of his own red bathing suit, which he'd bought in Chicago that spring after considerable shopping around. It gave him, he thought, a very nifty, not to say sexy, appearance. His mother thought it was too small. His father was more explicit. He had talked to Jerry about the need to avoid confining clothes. Tight underpants and tight bathing suits were just not what Jerry needed at this stage of his life, Mr. Engels said. "It's not tight," Jerry protested. His suit fitted him perfectly. It left his legs free. It was a serious suit. It was a swimmer's suit. He was a swimmer. "I mean, this is like what we wear at our meets," he told his father. "It gives you a suggestive look," his father said. Jerry shook his head. Could he help that? "I mean, is it my fault how I look? I mean, I'm just big. You've seen me. I'm big now." "And you need a bigger suit," his father said, but that was an old-fashioned point of view. People wore small bathing suits these days. Look at Mrs. Kincaid, a respectable married woman, the mother of four. Did she look suggestive?

Well, actually, yes. It was a real pleasure to see her in her suit and to carry her umbrella for her and then to set it up on the beach. He tended to show off as he did it. Instead of digging a hole for the umbrella pole, he liked to hold it in both hands and ram it into the beach like Tarzan driving a stake into the heart of a savage lion. Then he would fix the umbrella part to the pole, open it out, and give Mrs. Kincaid a big smile. "There you are," he would say, after which he would run into the lake, hit the water with his flat stomach, and put on a little swimming exhibition for the Kincaid family.

It was natural to show off a little. He wasn't the only one to do it. And anyway, what if his bathing suit was a bit smaller than anyone else's? Who was harmed by that? None of the women he met on the beach seemed to be driven out of their minds by the sight of him. He saw Miss Jones and Miss Smith frequently and always paused to chat with them and so far as he could see they never even looked at his suit. They were nice old ladies who just didn't notice that sort of thing, and why should they? Why should anyone notice; why should anyone be bothered by the sight of Jerry Engels in his new red swimming suit?

Though, on the other hand, he had to admit that the sight of Shirley in her two-piece suit bothered him. He would come out of the lake feeling good, only to find Shirley stretched out on a towel working on her suntan. She used a white plastic nose guard and a pair of eye cups to protect her face. This gave her head a kind of outer-space effect but left her midriff looking warm and reassuringly human. He would approach her and stand looking down into the winking eye of her navel. "Want to do something?" he would ask. "No," she usually replied, without bothering to remove the eye cups. "And don't drip on me," she would add. "I'm not dripping on you," he said. He was not a crude guy. He didn't drip on girls. But he did stand over them, he did look, and it bothered him sometimes. He would sigh as he gazed at Shirley. "Are you still standing there?" she would ask. The answer was *yes*. She would remove her eye cups and look up at him. Their eyes would meet. "Sure you don't want to do anything?" he would ask. "Please leave me alone," she would say.

Sometimes he did. Sometimes the sight of her would send him hustling back to the cabin to do some work. Sometimes it would send him one direction down the beach for a nice, long, lonely run. Other times it would send him the other direction down to the State Park to look at the girls there. Girls that didn't have his number the way Shirley did. Often he stopped at the Walker Hotel in Horton's Dock to pick up Alec. Expeditions to the Park were generally group affairs in which he and Alec, or he and Phil, or all three of them scanned the beach like explorers, searching for that slightly mythical pair or threesome of girls who were out for a good time. They never turned up, but still there was a lot to see at the Park. Sometimes, walking among the sprawled bodies, Jerry would get so wrapped up in the sight of a girl that he would simply stand in wonder. They were so pretty as they lay on their stomachs reading a magazine with one foot raised to brush off flies. Or how about when they knelt, fixing their sandals to their feet? Or when they stood and adjusted their bathing suits around their legs or breasts? They were just so nice in every position that he sometimes wondered how he could want to get on top of one of them, and . . . Lost in the wonder of it all, he sometimes stared too long at particular girls. On those occasions some rather frightening things could happen. The girl herself might look right at him and say something cutting. Worse, he might hear a rough male voice saying, "What are you looking at, Mac?" Then the mental blinds which prevented him from seeing the men on the beach would go flying up, and he would find himself focusing on some irate steelworker type sitting beside the girl he had been staring at. There was nothing to do then but flee . . . back to the Shores.

There he would find Shirley still working on her tan. Nancy might have come down. Sue Channing might be there. They were nice girls. He knew them. He could drop onto the beach beside them. He could talk to them. He could look at them. But there wasn't much else he could do. Sue Channing had broken her leg that spring and was still on crutches. Nancy was frequently out water skiing with Kevin O'Brien, who had begun coming down to the Shores in his family's Chris Craft. That left Shirley who was provokingly uncooperative this summer. Sometimes she provoked him so much that he teamed up with Phil who had always had a slightly quarrelsome relationship with Shirley. Together they would grab her by her slim ankles and her wrists and carry her down to the lake where they threatened to toss her in the water sizzling with sun and irritation. "I'd like to know what you two think you're doing?" she would demand loftily as she hung there between them. "We're saving you from

119

sunstroke," Phil said one day. "That's right," said Jerry. "If
you get any darker they won't serve you at the Spa." "Very
funny!" was Shirley's reply. She was not amused when they
manhandled her. "I wish you goons would put me down,"
she said.

"It's as though she thinks we're trying to make passes or
something," Jerry said to Phil one afternoon when they were
back in the woods once more. "Maybe we are," said Phil.
"With Shirley?" said Jerry. "Shirley"? "She's pretty sexy,"
Phil pointed out. "Yeah, but Shirley . . ." Jerry said. "I like
grabbing her," Phil admitted. "Well, so do I," said Jerry.
Grabbing Shirley and carrying her around and throwing her
in the lake and ducking were recognized summer pleasures,
but it was all just horseplay. "I wouldn't ever try to do anything with her, would you?" Jerry asked. Phil considered the
matter. Then he said, "What about Nancy?" Jerry fell silent.
Nancy was a different proposition. Nancy was the sort of
girl you could hope to do a little something with. She was
nice, but she was kissable. She liked boys. The trouble was
that currently she seemed to like O'Brien. Jerry pointed this
out. "I mean, we've just got no opportunities here at the
Shores," he said, "and we're getting nowhere down at the
State Park." "You can't tell," said Phil. "Listen!" said Jerry.
"In all the years we've been going to the Park have we ever
even talked to the girls there?" Phil didn't answer. "I mean,
be realistic," Jerry said. In his mind Michigan City was
beginning to loom as the only port for them in the particular
storm through which they were passing. "Let's face it," he
said. "You know what?" Phil said, going off on his own tack.
"Our problem is that we don't have jobs."

"Jobs? What good would they do?" "If we were working,"
Phil explained, "we wouldn't have so much time to think
about sex." "You think so?" Jerry asked. "Well, it figures,"
said Phil. "But where could we work?" Jerry asked. There
weren't any jobs at the Shores. "We could go up to Michigan," Phil suggested. "They hire lots of migrants during the

120

fruit season." "Hey!" said Jerry, impressed by this idea. They began to talk it over. They could go up to Traverse City in July and pick cherries. The idea excited them both. They would live in barracks with other migrant workers. There would be girls around. Mexican girls. All sorts of possibilities opened up, except that in July Rosalind would be at the Shores. That seemed quite a drawback. "We should get jobs around here," Jerry said. "Actually we should get jobs at the refinery," said Phil. "But we're not eighteen," said Jerry. Then Phil showed the kind of foresight for which Jerry admired him. "We'll be eighteen next summer," he pointed out. "Hey, yeah!" said Jerry. They decided that next summer they would prevail on their fathers to get them jobs at the refinery.

That prospect really dazzled them. They would work on the Ash Gang. They would clean hot stills and shovel ballast and do the hard, dangerous, smelly work at the refinery. Then, in the evening, they would come back to the Shores with the other men for a dip in the lake before dinner. They might even save up and buy a car. And with a car and real industrial jobs they would not only be men, they would be working stiffs. The thought excited them both, but the excitement was half erotic to begin with and before very long it became totally erotic in Jerry's case.

He saw himself in sweat-stained work clothes, wearing boots and a hardhat and punching a time clock while a trim secretary, perhaps in the timekeeper's shack, looked up from her desk. His body would speak to hers, hers would speak to his, and gradually a silent communion would be established between them until one day they would meet coming out of the main gate of the refinery. "Hi! I'm Jerry Engels," he would say. "I'm Betty Pavlochik," she would reply. "Betty Pavlochik!" he'd cry, slapping his forehead. "I used to know you in third grade." Her eyes would widen. "Jerry!" she'd squeal. "Jerry Engels! I haven't seen you in years."

On Saturday night he would take her to dinner at Vogel's

on Indianapolis Boulevard. Then they would go dancing at the Slovak Dom on Fishrup Street. Afterward they would park in the Water Gardens near the shore of Wolf Lake. "You know," he said to Phil, "you're right. We really ought to work." Phil, presumably immersed in his own fantasy, merely grunted. They tramped along in companionable silence, leaves rustling underfoot as their minds roamed ahead down the golden corridors of the future. Betty Pavlochik gave way both physically and imaginatively, and Jerry moved on from her to the current leading ladies in his internal dramas. There was Irma the Hard Blond whose proud boast was that no man had ever softened her up. . . . She melted like butter in Jerry's hands. Next he turned to Melissa, the Caramel-Colored Cupcake, whom he devoured like one of Verlene's frosted brownies. Finally he turned to Mischievous Mabel with all her tricks, some of which were so remarkable that he couldn't even imagine what they were. She was just a sort of kinetic blur out there on the periphery of his consciousness. Then, after putting all these ladies through their paces, he would sigh. He shouldn't be thinking like this. It was approved doctrine, even among guys, that there were other things in the world besides women. What other things, he wondered.

The problem (if it was a problem) was that there were women everywhere. Everywhere he went he saw a woman. He saw them on the beach and in the lake and on water skis. He saw them on the roads behind the wheels of cars, or perched on bicycle seats, or sometimes just strolling along. They were in every house he visited, reading books, making beds, telephoning, and sometimes just staring into cupboards or out windows. And of course women were not a local phenomenon. There were women in the streets of Chesterton and Porter. There were women in Gary and Michigan City, especially Michigan City. Chicago teemed with women. The world was filled with them. They were everywhere. Everywhere Jerry went he saw a woman.

Even deep in the woods he often came across old Mrs. Hollings bending mysteriously over some rare plant. "Have you seen this?" she would say, raising her head, her face beet red, her white hair disheveled. "Have you seen it?" Then he would be looking down at some wake-robins, or trilliums, or a clump of yellow lady slippers, their pursy blooms framed by twisted brown petals. "Nice," he would say, "that's nice," and Mrs. Hollings would give him a conspiratorial smile. "Don't tell everyone where they are," she would say, and he would promise not to. He understood that the secrets of the woods and swamps had to be preserved. He and Phil were jealous of their own secret places: a deep bed of sphagnum moss on which they had once rolled naked, a hollow oak in which they used to hide Sucret boxes filled with treasure. They had their own inaccessible blueberry patches and lookout spots to which they had given their own names: The White Throne, The Maze, The Hidden Valley. This was their world, and it was not a masculine world. Nothing was flat, nothing was straight, nothing was fenced. They roamed freely across the landscape of the Shores, a landscape which to Jerry's mind was like the great, sprawled body of a woman. Rounded drifts of white sand spilled forward from the burst bodice of a grass-covered hill. Fern-fringed, sun-warmed pockets of sand invited you to rest a while . . . and think of women.

He was an erotic pantheist or a pantheistic eroticist. As far as he was concerned there were women in the wind that filled the sail of his Dolphin and blew him to and fro on the lake. They were in the water through which he swam and in the warm sand on which he rolled. They were in the storms that burst overhead and in the rain that poured down over him while he heaved at the rope of his sledge. "Jerry," his mother called to him from the porch, "why are you working in the rain?" He straightened, feeling rainwater drain down the furrow of his back and into the cleft of his buttocks. "I love it," he called back. Swamped by desire, drenched in

123

the soft June rain, treading water in the lake, he felt surrounded by women, up to his neck in them, drowning in them. Why struggle against them, he wondered. Why hold out? They couldn't hurt.

One day he took a run down the beach. When he was opposite the Ingleside house it occurred to him that by some miracle the Inglesides might have changed their plans. Maybe they'd opened their house. Rosalind could be up there. He climbed the beach steps. The house was still closed, but now that he was there he didn't feel like leaving. He prowled around the place. It seemed to him that he might miss Rosalind less if he were to get inside—perhaps through this cracked basement window—and go lie for a while on her bed. He squatted to examine the window. He reached out to test whether the glass was loose in its frame. At first it didn't seem loose. Then when he pressed harder, it felt loose after all. Suddenly a sizable sliver fell inward and smashed musically on the cement floor. *I may have pressed too hard,* he thought.

He was sorry the pane had gotten broken that way. Since it was broken, however, he couldn't see the harm of reaching into an unused maid's room with dead flies on the floor. He himself into the basement, being careful to avoid the broken glass on the floor.

He was in the furnace room. The Inglesides had a good furnace, especially considering that they no longer used the house in the winter. Then he was in a dark hallway. He opened doors at random to get some light. One door opened into an unused maid's room with dead flies on the floor. He was surprised. The Moxons lived in some rooms above the garage. He hadn't even known there was an extra maid's room in the basement. Then he was ascending the steps into a pantry between the kitchen and dining room.

The dining room door squeaked on its hinges. That halted him for a moment. It was as if the house were registering a tiny protest against his intrusion. The dining room chairs, pushed tight against the table, had a stiff and forbidding look to them. Finally he went on through the dining room and living room and out into the hall. There was a curious smell that was not just the usual closed-house smell, familiar to him from opening the cabin every spring. This was an acidy, arsenicky smell as if someone had thrown handfuls of rat poison around the place. Someone had. He could see white powder. What was this? he wondered. Were the Inglesides invaded by rats? But the powder shouldn't smell this way if it had been put down last September. Very odd. Then something clicked in his mind. (His mind was working very clearly and lucidly, he felt.) *Eric Anderson*, he said to himself. Eric had checked the house recently, seen a mouse, and gone overboard with the poison bit. That solved, he headed toward the second floor.

Rosalind's room was at the back, overlooking the lawn and the tennis court. He hesitated on the threshold, deeply moved by the sight of her bed, and her dresser, and her bookcase, and her writing table, and her lamp and chair and rug. He sniffed. No rat poison up here. The air of her bedroom had a sort of dim musty flavor to it. The afternoon sun glowed orange against the drawn blinds. Finally he went in.

He stood for a while beside the bed. It had been stripped and was covered with a dust sheet. He let the tips of his fingers rest against the sheet. He was having trouble breathing now. Then, like a falling tree, he toppled across the bed, groaning slightly. "Rosalind," he groaned as he hit her mattress, but no smiling image of her came to his mind. "Rosalind," he said again, spreading his arms as if to embrace the mattress, but he was lying at the wrong angle for that. He moved until he was lying lengthwise on her bed, his cheek resting against the sheet through which he could feel a hard round mattress button. Once more he tried to summon Rosalind by invoking her name, but she would not come when called for, so he lay a while just wondering what he was doing. His mind no longer seemed to be working clearly and lucidly.

At last, almost reflectively, he got up from the bed and

moved toward her dresser. There was a mirror above it. He saw reflected there a young man in a sharp-looking red bathing suit. Himself, of course, but somehow not the usual self in which he took a friendly and sometimes puzzled interest. This was someone who seemed to know what he was doing, strange as that was. This self moved straight to the dresser and with scarcely any hesitation opened the upper right-hand drawer.

Inside the drawer were various hard little things, some of which rolled against the bare bottom. He could see a comb, a lipstick, a compact, a barrette, some hairpins, a narrow leather belt, a pair of turquoise earrings, and a coin purse. Inside the coin purse were three slightly discolored zinc pennies minted during the war. Inside the lipstick tube there was lipstick—tangerine colored. He applied some to the end of his nose. Then he wrote the letter R on one side of his forehead and the letter I on the other side. He studied the effect. On the whole it did not please him, so he tried to rub off the lipstick. This only smeared it and made it worse. Giving up on his face, he put away the lipstick and opened a box on top of the dresser. Inside he found a metal chain, perhaps of silver, and a small vial of eau de cologne. Thinking the cologne might cut through the smeared lipstick, he rubbed some on his forehead. The lipstick smear widened but did not disappear, and now he smelled strongly of cologne. Things were getting a little out of hand. He switched his attention to the drawer on the left.

It was more rewarding. He found the yellow bathing suit Rosalind had worn all last summer. He took it out and held it up by the straps. Of course he had not been in love with Rosalind last summer, but still this was a precious bathing suit which deserved to be handled tenderly, even reverently. He kissed the cloth that had cupped Rosalind's breasts. Then he searched out the most secret part of the bathing suit and kissed it there. Feeling much better about everything, he put the bathing suit away and knelt to open the first full-

126

length drawer. Inside it he saw folded blouses and shorts and other summer clothes but no real underthings. Probably she took her bras and panties and stockings to Chicago with her. Unless they were in the lower drawer. He looked in it, but was disappointed to find only a folded bedspread.

He was aware that you did not break into your girlfriend's house and rummage through her drawers. Nor did you explore her closet. This was not how he had been brought up. On the other hand it did not seem wrong. It seemed curiously right. It was as if he were being carried forward by some great power that was elevating him above himself and providing him with a flood of fresh ideas and new impulses. He knelt to examine a pair of sandals in Rosalind's closet. He picked one up. He sniffed the leather. Finally he fastened his teeth into the thong that had separated Rosalind's great toe from her other toes. Next he unzipped Rosalind's clothes bag and started to go through her summer dresses. He found an orange dress he had never seen her wear. He took it out of the clothes bag and went to stand in front of the mirror where he held the dress up to see how it might look if he were to put it on. He cocked his head as if listening to some voice that would tell him what to do next. Put the dress on? No. Stroke it? Yes. Squeeze it? All right. But he had to be careful not to rumple the dress. He liked this dress. He meant it no harm. He was only sorry that Rosalind evidently did not like the dress as much as he did. Apparently she was like his mother. She bought things she thought looked nice in the store and then turned against them when she got them home, leaving them to hang in her closet until they were old and out of fashion. It was a pity because she would look nice in this dress. Perhaps if he stroked it some more and pressed it against his body, some of his own affection would rub off on the dress so that Rosalind would look at it this summer and see how nice it really was. Then she would wear it, and he would murmur in her ear, "I like you in that." She would think he was merely complimenting her on her clothes. She would not guess he had a secret relationship with this dress. He smiled at the thought. Then he looked around the room. What to do next?

The silence seemed intense. He could hear his own breathing and feel his own heart thumping. The warm, intimate stuffiness pressed in on him, loaded with suggestions and possibilities. He closed his eyes as if to sort things out. He felt he was maybe passing into an ecstasy of some sort as he held the orange dress to his body. He held it with both arms. He was swaying a little, as if he were dancing with the dress. He thought he heard music. Then he really heard the sound of an automobile, and his eyes opened wide in sudden panic. Had the Moxons come out early to sweep up the rat poison and get the house ready? Could it be the Inglesides themselves? Or the police? Had that broken window been discovered and was the house now surrounded by the FBI? He let the orange dress slip to the floor where it crumpled into an empty sheath of bright cotton. The spell was broken. In two steps he got to the window.

He was about to raise the blind when wiser thoughts prevailed. Instead, like a gangster, he stood with his back to the wall. Then, with one finger, he gently pulled the blind inward until he could peer out sideways. He had apparently been holding his breath because he could hear it escape audibly as he saw it was only Valiant Foo in the driveway. Nancy, Shirley, Phil, and Kevin O'Brien had arrived to play a set of mixed doubles.

Faint with relief, he let the blind drop back into position. Feeling a little weak, he sat down on the edge of Rosalind's bed. Then he heard his mother's voice admonishing him to sit on his chair, not on the mattress. It was hard on mattresses when you sat on them. Not wanting to be hard on Rosalind's mattress, he shifted to a chair. He looked around the room, lately the scene of such mysterious pleasure. Now the room was somehow as reproachful as those stiff dining room chairs. The dress lay on the floor like an abandoned toy. He picked it up, straightened it, and rehung it. He shoved in the dresser drawers and arranged the sandals neatly side by side. He smoothed the dust sheet on the bed. Then he went back to the window.

The game was under way. It was Shirley and Phil against Nancy and O'Brien. He couldn't tell who was ahead. One thing, though, O'Brien had a really terrific physique. He had taken off his shirt to play. He was serving. He aced Shirley. He had a good serve. Phil managed to return his next serve, however, and Nancy muffed an easy volley. It looked sort of even. While he watched, Jerry used his free hand to rub at his forehead. He was beginning to feel a little discontented about being trapped inside the house while his friends played tennis outdoors. He should be there with them, except that he could scarcely join them looking the way he did now. Besides he couldn't pop up out of the basement window, which was practically in full view of the court. He would have to find another way out of the house. Sighing, he let the curtain fall back into place.

What he really needed to do, first of all, was to clean up. He went to Rosalind's bathroom. As he anticipated, the water was turned off. Well, he could wipe his face with a rag. Where did the Inglesides keep their rags, he wondered.

He found one in the kitchen, and while he rubbed his nose and forehead he took another look at the tennis match, this time raising the blind on the window above the kitchen sink. Shirley was serving. She stood sideways, put her foot near the baseline, looked down, bounced a ball, rocked, then tossed the ball into the air and let it fall without even trying to hit it. What was the matter, he wondered, and why was she staring his way? Then he realized he had raised the blind too far, and either the movement of the blind or the rubbing movement of his hand had attracted her attention. Funny how, even when you were concentrated on a game, you could pick up odd movements off in the distance, especially when you knew that nothing at all should be moving in that direction. *Damn*, he thought, pulling the blind down with a jerk that detached it from its roller.

That really tore things. Ducking, Jerry fled from the kitchen back upstairs. When he had gained what he now considered to be the relative safety of Rosalind's bedroom, he paused to reflect. His first instinct had been to get as far away from that broken basement window as possible. He expected them to discover it and come pouring into the house in pursuit of him, but now he realized that was unlikely. Shirley could hardly have recognized him. All she knew was that someone in the closed house had been peering out at her. Probably all of them out there were as alarmed as he was. Maybe even more alarmed. For all they knew he could be an escaped convict from Michigan City, hiding out at the Shores. Convicts were always escaping from the Michigan City penitentiary. Dillinger had escaped. They could think it's someone like Dillinger in here, Jerry thought, or a sex maniac like that William Heirens who used to break into apartments in Chicago and write things in lipstick on the mirrors of the women he killed. Before he did anything else, Jerry thought, he'd better check on what his friends were doing. Exercising extreme caution, he got back into his full gangster position and fingered Rosalind's blind until he could peer out again.

He was right. They were scared. O'Brien had his shirt on, and they were clustered in the center of the court looking up at the house. He could imagine the conversation. Shirley would be saying, "You boys watch the place while we go get the police." She'd have the National Guard on the spot in no time. He really had to escape, only he was riveted to the window, waiting to see what was happening outdoors. He was beginning to feel sorry about the situation, but he simply could not raise the blind and open the window and shout out to them that they had nothing to worry about. Shirley would never let him live it down. O'Brien would think he was a cuckoo. He just had to watch to see how things would develop.

They developed more or less as he had anticipated, except that O'Brien hopped into Valiant Foo right after Nancy and went driving off with her while Phil and Shirley kept watch in the driveway. They maintained a respectful distance from the house. Jerry let the blind fall a final time and took a last look around Rosalind's bedroom where so much seemed to have happened so recently. Then he padded down the hall to her parents' bedroom. He was surprised to see that Mr. and Mrs. Ingleside had twin beds. There was something questionable about parents using twin beds, he thought, but he felt in no position at the moment to criticize the Inglesides about anything, even the maintenance of their tennis court. He let himself out one of the front windows, tiptoed across the hot red tile of the porch roof, jumped to the narrow strip of lawn, landed unhurt, and slipped down the dune to the beach.

What troubled him about this experience was the way everyone talked about it afterward. Shirley was eloquent on the subject of the horrible face she had seen at the window. "It was probably just some kid," Jerry said. "You weren't there," said Shirley. "That was no kid!" "I would have been terrified," Linda said. "I was," said Shirley. "Why didn't you run away?" Joanne asked. Joanne was Jerry's cousin who had just arrived at the Shores. "I couldn't leave Phil alone," Shirley explained. "Someone had to stay with him after that O'Brien went running off with Nancy." "Maybe he thought you were all going to go," Jerry suggested. "He did not!" said Shirley. "Phil said he would stay to watch the house while Nancy went to get Eric Anderson." Jerry shrugged. Things looked bad for O'Brien. He couldn't really think of a way to save the guy's reputation. Finally he decided O'Brien would just have to sustain himself if he could. Still he felt a little guilty for having indirectly exposed the guy. He was not at his ease in O'Brien's presence. For the next few days he kept to himself, working on the yard and daydreaming on the couch.

One afternoon while he was resting he had a daydream

that involved a whole troop of girls with flowers in their hair and long filmy white garments, like nightgowns, that left their bodies as good as naked. They were strange, nameless girls who danced around him while he stood with his back to some kind of maypole that was decorated with wreaths of ivy. He seemed to be fastened to the maypole with a sort of loose silken scarf tied with a butterfly knot that could come undone pretty easily. The girls knew this, but it didn't bother them as they danced around almost naked. Some of them held flowers in their hands. One girl had a rose between her slightly parted lips. Her name was Flora. In fact they were all named Flora. It was Flora, Flora, Flora, and Flora dancing around him as he stood, naked it seemed, loosely tied to that maypole.

He was about to slip the knot and join them in their dance when he heard the screen door slap open beside him and then bang shut. Joanne stood beside the daybed looking down at him. "Jerry!" she said, in her penetrating Southern accent. "Jerry, Linda and I want to sleep out in the blow-out tonight. Will you sleep out with us?" He could see her standing there. He could hear what she said, but he could not answer her as he struggled upward through the thick medium of his daydream. "Jerry," she said again, "Linda and I want you to sleep out with us." "What?" he said, finally breaking the surface of his dream and taking in air. "I told you," Joanne said impatiently. "Linda and I want you to sleep out with us tonight. Phil won't do it. He's going to Shirley's." Shirley was giving a party that night. She paused expectantly, her eyes fixed on him. "Mother says I can, and Linda's mother says she can, but we want you or Phil to sleep out with us." He knew they were afraid of the Face at the Window, and perhaps of Diana of the Dunes, a beautiful and educated woman who had lived with a gangster in a remote dune cottage and was still supposed to walk the dunes at night. "Will you?" Joanne asked. "Tonight?" Jerry said. "Yes, tonight," said Joanne, her tone even more impatient because he was behaving like such a dope. Then, because she was asking a favor, she said, "Please." Their eyes met. "Please, Jerry," she said, and Jerry heard himself saying "Yes" because he liked to please and because he wanted to keep away from Shirley's party.

It was Midsummer Night. The sand glowed like silver in the moonlight. They unrolled their sleeping bags and then sat down on them to eat the sweet white grapes and chocolate chip cookies Joanne and Linda had brought down with them. They competed so see how many unbroken grapes they could stuff into their mouths. Then, when they had finished all the grapes and cookies, Jerry lay back on his sleeping bag feeling contented. "What do you want to do now?" he asked them. "Could we play Cut-the-Pie?" Joanne asked. "The sand's too tracked up," said Linda. You needed a smooth stretch of untracked sand for Cut-the-Pie. "Then let's play Shadow Tag," Joanne said. Linda and Jerry agreed. They left their sleeping bags in the blow-out and went over to the Live Dune, which was the best place for Shadow Tag. Jerry was *It*. He closed his eyes and began to count. He heard the girls running off lightly, the sand whispering as they went. When he reached a hundred he opened his eyes. He was alone on the wide, windward slope of the dune where dead tree trunks threw sharp, fantastic shadows. The trees had been buried by the dune and were now emerging, sea-changed, from the wave of sand that had passed over them. The Live Dune was a great, wind-driven sand wave, Jerry thought. Walking on the Live Dune, particularly on moonlit nights, was like walking on the bottom of some mysteriously empty sea. The litter of brittle old wood surrounding each tree was like sea wrack, and the wind-rippled sand was like the familiar wave-rippled bottom of the lake. He loved it there at night where—if anywhere—Diana of the Dunes *ought* to come gliding out from behind one of those hummocks where wild grapes and snake grass had taken root. This was her sort of place and her sort of night, so beautiful that he almost hated to disturb it by going to hunt for the girls, who must be crouching behind one of those hummocks or standing sideways behind one of the tree trunks. Just to look at this scene was enough, but Linda and Joanne were waiting for him to find them and chase them and try to step on their shadows. They would be disappointed if he didn't come.

He went looking for them. When he found them, he routed them out of their hiding places and began to chase them in short bursts up toward the crest of the dune where the girls finally dropped to the sand, sitting on their shadows so that he couldn't catch them. Then they let the game die as they sat together looking out over the dark forest below. They were sitting at the top of the moving face of the dune where the sand dropped away steeply, lying at the angle of repose. When you ran down this dune you sent long tongues of dry sand shifting downward. Then you could see the dune moving. You were helping it move, helping it lick its way forward into the grass and flowers and blueberry bushes below. Each season you could see the dune piled up higher around the trunks of those trees already caught in the sand. Gradually, as their trunks disappeared, the trees became mere green canopies above the sand. Then the grapevines found them, turning them into green vine-enclosed tents and killing the trees a few years before they would have been drowned in sand anyway.

They sat for a while just throwing handfuls of sand down the dune. Then they began to talk. Joanne went on with her saga of what life was like at Ashley Hall in Charleston, where her mother had put her in school. To Jerry and Linda, from their own perspective of the Lab School and U-High, Ashley Hall sounded as weird as life in another world. Ashley Hall was a penitentiary, surrounded by ten-foot walls and an overgrown garden full of poinsettia and pomegranate trees, with a grotto and a fountain, with orioles nesting everywhere. Ashley Hall was an inferno of ringing bells and cold vege-

134

table salads, presided over by the "Puffin" and her sister, Miss Estelle, who was mean about handing out fresh towels and cross when girls began to bloody their sheets. Ashley Hall was a horror house of huge pillars, great circular staircases, high ceilings, marble fireplaces, and dark wooden attics into which everyone crept at night to smoke cigarettes. "Do you smoke?" Jerry asked. "Of course," Joanne said, but she could not put up pictures of movie stars on her walls, and she was graded every day on how neatly she kept her room. "I wouldn't put up with that," Linda said. "You have to," said Joanne. And it was all girls. Ashley Hall was a death trap from which girls could never escape except in groups, all wearing hats and gloves and stockings and *no* lipstick. It was impossible ever to be alone with a boy from The Citadel or from Porter Military Academy. You were not even supposed to write a boy unless he was known to your family. "I think that's terrible," said Linda. It was. Joanne just knew she would never get married. "But why did your mother put you there?" Linda asked.

That, too, was a long story. Joanne's mother and grand-mother thought she needed an environment like Ashley Hall. "You know how they think in Kentucky," Joanne said to Jerry. And anyway there had been Dale, a boy next door in Lexington who could do anything. He had made his own radio out of parts, and it worked. He and Joanne had lis-tened to the "Hit Parade" on it, but now she hardly saw Dale and he didn't even write her. "No one writes to me," she said. "I'll write you," Jerry said, feeling it was the least he could do. "You didn't answer that letter I wrote you in March," Joanne reminded him. "I'll answer your next letter," he promised. He liked the idea of Joanne writing him long letters from Ashley Hall because he was the only boy who would answer her. Faithless Dale had lost his chance. Jerry lay back with his head in the sand, seeing himself as the one true boy in the world. Hadn't he written to Rosalind only the day before? His conscience was clear. He sighed contentedly. He began to see himself as a sterling character, the only boy in a world of girls, young girls mainly, all of whom wrote him letters and counted on him to protect them and to be nice to them in the summer and to teach them how to swim and to sail and then to kiss them when they were old enough. . . . This reverie was interrupted as Joanne punched his shoulder. "You're always daydreaming," she said. "I am not," he answered automatically. "Well, do you want to go swimming?" "Yes, sure," he said.

Moonlight swimming always meant skinny-dipping, though this midsummer night was so bright that Jerry, as the responsible person present, felt maybe he should have thought twice before agreeing. "Don't look," he did think to say as he undressed a few yards from Joanne and Linda, though he was pretty sure they did look as he ran ahead of them into the water. He looked at them, coming down the beach and splashing in after him, their bodies white in the moonlight, their small breasts like round little pears, not even jiggling as they ran. They were so cute. He felt a sort of brotherly, possessive pride in how cute they looked. "You looked," Joanne said, but he assured her it was all right for him to look. Then he teased her, nicely, by paddling backward with just his head and his feet out of the water, his big toe crooked, challenging her to catch him by his toe.

They frolicked in the water, the water feeling warmer than the air once their bodies adjusted to it. Occasionally the girls would rise up enough so that he could see water streaming down over their young breasts, but mostly they kept shoulder deep, each of them sinking completely underwater from time to time to swim a little and then pop up with a splash a few yards away. When Jerry sucked in air and sank underwater, he knew they expected him to pop up right beside them, or maybe even grab at their legs underwater, but he didn't do that. He was just sporting with them, that was all.

Then he felt like swimming farther out. He left them in the shallows and swam a hundred yards out into the path of

136

the moon. He felt that the lake was alive and warm all around him, and when he turned onto his back he could see the bright moon and some stars. Then he saw, sweeping across the sky, the finger of light that was the beacon on the Palmolive Building in Chicago. The sky was alive as well as the lake. And the shore was alive, too. Down in Horton's Dock he could see a ruddy bonfire on the beach. The whole world —lake, sky, and shore—was alive and almost humming with life, and from inshore he could hear the voices of Joanne and Linda calling out, "Jerry?" He began to swim in.

When he reached the shallows he could see the girls again. They were up on the beach by then, flicking water off their bodies before they put on their clothes. From where he rested in the foot-deep water above the sandbar, he could see them very clearly standing in the moonlight, brushing at their arms and legs. In a few years they would both be beautiful young women. They were beautiful now in a different way. "Jerry?" Linda called out, "are you watching us?" He had to admit he was. They turned their backs on him, and they were as beautiful as before. Then, giggling, they grabbed their clothes and ran up into the low beach dunes where he couldn't see them anymore.

He rose and waded out of the lake. He knew they were spying on him as he brushed off his own body. They were up there in the dunes, peering at him through the marram grass. It was all right, he thought. Probably he should not have undressed so close to them, but it was all right for them to spy on him now. After all, Linda had probably seen Phil naked, so this could be no news to her, and Joanne didn't have a father or brother, and besides she was locked up at Ashley Hall, so if she wanted to look at a man she should get the chance to look at her own cousin. Besides, he liked to be looked at, though there was no point in showing off. He gathered up his clothes and began to put them on.

Then later, lying in his sleeping bag in the blow-out beside Linda and Joanne, he couldn't get over the sensation that the whole night was murmurous with life. A faint breeze stirred the sand grasses, and in the distance he could hear bull frogs going *blump, blump* in the swamp. The party at Shirley's was still going on, and in addition to that he could hear his own parents, talking on the porch with Aunt Madge, Joanne's mother, who was going to stay until the wedding. Once he heard her loud, humorous sounding voice raised as she emphasized something she had to say, probably about the oddities of a relative or neighbor in Kentucky. She was full of funny stories about Kentucky people. Her voice, the music and laughter from the Hyatts' house, the sound of the wind and the grass and the bullfrogs and the peepers and a single droning mosquito all blended together into a background of murmurous life which both lulled and excited him and made him want more, though he could not have said *more what?* Just more. More.

Then, as if this were a prayer which life was answering, so much began to happen that he hardly had time to ask for more.

Nancy became friendlier. Perhaps she was disillusioned with O'Brien, or perhaps it was something else. Anyway Jerry sensed a change in her. She had always been friendly, but now she seemed to want a bit more from him. He felt it particularly one night when he sat next to her in the Aron Theater in Chesterton. Their shoulders touched. From time to time their legs brushed together. Gradually he became more absorbed by the feel of Nancy beside him than by the movie he was watching. Afterward, when they went to have ice cream at Brunks, he sat next to her again. She ordered a Coke, saying she was not hungry and that anyway she had to watch her weight. She was not heavy, she was not even plump, but she was the sort of full-bodied girl who would have to watch her weight eventually. He saw her eyeing his banana split when it came. "Want some?" he asked her. "All right, a bite," she said. He dug out a spoonful of ice cream and banana and chocolate syrup. "Here," he said, pointing the spoon at her mouth. She let him feed her. She even accepted a second spoonful, bending and opening her mouth a second time. Shirley looked pained. Probably she thought it was unhygienic for Jerry to be feeding Nancy from the spoon he himself was using, or maybe she thought it was disloyal to Rosalind. Jerry didn't care. "Want some more?" he asked Nancy.

Then, when they were all back in Valiant Foo, he rode home with his fingertips resting on Nancy's shoulder. She dropped off Phil and Linda in front of their cabin. She stopped in front of the Hyatts' house to let off Shirley. Joanne and Jerry got out at the same time, but at the last moment Jerry climbed back into Valiant Foo and went riding off with Nancy. "Well!" she said, not particularly surprised. He slid closer to her. "I'll see you home," he explained.

When she had maneuvered Valiant Foo so that it was pointing down the driveway in front of her house, she killed the lights and turned off the engine. She reached for the door handle. "Don't get out yet," Jerry said, trying to kiss her. "What about Rosalind?" she asked in her calm way. "Nancy!" he said in a special tone of voice he used when he was asking girls to kiss him. Nancy turned her face away from him. "You and I are good friends," he told her, leaning close and breathing on her cheek. "Please, Nancy." She faced him. "All right," she said, "a goodnight kiss." But it was more than that. He walked home across the blow-out, feeling the elation that always came over him when he was getting involved with a new girl.

Joanne teased him about it. She even reported to his family that he and Nancy had gone off together in Valiant Foo to do some necking. She was telling everyone about it when he walked into the cabin that night. He felt Anne's eyes on him, and his mother's. A sensation of sweet shamelessness came over him at being exposed this way in front of them. They knew he loved Rosalind, and moreover neither

of them had a very high opinion of Nancy. He smiled as
they looked at him. His Aunt Madge said, "Well, I don't see
any lipstick on his face." "He's rubbed it off," Joanne said.
Jerry blushed, but if anything his pleasure increased.

From then on he flirted with Nancy at every opportunity.
When he saw her settling herself on the beach, he hustled out
of the lake, arriving wet and almost breathless just in time
to help her with her suntan lotion. "Here, I'll do that," he
said, plucking the tube from her hand. "Ooooh, your hands
are cold," Nancy said, but she let him rub her back. One day
he finished her back and started in on her leg while she
chatted with Shirley. Nancy seemed unaware of what Jerry
was doing, though Shirley certainly noticed it. He could see
Shirley's eyes flicking continually to the sight of his hand
moving up Nancy's warm leg. When he was over the knee
and onto her thigh, Nancy seemed to become aware of the
situation for the first time. "What do you think you're doing?" she asked him, taking her suntan lotion out of his
hands. "Ummmm!" he said, running his hand back down
her leg and squeezing her ankle. "Behave yourself," she told
him.

He felt he *was* behaving himself when he rubbed her
back and squeezed her ankle and danced cheek to cheek with
her in the Hyatts' game room at night. This was how she
wanted him to behave and how he wanted to behave. Between dances he lounged next to her on the daybed and
made little advances which she parried in a rather casual way.
The others grew accustomed to their behavior, though Shirley continued to give him sour looks. He could afford to
ignore Shirley, however, and when Joanne teased him he
played the role she wanted him to play. "You've got a crush
on Nancy, haven't you?" she asked. "Yeah, we've got a crush
on each other," he said. Joanne's eyes sparkled. She thought
of Nancy and Jerry as a scarlet couple.

Then one night Anne talked to him about it. "Why are
you paying Nancy Train so much attention?" she asked. "I

don't know," he said. "She likes it," he added. "But you like Rosalind," said Anne. He agreed with that. "But don't you just like to flirt sometimes?" he asked. "No," Anne said. Jerry sighed. His sister and his mother, though very different from each other, were both serious women. He felt sometimes that he was in the wrong family. "Don't worry," he told Anne. "I mean, Nancy means nothing to me, and I don't mean anything to her. We're just having fun." Anne frowned. "But I don't even see why you want to flirt with her." He stared at his sister. "You don't?" " No," said Anne.

He felt the hopelessness of trying to explain something like this. Also, it seemed a little unfair that he should have to explain. After all, Anne had always encouraged him to call girls up and to kiss them. Why should she be surprised now that he was a bit of a flirt? Finally he said, "I like girls, Anne." "But you just said you don't really like her," Anne argued. "No I didn't. I said she doesn't mean anything special, but I like her." Anne said, "Well, I think it's wrong, Jerry. Don't you really care about Rosalind?" "Of course I do!" he exclaimed. "Listen, I broke into Rosalind's house. I miss her so much I just wanted to get inside and lie on her bed." "What?" said Anne. "Honestly," Jerry said. " Rosalind means everything to me." "You broke into the Inglesides' house?" Anne said. "Yes. I mean, I love Rosalind." " Jerry!" said Anne. "What have you been doing?" "I told you," he said, "and don't tell the parents either." "You broke in?" "It wasn't any big deal," he said. "The window pane was practically falling out already." "That was *you* Shirley saw?" "Yeah." "Jerry!" "You're not going to tell, are you?" he said.

They had taken a walk after dinner. They were now sitting on the jump-off, a high sand bluff from which they could look up the blow-out toward the dark lake. Below them sand swallows swooped in the air before darting into their burrows in the face of the bluff. "You're too old to still be breaking into people's houses," Anne said. At eleven and twelve he and Phil had gotten into many of the houses at

141

the Shores and, as usual, Anne had found out about it. "It's childish," she said. "No, it isn't," said Jerry. "I mean, this was different." Then he told Anne some of the things he had done while he was in Rosalind's bedroom. Anne listened with fascination. "That's incredible," she said. "Do you think so?" he asked. In his own mind the experience had gradually begun to seem normal and rather nice. "But Jerry," said Anne, "you put lipstick on your face?" "And I kissed her bathing suit." He looked at his sister. "Listen, if you were in Michael's room wouldn't you go through his things? I bet you would. You'd want to look at his shorts and so on." Anne seemed dubious. "I'm not so sure I would." "I bet you would," he said. "I don't think so," said Anne. "Well, maybe it's different for girls," Jerry said.

He lay back with his head on the sand and gazed into the dark sky. Then he looked at his sister's form. She was sitting with her arms around her knees, presumably brooding on what he had told her. He felt moved by the sight of her, and then said that he was going to lose her. Who else could he tell everything to? "Lie down beside me, Anne." She looked around at him. He put his hand on her shoulder and pulled her gently until she was lying beside him, her head on his arm. "I'm going to miss you so much," he told her. Then he turned slightly so he could look down at her face. "Oh Anne!" he said. He wanted to kiss her. Their whole childhood was in his heart: the raft, Orphans, his first swim out to the nets. "Will you always love me?" he asked. "Jerry," she said, moved by the same feelings that moved him. "Of course I'll always love you. We'll always be close. We'll always be brother and sister." He bent to kiss her cheek. "You know I love you," she continued, and then somehow they were hugging each other. He couldn't decide who started it. Finally, at about the same moment, they each became embarrassed by what they were doing. They separated. Anne was breathing deeply. She said, "Maybe we love each other too much." "I don't think you *can* love anyone too much,"

Jerry said. "You know what I mean," said Anne. She sat up. Presently she began to talk about Michael.

He lay listening to her, glad that she was opening up at last. Ever since she'd come home from Swarthmore she'd been involved in preparations for her wedding, and in seeing old U-High friends. She had not really spent much time with him or told him a lot about Michael. Now she seemed eager to talk. "It's been so good for me to have someone like him," she said. "I've always been afraid, but he's so good, Jerry." She looked around to where he lay. "Do you know what I mean?" He thought he did. He knew she had always been a little afraid of boys. "He's really better than I am," she said. Again she looked around at him. "Do you ever feel that way? Do you ever feel you're just not at someone's level, that they're above you?" "All the time," he said. Anne sighed. "That's how I feel about Michael. He really knows a lot, Jerry. He's . . ." She searched for the right word. "He's wise."

Jerry wondered how well he would get along with a wise brother-in-law. "He's so wise," Anne said, liking the word now that she had used it. "And so good." "You really must love him," said Jerry. "I do." Then, by means of some interior transition Jerry could not follow, she said, "And we're going to have children. We both want to have lots of children." He nodded, though she was no longer looking around at him. "And we're going to bring them up differently from the way you and I have been brought up." "Why?" he asked. He could see no flaw in the way he and Anne had been brought up. "We've been too sheltered," Anne said. "Oh," said Jerry.

There was a long silence. He imagined Anne meditating on her children and on Michael's goodness and wisdom, but when she spoke it was to repeat what she had last said. "We've been much too sheltered." He had nothing to say to that, so he kept silent. "Both of us," Anne said, as if challenging him. "I don't feel sheltered," Jerry said. She looked around at him. "You are, Jerry. That's why you're the way

143

you are." What way was that, he wondered. Anne went on to explain. "The reason you're so uninhibited is that you've never had to protect yourself." "I'm not uninhibited," Jerry protested. "Gee!" he said, sitting up at last. "I'm inhibited about a lot of things." "You do whatever you feel like doing," Anne said. Her tone was almost severe. "I do not," he said. "And then you tell people everything you've done." "I only tell you!" he exclaimed. "You're the only person I've told about breaking into the Inglesides'." "Well, how many people would tell anyone?" Anne wanted to know. "I don't think that makes me uninhibited," Jerry maintained. "And there are some things I don't even tell you," he added. "What?" she said. "I'm not going to tell you," he said, feeling really cheered up and lighthearted compared to the heavily emotional mood he'd been in when he and Anne hugged and kissed. In fact, it occurred to him that now he was almost flirting with Anne, which seemed to prove that love and flirting could exist side by side perfectly well.

He went on flirting with Nancy. He was finished now with his yard work, and had more time to spend on the beach and at the tennis court. He could devote himself almost full time to playing around, and he saw to it that Nancy was his partner most of the time. He did not feel he was behaving badly toward Rosalind. Indeed, when he was using the Inglesides' court, he had the sense that Rosalind was actually overlooking his little romance with Nancy. The drawn blinds of Rosalind's bedroom windows seemed like sympathetically lowered eyelids. Yet, at the same time he was beginning to wonder what would happen when Rosalind finally arrived at the Shores. One afternoon while he and Nancy were sitting on the green bench beside the court he asked her what had become of O'Brien. "Did you two quarrel or something?" he asked. It had occurred to him that it would be convenient if O'Brien were to reappear in July. Besides, Kevin was the kind of fellow Nancy really ought to be interested in. He

144

was Catholic, for one thing, and while her family's religion probably didn't mean much to Nancy, her mother was pious and would presumably have a fit if Nancy were to get seriously involved with a Protestant boy. "What's become of Kevin?" Jerry asked. Nancy shrugged. "He's a good guy," said Jerry, who could afford to be generous now.

They were relaxing in the sun. He looked down at her bare leg next to his. His thoughts wandered a little as he studied her kneecap. Girls had smooth kneecaps with a little layer of flesh over the bone, whereas boys had knobby, bony knees until a muscle in the lower thigh developed to fill in and half cover the kneecap. It was one of the small but fascinating differences between boys and girls. He put his hand on Nancy's knee. She brushed it off. He touched her knee again, and after a while she brushed off his hand a second time. Then he stretched comfortably. "What would you do if you could do anything you wanted?" he asked. "Go to Europe," Nancy said promptly. He looked at her with surprise. "Europe?" The farthest he wanted to go was Michigan City. Why would anyone want to go as far away as Europe? "Why?" he asked Nancy.

She explained that her best friend at Francis Parker was spending the winter in Paris. At one time Nancy had been promised that she, too, could have a European sojourn, but at some point that spring one of Mr. Train's big deals had fallen through, and now there was not enough money for Nancy to live in Paris with her friend. Instead she would be entering Wheaton in the fall. She was nine months older than Jerry and a year ahead of him in school. "I know I'm going to hate Wheaton," she said. "Why?" he asked. "Oh, I've heard you have to work hard. And there are no boys. . . ." She made a dissatisfied gesture with her tennis racquet. Jerry nodded sympathetically. Looked at in this perspective, Europe made sense. Europe would be easier than Wheaton, and there would be more boys. "But you'll be seeing boys on weekends," Jerry pointed out. "I know, but it would have been fun with Eileen in Paris. It's just that Daddy's so broke now."

That interested Jerry. The Trains had two servants working for them. One was Miss Dietz, who had been with them for years and seemed to be a kind of governess for Nancy and her younger sisters. The second was a young man Nancy referred to as the chauffeur, although her father still drove himself into Chicago every morning in his big new Packard, leaving the "chauffeur" behind to paint the trim, wash the windows, and do yard work. But how could Mr. Train afford even a pseudo-chauffeur if he was broke? Jerry asked. Again Nancy gestured with her racquet. "Charles owes Daddy some money. We're not paying him anything." "Really?" said Jerry. Owing money and being owed money was just not something that happened to his family. "What does Charles owe your father for?" Nancy became vague. She was honest up to a point, more honest than her father probably, but she was not prepared to tell all. Mr. Train, Jerry gathered, had done some legal work for Charles, who couldn't afford to pay the bill. There was more to it than that, Jerry felt sure, but he knew better than to pry for information. Maybe Mr. Train had kept Charles out of jail, he thought.

This was what made flirtations and love affairs so exciting. You learned so much. You learned about the girl, you learned about her family, and you even learned something about yourself. Flirting with Nancy had showed him that he could be happy with a girl like this, just as he had been happy with Carolyn Webster. He was not like Anne, who had to think the person she loved was good and wise. He knew Nancy was no better than himself, but he felt he could be almost as happy with her as with Rosalind who was better than anyone.

— He went into town to see her when she got back from New Mexico. He had other things to do as well. He had to pick up his wedding suit from Fields', and collect some cases of

146

champagne from Zimmerman's, and meet his cousin Polly who was arriving from St. Louis. There were also some odds and ends to be gotten from the apartment in town: cake knives and silver salt cellars, and other utensils they generally did not need at the cabin. He had quite a list of things his mother wanted from in town. Rummaging through her silver box in the stuffy closed apartment, he was reminded a little of how he had felt rummaging through Rosalind's things. When he had collected everything on his mother's list, he set off for the Inglesides' house on Woodlawn, buoyed up by a happy, excited feeling.

Rosalind met him at the door and hugged him back when he hugged her. They had not seen each other since the evening in May when they had been menaced by the neighborhood guard. He thought she looked even better than usual. "You look terrific," he told her. "You're tanned." She smiled. She was not one of those girls who had to disclaim every compliment by saying that her hair was a mess or that she hated the clothes she was wearing.

They went into the Garden Room to talk. She had been on the phone with Shirley so she knew things he had not included in his letters to her. "How's Nancy?" she asked. "Nancy's fine," he said. "Is she?" said Rosalind. "What do you mean by that?" he wanted to know. "Oh, nothing," she said. "Nothing at all." She crossed her legs, popped an elbow on her knee, rested her chin on her hand, and stared at him. It was a position he had seen her mother assume. "And how are you?" she asked. It struck him he was going to have to do some explaining about Nancy, but he didn't feel like it just then. "Gee, I'm glad to see you," he said. "Did you get my letters?"

"Your letters!" said Rosalind.

They had been about the state of the tennis court and the controversy in the Town Board over what to do about the beaver dam that was flooding the road into town. He had written her about the new house that was going up along

West Road and about the new family in town—the Kincaids. He even mentioned Mrs. Kincaid's two-piece bathing suit. They were long, detailed letters, but they had not been eloquent or passionate. "I told you they wouldn't be good love letters," he said. "You didn't even tell me someone had broken into our house," said Rosalind. "Oh that!" He shrugged. "Shirley's hepped on the subject. It was just some kid having fun." He got to his feet. This conversation was making him feel uneasy and at fault in various ways. He sat down on the couch next to Rosalind. She uncrossed her legs and stopped looking at him the way her mother looked at people, but she did not seem ready to be kissed. "Well, I'm glad we weren't there," she said, referring to the break-in. "If you'd been there no one would have broken in," he said a little impatiently. He was tired of that subject. "Listen," he said, "when are your parents opening the house?" "On the second." "And when will you be there?" She wasn't sure. It might be the seventh or it might be the eighth. It depended on her grandparents. "And you'll be all alone with them on their yacht?" Jerry asked. "Well, there's a crew," said Rosalind, "and I think they're taking a friend of theirs with them." It still seemed pretty dismal to Jerry.

His eyes were on her face, waiting for some sign that she wanted him to move closer on the couch, but she made no such sign. She asked him about the wedding, and he told her he was picking up Polly that afternoon. "She's Anne's bridesmaid," he said. Then he started to tell her everything about the wedding. "There's been a lot to do," he said, feeling knowledgeable about weddings. "My mother's been going crazy all month." Rosalind looked interested. Weddings interested girls. "I mean, just deciding where to put everyone . . . our cabin is pretty small, you know, and practically my whole family is coming." He described the sleeping arrangements that had finally been worked out. He and his cousin Rufus would sleep on the porch. His grandmother would have his room. Polly would sleep with Anne. Aunt

Madge would move to the loft so that his Aunt Grace and Uncle Mac could have the room she had been in. Joanne would move from the loft to the Forsons' cabin to sleep with Linda. Michael and his best man would also be at the Forsons'. Michael's family would stay at the Guest House. The minister would be at the Hyatts'. That led Jerry into a digression. "I mean, we don't belong to a church now, but we used to belong to the Congregational Church in Whiting, and Mr. Paul is going to marry Anne. He isn't minister there anymore. He does psychiatric social work up in Michigan, but he still marries people when they want it."

"And what about Michael?" Rosalind asked. "You haven't met him yet?" "It's driving my parents crazy," Jerry said. "They think he should have come to see us in the spring. You know, to be looked over. And my father thinks the honeymoon idea is for the birds. Michael and Anne are going straight to Campobello Island for a youth conference." Jerry shook his head. "Daddy thinks Michael should take Anne to Lake George or some place like that." Privately Jerry agreed with his father. Who wanted to spend his honeymoon at a youth conference? Publicly, though, he supported Anne and Michael. "They're both real interested in politics," he said. "Michael may even go into politics eventually. Everyone's afraid he's a radical." "Is he?" Rosalind asked. "I don't know," said Jerry. "I guess we'll find out." He was looking forward to the meeting between Michael and the Engels family, but this was not what he wanted to talk about with Rosalind. He moved closer to her. "Listen," he said, "you're not mad at me or anything, are you?" He was thinking of Nancy. "I mean, you and Nancy are just so different." It seemed to him obvious that by flirting with Nancy he was not being unfaithful to Rosalind. The feelings Nancy evoked were just different feelings from those Rosalind evoked. "You understand, don't you?" he said.

Rosalind said, "Well, I think you could have waited for me." She seemed serious. She was not kidding. She didn't understand. "Gee, Rosalind," he said, "you're better than Nancy. You're a better person." "Well thanks," she said. "I mean it. You shouldn't compare yourself to Nancy." "Was I comparing myself?" "Well, you sounded a little jealous," he said. "Why shouldn't I be? Shirley says you've been doing everything with Nancy. You've been oiling her back." Jerry leaned forward to emphasize his point. "You wouldn't want me to oil your back. You're not that sort of girl." Rosalind looked impressed by this insight, but then, rather illogically Jerry thought, she said, "Well, why are you oiling Nancy's back?" "Because she *is* that sort of girl." There were girls whose backs you oiled and girls whose very bathing suits you worshipped. "I mean, boy, I'd do a lot more for you than I'd ever do for Nancy." He felt like telling what he had done for her, but this didn't seem like the moment to reveal he had broken into her house. "You shouldn't be jealous of Nancy," he said.

He seemed to have convinced her. There was a softening in her face, and he was about to kiss her when her mother came into the room. He got up to shake Mrs. Ingleside's hand, and that broke up the moment with Rosalind. He looked at his watch. He had things to do in the Loop before he met Polly at the LaSalle Street station. He had to be on his way. "Walk me out to the car," he said to Rosalind. Then, outside in the hot June sunshine, he put his arm around her waist. "I'll be waiting for you," he told her. "You don't have to worry, I'll be waiting." She let him brush her lips. "Be good," she told him. Then he drove off to do his errands in the Loop and to pick up Polly.

Polly was a kind of supplementary older sister, a bit softer on him than Anne had been. Polly had never encouraged him to do frightening or taxing things such as fight with other boys or swim out to the nets or tell girls he loved them. Polly had helped him in less challenging ways, for instance, by teaching him to dance during the summer after fifth grade when he was still smarting from his failures at the Lab school. For hour after hour that summer they had danced barefoot on the sweating cement floor of the game room in the basement. Polly played "Stormy Weather" and "Amapola" and "Begin the Beguine" over and over as she showed him various steps and got him to keep time and lead her properly. She seemed to enjoy it as much as he did, though she was sixteen then and he was only eleven. That was the sort of person she was, willing to dance with a skinny little cousin and make him feel like a million dollars just when he needed it most. He had been looking forward to her arrival.

So had she. She was wild with excitement about the wedding, about seeing everyone, about being bridesmaid, and even about her new suitcase, a gleaming leather object with straps and brass buckles. She had blown all her money on it, she said. Suitcases had always been a big thing for her. In the old days, when she first began to spend her summers at the Shores, she had always arrived with two huge suitcases plastered over with labels from hotels in London and Paris and Biarritz. They were her father's suitcases, left over from the days before he'd gone bankrupt and lost his shoe business. To Polly they had been a source of great pride and joy. She lugged them around for years, and it was typical of her that now when she was working full time in an advertising agency and had a little money to spend, she had splurged on a suitcase. "Isn't it a beauty?" she asked Jerry, as he placed her suitcase above the champagne cases in the trunk of the Oldsmobile. He agreed it was a nice suitcase. He wished he could feel this way about luxury items. His trouble was that his parents had never wanted him to feel rich. He had been brought up to think his family really did not have much money. Now, when they had a lot more than they used to have, he couldn't quite rejoice in the signs of affluence that were beginning to multiply. It didn't seem right to him for his mother to have a mink coat or for both his parents to talk about selling the cabin to buy a real house at the Shores. Polly had no such problem. She'd felt rich as a kid, and though she had been poor ever since her father's crash in 1938, she still considered that her swanky new suitcase was just the sort of thing she ought to have.

In the car she lit up a cigarette and settled back. "All right," she said, "now I want to hear absolutely everything." Jerry knew just what she meant. He was supposed to tell her Anne's innermost feelings about marriage. He was supposed to describe and analyze just how his parents were reacting to the situation. He was supposed to tell her everything he knew and had guessed about Michael. And so on. And he was willing, except that Polly would soon find out all this for herself in long bedtime conversations with Anne and in heart-to-heart conversations with his mother. Polly was a genius at finding out exactly how everyone felt about everything, and it was a waste of time for him to give her his views. "You'll find out for yourself," he said. "You bet I will," said Polly. She was practically champing at the bit. In fact she wasted no time in finding out what was going on inside Jerry. She got the story of his great love for Rosalind and his current flirtation with Nancy Train. She even got a fairly clear hint that Jerry longed to meet the catwoman of his dreams. By the time they were heading out of Gary she was in more or less full possession of the facts of his case. He had not told her about breaking into the Inglesides' or the exact address of that cathouse in Michigan City, but she knew all she needed to know in order to say, "Well, if you ask me, you're headed for trouble." She lit up another cigarette. "Have you told your father about all this?" Jerry shook his head. "He just doesn't understand, Polly. I mean, he even thinks my bathing suit is indecent." "What's this?" she asked, so Jerry filled her in on the bathing suit controversy. "I can't wait to see you in it," she said. "I look good," Jerry told her. "I bet you do," she said. "That's one of your problems. Girls like you too much." She slid closer to him and touched his arm and batted her eyelids. "I'm crazy about you!" Then she began to laugh. "It's serious," he told her. "I know it is," she said, and she went on laughing.

He was used to this. Polly found almost everything funny, even things she was really serious about. "You know me," she said when she'd calmed down, "I can't help laughing." "Yeah, but what do you think I should do?" Jerry said. That started her off again. He shook his head at this fresh sign of her incurable high spirits. "I mean, if you've got any advice, I could use it," he said. "Talk to your father." "I just can't!" he told her. "I don't know why. He's such a sweet man. I think your father is one of the nicest men I've ever known." Jerry had heard this before from women of all sorts. Miss Smith, for instance, had told him much the same thing at a Club House dance the summer before. Jerry knew there were lots of women, besides his mother, who found his father charming and lovable, but that did not mean he was an easy man to talk to about girls and sex. "He just isn't sympathetic about it," he told Polly. "He thinks it's all wrong to do anything before you're married." "Well, it is," said Polly. "Henderson's right." She called Mr. and Mrs. Engels by their first names. "Anne doesn't think so," said Jerry. "Well, Anne is a revolutionary," Polly said. "Don't listen to Anne. Anyway, I notice Anne is getting married, and pretty young, too." "I can't get married," Jerry said, "and anyway Rosalind wouldn't marry me." "Neither would I if you were flirting with Nancy Train," Polly said. "But I like it," Jerry objected. "It's fun." "We're going to have to do something about you," Polly said.

She said it again when they went down to the beach for a quick dip before dinner and she saw him in his bathing suit. "It isn't indecent, is it?" he asked. "No," said Polly, who had an eye for style and always knew what was being worn. "Then why don't you tell my parents that?" Jerry suggested. "All right," said Polly. "You just hold the fort and we'll let you prance around in anything you want to wear." He looked at her a little doubtfully. He didn't prance, but he was afraid if he said so Polly would begin to laugh again. He could see she was on the verge of laughing now. "What's funny?" he asked. "Nothing, Jerry," she said. She slipped an arm around his waist. "I love you. I'm just happy to be here."

With her arrival the wedding had really started for him. That night he lay in his bunk bed listening to her talk to Anne. It was like the summers of old when Polly and Anne had talked endlessly at night, often bursting out into smothered laughing that kept everyone awake until his mother eventually came into the hall to whisper fiercely at their closed door. "Girls! It's midnight. Henderson and I have to be up in the morning." Then there would be silence for a while until suddenly something struck one of the girls as funny. Smothered laughter would erupt more violently than ever from their room. Polly was the only person who could make Anne behave that way. With Polly, Anne had talked and laughed and even giggled like an ordinary adolescent. Night after night Jerry had fallen asleep to the sound of the girls in the next room, murmuring and laughing together. He could even hear the rustle of their bedclothes and the squeak of the bed frame as they rolled around together. To his mind those were the sounds of summer, of hot nights and open windows. He'd missed them in recent years when Polly had begun to work during the summers. Now the sounds had started up again, and they were just the right sounds for a wedding party, he thought. All they needed now was the bridegroom.

He arrived on the first of July. He and his best man had driven clear across Ohio and Indiana that day. They were hot and stiff from their trip and went to the beach as soon as possible. The temperature had been ninety-two degrees in the early afternoon, and even at five o'clock it was not much cooler. The sun was still high in the west and the sand of the beach was still hot. Michael and Bill Treadway waded straight into the lake and began to swim out. They could swim well. Jerry joined them, and together the three of them swam several hundred yards into the lake, leaving Anne and Polly and Joanne on the sandbar. When at last they stopped swimming, Michael moved his arms back and forth through the clear water. "And it's all fresh?" he said. He cupped some water in his palm and tasted it. He did not swallow. "You can drink it." Jerry said. He drank some water to prove his point. Then Michael drank some. "What it reminds me of," he said at last, "is a lagoon. A South Pacific lagoon." He had been in the South Pacific during the war. "Except the water is sweet," he added, drinking some more. Jerry had been on the alert for any sign of condescension toward Lake Michigan. Now he relaxed. Michael could swim. He was obviously impressed with the lake. He was not an Atlantic seaboard snob. He was okay.

He was tall and somewhat bony, but not really bad-looking. He talked and behaved well. At dinner he was complimentary about the food. He turned to Mr Engels halfway through the meal and said, "Anne tells me you're interested in the Civil War." His grandparents, he said, lived in Fredericksburg, Virginia, and he knew the Battle of Fredericksburg inside out. He and Mr. Engels talked for some time about the war. Michael admitted that sentimentally he was a Confederate, even though he was a Socialist who would vote for Norman Thomas in the fall. That brought up current politics. Polly, a Republican like all of Jerry's mother's family, shook her head in mock sadness. "Well, I guess you're right for my Red cousin here." Then she slipped her arm around Anne's waist. Everyone looked at Anne who blushed, not because she was a Red but because Michael was now looking at her in front of her family. He had a fond, almost possessive, intimate look on his face. "I hope I'm right for her," he said. Anne blushed even more.

She was not at ease, surrounded by her family, with Michael smiling at her. After dinner she and Michael went for a walk together. Soon after that, Bill Treadway excused himself, saying he was tired. He went off to the Forsons, and then Jerry's family settled down to a discussion of Michael. Aunt Madge thought he had handled himself beautifully. Joanne said he looked like Humphrey Bogart. Polly thought he was

brave. "Imagine what it takes to come here and face us all."
Jerry noticed that neither his mother nor his father joined
in this conversation, though they were obviously more concerned than anyone about what sort of man Michael was.
"You can tell he comes from a good family," Aunt Madge
said. She was convinced of this not just by his manners but
by an antique silver coffee pot his grandparents had sent to
Anne. She had studied the hallmark. It was a genuine
eighteenth-century coffee pot, which told her more about
the Goodfellow family than anything else she had been able
to learn. After all, anyone could work for the New Deal
the way Michael's father had, but not everyone came from
a family that had heirlooms like that coffee pot. Aunt Madge
was convinced Anne was making a good marriage, a better
marriage than anyone in the Kentucky branch of the Engels
family had expected.

When Anne came back from her walk she was alone.
Michael had turned in, she explained. She surveyed her
family sitting around the porch. Her attitude was a bit de-
fiant. She knew they had been talking about Michael. "It's
all right," said Polly. "He passes." "I just don't like the feeling
you've been talking him over," Anne said. Polly said, "You
know we're going to talk about him." She pulled Anne down
onto the daybed with her. Aunt Madge said, "I think he's
very nice." Anne looked at her father. "He seems to be a
sensible young man," Mr. Engels conceded. There was an
awkward pause, which Joanne broke by saying, "He eats
cantaloupe with a knife and a fork." Anne leaped up from
the daybed. "I'm going to bed," she announced, "and you
can talk him over all you want." She fled from the porch.
Polly looked around with a smile on her face. "You go,"
she suggested to Jerry's mother, who got up to follow Anne
to her bedroom. "Heavens!" said Aunt Madge, "she's certainly touchy about him." "Well, wouldn't you be?" Polly
asked her. Aunt Madge shook her head. "This is nothing,"
she said. "I remember bringing Sheldon to Mount Sterling
to meet Mother and Auntie and Mac and Grace and Cousin

Webster and all of them." She was referring to her dead husband's first meeting with her relatives. "Anne should thank her stars she doesn't have to go through that." "She will," said Joanne. "They're all coming." "Cousin Webster is not coming, thank goodness," Aunt Madge said, "and poor Auntie is dead, and anyway, this is not Mount Sterling. I had to take Sheldon to every single house, and they fed him beaten biscuit and country ham everywhere he went until his throat was so dry he could hardly talk. Nothing to drink, of course. No alcohol, and everyone watching his every move. Michael is getting off very easily, I think." "He handled himself quite well," Mr. Engels said. Polly rose and gestured toward the back of the house. "I'm going to go get in on this."

Gradually over the next half hour the whole family collected in Anne's bedroom. When Jerry went in he saw his mother sitting on the edge of the bed with Anne's head in her lap. Polly was lying beside Anne. Anne had been crying. "Oh Jerry," she said when he appeared. She stretched out her hand to him. "I want you all to love him the way I do." Her mother patted her cheek. Polly patted her hip. Presently Mr. Engels appeared. At the sight of her father Anne burst into tears. "He's so good," Anne said. "He's so good." She seemed to be referring to Michael. Mr. Engels said, "You mustn't think we're criticizing him." He seemed very moved himself. "I just want my daughter to be happy." That made Anne weep even more. Jerry had never seen her so vulnerable. Then Aunt Madge put her head into the bedroom. "There's more room on the bed," Polly called out cheerfully. "Why don't we all cuddle up?" "I just thought I would say goodnight," Aunt Madge said. Joanne asked, "Why is everyone crying?" Jerry, who felt close to tears himself, thought it was a good question. Why were they crying? Then, from the bed, Polly answered him. "It's just not a marriage unless everyone has a good cry ahead of time."

The next day Jerry drove into Chicago again, this time to meet Michael's family who were arriving by airplane. Michael

157

had intended to meet them, but Anne wouldn't let him go. "Jerry would be glad to go," she said. "You drove all day yesterday. Let Jerry do it. He knows the way." So Jerry set off with a photograph of the Goodfellow family to help him identify them at the airport.

It was another very hot day, and as he drove slowly through Whiting, Jerry could hear the tires of the Oldsmobile making a special kind of sound, like ripping silk, as they rolled over the softened asphalt of Indianapolis Boulevard. He took a brief detour to drive by his old home on Davis Avenue. The events of the night before had left him feeling sentimental, and now he wanted to look at the place where he and Anne had grown up. He thought maybe the sight of the house would enrich and deepen his feelings about his sister and his family. He was afraid that his preoccupation with his own life had kept him from reacting as strongly as he should to the big event that was about to take place in the Engels family.

Unfortunately, as soon as he stopped in front of the house on Davis, he saw a little girl playing with some friends of hers in the yard of what used to be his house. The yard was now enclosed with a white picket fence. The Chinese elms along the parking strip were larger than when the Engels lived there, and the house itself looked more imposing because the doctor who owned it now had built an addition on one side, where he had his office and consulting room. To Jerry, it no longer seemed like home, and moreover, after he'd been staring at the house for a minute, the little girl in the front yard came out on the sidewalk and asked him why he was looking at her house. He felt confused. She was only ten or twelve, but she intimidated him a little. "I was just looking for an address," he told the girl. Then he drove off.

He had no trouble identifying Michael's family. They looked just like their photograph. Mr. Goodfellow was plump and wore a bow tie, Mrs. Goodfellow was angular and intelligent looking, Paul was a much younger version of Michael, and Mary a younger version of her mother. They were all wilted by the heat. Jerry promised them it would be cooler at the Shores. He felt very much in charge, helping them to get their suitcases, bringing the car around to the terminal entrance, packing their suitcases into the trunk of the Oldsmobile, and getting them on their way with great efficiency. He found out that only Mr. Goodfellow had seen Chicago, so when he got to Washington Park he gave them a little tour to show them the hospital where he and Anne had been born. Then he stopped so they could admire the Saint-Gaudens fountain at the Washington Park end of the Midway. "Now all that is the University," he said, gesturing at the line of gray stone buildings along 59th Street. He drove slowly along 59th, identifying the buildings for them, and stopping in front of Rockefeller Chapel. At the corner of 59th and Kimbark he stopped again. "That's Ida Noyes Hall," he said, "the girls' gym, but we used the pool there during the war." He was remembering the screens that had been set up along the back of the girls' basketball court to protect the girls in their blue gym clothes from the sight of wet, shivering boys in bathing suits, running back and forth from the pool to their temporary locker room in the basement. In spite of the heat he felt himself almost shivering. Then he returned to the present. He gestured across the street. "That's Blaine Hall," he said. "I went to school there." He was looking right at the windows of M. Coppée's French classroom. "Anne and I both went to school up there," he said, gesturing toward Belfield. At the next corner he identified Sunny Gym for them. "And this is where we play soccer," he said. "That's our track," he added. He was fascinated to see the athletic field deserted, the grass higher than it ever was during the school year. "Would you like to see where we live?" he asked the Goodfellows. "It's only a couple of blocks from here." Mr. Goodfellow said, "Maybe we ought to be getting out to Indiana Shores." "All right," Jerry said, but instead of taking the Inner Drive through Jackson Park, he backtracked a little to get them on the Outer Drive. This would give the Goodfellows a view of the Museum of Science and Industry and of the lake. "There's a coal mine in the museum," he told Paul Goodfellow, "and that's a captured German submarine at the side." He slowed the car so that Mary and Paul could look at the submarine. Then he gestured ahead. "That's the lake," he said.

In Whiting he took them a little out of the way to show them the new research buildings. "The old laboratory where my father used to work is right inside the refinery," he explained. "You can only see it from Route 12 and we're taking Route 20 out of town." "Does it always smell like this?" Mr. Goodfellow asked. Jerry sniffed the air. "Sometimes it smells worse," he said. "When the wind is from the west you smell the Amaizo plant. That's worse than the refineries." He got them back onto Indianapolis Boulevard, where again he could hear the ripping silk sound of tires on hot asphalt. The bridge over the industrial canal was up, so he had time to point out things of interest. "Sinclair's on that side," he said, "and everything on the left is Standard. That tall thing is a catalytic cracker. It's new." "What's the holdup?" Mr. Goodfellow asked, trying to peer ahead along the line of motionless cars. "The bridge is up," Jerry explained. "Sometimes during the war, what with the bridges and the railroad crossings, it used to take us half an hour longer to get to the Shores. A lot of oil for the East coast was shipped out of Whiting during the war. You used to see freight trains with a hundred tank cars going through all the time." He felt the Goodfellows were not being as responsive to Whiting as they ought to be. He wanted them to understand that they owed something to this town.

The line of cars began to move forward at last. "This is the industrial canal," Jerry explained as they crossed it. This was where he had once seen a pretty girl watching her brothers wrestle. The shack was gone now. It had disappeared

160

during the war, but the cottonwoods were still growing on the canal bank. "We're in East Chicago now," he announced as they came down off the bridge.

Through East Chicago and Indiana Harbor and Gary he tried his best to interest the Goodfellows in the industrial sights around them, but the heat had gotten to them, and anyway, he reflected, you probably had to grow up in the Calumet to really appreciate it. It was only after Gary that his passengers showed some signs of reviving. "We're in the dunes now," he told them. As they approached Baileytown, which was the last village before you turned north into Indiana Shores, he said, "Maybe you can see the Club House and the Guest House. We're near the Shores now." In the old days, when his family drove out for spring weekends at the Shores, he and Anne had always kept on the lookout for the Club House. They chanted:

Here we come to Baileytown, Baileytown, Baileytown,
Here we come to Baileytown, Baileytown, town.

Then at Baileytown they would stop their chant to look for the Club House. Anne always saw it first. "First on the Club House," she would cry, "first on the Club House." Then Jerry would see it and begin to shout, "Second on the Club House, second on the Club House." By then they would both be wild with anticipation. He wished the Goodfellows could understand all this.

At the cabin they sorted themselves out a bit more. Mr. Goodfellow turned out to be a sort of teasing, good-humored man who said to Jerry's father, "Well, your son has given us a whole tour." Mrs. Goodfellow stood on the porch looking out over the blow-out at the live dune. "Why, it's like Cape Cod," she said. "Want to go swimming?" Jerry asked Paul and Mary. He took them down to the beach. "Listen to the sand," he told them, shuffling his feet through it and making it sing. "There are only two other places in the world that have singing sand." It was an article of faith he had been brought up on, and neither Paul nor Mary disputed it. They shuffled their feet and listened to the sand. "That's my Dolphin," Jerry said, "and that's Phil's. He's my friend. And this is where we have beach picnics." He pointed to a weathered tree trunk, washed down from the northern part of the lake and cast up here by some storm. It was now deeply embedded in the sand and made a nice backlog for their beach fires. Then he led them toward the water. "You don't have to be afraid of anything here," he said. "There are no undertows or tides or anything."

He was still on the beach with Paul and Mary when Rufus appeared. He had just arrived from Kentucky 10 minutes before with Jerry's grandmother and his uncle and aunt. "We had two flat tires," he announced. "I got to cool off." He plunged into the lake and began to swim vigorously but without much science. "That's my cousin," Jerry explained to Paul and Mary Goodfellow, "He goes to the University of Kentucky."

Rufus had been a very red baby who had gone on being ruddy all his life. His name was the same as his father's, William Macmillian Engels, but nobody had ever called him anything but Rufus, and it fit him perfectly. His hair was red, his face was red, his arms were red, and though the rest of his body was white, you could see it would turn red at once if exposed to the sun. He wore a voluminous bathing suit that began at his navel and went several inches down his thighs. Once he had cooled himself off enough to talk, almost the first thing he said to Jerry was, "They let you wear a bathing suit like that up here?" Jerry said, "You should get yourself one. It leaves your legs free." "I'd feel naked in it," Rufus said. Then he began questioning Paul and Mary about their trip. "You flew?" he said. "I've never flown. Beats driving I bet, especially on a day like this." He turned to Jerry. "We had a blowout near Muncie. Scared us all to death. At least I was at the wheel." He stood with his legs apart in waist-deep water, looking about at the beach and the dunes as he talked. "That's a new house," he said, pointing to the Kincaid place, high up on the dunes near the Forson's cabin. "She lives there," said Jerry, pointing to Mrs. Kincaid, who was collecting her children. Rufus nodded silently. He said nothing for a while until Mrs. Kincaid started toward the parking lot. Then he said, "I've never seen a woman that age in a bathing suit like that." "She looks pretty good in it, doesn't she?" said Jerry. "Yeah," said Rufus, "but how'd you like to see your own mother's navel?" Jerry said nothing. The likelihood wasn't very great in Jerry's case, and it was nil in Rufus's. His mother probably didn't even own a bathing suit. Then, as if to confound them all, a party of adults came down from the cabin, and Jerry and Rufus saw that Mrs. Goodfellow was wearing a two-piece bathing suit. It was bigger than Mrs. Kincaid's, but it was still a two-piecer. Rufus looked at Paul and Mary, started to say something, and then stopped.

That night there were seventeen people for dinner at the cabin. By pushing two tables together, Verlene and Mrs. Engels were able to seat twelve on the porch. Jerry, presiding over a small table in the living room, felt like a host. He tried to draw out Mary and Paul, but he could never give them the limelight for very long because Rufus dominated things, speaking in a loud, confident voice even when he was discussing people who were seated right out on the porch. "Now, I hope your brother can hold Anne down," he said to Paul and Mary, "because Anne can be a terror." That was Anne's reputation in Kentucky. "Anne's something," said Rufus, shaking his head. "She's worse than Joanne." Joanne bridled. "You're no one to talk." Rufus paid no attention to her. Addressing his remarks to Paul and Mary Goodfellow, he explained the whole ranking structure of the Engels cousins—as seen from Montgomery County. Anne was a terror who could only be held down by a strong man. Joanne showed signs of wildness, which everyone hoped would be cured by Ashley Hall. Jerry was a lady's man that you shouldn't rely on. "And tell them what you are," Joanne said. "I'm just a country boy," said Rufus, obviously satisfied with this view of himself as a diamond in the rough.

Jerry had always felt that if he couldn't be a brilliant student like Anne, his father would have preferred him to be a solid character like Rufus. That night he was pleased to discover even solid characters had problems with girls. Rufus was involved with a nice girl at the University of Kentucky. She was the sort of girl you could take home to meet your family, Rufus said. Her father was a doctor in Cincinnati, and Rufus really liked her. He had even thought of marrying her. "And I ought to marry her, if you know what I mean," he said. Jerry knew. Only the trouble was she had been raised in a city. Rufus didn't think she'd be happy as a farmer's wife, and all he had ever wanted to do was farm. And besides, if he married Laura he didn't seee how he would ever get his hands on a farm. His father's farm was too small to support two families. He couldn't go into partnership with his father. "What it is, Jerry," he said, "is that I should court one of the local girls. Sally Church, for instance. I don't like her father much, but they've got land. They're renting one of their farms. They'd probably let me work it for them, and I know Sally and I could get along together, if she'd have me." He sighed heavily. His shoulder touched Jerry's as they lay side by side on the porch daybed which opened out to accommodate two. "Only I feel like a dog, letting Laura down," Rufus said. "She likes me," he explained. "I guess I took advantage of her." He fell silent. Then he asked, "You done that yet?" "No," said Jerry. "Well, see you don't deceive anyone," Rufus said. Then he asked, "What do you think about this Michael?" "I like him." "He's sort of thin looking," sail Rufus. "You reckon he and Anne will be all right together?" "She thinks so," Jerry said. Rufus sighed again. "I wish I was settled," he said. "You know what land costs now in Montgomery County? Five hundred an acre. That's what the Travers got when they sold. Now, how is someone going to start out farming with land sky high like that? Even if I could get a mortgage the payments would kill me." He shifted on the daybed. "You're lucky," he told Jerry. "You don't have to think about getting a farm. There are lots of things you could do." "But I don't know what I'm going to do," Jerry said. "Good-looking like you are, you could just marry some rich girl," said Rufus. "I'd never do that," said Jerry. "That girl you have now, isn't her family rich?" "But that isn't why I like her," said Jerry. "Well, it isn't why I like Sally Church," said Rufus. "I thought you liked Laura," said Jerry. "I like them both," said Rufus, "only maybe I like Laura more." He stirred some more in the bed. "What it is, Jerry," he said, "is that it's tough until you're settled down."

Settled down! Long after Rufus had fallen asleep, Jerry lay awake wondering what it would feel like to be settled down. His father was settled, his uncle was settled, Mr. Forson and Mr. Hyatt were settled, and Mr. Goodfellow looked like a settled man. Michael was settling, Phil would settle, Rufus was already more settled than most guys his age and probably would settle down completely in a few years. Only Jerry Engels did not seem to be settling. He didn't even know what it was like to *want* to be settled. Was he missing something?

He thought about it. If you were settled you would have a wife and some work you were interested in and a house and a car. That could be interesting, he thought. You'd have a sort of regular life. You'd go off every morning to do something, and you'd come home every evening to your wife and you'd sleep with her every night. You wouldn't be surprised all the time by what you were doing and what was happening to you. You'd know what to expect. That could be pleasant: to know what to expect. Jerry never knew what to expect next. Anything might happen, and even when he

165

knew what was going to happen next—like Anne's wedding—he had no idea what to expect from it. Was he going to be deeply moved in some way? Would he cry? Would he feel as if Anne were lost to him? Well, he'd find out, he thought.

He did find out. Weddings were chaotic, he discovered. There were so many people around and so much going on that a wedding did not allow you to feel anything but a generalized sense of excitement. You felt something important was happening, but that was about all you felt. There was too much hubbub to sort things out, too much coming and going, too much waiting to get into the bathroom. The bathroom was in constant use, and the hot water supply, never very copious, kept giving out. On Saturday Jerry's mother was trapped in the shower with nothing but cold water to rinse herself off in, and on the morning of the wedding Jerry had to go to the Hyatts to shave. There was also a constant opening and closing of bedroom doors as people dressed for the brunch that Mrs. Forson gave on Saturday, and then got into cooler clothes for the wedding rehearsal, and then dressed up again for dinner at the Spa. Jerry caught a glimpse of his mother in her slip and of Polly and Anne in their bras and panties. Aunt Madge complained that every time she started to change clothes in the loft someone came into the living room and found her at it. Jerry finally nailed up a blanket that gave her some privacy, but it cut off the circulation of air. That was a problem because the weekend of the Fourth was very hot. And this in turn meant that parties of people were constantly going off to the beach and then coming back with sandy feet and wet towels and bathing suits. Only Jerry's grandmother and Aunt Grace seemed immune to it all because they didn't swim or change into cooler clothes. Between events old Mrs. Engels sat on the porch fanning herself and talking to anyone who was available. Aunt Grace studied the wedding presents and made interesting comments about people's tastes. From time to time she seized a broom to sweep out the sand that was constantly being tracked into the cabin by all the coming and going. "Oh, Grace, don't!" Jerry's mother cried. "Let Jerry or Verlene do it." "I'll do it," Verlene offered, but it was impossible to wrest the broom from Aunt Grace. "Verlene has more than enough to do," she said, "I can make myself useful this way." Aunt Grace was like a West Point general watching raw troops maneuver. Events were not evolving the way they did in her house. The telephone rang, people went off in different directions, a car was sent to pick up the Goodfellows at the Club House, and the Goodfellows appeared on the porch, having walked down the beach. "In this heat?" Jerry's mother exclaimed. "It was lovely," said Mrs. Goodfellow. She liked beaches. Then the car that had been sent to get them was needed to go to Chesterton on an errand, only now it was down in the beach parking lot while Mr. Engels and Uncle Mac and Rufus and Joanne had a short swim. Finally, where were the flowers? They were supposed to have been delivered that morning.

Verlene had never seen a wedding quite like this one. (Neither had Jerry's Kentucky relatives.) On the morning of the Fourth when Jerry picked her up, Verlene hopped into the car full of anticipation. "Well, how's it going to be?" she asked. Jerry shook his head seriously. "I'm not sure if my mother is going to make it." He had never seen his mother so worked up and tense, not even during their semi-annual moves from Chicago to the Shores and from the Shores back to Chicago. She was in a real swivet, he told Verlene. *Swivet* was an Engels family word meaning *state of frenzied activity*. Yet, by late afternoon his mother seemed to have pulled herself together. In her long dress and hat she looked calm and dignified. He escorted her and his grandmother out onto the lawn.

He stood between them as the wedding march began to play from the phonograph, which he had positioned at the loft window that overlooked the yard. Verlene was up there working the phonograph. Then Polly appeared, holding her

167

bouquet with hands that visibly trembled. There was a sweet, if slightly fixed, smile on her face. Then Anne appeared in her wedding gown, looking more solemn than Jerry had ever seen her. His father looked solemn, too. They moved slowly across the lawn toward Mr. Paul, who was standing with his back to the wall Jerry had built. Mr. Paul was easily the most relaxed person involved in the wedding.

Jerry listened to the ceremony for a while. Then he found his attention wandering to the people around him. His grandmother had been to so many weddings that probably this one could not mean much to her even if Anne was her first grandchild to get married. And his mother was probably just glad it was almost over. What about Aunt Grace, he wondered. She was standing very erect with her eagle eye surveying everyone and everything, storing it all up to be recounted to people in Montgomery County. Home weddings were not unknown in the County, but they took place indoors, especially if there was a fine staircase for the bride to descend. You had receptions on the lawn, but then the lawn was always a lot bigger than this one, and the guests formed a more homogeneous crowd than this mixture of Standard Oil people and Engelses and Goodfellows and friends of Anne from U-High days.

Then Michael slipped the wedding ring on Anne's finger and Mr. Paul pronounced them husband and wife. Anne lifted her veil and Michael kissed her. What did it mean, Jerry wondered. Did they feel married now? What did they feel as all their friends and relatives moved up to kiss them and congratulate them? He kissed Anne, thinking, *Now she's Mrs. Michael Goodfellow.* How strange! Did Anne feel she was settled now? But how could anyone feel settled on an occasion like this? The caterer's men had begun to pass glasses of champagne. Toasts were proposed. The Engels family posed for a picture. The wedding party posed. Anne and Michael posed. The Goodfellows were rounded up and made to pose together. It went on and on. Food appeared.

Jerry saw his mother seated next to Mrs. Goodfellow, their heads turned toward each other as if they were deep in some interesting conversation. He took another glass of champagne. He talked to Emmy Motherwell, Anne's best friend from U-High. Emmy was the one girl Anne had never encouraged him about. She had stared at him in amazement when he told her he liked Emmy. "Jerry," she said, "you don't come up to Emmy's shoulder. You're in sixth, Emmy's in tenth." Now, however, he came up to Emmy's shoulder, and beyond. He talked to her about Northwestern, where she was going. He talked to Anne. He talked to Phil and Shirley. He kissed Joanne, who was looking very grown-up and ladylike in hat and gloves. He kissed Linda for good measure. He went back to talk some more to Emmy. Then he kissed her. It was all right to kiss everybody at a wedding. He kissed Shirley. He kissed his mother. He kissed Mary Goodfellow. He and Polly hugged and kissed. "Oh, I'm so happy!" Polly exclaimed. Then he kissed Mrs. Goodfellow and Mrs. Forson. Mrs. Forson was like an aunt to him. He called her Aunt Beth. He found his grandmother sitting down on the porch and kissed her and Aunt Grace and Aunt Madge. He realized that his face was getting covered with lipstick, so he went into the bathroom to wash it. When he looked at himself he thought he was almost as red-faced as Uncle Mac, though still not as red-faced as Rufus. Still, he was pretty red-faced. The Engels were ruddy men.

It was growing dark now, and Anne had disappeared from the porch to change into her traveling clothes. "Come on!" said Rufus, "we got to fix up Michael's car." They went down into the road. They did what had to be done on these occasions. They put pebbles into the hubcaps of Michael's car. They wrote *Just Married* in lipstick on the back window. They wrote it again on the hood, and only Rufus prevented Jerry from writing it a third time on the side window. Then they tied a white bow to the aerial and a pink bow on one door handle. "That's good enough," said Rufus, who was more experienced with weddings than Jerry or Joanne or the Goodfellows. Then they shared the rice and gave handfuls to the adults who had begun to collect in the road around the car.

Anne was smiling as she came down the steps with Michael. In her traveling clothes she looked more grown-up and stylish than Jerry could ever remember seeing her. Both she and Michael had happy, self-conscious expressions as they kissed people and said goodbye. Showers of rice fell on them. It was all so unusual that Jerry didn't know what he was feeling as he hugged his sister and heard her say, "Oh, Jerry," in that sentimental voice she used sometimes when they were about to have one of their heart-to-heart talks. He thought he might cry, but he didn't. Instead he crowded around the car throwing rice in the open window. He was beside his mother, who bent down at the last moment to give Anne another kiss. Then Michael started up the car. It moved off with a remarkable banging and clattering coming from the hubcaps. Then it turned the bend and was lost to sight. The wedding seemed to be over.

Yet everyone was still there. They went back up to the cabin. "A very handsome young couple," Jerry heard his grandmother saying. "They look so young," Aunt Grace said. "They are." "Well, Brother!" said Uncle Mac, clapping Jerry's father on the shoulder. "I think I'm going to collapse at last," Jerry's mother said, but in fact a new sort of party began in which people sang and drank the remainder of the champagne and ate cold chicken and fruit salad. Fireworks were going off in the distance. Jerry moved around from group to group, feeling happy and aimless. Then Rufus appeared at his side. "We've got to get Joanne out of sight," he told Jerry, leading him outdoors. Joanne was sitting on Jerry's wall, her hat cocked on her head, a loopy expression on her face. While no one was looking, she had had another glass or two of champagne. "We can't let Grandma see her like this," Rufus said, hoisting her to her feet. "You take her other arm." They walked her around the house and brought her in by the front door. "I'm all right," she kept saying. "Sure you are, honey," Rufus said. "All you've got to do is lie down for a while." They took her into the bunk room and put her on the bed. They removed her hat, her corsage, and her shoes. "Everything's spinning," she complained. "You put one foot on the floor and it will stop," Rufus advised her. She did as he told her and it seemed to stop. "Am I drunk?" she asked. "You've had a little too much champagne," Rufus told her. Joanne looked pleased. Then she closed her eyes. "She'll be all right," said Rufus.

Out in the hall he moved close to Jerry and in a lowered tone of voice said, "We've got to do something." Jerry beamed at him. He had had more champagne and was a little high himself. "Where do you all go?" Rufus asked. Jerry went on beaming. "Down home," Rufus said, "the fellows in a wedding party generally go off afterward. You know . . ." "Good," said Jerry. "Well, where do you go around here?" Rufus asked. Then Jerry realized he was suggesting they visit a cathouse. "Michigan City," he said. "Who should we take with us?" Rufus said. "You think Paul is old enough?" "No," said Jerry. "What about that Tread-way fellow?" "He's too old." This was strictly a young man's expedition. "Just you and me, then?" Rufus asked, his red face smiling. "And Phil," said Jerry. "That's right. You go get Phil. I better drive."

Phil was on the porch, singing with the others. He held a plate of chicken in one hand and a fork in the other. "Come on outdoors," Jerry told him, "I've got something to say to you." But once outdoors he was so excited he couldn't speak for a moment. He just stared at Phil. Then he said, in slightly awed tones, "We're going to Michigan City. You and me and Rufus. It's what you do after a wedding." There was a hush. Phil didn't say anything. How could you say anything now? The time had passed. The decision had been arrived at. It was what you always did after a wedding. Theirs not to reason why. They started for the road. Then Phil said, "I don't have any money with me." "Neither do I!" Jerry said. He turned back toward the cabin. Phil hurried off to the Forsons, still carrying his plate and fork.

When they were all in the car, Rufus said, "Okay, let's go get us some poontang." The word delighted Jerry. Everything delighted him—the rush of night air on his hot face, the feel of being surrounded by his friends whose thighs pressed against his, even the whiff of paw-paws as they crossed the swamp. They were off to Michigan City to get some poontang. He began to sing:

> Going to get some poontang, poontang, poontang,
> Going to get some poontang, poontang, poon.

"You're higher than Joanne," Rufus told him. "I am not," said Jerry. "That's a real song Anne and I used to sing." "That?" Rufus said. "Well, the words were different," Jerry admitted. It was the Baileytown song. He sang it for Rufus. "That's not the same at all," Rufus said, only it was the same, and Jerry felt the way he had felt on those spring weekends when they drove out to open the cabin. Something wonderful was about to happen.

In fact this was even better than those weekends, because it was unexpected. For the last few days, as he'd gotten swept up in the wedding, he'd stopped thinking about Michigan City. Now, as if to reward his goodness, he was being taken there. He felt buoyed up and borne along. It was how he felt in Scammons Gardens among the Hard Core; it was how he felt after practice when he and his pals went off to Stineway's; it was how he felt on Halloween when they all roistered through the streets of Hyde Park. His strength was trebled by his companions. He would bound up the stairs of the house. He would not be afraid of catwomen. What was there to be afraid of? "Do you think we should wear something?" he asked suddenly. *Wearing something* meant using a contraceptive. "I mean, I haven't got one with me." "You don't need one," Rufus said. Jerry relaxed. He didn't need one. Everything was all right.

But when they finally found the house and parked across the street from it, he was not so sure. "It doesn't look like much," said Rufus, surveying the place. It was an ordinary-looking two-story house on what appeared to be a rundown residential street. Lights shone from behind drawn blinds, but the porch was dark and there was no welcome mat out, no doorman in a braided uniform to say, "Right in here, boys." Rufus shook his head. "It sure doesn't look like much." To Jerry it didn't look like anything. Indeed, as the three of them crossed the street, a terrible suspicion began to gather in his mind. Suppose Walker had lied? Suppose it was a hoax? Suppose this was just an ordinary home? Suppose, in fact, that there were no cathouses anywhere? Maybe they were just myths—like undertows on the lake. All his life Jerry had heard people talking about undertows. He'd been warned about them, but he knew they just didn't exist. Maybe prostitution was like that. Guys talked about cathouses, and fathers warned you against going to them, but in fact there were no such places. The house they were approaching was probably just the home of a poor family getting ready for bed. That was why lights were on in an upstairs window. "Maybe we shouldn't bother them," he said to Rufus and Phil. "Bother who?" said Rufus, starting up the porch steps. "The people who live here," said Jerry. Rufus paused. "Aren't you sure of the address?" Jerry said, "It doesn't look like the right place." "Well, hell!" said Rufus, "you ought to know the right places." Then Phil spoke up. "I think this is it."

Jerry watched from the sidewalk while Rufus and Phil went up to the front door and knocked. It was opened, rather promptly, by a man who stood in the doorway, light shining out around his big frame. Jerry got ready to run. He was sure the man was going to give a cry of rage when Rufus or Phil asked to see the girls. Instead, however, the man stood back. Rufus went in first, then Phil. Jerry hastened up the steps and slipped in after them.

He was in a bare hallway with a staircase on the left and on the right an arched doorway into a shabbily furnished living room. The man called out, "Gretch!" and then settled himself in an armchair. He was like a householder letting his wife deal with salesmen at the door. From the back of the house Gretch appeared with metal curlers in her hair. She looked not at all like Belle Watling in *Gone with the Wind*, who up until that moment had constituted Jerry's sole model for what a Madam should look like. Except for those curlers in her hair, Gretch did not even look specifically female, and the curlers, though feminine, were scarcely an attraction. They made her look about as lovable as an egg beater. "Okay, boys," she said, "that'll be ten dollars." For what, Jerry wondered. "Don't we get to see them first?" Rufus asked. "You'll see them," said Gretch, holding out her hand.

They paid her, but now Jerry's doubts were reviving. Was this really a cathouse? Where were the mirrors and the chandeliers and the piano? Where, above all, were the girls? Gretch seemed to him like some sort of terrible landlady. Maybe they were just renting rooms in her seedy boarding-house. How did they know what they were paying for?

"This way," said Gretch, leading them up the staircase. Jerry went last, feeling that some terrible deception was about to take place. He would be shown into some bare room and Gretch would lock him in and hold him for ransom. He and Phil and Rufus were all dressed up in their wedding clothes. Maybe Gretch thought they were rich kids who could be exploited in some way. One thing was sure: there could be no real catwomen in a place like this. It wasn't an erotic kind of house. It was a dump.

And yet there were girls upstairs. "I'll take that one," Rufus said, making up his mind quickly. Gretch handed Jerry over to another. "This is Elaine," she said, and Jerry scarcely had time to exchange one final blank look with Phil (being led off by a third girl) before he found himself alone with Elaine in one of the upstairs bedrooms.

It had all been so quick and chaotic and unbelievable that he found himself trembling in every limb. He was shaking so violently he wasn't sure he could even stand up. What if he fainted? He had to lie down, anyway. Tottering forward past Elaine, he flopped onto the bed, which was as unimpressive as everything else about this place. Only, what was happening to him? He'd die of shame if he fainted with his first woman, who, comfortingly enough, didn't seem to notice that there was anything wrong with him. She just sat down on the bed beside him and began to open his trousers. He would have been just as happy to open them himself, but given the fact that he had all he could do just to keep himself together, he decided to let her go ahead. He felt like he was shaking the bed. Then abruptly he stopped shaking. "What are you doing?" he asked her, for not only had she opened his trousers, she'd reached into his underpants, and now it looked almost as if she were actually going to put his thing into her mouth. He could not have been more disconcerted if she had tried to stick it up her nose. "Stop that!" he said. She looked up. "Isn't it what you want?" "No!" he said loudly. This was what a terrible man in a stinking Men's Room once offered to do. He hadn't come to Michigan City for that. He wanted the real thing.

When she understood as much, Elaine said, "Okay, Buster, but let's get our shoes off first, shall we?" "My name is Jeremy," Jerry said, "but everyone calls me Jerry." She wasn't really listening, however, for all she said was, "Okay, Jeremy, but I don't lay guys in their shoes."

Fair enough, he thought, getting up. In fact he respected her for making him take off his shoes. Things were still far from good, but they were certainly a lot better than they had been a minute earlier. She had slipped out of her robe and was now sitting naked on the edge of the bed, watching him remove his shoes and socks, and then lower his trousers and finish removing his shorts. He was naked from the waist down and she seemed to be really seeing him now, though what she chose to comment on was his age. "You're pretty young, aren't you?" she said. "I'm eighteen," he replied, giving himself an extra ten months. "How old are you?" "I'm twenty-five," she said, robbing herself of ten years. Though maybe she *was* twenty-five, he thought, and the life she was leading had had an aging effect on her. Anyway it wasn't exactly his business, though he seemed to be making it his. "Do you like this?" he asked her. "Like what?" she said, sort of sharply. "I don't know . . . this . . ." and he gestured around the room they were in. "What's the matter with it?" she asked him. "Nothing," he hastened to assure her. Their eyes met, and then he lowered his gaze to her body. He was chiefly conscious of its whiteness and of a prominent scar on her abdomen. Could that be an appendix scar? He felt like asking what had happened to her there, but then he thought that might not be tactful. "Should I take off the rest of my clothes?" he asked. She seemed so much older that he felt he really had to ask her permission. "Do what you want," she said. He hesitated, and then finished undressing.

Now she was really looking at him, and he felt much better all over. His trembling was gone, and he felt a rising excitement that it was really going to happen, and when he glanced at her body again it didn't seem so unappealing as it had the first time. Her legs and arms and middle were too soft and shapeless, but her breasts looked rich and heavy as she sat there, and her expression was not really dumb or unkind, it was just sort of far away or painted over as if she didn't want anyone to see her face. "Well?" she said. "I've never done this before," Jerry told her.

She nodded. "That figures. What did you say your name was, anyway?" "Jerry," he said. "Well, look Jerry," she told him, "there's nothing to it." She had fallen back on the bed Now she opened her legs. "See? That's all it is," she said "There's really nothing to it."

He was not sure he believed her. There was a lot more to it than she said. A lot. He was sure of that. But her attitude did help him mount her, because he could see that from her point of view there might not be so much to this. Everything, every tiny detail seemed fantastic to him, but as her arms and her legs pinned him into position and it actually began, he had a flash of insight. This was just a sort of habit for her. Then things began to get rather violently mixed up, and he found himself realizing that this could become habit-forming very, very quickly.

And yet there was a disappointment involved in it all. Should an experience you'd waited seventeen years to have be over so soon? It seemed to him he'd hardly had time to start getting used to it before it was finished. That was saddening. There should be more to come. Actually there *was* more to come. Nothing prevented him from coming some more except the fact that he was being ejected from the deeps and cast up on the shallows of her sheets. "Is that all?" he asked. "It's what ya wanted, isn't it?" she said with some surprise. "Yes, but . . ." He gestured at himself. Elaine stared at the two faces of Jerry Engels, and then, concentrating on the one with two eyes, she said, "It's really your first time, hunh?" "Yes!" he said, his whole face, his voice, his eyes, everything about him breathing such a heartfelt air of truthfulness and sincerity that she had to believe him. She glanced at a clock on a terrible night stand beside the bed. "Well, okay," she said. "Since it's your first time we'll give you one on the house."

The second time seemed even better because she was concentrating on him more. Before, she had just been sort of doing her thing without paying a whole lot of attention to him, but this time he felt she knew he was there. She wasn't thinking about tomorrow or wandering around inside her mind, looking into store windows. She was with him, and he was with her and for a moment it seemed to him they were really together.

Yet it was somehow a more localized experience than he'd

expected. There was not that all-over, ecstatic voluptuousness he felt when he was just thinking about Rosalind, or biting her sandals. This was both less and more than he'd expected: less because less of him was involved; more because the part of him that was involved was so deeply and thoroughly involved that he could hardly bear to disinvolve it even now. "Satisfied?" he heard Elaine saying. The answer was *no*. He wondered whether, if properly appealed to, Elaine would give him one to grow on. Why not? She had so much to give and he had so much to get. Why shouldn't they just go on doing this for a while longer? But there he was again, getting heaved off and tossed out. "That's it," she said with finality, sitting up and then standing to drive the point home.

He looked at her more closely, wondering how such a nice woman could have become a prostitute. "Do you live here?" he asked her. "Here?" she said, her look taking in the room with a contempt that confirmed his feeling that she was really an awfully nice woman. She could see what a terrible room it was and how it smelled. There was a cloying odor of cheap powder and perfume that masked something deeper and worse. He'd noticed the smell downstairs and it was really marked in the bedroom. "Well, where *do* you live?" he asked. He envisioned meeting her on her day off, maybe taking her to the movies or something, and then going back to where she lived—a nice little beach cottage maybe—where they could settle down and do this as often as possible. "I live at home," she told him in tones that closed that door. The way she said "home" told him it was private. There was probably someone else there. A husband? A child? She could easily have a child, after all. Imagine having a mother who went off to work at Gretch's house!

She had shrugged on her robe. She was looking down at him. "Come on—what's your name? Jerry. Fun's over for tonight." He nodded. He knew he had to get up and dress and leave, and yet he felt so close to her in a way that it was hard to believe they were about to part. "Ya liked it, didn't ya?"

she said. "Yes!" he said. "Okay, come back again, and I'll give you a real whirl. I'll make it even better for ya." His eyes opened at that thought. She could make it better for him? But no, she was probably just boasting. Though she was such an honest sort of person that if she said she could make it better she probably could. And what would *that* be like? "Now come on," she said to him. "Time's up, fella." "I know," he said, reaching for his clothes. She watched him dress. When he was back together again she gave him her professional smile. "Now you ask for Elaine next time," she told him. "Don't ya forget." "I won't," he said. He felt her hand on his arm. He saw her nostrils move as she suppressed a little yawn. Her door was open and they were parting without having ever kissed. And they didn't even know each other's last name. Elaine what, he wondered as he found himself once more in the upstairs corridor of Gretch's house.

Downstairs he encountered Rufus and Phil, those other survivors of the recent whirlwinds, submarine earthquakes, and volcanic eruptions. He followed them out into the darkness—a man at last.

Jerry in Love

ON THE ninth of July the Calypso appeared, steaming in toward the Shores. Jerry, like some island native, leaped to his Dolphin to sail out and perhaps dive for coins, should Rosalind or her grandparents throw him any. In the event it was Rosalind he picked up. As he tacked toward the yacht he saw Rosalind disappear from the deck. A few minutes later she reappeared in a royal blue bathing suit. He saw her speak to her grandmother as she tucked her hair into a white bathing cap. Then she climbed down the side ladder of the Calypso. A few feet above the water she paused briefly, dove, and then began to swim away from the yacht. He brought his Dolphin into the wind, the sail slatted, he lost way, and the Calypso moved steadily on.

He watched as Rosalind swam toward him, laying each hand on the surface of the lake before pushing down. *Pull, don't push,* he thought. *Dig,* he felt like calling out. Then she was resting her forearms on the low deck, and Jerry the swimming coach disappeared to be replaced by Jerry the waiting lover, the lovelorn waiter. "Am I glad to see you," he said. He helped her aboard. Water glittered on her smooth limbs. She tugged off her bathing cap and shook out her blond hair. She smiled at him. "Am I glad . . ." he started to say again, his voice going up as he spoke. He stopped himself. "Hello," he said. She looked at him a little quizzically. "Hello," she said.

He felt shy. He saw the world now through the eyes of a man who had proved himself. Yet he felt shy. "I've been looking out for you all afternoon," he told her. He had found out from her parents when she was expected. "I've been sitting on the beach looking out for you," he said. "You look good," he added. His eyes were on her hair, on her shoulders, and on the delicate V-shape at the base of her throat. "How are you?" he asked. "How are *you?*" she said.

"I'm okay," he answered, his mind really elsewhere. Rosalind laughed. "You look so funny." Instantly he was on the spot. "What do you mean?" She shrugged. "As if you've never seen me before." "Oh," he said. "What is it?" she asked. "What have you been up to?" "Nothing," he said, wondering how she could possibly have divined that he was a changed person. Did it show? Was it that obvious? "I've been doing nothing," he repeated. "Waiting for you," he added. "Well, here I am," she said.

The Dolphin had been drifting. Now Rosalind leaned forward and put her hand on the tiller. "Let me take it," she said.

He watched as she got the boat underway. Because of all her experience with her father aboard his three-meter, she was really a better sailor than he was. She could do a lot of things better than he could. She could ride horseback better, and sail better, and sing on key. She was almost an all-A student. In fact, at the moment he could think of nothing he was better at, except swimming. "Listen," he said, "you've really got to work on your stroke." "Do I?" she said. "Well, it's not good. I mean, you should swim better than you do." He wanted her to be perfect. "I'll help you, okay?" "Okay," she said. Then, "Listen, tell me why you're so solemn? I thought you were glad to see me." "Solemn?" "You haven't said anything except *hello* and *how are you?* You've hardly smiled. What's the matter?" "Nothing," he said, "nothing's the matter." "You're very mysterious," she told him. "Are you still chasing Nancy around?" "Don't begin that," he said. Then he remembered a message he had for her. "Shirley wants you to come down to her house tonight." "I'll try," she said, "but I may be late."

They were talking more naturally by the time she sailed the Dolphin in over the bar. When it grounded, she dropped the sheet and began to wade ashore to greet her parents who had come down to the beach to meet the yacht party. Jerry followed her, towing his Dolphin. A school of minnows was moving slowly along the channel between bar and beach, and when Rosalind stepped down into their path, the minnows broke and scattered wildly. To Jerry, it looked as if Rosalind's legs were striking silver sparks in the water.

Mr. Ingleside kissed Rosalind and then put a possessive arm around her shoulders. "So," he said to Jerry, "you're here already." "Jack, that isn't fair," said Mrs. Ingleside. "You told him yourself when she was coming." Mr. Ingleside said, "But I didn't expect him to sail out and bring her in on that aquaplane, or whatever he calls it." "It's a Dolphin," said Jerry. Mr. Ingleside paid no attention. He ran his eye down Jerry's body. "Where'd you get that bathing suit?" he asked. "In Chicago," Jerry said. "It doesn't look like a Chesterton suit," said Mr. Ingleside. "I think it looks nice," said Mrs. Ingleside, putting her own hand on Jerry's shoulder. He appreciated that. "My mother thinks it's too small," he said. "So do I," said Mr. Ingleside. "Really, Jack!" Mrs. Ingleside said. "You're embarrassing him." Mr. Ingleside shook his head. "It's impossible to embarrass Jerry." "That isn't true," said Mrs. Ingleside. "Jerry's very sensitive." "I am," he said. He had to say something.

Mr. Ingleside continued to regard him with genial ferocity. "All right," he said, "since you're here we may as well get it straight. No telephone calls during meals. No calls after ten o'clock, and I don't want you using the court before ten in the morning." Feeling that you had to talk back to this kind of thing, Jerry shook his head seriously. "Your court is in really bad shape," he said. "We'll try it out tomorrow morning," said Mr. Ingleside. "At ten." "Stay for lunch," Mrs. Ingleside added.

The Calypso had anchored fifty yards offshore. Now Mr. and Mrs. Elbridge and a third old party, a gentleman, were being ferried toward the beach. Jerry accompanied the Inglesides down to the water to greet them. He helped the crewman from the Calypso run the boat up onto the sand so that the yacht party could step ashore dry-shod. Mr. Elbridge got out first, landing and taking command of the situation in one step. "Imogene," he said to his daughter, "you know Horace Robertson. Horace, this is Jack Ingleside." "Welcome to Indiana Shores," Mr. Ingleside said to Mr. Robertson. Mr. Elbridge went on with the introductions. "And this young sailor," he said, pointing to Jerry, "this young sailor is . . ." He held up on the name. "Jerry Engels," said Mrs. Ingleside. "Of course!" said Mr. Elbridge, shaking Jerry's hand. "Clever little boat you have there," he said, leading Jerry off toward the Dolphin, which was beached a few yards away. "What's it made of?" Mr. Elbridge wanted to know. "Fiberglass?" "Yes," said Jerry. "Ha!" said Mr. Elbridge, "that's one for you, Horace." Mr. Robertson had also come over to look at the Dolphin. Had he invented fiberglass, Jerry wondered, or did he manufacture it, or had he perhaps cornered the fiberglass market? He looked uncertainly at Mr. Robertson, who said, "Very nice." Mr. Elbridge put one well-shod foot on the low deck and rocked the Dolphin back and forth on the sand. "Jack!" he said over his shoulder, summoning his son-in-law and getting all the men around him as he liked to do. "Come look at this little boat." "It's not a boat, it's a joke," said Mr. Ingleside, whose own three-meter was now resting high up on the beach, attached to a stout winching post. "But convenient," Mr. Elbridge pointed out, rocking the Dolphin again. "No trouble getting this out of the water." "Or finding a harbor for it," said Mr. Ingleside, putting his own foot on the Dolphin and rocking it the other way. "You should get yourself one," he told Mr. Elbridge. "Ha! you think so?" Mr. Elbridge said. "But what would I do with it?" "Sail it," said Mr. Robertson. "Oh, I was a sailor once before I took to steam," said Mr. Elbridge. "Oh, yes. Remember the J-boat, Jack?" "Do I not?" said Mr. Ingleside. Mr. Elbridge turned to Mr. Robertson. "Jack here crewed for me when he was in college." He nodded several times as if to confirm his own statement. "That was quite a boat," he added reminiscently. "Too big for these days, of course." "Too big for those days, too," said Mr. Ingleside. "Oh, we handled her, we handled her," said Mr. Elbridge.

Listening to this conversation and watching his Dolphin being rocked on the beach, Jerry felt what he often felt in the company of successful older men. They seemed to know so much more than he did and to have so much more money and power and assurance that compared to them he was really nothing. What had he done so far? Slept with Elaine. What did he know? Practically nothing. He'd never heard of a J-boat, and he wasn't a good sailor, and when it came right down to it, he wasn't even a top-flight swimmer or tennis player. He was nothing really. All he had was his Dolphin, and his feelings, and his body. But a breath of wind could upset his Dolphin, a harsh word collapse his feelings, and a thorn pierce his flesh.

Then they were back among the women and he began to feel better. Mrs. Ingleside liked him. Rosalind more than liked him, and Mrs. Elbridge . . . ? He smiled at her. She nodded slightly. He felt cast down. Then the crewman who had ferried the yacht party ashore returned from carrying Rosalind's suitcases up to the house. Mr. Elbridge began to give him orders. The Calypso was to be moved to the harbor in Michigan City, but the Elbridges and Mr. Robertson would sleep aboard it that night. They were leaving the next day for Chicago and did not propose to shift ashore for a single night. They would be driven to Michigan City after dinner. "Be on the lookout for us at nine," Mr. Elbridge said. The crewman saluted. Then he smiled as Rosalind shook his hand and said goodbye. As he shoved his rowboat back into the water, he glanced up the beach to look at Rosalind once more and at Jerry standing beside her. He thinks I'm a lucky stiff, Jerry thought. Then he thought, *I am*. He was incredibly lucky, maybe too lucky.

That evening he went over to Shirley's house right after dinner. He wanted to find out if Shirley had invited Nancy for the evening. He also thought that a preliminary chat with Shirley might give him some ideas about how he was going to handle his problem of having two girls at the same time. Not that he really thought of Nancy as his girl, but still the situation promised to be a little awkward at first.

He found Shirley in the living room reading Agatha Christie. Her father was seated in an armchair reading Chaucer. Chaucer was Mr. Hyatt's favorite poet. Uncle Paul, which was what Jerry called him, was not a typical refinery superintendent. Jerry said *hello* to them both and then went into the kitchen to greet Mrs. Hyatt—Aunt Helen—who was putting things away. Then he went back to the living room. Shirley and her father continued to read. Jerry sat down. Minutes passed. He could hear a clock ticking. Occasionally Shirley or her father turned a page. In the kitchen Mrs. Hyatt finished putting things away and came into the living room. "Well, things must be quiet at your house now," she said. Not as quiet as this, Jerry thought. "Have you heard from Anne yet?" They hadn't. Mr. Hyatt turned a page rather noisily. "Shirley," Mrs. Hyatt said, "why don't you take Jerry downstairs?"

Downstairs in the game room Shirley put a record on the player and then sat on a broad couch with her legs tucked under her. "I saw Rosalind this afternoon," Jerry said. "She's coming over when her grandparents go back to their yacht," Shirley told him. Jerry fiddled with an ashtray. "Who else is coming?" he asked. "I didn't call up Nancy, if that's what you mean," Shirley said. "Good," said Jerry. "What do you think I should do?" he asked her. "That's *your* problem," she said. "Yeah, but what do you think?" he asked. In his experience girls generally had good ideas about how to handle the kind of situation he was in. "They're both my friends," Shirley said. "I'm not going to tell you what to do." "I wish O'Brien would turn up again," Jerry said. Except for one brief reappearance, O'Brien had definitely faded from the scene. He sighed. Then he glanced at Shirley who was looking at him with a considerable lack of sympathy. "Nancy liked him." "He was an impossible show-off," said Shirley. "All those rippling muscles!" Jerry shrugged. "Well, what do you think I should do?" he asked again. "Be ashamed of yourself," Shirley suggested. "Be serious," he told her. "I am serious," she said.

This was getting them nowhere. "What do you think of Alec Walker?" Jerry asked. "Ugh," Shirley said. "He likes you." Jerry knew this was not strictly true. Alec was attracted to Shirley, but he didn't seem to like her, He claimed she was a tease, also flat-chested, but then he was the sort of guy who always resented and felt a little hostile toward the girls who attracted him. "He's horrible," said Shirley. "Do you think Nancy would like him if he started paying attention to her?" Jerry asked. Now that he knew Alec had no chance with Shirley, it seemed to him that he might be doing everyone a favor if he could subtly switch Alec's attention from Shirley to Nancy. "What do you think?" he asked Shirley. "How should I know?" she said. "*I* can't stand him." "But you couldn't stand O'Brien either," Jerry pointed out. Nancy was less hard to please. "I can see what *you're* thinking," Shirley said. He smiled at her. "Don't you think it's a good idea?" "I think you're impossible," said Shirley, getting up to change the record.

She put on "Nature Boy." "Want to dance?" he asked her. "No." "Oh, come on," he said. He put his arm around her waist, and after a moment she began to follow his lead. They were dancing when Phil came in through the downstairs door. Jerry spun Shirley in Phil's direction. Her skirt brushed against Phil's legs, and then Jerry drew her back and ended the dance with a big dip. He smiled down into Shirley's face. "Who's coming over?" Phil said. Still arched backward, her hair falling looking at Phil upside down, Shirley said, "No one except Rosalind."

They went on dancing while they waited for her. At first Jerry and Phil took turns dancing with Shirley. Then Phil dropped out while Jerry and Shirley continued to dance barefoot on the soft carpet that covered the cement floor. As he danced, Jerry could feel everything getting straightened out between himself and Shirley. On the beach he was always tempted to roughhouse with her, and when they played games she was always trying to win, and when they just talked, things went wrong in other ways. Either Shirley treated him as if he were feebleminded, or else she browbeat him and tried to make him feel ashamed of himself for things like his flirtation with Nancy. But when they danced everything came right. Shirley was a very good dancer, and so was he. They became partners, equals. It was lovely.

Then suddenly Shirley broke away from him. "Rosalind!" she screamed. Rosalind had just stepped through the screen door. "Rosalind!" The two girls hugged and kissed each other, and then, with their hands on each other's waists, they leaned back to look at each other. "Your hair!" Shirley cried. "You like it this way?" Rosalind asked. What way, Jerry wondered. "Your skirt!" Shirley cried. "Your tan!" Rosalind responded. "Oh, let me see this," said Shirley, backing off. Rosalind took hold of the hem of her skirt and opened it out. "It's wonderful," said Shirley. "I found it in Santa Fe," said Rosalind. Rosalind and his mother were alike, Jerry thought. They never bought anything. All Rosalind's clothes were finds.

With her arrival the dancing stopped. Even the record player went temporarily unattended while Rosalind answered questions about her stay in New Mexico and her cruise. Jerry learned that the Calypso had stopped at Manitou Island and that Rosalind had spent a night at Manistique and another night at Ludington. It began to sound less terrible than he had imagined it as being. "Why didn't you tell me that?" he asked her. "You didn't ask," she replied. She was in a cheerful mood. They all were. "So, now, tell me everything," she said to Shirley. She glanced at Jerry and Phil. "You boys can leave if you want." "Let's do something," Jerry suggested. "Want to drive somewhere?" "She's been traveling for weeks," Shirley said. "How about dancing some more?" Jerry said. He had not danced with Rosalind since the Junior Night party at U-High. "Come on!" He moved toward the record player. "We want to talk. We haven't seen each other," Shirley said. "I think they may really want us to go," Phil observed. "Well, I'm not leaving, are you?" Jerry said. Shirley said, "We can always leave you, you know." She rose from the couch on which she and Rosalind had been sitting. It was not clear what she intended to do. Probably she was merely going to put on a record, but Jerry chose to see this as a move toward the stairs. He blocked the steps. Then his hand brushed the light switch, and he plunged the room into total darkness. "Jerry!" It was Shirley's voice warning him not to try anything. "Got you!" he cried. "Oh, act your age," Shirley said, trying to extricate herself from his grasp. Rosalind laughed in the darkness. Then she turned on a lamp. "I know!" Jerry said, "let's play Murder." It was a game that involved turning off the lights and wandering around in the dark. Shirley shook her head sadly. "He's been like this all summer," she said to Rosalind. "I hope you can calm him down." "I'll do my best," Rosalind said.

Her best was none too good. Jerry played an inconclusive match with Mr. Ingleside the following morning, and then went down to the beach with Rosalind. "Look," he said, "this is how you swim." He lay in the water, scarcely kicking. He made exaggerated, dainty patting motions with his hand. He slapped the water a few times and then rose, his face dripping. "See?" he said. "And this is how you *should* swim." He launched himself in a flat-bellied dive and went plowing off through the lake. "See?" he said again, rising and wading back toward her. "Now try it," he urged. "Dig in. Reach. Don't pat the water, reach and dig in." "Like this?" said Rosalind, falling forward and slapping at the lake as he had done the first time. "You weren't really trying," he told her when she rose and looked at him. "Well, show me again," she suggested. He looked at her a little doubtfully, but got down in the water again to give a demonstration of how it should be done. Then he felt her hand on his head, pushing him under.

He knew what to do about that. He hooked her legs out from under her and his swimming lesson turned into a wrestling match. "Are you trying to drown my daughter?" Mr. Ingleside asked. He had come down for a dip before lunch to find Jerry holding Rosalind in a full nelson and bending her forward, trying to push her face underwater. Jerry had not noticed Mr. Ingleside's arrival. "I was just trying to teach her to swim," he explained. "He was drowning me," said Rosalind. Jerry, who had let go of her as soon as he was aware that they were not alone, splashed water in her face. "See?" said Rosalind. "He treats me mean." "She just won't try," Jerry explained. Mr. Ingleside waded on past them. "The way to break a full nelson," he told Rosalind, "is to dig your heel into your attacker's foot. I'm not sure if it works in the water, though." Then he went on with his swim.

Lunch did subdue Jerry a bit. He had changed back into his clothes in the downstairs maid's room. He sat between Rosalind and Mr. Elbridge and generally listened to the conversation which ranged over topics he had nothing much to say about. The wine they were drinking came in for discussion. Then there was an asparagus tart which Mr. Robertson praised. Peter Elbridge, Rosalind's uncle, was in Germany that summer to hear the Bayreuth Festival. Mr. Robertson and Mrs. Elbridge talked about prewar festivals at Bayreuth. That led them into a discussion of Toscanini. From there the conversation skipped back to wine. Mr. Ingleside had opened another bottle. "This is very good Sancerre," Mr. Robertson said. "If I'd known you liked wine I would have opened something really interesting," Mr. Ingleside said. "I sympathize with you after ten days on the Calypso." "Ha! What's that?" said Mr. Elbridge. Then they discussed what happened to wines when they were disturbed by being carried around on board yachts. It was interesting, but not the kind of subject Jerry could contribute to. Only when they got around to local topics did he have anything to say.

The new house that was being built nearby came in for criticism both for its location and for its design. "Thank God we won't see it," said Mrs. Ingleside. "And does anybody know who the people are?" Mr. Elbridge asked. "Their name is Fine," said Jerry. "F-E-I-N or F-I-N-E?" Mr. Elbridge inquired. "F-I-N-E," said Jerry. "Well, I suppose it amounts to the same thing," said Mr. Elbridge. "He's supposed to be a psychiatrist," said Jerry. "Yes," said Mr. Elbridge. "Another barrier fallen," said Mr. Ingleside cheerfully. "Please don't think I'm prejudiced," Mr. Elbridge said to the table at large. "I was the first man to suggest a Jew as Director of the Art Institute. I wish they had listened to me." "Did you have any particular Jew in mind?" Mr. Ingleside asked. "Ha!" said Mr. Elbridge, not much amused by this. He looked at Jerry sitting next to him. "I suppose you're like everyone else now? You think it's prejudiced just to recognize differences?" Not up to dealing with that question, Jerry said, "There are already two Jewish families at the Shores—the Bakers and the Longstreets." Mr. Robertson laughed. Mrs. Elbridge frowned. "I think it is so wrong for people to change their names. One should be proud of what one is." It seemed to Jerry that she

191

was looking straight at him. He nodded vigorously to show his agreement.

After a dessert of raspberries, they went out to the porch for their coffee. It was served by Mr. Moxon. What surprised Jerry was that Malcolm Moxon, Mr. Moxon's grown-up son, joined the party on the porch and even accepted coffee from his father. Malcolm had eaten in the kitchen with his parents, but now he was operating as a member of the family, someone who had practically grown up with David Ingleside. He called Mrs. Elbridge "Marianne" and sat beside her, talking about the program at Ravinia that summer. Malcolm taught music at a Chicago high school. He also played the flute, which seemed to Jerry a sad instrument for a man—if Malcolm was a man. Jerry had his doubts. Now, however, he was impressed by Malcolm's social ease.

He and Rosalind left the porch after a while. They walked down the road to look at the new house. "He calls your grandmother Marianne," Jerry said. "She told him to," said Rosalind. "She thinks he's a very good flutist. If there weren't so much prejudice he might be able to play in the Chicago Symphony." "Yeah, but you don't call her Marianne," Jerry said. "I call her Grandmother," said Rosalind. It still seemed strange to Jerry, but since there was so much that was strange about Rosalind's family, he let it pass. The Inglesides and Elbridges were just different from the Engelses. He looked sideways at Rosalind. Then he cocked his head a little. "Well?" she said. He went on looking at her with his head cocked. "Yes?" she said. His lips felt full and almost tingling with anticipation. Gradually Rosalind got the idea. Then she pretended not to understand. "Isn't it a nice day?" she said. He refused to answer. "So nice," said Rosalind. He was not going to demean himself by asking for a kiss. After all, her grandmother had practically urged him to be proud. Then they came in sight of the new house and Rosalind stopped to deplore it. Every new house that was built at the Shores was regarded as a catastrophe by those who lived nearest to the site. "It's so ugly!" Rosalind said.

It was a very modern house with strange angles and lots of oddly placed windows. "It's just horrible," Rosalind decided. Jerry followed her as she walked up the unfinished driveway to get a closer look. It was Saturday so there were no workmen around. Rosalind climbed onto the wide deck that went around three sides of the house and peered through a sliding glass door. Jerry stood behind her. He could see a couple of sawhorses in the living room. He could see Rosalind reflected in the glass door. He could see himself standing behind her. There was an odor of freshly cut pine and creosote in the air. "Want to get in?" he asked. "Can we?" she said. "Sure." There was always a way. While he scouted around for an entry, Rosalind turned to admire the view from the deck. She was framed between two pines. Beyond her he could see the lake, as soft and blue as a baby's blanket. Then she looked over her shoulder at him, and he walked across the deck to kiss her. The taste of raspberries and cream was still in her mouth.

There was nothing calming in that, though later in the day after her grandparents had departed for Michigan City Rosalind did have a serious talk with Jerry. "I've been thinking about us," she said. This was generally an ominous prelude. When a girl said she had been thinking, it generally meant she was about to blow the whistle on something or other they had been doing together. "We're going to have to be careful this summer," Rosalind said. Jerry agreed. It was always best to agree. "You know what I mean?" Rosalind asked. "Sure," he said.

They were walking hand in hand along the beach. Ahead of them each gull and sandpiper kept one bright bird fixed in their direction. "I wouldn't want anything to happen," Rosalind said, "anything we'd be sorry about later." "Neither would I," he said. He felt the crunch was still to come and wondered what it would be. She couldn't very well think they should stop kissing, and that was practically all they did. "I'm glad you feel this way, too," she said. He smiled at her and squeezed her hand. Ahead of them some gulls that had been resting on the beach got up and began to move away uneasily. Most of them birdwaddled toward the lake; a few moved toward the dunes. Two birds kept in the center of the beach, moving sideways, always with one eye fixed on Jerry and Rosalind. He thought it was as if his body and Rosalind's formed the focal point of some inimical force that was pushing the gulls out of their way, clearing a semicircular area into which they steadily advanced. "I'm glad you're not mad about it," she said. "About what?" he asked. She had still not said anything very alarming. "Well, I don't think we should date this summer."

He felt very relieved. It was even less threatening than he had anticipated. He never dated in the summer. Dates were for Chicago. At the Shores you piled into a car with half a dozen kids and went off to the movies in Chesterton, sometimes barefoot. You met at Shirley's house in the evening, or in the blow-out where you played baseball or Wave-Me-Out or Stealing Sticks. He had not even been thinking of taking Rosalind out on dates that summer. "Is that all?" he asked. "We shouldn't be alone together too much," Rosalind said. That was a bit different, but he felt he could agree with that, too. After all, everything depended on how much was too much. "You're right," he said. She squeezed his hand. "I'm glad we feel the same way," she said. He squeezed back, thinking how differently her hand felt from that of a guy.

The next afternoon Jerry and Joanne went down to the beach where they found the normal Sunday scene of umbrellas and family groups and a few boats out on the lake. Nancy and Rosalind and Shirley were sitting together in the sun, having a nice talk. Jerry looked around for Phil, but Phil was out sailing, apparently with Linda on board. Joanne looked at Jerry. "There's Nancy and Rosalind. What are you going to do now?" "What do you mean?" Jerry replied. He dropped his towel near the girls and went right on into the lake. When he was fifty yards out he turned onto his back and floated for a while. When he looked shoreward he could see the same familiar line of bright beach umbrellas, the same family groups, and the same three girls sitting together. He swam a little farther out. From there things were not as clear. He floated some more. Then at last he swam in. He would just have to face things.

"Hi!" he said to the girls as he returned from the lake, dripping. He stood above them, toweling himself with great thoroughness. Phil was still well out in the lake. There was a good light breeze. "Anyone want to sail?" he asked. "I do," said Joanne. "Fine." He took her out for a sail. She said, "You like Rosalind more than you like Nancy, don't you?" "Sure," he said. "They're both going to be mad at you," Joanne predicted. "You don't know anything about it," he said. He sailed Joanne around for fifteen minutes and then headed back toward the beach. "Who's next?" he called out. None of the big girls spoke up. He approached them, leaving his Dolphin drawn halfway out of the water, its sail still up and shivering in the breeze. "You want to sail?" he asked Rosalind. She was comfortable where she was. "Do you?" he asked Nancy. She, too, was comfortable. "What about you?" he asked Shirley. She shook her head. None of them wanted to sail with him. "Come on, sail with me," he said to Rosalind, reaching for her hand. His eyes were as much on Nancy and Shirley as on Rosalind. "Come on!" He tugged at her arm. She resisted, and he let her pull him off balance. He fell beside her, but when he tried to get comfortable by resting his head on her leg, she brushed him off. "Okay," he said, rolling onto his chest. He did some meditative pushups. Then he lay face down, staring at grains of sand while the girls went on talking.

Girls listened to each other more than boys did. Nancy was telling Rosalind and Shirley about some friend of hers who had dieted until she was sick. It was a long story and to Jerry not a very interesting one. He could not imagine telling Alec Walker anything like that. He could hardly imagine telling Alec about anyone Alec didn't know, nor could he imagine Alec listening. Yet both Rosalind and Shirley listened. Girls were just more polite or maybe less self-absorbed than boys. They seemed to be interested in hearing about people they didn't know. Shirley began to talk about her cousin Jessica who was studying ballet. Nancy listened to that. So did Rosalind. Next it would be Rosalind's turn, Jerry thought. He rolled onto his side and propped himself up with his elbow. "What about a game of Underwater Tag?" he asked. They turned him down. Then Phil sailed in, and Alec Walker turned up, and they had enough people for Keep Away.

It was like water polo, only there were no goals. You just tried to keep the ball away from members of the opposing team. And as in water polo, a certain roughness was permissible. Jerry splashed and ducked Nancy. He tied her up with his arms and wrestled the ball out of her hands. He tossed it to Rosalind who was on his team. Then he turned back to Nancy. "No hard feelings?" he asked, putting his arm around her shoulders. It seemed to him that Keep Away provided a nice, legitimate way to maintain friendly contact with Nancy without offending anyone. He was all over her as long as the game lasted.

That night Rosalind commented on his behavior when he drove her home after an impromptu party at Shirley's at which he had also danced several times with Nancy. "Are you trying to make me jealous?" Rosalind asked. He assured her it was the last thing he wanted. "You should never be jealous of anyone," he said. "Oh?" said Rosalind. She was above all that, he told her. "Well, that's nice," she said, but she did not seem fully mollified. "I just don't like it," she told Jerry. "And I don't think it's nice for Nancy, either." "Well, I can't ignore Nancy," he pointed out. "You wouldn't want me to do that." Rosalind looked at him seriously. "But why are you like this, Jerry? I don't see why you started to pay her so much attention." It was like his conversation with

Anne, he thought. Then he thought of how he had told Anne about breaking into Rosalind's house. Should he tell Rosalind? But Rosalind was not Anne; she might take it in the wrong way. To gain time, he said, "Look, let's go down to the beach." They had been talking in the car. "Well, all right," said Rosalind.

On the beach he was still hesitant. He ran his hand up Rosalind's arm. He squeezed her elbow. He bent to kiss it. "What are you doing?" she asked. "Kissing you," he said. "My elbow?" She seemed faintly perplexed why anyone should want to kiss her elbow. "Why not?" he asked her. He kissed it again, first on the outside just above the bone, then on the inside where he could taste the faint saltiness of her skin. "Jerry . . . " she began. Then she stopped. He could follow her reasoning. After all, it was only her elbow, and above them the porch lights of her house shone in the darkness. "Know something?" he told her, "I could feel your pulse with my lips." Rosalind didn't reply. He touched her cheeks with his fingertips. It seemed to him she was being deliberately still, but when he bent to kiss her throat she stepped back. "I think we should talk, Jerry."

He agreed with that. "I wanted to tell you something," he said, "only I'm not sure how you'll take it. That was me in your house. I broke in because I missed you so much." At first she didn't understand what he was talking about. The incident had now faded even from Shirley's conversation. When she understood, she was simply surprised. "I mean, if you think I don't really care about you, I do," he told her. "I wanted to be closer to you. I kissed your bathing suit." "My bathing suit?" "Your yellow bathing suit," he said. He put his arms around her waist. "I was really thinking of you all last month. That's why I did it. You aren't mad, are you?" "It's so strange," she said. He held her closer. "Tell me you're not mad." "Jerry . . . " she began. Then they heard someone descending from the house.

It was Malcolm, carrying his flute. He paused on the

bottom step, obviously surprised to find Jerry and Rosalind on the beach. "Hello, Malcolm," Jerry said. Malcolm stepped off into the sand and came scrunching toward them. He was wearing shoes, a white shirt, and bermuda shorts. "Are you going to play?" Rosalind asked him. "I thought I might," Malcolm said. At night, when he wanted to play without disturbing anyone, he often came down to the beach. "I didn't know you were here," he said. "We're just going up," Rosalind said, but when Malcolm moved off down the beach she made no move to go up to the house.

"Are you mad at me?" Jerry asked. Again his arm was around her waist. "It seems like such a funny thing to do," Rosalind said. "But it was for you," Jerry said, "I was thinking of you." He felt she was moved in some way. Maybe it was the warm night, and the mild slap of waves against the sand, and the sound of Malcolm's flute in the distance. The music he was playing was like a bright skein of light in the darkness. Then it grew fainter as he moved farther off. "Let's follow him," Jerry suggested.

They moved off in the direction Malcolm had taken. "I don't know what to say," said Rosalind. "I just want you to know I love you," Jerry said. He felt his soul sort of expanding in the night. "I just want you to know that, and you don't have to love me or anything." He felt almost rhapsodic. "I'll love you anyway. . . . Hey, look!" Ahead of them the western sky suddenly began to glow crimson. "They're pouring steel in Gary," Jerry said. They watched the glow of molten steel reflected against the clouds. Then the glow faded almost as quickly as it had bloomed. Beside him Jerry could hear Rosalind breathing deeply. Ahead, the sound of Malcolm's flute was louder. "He's sitting down now," Jerry said.

They stopped. He drew Rosalind away from the middle of the beach. They sat down on the sand, then they lay back against the rise of the beach dune. "Do you know what he's playing?" Jerry asked. "I think it's Debussy," said Rosalind. He looked at her profile as she lay beside him, her head on his arm. He felt great pride that she could almost recognize the music Malcolm was playing. He reached for her hand and kissed it. Again he could taste the faint saltiness of her skin, especially when he licked her palm. "Jerry . . . " she began. He sighed heavily, and then so did she. "It's funny," she said. "What's funny?" he asked. "I was annoyed with you." "I know you were," he said. "I wish you'd always be like this," she said. "I will be," he promised. Then they lay for a while looking up at the overcast sky and listening to the lake and to Malcolm's flute. He felt they had never been quite so close.

Debussy, or whatever it was, came to an end. Something else began. This was quicker, also louder. "He's coming back," said Jerry. He rose and put out his hand. Rosalind accepted it, and together they left the beach. They found a little hollow in the dunes and sat down there, waiting for Malcolm to pass by. Jerry began kissing Rosalind's throat. He put his lips to the base of her throat and murmured, "I love you," as if he were talking directly to her soul without having to go through her ears and her brain. Nearby Malcolm's heavy footfalls added a new sound to the night. A droning mosquito added something more. Then somehow they were no longer sitting up. Enormous things seemed to be happening. Rosalind grew still beneath him. Then he felt her arms around him, and at that point he didn't see how he could not go ahead.

He woke up the next morning feeling very serious. His first thought was, *I may have gotten her pregnant.* His second thought was, *then we'll have to get married.* His third thought was, *only they won't let us marry.* Then he got up and went to the bathroom where he showered for a long time. Finally he put on clean clothes and went out to the porch to face the new day. His father had left for work. Verlene was singing in the kitchen. His mother was watering the lawn. Joanne was still at the breakfast table, shaking cinnamon sugar onto a heavily buttered piece of toasted raisin bread and then studying the result. He slid in opposite her and reached for a plum. "Hey, Verlene," he said, "got anything for me?" "I've got pancake batter left," Verlene told him. "Any sausages?" Jerry asked. "It'll take no time to cook 'em up," said Verlene.

While he waited for his sausages and pancakes, Jerry watched Joanne shake still more cinnamon sugar onto her toast. "You'll make yourself sick with that," he warned her. She bit into the toast and then reached out for a glass of milk. "What did you do last night?" he asked her. Her expression suddenly changed. "You know what we did?" she said. "We got Marky Kincaid to believe in snipe hunts. We were going to take him snipe hunting and ditch him in Skull Valley, only Betty Train ruined it." "How?" Jerry asked. "She told him," said Joanne. "She's a jerk. Linda and I are going to boycott her." She took another bite of her cinnamon toast. Then she said, "What did you do last night?" "Nothing," he said.

After breakfast he considered where to go and what to do. He should probably hurry over to the Inglesides to reassure Rosalind and see how she was, only it wasn't ten o'clock yet, and Mr. Ingleside's prohibition about visiting before ten was still in force even if Jerry and Rosalind had become lovers. He could go to the Forsons, but he didn't exactly have anything to say to Phil this morning. Finally he went off on a solitary walk across the blow-out to the live dune. He wandered around among the grape-covered hummocks at the top of the dune, looking for the site where he and Phil had once built their best secret hideaway. They had chopped down practically a whole glade of poplars at the foot of the dune, laboriously dragged the trunks up the steep sand face, and then cut them up into the right lengths for the walls of their cabin. They had thatched the cabin with sweet clover cut from a patch that grew along the beach road. Then, during the winter, some vandals from Horton's Dock had destroyed their hideaway, taking the logs for firewood. You built things, he thought, and then people came and destroyed them.

After a while he ran halfway down the dune and then slipped into the shelter of an oak tree half submerged in sand and covered with grapevines. He felt enclosed in a green tent, safe from inquisitive eyes. Lying back against the dune he began to think more seriously about Rosalind. Why had she let it happen, he wondered. She had not been driven by passion. Neither, for that matter, had he. Why had he done it? It was a crazy thing to do, without precautions, with mosquitoes biting his back, and no blanket for Rosalind to lie on. His knees were chafed. It had really not been much fun for either of them, particularly for Rosalind. He'd enjoyed it with Elaine more than he had with Rosalind, yet there was just no comparison between the two experiences. Elaine meant very little; Rosalind meant everything.

As he lay there in his green tent his memories began to rearrange themselves. Gradually he forgot about the sand and the mosquitoes and all the awkwardness he had felt in undressing Rosalind. A grave, almost solemn feeling came over him. Now they were lovers, he thought. She was his. The idea affected him in some strange way he couldn't understand but rather liked. She was his, and he was hers. Nothing separated them anymore. There were no secrets between them. It was all open. It was all sort of grave and solemn and open. This was not at all the way he'd thought he would feel if it ever happened between them. He had thought it might happen as the result of some overpowering longing, and that it would leave him feeling ecstatic, but in fact the longing had not been overpowering and this morning his feelings were not ecstatic. He felt almost calm, though when he thought about the fact that he hadn't taken precautions, he realized the whole thing had been crazy. Maybe even wrong. Probably wrong, he decided. Well, definitely wrong. No, not that wrong. Finally he gave up trying to decide how wrong it had been.

As soon as he stopped thinking about the degree of wrong in what he'd done, his mind began to work the other way. How could he make things better? Yet, as soon as he asked himself that question, the answer stared him in the face. Things were bound to get better as he and Rosalind got more used to doing it. They'd find some sheltered spot like the one he was now in, with green sunlight filtering down on them and no mosquitoes droning about. They'd get a beach blanket. And in the daylight they'd be better able to see what they were doing. It would get better and better, he thought, and he felt like hurrying off to tell Rosalind the good news that there was really nothing to worry about. It would be all right, and from now on he'd take precautions so they would not have to worry about having a baby, which he didn't think either of them was ready for yet. Though he liked babies, and probably so did she, so eventually it would be a real pleasure to have them. If they got married. That contingency sobered him a little, and instead of hurrying off to the Ingleside house, he lingered a while in this green tent. Even when he left it, he moved rather slowly back toward the cabin.

He took his bicycle and set off for the Inglesides without bothering to tell his mother where he was going. If she missed him she would assume he was there anyway. Already she had told him he was not to impose on Mrs. Ingleside by eating lunch there all the time. "She invited me," he said. "They both invite me." His mother shook her head. "Tell them you're expected at home." It seemed foolish, but he'd agreed. Now, pedaling his way to the Inglesides, he felt rather glad he'd agreed. Today he didn't feel like lunching with the Ingleside family. In fact, as he neared the house, he felt his anxiety rising. What would Rosalind look like this morning? And what would her mother say when he arrived? Would Mrs. Ingleside be as friendly as ever? Or would she already know what had happened? The night before, Rosalind had seemed upset as they parted. Suppose she'd gone straight to her mother and poured it all out? And what if Mrs. Ingleside had then told Mr. Ingleside? At that thought Jerry abruptly veered off the road and down a track that quickly turned to soft sand where he could no longer pedal. He leaned his bicycle against a tree and walked off into the woods.

He was scared, but he would just have to face it. Mr. Ingleside couldn't kill him. Or could he? Mr. Ingleside was an unpredictable man, or at least an unusual one. What if he had a gun and decided to use it? To die at seventeen, Jerry thought, and all because he'd done something wrong that hadn't even been as pleasurable as he'd expected it to be. To be killed before he'd gotten Rosalind used to it so that the experience would be really worthwhile. What a tragedy! Yet, even as the tragic possibilities struck him, he was noticing that some blueberries were ripe. Perhaps he should pick some berries and bring them to Rosalind? Only what could he carry them in? His shirt?

He took it off and used it as a bag. It was going to be a good season, he thought. There were about five kinds of blueberries at the Shores, from the very low bushes that bore sky-blue berries as round as pearls to thigh-high bushes that bore clusters of dark, almost purple, berries, faintly pear shaped. These latter were now ripening. He stripped them from the bushes. He gathered almost a quart, enough for a good deep-dish blueberry pie, which he happened to know that Mr. Ingleside liked. Not that he was picking these berries for Mr. Ingleside, but still it wouldn't hurt to make sure Mr. Ingleside went on liking him. It was worth getting more mosquito bites for that.

He knocked at the kitchen door. Mrs. Moxon let him in. "Hello," he said to her. "I picked these berries on the way over." He handed his shirt to Mrs. Moxon and then followed her into the kitchen where Malcolm was sitting at the table, drinking a cup of coffee. "Hello, Malcolm," he said. He almost went on to compliment him on his playing the night before. He stopped himself in time and merely smiled. "Hello, Jerry," said Malcolm. "Your shirt's all dirty," said Mrs. Moxon who had emptied the berries into a bowl. "It's all right," said Jerry. He brushed off a few remaining leaves and twigs and started to put it on. "You want some calamine lotion for all those bites?" Mrs. Moxon asked, observing the state of his back and his arms. "Well, all right," said Jerry. Mrs. Moxon went off to get the calamine lotion and Jerry sat down across from Malcolm. "You staying long?" he asked. "A few days," said Malcolm. Jerry smiled agreeably. He felt better disposed toward Malcolm than he usually did. He wished he knew what to say to him. "It's hot," he said. Malcolm agreed it was hot. Then Mrs. Moxon came back with the calamine.

She was rubbing it on Jerry's back when Mrs. Ingleside came into the kitchen, smoking a cigarette in a long holder. "Why, Jerry!" she said, "I didn't know you were here." "He brought us some blueberries," said Mrs. Moxon. "How wonderful," said Mrs. Ingleside, looking at the bowl of berries. "Jack will be pleased. Too bad there isn't time to do anything with them for lunch." Then she got down to business. "Mildred," she said to Mrs. Moxon, "Jack wants a cheese souffle for lunch. I'm sorry, but I couldn't argue him out of it. Can you stand the heat from the oven?" "It's all right," said Mrs. Moxon. "So forget about the salmon," said Mrs. Ingleside. "He wants the salmon with boiled potatoes anyway, and he can't have both a souffle and potatoes. Just mix up a big salad. A salade Niçoise, maybe." Mrs. Moxon nodded, and Mrs. Ingleside turned to Jerry. "What did you do to your back?" she asked him. He explained how he had gotten bitten. "And all for us!" said Mrs. Ingleside. "We'll have to have you for lunch." "Mother's expecting me," he said. "Anyway, my shirt is dirty." "Well, you're a hero," said Mrs. Ingleside. "Thank you for the berries."

He felt a lot better after being called a hero and feeling Mrs. Moxon's clean, strong hands rubbing the soothing lotion onto his back. Clearly Rosalind had not told her mother anything. He was still accepted in this house. He put on his shirt and buttoned it up and followed Mrs. Ingleside out of the kitchen. "Rosalind's on the beach," she said.

She was lying on a beach towel. She had been sailing with her father who was still fussing around with his boat at the

204

edge of the water. "Just in time," said Mr. Ingleside. "I was afraid I would have to winch it up myself." He motioned toward the winching post. "Just put your shoulder to the wheel, will you?" Jerry put his shoulder to the wheel. Then he helped Mr. Ingleside fix the tarpaulin over the boat. All this time Rosalind continued to lie on her stomach. Mr. Ingleside paused above her before he went up to the house. "Don't be late for lunch, Rozzie," he said. "There's cheese soufflé and salmon." Then he started up the steps. Jerry dropped to the sand near Rosalind.

At first she would not look at him. He took up a handful of sand and let it trickle through his fingers. "Rosalind?" he said at last. "I better go up," she told him, starting to rise. "Wait!" he said. She picked up her towel and shook it. She would not look at his face. "I'll see you later, Jerry." "It's too early for your lunch," he told her. "Mrs. Moxon hasn't even started it yet." Rosalind folded the towel and put it over her arm. Then she felt with her feet for her sandals. Jerry picked one up to keep her from slipping her foot into it and walking off. It was the sandal he had bitten. He could see his own tooth marks in the leather of the thong. "Don't go," he told her. "I just don't want to talk about it now," she said. "Then we don't have to talk about it," he said, "just don't go. You don't have to go. Honest. Your lunch won't be ready for half an hour." "Give me my sandal, Jerry." She extended her foot so he could put it on for her. Instead he enclosed her ankle with his hand. "Please!" he said. Then, looking up, he was horrified to observe tears standing in Rosalind's eyes. "You can't go up," he told her. "You're crying."

This was worse than anything he had expected, even getting shot by her father. He felt stricken by the sight of her remorse. He bent his head to kiss her foot. "I'm so sorry," he said. "I'm so sorry." He hadn't felt sorry until now, but now he felt so sorry that he wondered why he hadn't felt sorrow from the time he woke up. Obviously that was how he should have been feeling. "It will never happen again," he told her. "Never."

At last she sat down beside him, the towel draping her lap. She sighed, and he sighed as well. "I don't blame you for being mad at me," he said. "I'm not mad," she told him. "I could kill myself," he said. "Don't blame yourself for everything," said Rosalind. "It was all my fault," he asserted. She shook her head sadly. "Honestly, Rosalind, it was. You have nothing to blame yourself for. I took advantage of you." She touched his shoulder. "You're sweet to say that," she said. He shook his head vigorously. "No, I'm not sweet. I'm terrible." In his hand he still held her sandal with his tooth marks in it, sure proof of how terrible he was. "You see this?" he said, showing her the sandal. "Those are tooth marks in the thong. When I was in your house I went through your room. I made those marks." He felt she might as well know everything about him. She looked puzzled as she examined the sandal which he handed her. "How could you make these marks?" she asked. "With my teeth. I bit the leather." "But why?" she asked. "I don't know why," he said. He looked at her eyes for a moment. "So don't blame yourself for anything." He gestured at the sandal. "I mean, I'm like that."

If he had thought all morning he could have said nothing more calculated to ease her conscience and shake her free from her mood of self-absorbed remorse. He felt this as he saw a glimmer of interest in her eyes. "You bit my sandal?" she said. "I could do anything," he told her. "I'm the one you should blame. I wouldn't even blame you if you never wanted to see me again." Even as he spoke, he realized he was arousing her sympathy by making himself seem humble, and contrite, and unpossessive, which he didn't really think he was. He surprised himself. How could he be talking this way to Rosalind and admitting these things? Even more surprising, how could he be regaining her confidence by telling her terrible things about himself? Yet he was gaining ground with her. It was obvious. "Do you want me to go away?" he asked her. "No," she said.

206

He had a curious sense of power and certainty as he waited to hear what she would say next. And though what she said was not at all what he expected, he knew the moment she began to speak just how he would respond and how it would all work out. She said, "After this we're going to have to be super careful." At once he said, "Boy, are you right." A week later he made love to her a second time.

He did not understand the new power he had, but he could feel it at work in him almost all the time. At night when he lay in his narrow bunk bed he had no trouble controlling himself. Even with Rosalind he had no trouble. He did not have to make love to her. He was not driven by passion. Rather, passion seemed to be inside him, guiding him in quite deliberate ways so that his behavior seemed to him more controlled and less random than it had ever been. He seemed to know exactly what he was doing, though he surprised himself at almost every turn by what he did and how he did it. His second seduction of Rosalind, for instance, looked like a masterpiece of planning, though he was not aware of having made any plans except insofar as he had purchased a packet of Trojans one afternoon when Nancy Train was driving the whole bunch of kids to Chesterton to get some ice cream at Brunks. And even the purchase of Trojans happened almost by chance. Nancy decided she needed gas for Valiant Foo. She pulled into the Texaco station her father used, and then turned to the group in the car to announce it was time for them to chip in. She did this from time to time, and it seemed fair to Jerry. Valiant Foo consumed torrents of gasoline, and Nancy's allowance was not in line with the "chauffeur" and governess her family employed. He contributed some change from his pocket and then excused himself to use the Men's Room, where he observed a contraceptive dispenser on the wall. Fishing into his pocket he found he had a quarter left. He popped it in, got a packet of three contraceptives, and calmly rejoined the crowd in Valiant Foo.

Later he told Phil, "They had rubbers for sale in that Men's Room." "Did they?" said Phil, and then they looked at each other with amusement and some feelings of superiority. They agreed they had never seen rubbers for sale in a Standard station. Standard was a good, homey kind of company. For all they knew the company actually insisted that its dealers maintain respectable, noncontroversial Men's Rooms.

Jerry had made his purchase without having any particular idea in mind. It just seemed to him that contraceptives might come in useful sometime. They were still in the pocket of his shorts when he rode over to the Inglesides the next day to play tennis with Rosalind. He found her not in the mood to play—and for a reason that reassured them both. He smiled encouragingly at her as if to say, *You see, no harm has been done.* Then he settled down to chat with her on the porch. He had brought his bathing suit with him, thinking they might swim after tennis, but now he was prepared to give up swimming as well. Rosalind, however, encouraged him to swim, so he changed into his bathing suit and they went down to the beach together. They were still on the beach when Mr. Ingleside came down and suggested a sail. Rosalind didn't feel like sailing. She didn't feel well, she said. She thought she would go up to the house and lie down. So Jerry went sailing alone with Mr. Ingleside.

He liked doing things alone with Mr. Ingleside. When they were alone together, which was not often, Mr. Ingleside seldom said disconcerting things. He was much more like a father. The rigging of his boat was more complicated than the rigging of Jerry's Dolphin. Mr. Ingleside explained it all, and actually taught Jerry something about sailing. And when it came time to haul the boat out of the water he behaved very differently from the way he had behaved a few days earlier when Rosalind was lying face down on her towel. Then Mr. Ingleside had seemed to take pleasure in making it look like he was exploiting Jerry. This afternoon the two of them worked together. Jerry decided that probably Mr. Ingleside would have been a better man if he had not lost both his sons. Their deaths seemed to have left him playing a sort of greedy, competitive, boyish role in his own family.

When the boat was safely up on the beach and covered once more by its tarpaulin, Mr. Ingleside smiled at Jerry. "Coming up?" he asked. Jerry decided it was too late in the afternoon. It was time for him to get home. He trotted back to his end of the Shores and took a dip with his own father and Mr. Forson, who were just home from Whiting. It was only as he rode up to the cabin on the running board of the Forsons' Buick, that he remembered he had left his bicycle at the Inglesides' house and his shorts were hanging in the basement maid's room.

They continued to hang there for another three days. He seemed to forget about them every time he visited Rosalind. One afternoon he remembered them. He had arrived just after lunch to discover Rosalind all alone. Her father had gone into the University to do some work, and her mother had gone along at the last minute to see Mrs. Elbridge and do some shopping. The Moxons had taken the day off, driving into Gary for lunch and a movie. Yet, even as he learned from Rosalind that they would have the house to themselves for several hours, he did not immediately think of his shorts and his contraceptives in the basement. He merely smiled at her and bent to kiss her. They were now on affectionate, rather brotherly and sisterly kissing terms. "Feel like tennis?" he asked, sinking into a deck chair beside her. She didn't particularly feel like playing. They sat on the porch talking about their friends. "Shirley attracts dogs," Jerry said. He meant it both literally and figuratively. During her periods Shirley was always bothered by dogs sniffing around her when she came down to the beach. More than that, the boys she attracted seemed like dogs to her. At least that was how she was currently treating Alec Walker. "If she doesn't watch out, she'll end up unmarried," Jerry said. Rosalind said, "Well, she compares boys to you and Phil." "Me?" said Jerry. "Most of the time she treats me as if I'm a maniac." "Well, but you know what she means," said Rosalind. "What does she mean?" Jerry asked. "Well, she's grown up with you and Phil. She expects other boys to be like you two, and they just aren't." This was an interesting insight. Jerry shifted on his deck chair to look at Rosalind, wondering if a compliment to himself was implied in what she had just said. "Ernie Hill is like me, and Shirley wasn't much interested in him before he started going around with Carolyn." "Shirley has high standards," said Rosalind.

What Rosalind meant was that Shirley had probably refused to go all the way with Ernie, and so Ernie had turned to Carolyn, but the conversation might become dangerous if it went in that direction because Rosalind, despite her own high standards, had gone all the way with him. Jerry could see a sort of clouding on her face as she thought of this, and to distract her from contemplating her own fall, he suddenly felt his stomach. "Hey, I'm hungry," he said. They went into the kitchen. Rosalind opened the refrigerator and bent forward to inspect its contents. As she bent, her blouse stretched taut across her back and her shorts rose slightly on her legs. He stepped behind her and placed his hands on her hips. It seemed like the right thing to do. She straightened up at once and turned her head to remind him that this was just the sort of situation they were supposed to avoid. "I know," he said, and it was at that precise moment he remembered distinctly that there were contraceptives in the pocket of his shorts hanging in the downstairs maid's room. "I'll be careful," he told her, sliding his hands upward until they rested over her breasts.

It was all unplanned, and yet the contraceptives were there, and as he breathed in her ear and kissed her neck and moved his hands he seemed to know just how to appeal to her. "It will be safe," he said, "and it doesn't make any

210

difference now." Caught between the open refrigerator on one side and Jerry on the other, Rosalind gradually melted. When she heard of the Trojans in the basement, she gave in, and they eventually went up to her bedroom.

It was changed. The air was no longer musty, the bed was no longer stripped. Though neat, it had a lived-in look. He noticed the books in her bookcase. They had the worn, well-read appearance of books that accumulate in summer houses. He noticed other things that had escaped his attention before. On the wall over the headboard of the bed was a bright red reproduction of a painting of horses. It was in his mind as he made love to Rosalind. She loved horses, she loved riding. "Here," he said suddenly, turning until he was on his back and she above him. She looked more naked and vulnerable above him than below him, and yet as they went on he saw her suddenly lift her head as if she felt something of what he was feeling.

They lay together for a time. They had nothing to say to each other. Finally she went off to the bathroom, and he looked at his watch. They had plenty of time, he thought. Perhaps when she came back they could do it again. He had two more Trojans. Then he felt he should slip off his watch which might feel cold and hard against her skin. He put it on the little table beside her bed but did not like the sight of it there. It seemed wrong for his masculine-looking Swiss watch to be lying there right in front of a framed photograph of her parents. He got up and put the watch into the little box on top of her dresser. Then he lay back on the bed, waiting for Rosalind. He felt tender and loving as he thought of her and saw again, in his memory, the sudden lift of her chin as they had made love. But when she reappeared she was dressed. She stood in the door, looking at him. He felt like covering his nakedness, but he didn't. "We have to make the bed," she told him, averting her eyes. He wanted to point out that there was no hurry, but he felt too much at a disadvantage to say so. He got off the bed and pulled on his clothes with his back to her. The only time he had ever had to make beds regularly was during his month at camp in Colorado. He wondered how often Rosalind made her own bed? He smiled across at her as they tucked the bedspread in under the edge of the pillows. "There, that looks nice," he said. It was the first time he had ever worked with someone making a bed. It was sort of like being married, he thought.

Then they went downstairs. "It was an accident," he told Rosalind. He tried to touch her shoulder but she moved away from him. "It's not your fault, you know that," he said, worried about her now. "You know it was just an accident." There was a painful-looking frown on her face. "What are we going to do, Jerry?" "Nothing," he said. "It just happened, that's all. It won't happen again." And yet even as he said it, he remembered his watch, which was still upstairs in the little box on top of her dresser. He thought of going upstairs to get it, but it seemed to him cavalier just to walk into Rosalind's room to get his watch, and he couldn't ask her to go get it for him so he decided to leave it there for the time being. He went on reassuring her that everything was all right, that nothing would happen again, that in a way they were simply victims of fate. How often did it happen that the house would be empty this way? When he finally left her he felt he had almost persuaded her to accept his view of the situation.

Yet his watch was in her bedroom, his shorts and a pair of tennis shoes were in the basement maid's room, and his tennis racquet was in the garage. Normally he was careful about his possessions. He did not scatter them around; now he seemed to be leaving things all over Rosalind's house. They were like bridgeheads, he thought. He seemed to be moving in. It was almost as if he had no intention of ending their affair, despite his assurances to Rosalind that it was never going to happen again.

He waited several days before asking her about his watch.

212

He spent the intervening time doing improving things. He picked blueberries. He Simonized the Olds without being asked to do it. One night he even began to read *Anna Karenina,* which Anne had given him for his seventeenth birthday that spring. She had written in her birthday letter that Michael considered *Anna Karenina* superior to *War and Peace* and that it had less history in it. Those seemed like solid recommendations. Jerry read the first chapter with considerable pleasure, though he was not sure that happy families were all alike. His own family seemed to him rather different from the Forson family and the Hyatt family. Nor was he convinced that unhappy families were always unhappy in different ways. In the novel the Oblonsky family was unhappy because the husband was unfaithful to his wife. Jerry's experience of unhappy families was not extensive, but in the few cases he knew, the cause of unhappiness was exactly the same: unfaithfulness. That was why Ernie Hill's parents had divorced. Still, *Anna Karenina* interested him for an evening, and he almost regretted that he didn't have time to go on with it. But he just didn't have time. Every moment of his day from morning to midnight seemed full, and he really needed his watch to keep track of the time while he was out in the woods picking berries.

"Have you seen my watch anywhere?" he asked Rosalind one afternoon when he stopped by her house to sell her family a quart of blueberries. She hadn't seen it. "I must have left it somewhere else," he said. He didn't stay long. He was doing his rounds, still dressed in his blueberrying clothes—a long-sleeved shirt and long pants. Moreover he smelled of mosquito repellent and of the sulfur he rubbed on his wrists and ankles to keep chiggers from creeping up his arms and legs and burying themselves in his armpits and crotch. He smiled reassuringly at Rosalind. "Be seeing you," he said, as he got back into the freshly Simonized Olds.

Actually he saw relatively little of her for almost ten days. He was waiting for her to get over the crisis she was obviously going through after it had happened a second time. His only fear was that she might tell her mother, or find some way of leaving the Shores. She and her mother generally went to New York in September to see plays and to buy clothes. Maybe she would persuade her mother to go early this summer. She didn't, however, and one day toward the end of July when he sailed down to see her, he found her sitting on the beach, looking rather cheerful. There was a brisk wind blowing. He took her out for a sail, during which he tipped over the Dolphin once by accident and a second time on purpose because it was fun going over. "You're some sailor," Rosalind told him as they righted the Dolphin the second time. Then, when he deposited her on the beach once more, she told him to wait before he sailed off. "I have something for you," she said. She went up to the house. When she came back she handed him his watch. "Here," she said. Their eyes met, and he could not tell whether to pretend surprise or just accept the watch and put it on. Finally he said, "Thanks," and put it on.

That night he saw her again at Shirley's house. The wind had freshened still more, and when they stopped talking or playing records they could hear the lake roaring in the distance. They were all affected by the weather. They played Up-Jenkins. They played Concentration. Nancy was there, as well as the Rathko boys. Finally someone said, "Let's go down to the lake," and they all went down together. They found Joanne and Linda sitting above the reach of the waves with their arms around each other's waists. "You guys were nuts to stay indoors on a night like this," they said. "See the stars?" It was a black night. The sky was almost clear and filled with stars. "And feel the wind," said Joanne. "Listen to the waves," someone said. In the darkness you could see sudden lines of white appear as the waves broke. While they were standing on the beach a wave came hissing up the sand and sent them all moving backward. "It's still rising," Phil observed. "It's cold," said Rosalind. "The water

214

would feel warm," Jerry said. He wanted to swim. "Let's all go in," he said. No one took him up on it, however, so he abandoned that idea. "I'll walk you home along the beach," he said to Rosalind. "I drove over," she told him. "Let's do something," Jerry said. It was that sort of night. "What about Sardines?" someone said, but that was best played indoors and it was too dark for such outdoor games as Prisoner's Base or Poison. Gradually the group broke up. Jerry followed Rosalind to her car. Overhead the trees were thrashing in the wind. He wanted to ride along with her, but he couldn't ask and he couldn't just climb in. Shirley was there, as well as Phil. "Let's all go," he suggested. "We can walk back along the beach." "I have to go in," said Shirley. Then Phil drifted off toward home. Rosalind put her key in the ignition. "Can I come along?" Jerry asked. It was the situation they were supposed to avoid. They had agreed they should not be alone together at night. "I'll just ride with you," said Jerry. Rosalind said, "It's been nice tonight, Jerry. Let's just . . . " But he was in the car. "Well, all right," she said.

The trouble—they agreed about this later—was that she tried to resist him too completely. He could not kiss her, she said, so he grabbed the keys out of the ignition and stuck them into his pocket. She made a second mistake in trying to get them back. That just made things worse. "If you'd have let me kiss you that's all that would have happened," Jerry said. "I'm not so sure," said Rosalind. "Honestly," Jerry said. "Well, maybe," Rosalind conceded. They were by then in each other's arms, lying on the lap rug which had been in the trunk. The car was parked at the end of West Road and they were nestled in a sheltered spot halfway up a dune. "I mean, honestly, I wasn't going to try anything," Jerry said. "I just wanted to be with you." It was all that playful scuffling around in the front seat that had changed his mind. Rosalind sighed. "I just don't know what we're going to do," she said. What they had just done was to make love. Jerry had another Trojan left and had a pretty good idea of what they could do next, but he didn't mention it. Things were still at the critical point in which Rosalind might dip into gloom over her own frailty. "It's lucky you had those things with you," she remarked. He agreed it was indeed lucky. He had been transferring them from pocket to pocket as he changed his clothes. He felt it would be indiscreet to leave them at home in a drawer. They lay for a while in silence, holding each other tightly because it was a cool night. Finally he said, "I have one left."

They were all gone by the time they shook out the lap rug and put it back in the trunk. Rosalind seemed resigned to what had happened. Also, she had enjoyed it more. In the car as she started up the engine she heaved a final sigh. "After this it's going to be harder than ever to be good." Jerry agreed. In a way Rosalind's comment was a sort of tribute to the experience, or at least that was how he chose to respond to it.

"It looks like you need gas," he told Nancy Train a couple of nights later when they were all in Valiant Foo on their way home from the Aron Theater in Chesterton. He was in the back with Phil and Linda and Joanne and Betty Train. Rosalind was sitting up front with Nancy and Shirley. Jerry felt Linda kick his ankle as he called Nancy's attention to the gas supply. Linda hated it when Nancy dunned the Standard Oil kids for gas money and then spent it to buy Texaco. "You think she'd at least buy Standard Oil," Linda said. That evening, however, Nancy spent her own money, and while the tank was being filled up, Jerry strolled into the Men's Room and spent all the quarters in his pockets.

It was another ten days before Rosalind was willing to meet him by arrangement, and he was too wise to hurry her. He waited. They had another "accidental" encounter one night when her parents had gone out to dinner. The Moxons were in the house and Rosalind was very nervous about them.

He said, "We should really be more careful." She agreed wholeheartedly. "We'd be safer outdoors in the dunes," he said. She didn't reply to that, and he did not try to arrange anything. The idea had been planted, however, and by the second week in August they had their first fully deliberate meeting.

It took place on top of the White Throne, where there was a hollow that could not be overlooked from any surrounding dune. A pine tree provided some shade. The wind was undermining the pine, whose exposed roots now branched out several feet above the sand before they finally curved downward. It looked as if the tree were clutching at the sand or perhaps standing on its hands. It would probably go down during the winter storms, either this year or the next. Meanwhile it shaded them from the sun and provided a shelter for the beach blanket that Jerry rolled up tightly and stuck under the tree when everything was over. "This is a great place," he told Rosalind. "No one ever comes here." He felt they had reached a whole new level of confidence and intimacy which allowed him to discuss with her the pros and cons of various places, as well as little storage details such as the one he now revealed. "You see? I'll keep them here," he said, putting some contraceptives into a Sucret box which he buried in the sand. He smiled at her as he smoothed the sand over his buried treasure. She did not smile back. "It's all right," he told her. "It's really all right." He moved next to her and put his arm around her shoulder. She still needed reassurance. He thought that perhaps he should not have displayed his contraceptives. He had to remember that she was finer than he was and might not respond as he did to the thought of what fun they were going to have using them up. "I'm sorry," he told her. He kissed her hand. "I'd do anything for you," he assured her. "Believe me, I would." He tried to think of something he could do for her, but nothing came to mind. That was the trouble. When he thought of trying to save her life, the only way he could imagine it being imperiled was if he were to set fire to her house in the first place, or take her far out in the lake and somehow sink his Dolphin so that he would have to help her ashore. And she didn't really need that kind of help. He was not sure what she needed.

He worried about her. She was not a particularly independent or passionate girl. It was hard for her to be doing something so contrary to what her parents expected of her. It was a little contrary to her own nature. She was not the sort of girl who should be sneaking off into the dunes to meet her lover. He thought it might actually have been better for her if he had fallen in love with someone else, someone more like himself. Nancy, for instance. But that hadn't happened. He'd fallen in love with Rosalind. He was her lover now, and it was his responsibility to make her as happy as he could.

This sense of responsibility for her happiness occupied his mind during the hours they were apart and gave him a weighty, adult feeling. At times he felt he had to insist she meet him again the next day. His motives seemed to him quite divorced from lust. He knew better than she did what would make her happy. With this weighty, adult feeling heavy upon him, he told her one afternoon during the first week of their affair that he would be at the White Throne at ten o'clock the following morning. "I can't come," she said. He asked her when she could come. "Mother and I are going into town tomorrow," she told him. He asked what time they were leaving, adding that he could be at the White Throne at seven o'clock, or even six. He would give up his morning swim to be with her. "I just can't make it tomorrow," she said. "You'll be back in the evening, won't you?" he asked. "Jerry," she said, "don't pester me."

That hurt him a little. He was not pestering her. He wished she could understand that. Then he saw her smiling at him. Perhaps his expression was crestfallen. In any case he saw a glimmer of amusement in her eyes as she said, "I'll meet you the day after." "At nine o'clock?" he asked. "All right, nine," she said.

When they were having one of their secret meetings they did not walk off together. He always biked to the end of West Road and then tramped through the woods, approaching the summit of the White Throne from inland. Rosalind approached it from the lake. On the day after her trip to Chicago he lay against the slope of their hollow, looking down at the wide sweep of beach. Presently he saw her coming, a single figure dwarfed by the distance, a spot of deep blue against the sand and the pale lake. She was wearing her bathing suit. Quickly he removed his own clothes and pulled on his suit, which he had brought with him, thinking they might swim afterward. Then he lay down again to watch her climb the long open slope of the White Throne. It was almost as if he were spying on her, his head invisible in the fringe of grass. The slope was steep, so that she began to use her hands as well as her feet as she climbed up toward him. He could see great tongues of dry sand shifting downward, displaced by her climbing. He was so affected by the sight of her working her way toward him that he felt inarticulate when she came over the lip of their hollow and sank down beside him on the blanket. "Woof!" she said, panting a little from the climb. "I'll get my breath in a minute," she told him. He watched her breathe deeply. Finally he said, "Was it nice in Chicago yesterday?" "Lovely," she said. "We had lunch with Grandmother and then we went to the Art Institute." "What for?" he asked. She looked at him a little oddly. "To look at some pictures." He nodded.

He felt almost shy with her that morning. Somehow his feeling of responsibility for her happiness had deserted him. He was the recipient of what she had brought him. He put his hand on her shoulder, fingering the strap of her bathing suit. "I'm glad to see you," he said. His fingers worked gently at the strap. She smiled. "I missed you," he said. "I thought of you at the Art Institute," she told him. "Me?" he asked, temporarily distracted from his effort to ease her strap off her shoulder. "What made you think of me?" "A picture," she explained. "A Picasso." She smiled happily at him. "I thought of us, really. It's called 'The Lovers.'" "And it looks like us?" he said. A Picasso that looked like Rosalind Ingleside and Jerry Engels? She shook her head. "No. But it looks like two lovers. That's all."

Then she let him ease the strap off her shoulder. She turned her body slightly to let him ease off the other strap, and when he let down the front of her bathing suit, she had a shy smile on her face as he looked for a while at her round white breasts with their pink nipples.

He could not explain even to himself the feeling he got from looking at Rosalind sitting with her breasts uncovered, a fugitive smile on her lips. As such moments he felt more truly happy than he could ever remember feeling in the past. He felt unimaginably close to her during that first breathless moment when he saw her body. The thought that it was going to happen was more enchanting even than the recognition that now it was happening. Yet everything was enchanting: the sight of her lying back, her breasts differently shaped from when she sat up; the feel of the blanket against his knees, and of the sun on his back; the sight of her face so close to his, her hair spread out around her head; the feel of her body against his. At times it seemed to him wrong that this should be happening outdoors. For all her horseback riding and her tennis and her sailing, Rosalind was not really an outdoors person. When he saw her white breasts and pink nipples he longed to have her whole body pink and white and golden. Tan didn't really suit her. One day he said, "I wish you were white all over." He ran his hand along the white marks left by her bathing suit straps. "I'd love to see you all white." "I'll be all tan if we keep this up," she said.

Soon after the beginning of their regular meetings there was a new burst of heat as the August dog days began. The

220

sun rose red and fiery in the east, and already it was heating the sand when Jerry and Phil walked back up to the ridge after their morning swim. By noon the leaves on the cottonwood in front of the cabin hung motionless in the hot air. The birds were silent. Nothing moved except the heat pouring down from the sky and radiating back up from the sand. You could see waves of heat rising and shimmering in the air above the dunes, and on the path from the parking lot to the beach, little kids who had forgotten to wear sandals ran a few yards, dropped their towels, stood on them, and then when their feet had cooled, ran on another few yards before they dropped their towels again. One afternoon Jerry found Betty Train marooned on a towel halfway to the beach. There were tears in her eyes. "The sand's too hot to walk on," she said. He agreed, though he still pretended to stroll unscathed along the fiery path to the beach.

He gave Betty a lift. She clung to him as if he were a woman, riding his hip instead of getting on behind. Her weight pressed his feet deeper than usual into the hot sand, and before he had taken five steps he began to hurry. His feet were being fried. Yet when he and Phil were together they still went through the pretense that their toughened soles could stand anything. Even when it was agony, they strolled without sandals and without hurrying, though now they went straight into the lake to cool their feet. One day while they were cooling their feet in the lake, they looked at each other and just shook their heads.

But even on such days Jerry and Rosalind were meeting each other, and for a good Standard Oil boy he was visiting that Texaco station with remarkable frequency, even buying a tank of gas one day. "Fill it up," he said to the station attendant, hoping that Texaco would not clog the carburetor or foul the points of his family's Oldsmobile. Then he went into the Men's Room and cleaned out the dispenser there, hoping it would be refilled soon before he used up the six packages he got in exchange for his six quarters.

He and Rosalind met in the morning before the full heat

of the day, but even so it was hot. One morning as Jerry waited for Rosalind, he saw her appear in the distance and then stop before she began to climb the dune. She looked in his direction and then turned to look at the lake. He rose and stood for a moment, poised in his red bathing suit atop the dune, before he ran down to join her. He did not run so much as slalom down the dune, moving laterally back and forth like a skiier, because if you ran full speed straight down a dune like that you could not keep up with yourself. You fell. He arrived on the beach exhilarated by his run. "You want to swim first?" he said to Rosalind. "All right, let's swim," she said.

When they came out, however, she did not want to climb the dune. "It's too hot," she said. She sat down on the sand with her feet in the water. She began to search for Indian beads amid the tiny pebbles that edged the lake. "You don't want to go?" Jerry said, standing and looking down at her bent head. "It's too hot, Jerry," she said. "There's a little breeze up there," he reminded her. She went on sifting pebbles. "You really don't want to go up?" he asked her. She shook her head. Her blond hair moved slightly. He felt a constriction of desire. He had been looking forward to their meeting for twenty-four hours. "Are you all right?" he asked her. "It's too hot this morning," she said, still not looking up. He felt worried and a little exasperated at the same time. Was she sinking into one of her guilty moods, or was she just being perverse? He picked up a flat stone and skipped it out across the water. Then he said "Maybe we could meet tonight?" She didn't answer him. "You're sure you're all right?" he asked her. "Jerry, I don't feel like it," she said.

He sat down beside her. "I could get the car tonight," he said. "Would you like to see a movie? We could go to Michigan City for a movie." They had seen what was on at the Aron. "Would you like that?" he asked. "Just us," he added, meaning they would not invite Phil or Shirley or

Joanne or Linda to go along with them. It would be a date. "Wouldn't you like that?" he said. "We've been seeing too much of each other," she said. He didn't agree. In fact he totally disagreed. "We haven't been out on a date all summer!" he said. She looked around at him. "You're not thinking of a date." His feelings were hurt. "It would be a date," he insisted. She shook her head. "You know it wouldn't be." Then she repeated what she had said before. "We're seeing too much of each other."

"Don't you want to see me?" he asked. "I'm here, aren't I?" she said. "Well, what do you want to do?" he asked her. "Do we have to do something?" she said. She had found an Indian bead and was now holding it on her palm, looking at it. "Rosalind," he said, trying to get her attention away from the Indian bead, "Rosalind." She went on looking at her palm. "Are you just going to sit there?" he asked her. "Is that all you want to do, *sit*?" She glanced at him. "We could talk." "We *are* talking," he said, and a very unsatisfactory talk it seemed. "We practically never talk," she answered him. "All we've done this morning is talk," said Jerry. Her unreasonableness drove his voice up. Rosalind said, "I don't call this talk. You're arguing with me. You're pestering me again." He said, "I'm just asking you what you'd like to do. Is that pestering?" "Yes it is," she said.

Jerry looked up at the bright sky as if inviting the higher powers to take note of Rosalind's unreasonableness. "I don't call it pestering to ask someone what she would like to do. I'll do anything you want. That's not pestering." He bent to look at her face which was hidden from him by a curtain of hair. "Are you really all right?" he asked her. "Jerry," she said, "what's going to happen to us?" The question took him by surprise. He had been so absorbed in what *was* happening he had given no thought to what *might* happen. "We can't go on this way," Rosalind said. He thought about it. His family was going up to Red Crown Lodge for Labor Day. She and her mother were going to New York in the middle of September. Then school would start and it would be autumn. After that winter would come. They had only another week or so when they could meet like this. "I know," he said, realizing they couldn't go on in the same way. "But we'll find a way," he promised her. She shook her head. "Jerry, we should stop." "No!" he cried. The idea was one that had to be opposed as promptly and decisively as possible. "No," he said again. He seized her elbow to emphasize his point. "You scare me sometimes," she said. That made them even, for she had just scared him with the idea that they should stop.

He pulled himself together and began to think. "Rosalind, we can't stop," he said. They had to go on. They were just at the beginning. Ahead of them were things he had only dreamt about but which would gradually come true if they went ahead. "Don't you see?" he said. "We're together now." He reached for her hand and then placed it on his thigh. "I'm yours," he said. "You're mine." How could one stop that? "It can't stop." "But Jerry . . . " she began. "Feel," he told her, working his thigh muscle in the way Shirley so deprecated. "Don't you see?" He was staring into her face. Her eyes were fixed on her own hand resting on his brown thigh. "Oh, Rosalind," he said, suddenly falling back on the sand with his arms spread, "I want you." It was true, of course, but he was not reaching for her. He was lying with his palms up, his eyes actually focused on a gull circling overhead while he waited for her to want him. Her hand continued to rest on his thigh. He knew she was looking down at him. Words and images circled through his mind like that gull circling overhead. He opened his mouth. "I'd die if you left me," he said. Her hand tightened. He could feel her fingernails digging into his skin, and then he gave a happy sigh of relief as he felt her fling herself on top of him, weeping.

She wept now from time to time, usually after they had made love. He would roll aside and lie on his back, one arm flung across his forehead to shield his eyes from the sun overhead. Then he would feel her move. Generally she sat up. When he stole glances at her he could see her womanly shoulders, her full breasts, and sometimes a glistening tear on her cheek. He knew at such moments that he was not making her happy, that he was not good for her; yet she was so good for him that he simply brushed aside the possibility that they should end it. He clung obstinately to the belief that he could make her happy, that he could be good for her if only she would let herself go with him. He was not too sure what he meant by this, but one day when he saw a bright tear on her cheek he asked her, "Why don't you let yourself go more?" "How can I?" she responded. "Well, kiss me all over," he suggested. He had begun kissing her everywhere. "I can't," she said. He sat up and put a comforting arm around her. "You don't have to," he said. She turned to him and rested her cheek against his chest. "Jerry," she said, "I'm afraid."

She said that more and more frequently. Sometimes she meant she was afraid of her parents finding out, but more and more she meant she was afraid of what was happening between them. When it first began she had no idea of what she was getting into. He had practically no idea himself. The difference was that every new tenderness, every fresh gesture of affection he lavished on her felt somehow familiar to him, and right. It was like coming home. When he kissed her in some new spot, or held her in some new way, he had the sensation of having been there before. There was a welcoming familiarity about it all. But it was not like that for Rosalind. He surprised her. He startled her. And then afterward she might turn to him and say she was afraid.

He felt he was advancing very rapidly along a path he was meant to follow, whereas he was taking Rosalind in a direction that was not right for her. Finally he just had to talk to someone about it, even though it was wrong to tell anyone. One night when he and Phil were leaving Shirley's house, he said, "Let's sleep together." "All right," said Phil. The weather was the same as it had been for the last ten days: still and very hot. They lay without even a sheet over them, sweating gently in the breathless night. "How did Rosalind seem to you?" Jerry asked. She had left Shirley's earlier in the evening after they had finished planning the picnic they were giving for their U-High friends. "What do you mean?" Phil asked. "She didn't seem worried or anything?" Jerry said. "No." They lay for a while in silence. Now that he was at the point of exposing Rosalind to Phil, Jerry was full of doubts. "Why?" Phil asked. "Should she be worried?" "We're having an affair," Jerry said.

It did not surprise Phil as much as Jerry expected it would. "I thought so," Phil said. "Why?" Jerry asked. "I don't know. Well, for one thing you haven't suggested going back to Michigan City. And for another you and Rosalind seem pretty close, but you don't touch her as much as you used to." "Really?" said Jerry. He was impressed by Phil's observations and inferences. "Is she pregnant?" Phil asked. "Oh no!" said Jerry. "Listen," he added, "you won't tell anyone else, will you?" "What do you think I am?" Phil said. "And you won't think anything bad about her, will you?" "I guess not," said Phil, "but why are you telling me this? You shouldn't tell me." "I know," said Jerry. Phil said, "I mean, if you'd gotten her pregnant or something, I could understand, but why just tell me?" "I have to talk to someone," Jerry said. "Don't you talk to her?" Phil asked. "Well, yes. But I need someone else to talk to. You don't mind, do you?" "No, I don't mind," said Phil, "only I wish you hadn't told me." "But you guessed," Jerry pointed out. "Yeah, but now it's different. What do you want to talk about, anyway?"

It was not the most encouraging start. "If you'd rather, I could go home," Jerry said. "Hell!" said Phil, turning on the bedside light to get a good look at Jerry. They were both naked and their sweating bodies gleamed in the light. Phil's body suddenly struck Jerry as menacingly powerful. "What's the matter?" he asked. "Well, hell!" said Phil. "You say you're having an affair with Rosalind, and then you say you're going home." "Well, you sounded as if you didn't want to talk about it," Jerry said. "You sound angry," he added. "I am," said Phil. "She's a great girl." "She is!" Jerry agreed enthusiastically. "She's wonderful." "Then what do you have to mess her up for?" Phil wanted to know. Jerry hesitated. He had not expected Phil to be this stern and unsympathetic. "Look, turn out the light," he said.

Once it was dark, however, he found he could not talk to Phil without touching him. He put his hand on Phil's chest. "Look, I need advice," he said. "Do you think I should let her go?" He explained that she was afraid, that she thought they should stop. "Should I let her go?" he asked again. "It sounds like you have some power over her," Phil observed. "I do," said Jerry. He felt that no matter which way Rosalind turned he could bring her around. "What would you do?" he asked. "Stop feeling my chest," said Phil. Jerry removed his hand. This whole conversation was not going the way he had hoped it would. "Would you give her up?" he asked. "Would you give up Rachel?" Rachel Fein was Phil's girlfriend. "I don't have Rachel," said Phil. "Well, if you had her. Would you give her up?" He touched Phil's arm. "Could you do that?" "I don't know," said Phil. "I can't give up Rosalind," Jerry said. Then abruptly he rose and stood at the window. "I can't breathe," he said. "You want to swim?" "No," said Phil.

Jerry sat down on the bed. Phil's hairy legs were faintly visible. Jerry stared at them almost thoughtfully. He thought of Rosalind's smooth legs. "I don't think I could live without her." "You've got it bad," said Phil, his tone more sympathetic than it had been. "I know," said Jerry. "When I'm alone with her, I go almost crazy sometimes." He felt Phil was listening in the right way. "I scare her." His hand was now on Phil's leg. "Sometimes I almost scare myself." "Well, you're scaring me," said Phil. "Get your hand off my leg. I'm not Rosalind." "I know," said Jerry. "Her legs . . . " Again he got up and went to the window. "Let's swim," he said again. "Oh, hell, all right," said Phil.

On the beach they took off their clothes and waded out into the still lake. It was almost like a pool whose glassy surface they alone were disturbing. As he swam leisurely, barely kicking, his head up, Jerry could hear water dripping from his arms onto the surface of the lake. The only sound in the whole night seemed to be the dripping, mildly splashing sounds that he and Phil were making. Off to the northeast he could see heat lightning playing silently along the horizon. "Let's go out," he said to Phil. "We can't even see the nets," Phil objected. "Come on," said Jerry. He led them farther and farther out. The dark lake seemed to open up around him. He lost the sense of the dunes rising up along the shore. Soon he felt he was suspended in a featureless world that stretched out endlessly in every direction. Then he became conscious of the depths below him, and for once in his life the lake no longer seemed familiar and safe. It was not even a lake anymore. He no longer believed that below him, and not very far below him at that, there was a clean sand bottom. Now he felt himself swimming over oceanic depths. This smooth warm surface in which he swam covered something that went down into coldness and pressure and oozy bottom softness where Something stirred, awakened by the sound of his tiny surface splashing. Slowly the thing uncoiled itself. It opened out, its many tentacles alert as it began to drift slowly upward, searching now for the source of the splashing sound that had awakened it. Jerry could feel it rising beneath him. Momentarily he expected his legs to be brushed by something cold and slimy. Abruptly he stopped swimming.

Phil stopped, too. "We're far enough out," Phil said. Jerry couldn't answer him. He didn't want to move for fear of attracting those blind, waving tentacles. Near him Phil treaded water, serenely unaware of the danger. "Want to start back?" Phil asked. "All right," Jerry said. He couldn't remain suspended motionlessly forever in the lake. He heard Phil begin to swim away. Still Jerry lingered where he was. Then, as abruptly as he had stopped swimming, he started to swim again, this time at racing speed. The faster he moved and the stronger he kicked, the less chance there was that he could be grabbed from below. He caught up with Phil. He passed him. He heard Phil quicken his stroke to keep up. Then it turned into a race, and with a sense of relief that did not cause him to slow down, Jerry realized he was once more in a familiar world. This was the lake. Behind him Phil was doing his best to keep up, but he, Jerry Engels, was the real swimmer. There was nothing below him but little white fish and clean sand, while behind him his best friend—a football-playing, shot-putting athlete—was struggling to keep up. Everything was all right.

Yet later, after he had parted from Phil to go home and sleep in his own bed after all, he lay awake for some time, wondering why he had been afraid of the lake. Then he thought of Rosalind. His thoughts were never very far from her these days. He thought of her lips, her hands, her feet. He thought of her blond hair spread out on the beach blanket. He thought of her breasts, her waist, her hips. A longing to see her came over him, but she was asleep now in her own bed, and she had made it very clear that he was not to turn up in the middle of the night to throw pebbles at her screen. Still, she couldn't know or object if he just went down to her house and looked up at her windows. He slipped out of his narrow bunk and left the cabin, feeling a surge of tenderness at the thought of his parents sleeping peacefully with each other, and of Joanne curled up alone in Anne's room, where she had moved now that Anne was gone.

He had the same feeling about Mr. and Mrs. Ingleside and the Moxons as he approached the Ingleside house. They were all asleep, he thought, all peacefully sleeping. Rosalind was asleep, too. It made him feel better about her. She could sleep while he sat on the grass below her window, slapping at the mosquitoes that promptly began to collect around him.

He thought he was probably the only person awake in all of Indiana Shores. You could never have this feeling in Chicago, but at the Shores it was possible. He was awake while everyone else slept. It gave him a good feeling. He began to see himself as a kind of guardian, watching over the Shores and particularly over Rosalind while she slept peacefully indoors where she belonged. The fact that he was getting badly bitten by mosquitoes added something to his sense of watching over her and protecting her. He breathed deeply, savoring his own strength and patience and ability to endure. He could keep watch for hours. He didn't feel sleepy at all. What time was it? Two o'clock? Three? He could watch until dawn, and then steal home. He could come again the next night, and the night after that. He would spend every night watching the house. It would give him something to do during the nights when he couldn't be with Rosalind. He sighed heavily and accidentally inhaled a mosquito which made him cough. He would have to remember to bring mosquito repellent with him and maybe something to eat as well. He was not sleepy, but he was hungry. But then he rejected the thought of bringing sandwiches with him as he kept his vigil below her window. This was not meant to be a picnic. He *should* be hungry and uncomfortable, though maybe not *this* uncomfortable. He waved off the mosquitoes and got to his feet to move around and restore circulation. Guards didn't have to stay in one spot all night.

He wandered down to the tennis court where he thought lovingly of Rosalind's imperfections as a tennis player. She didn't get down far enough on her returns, and her forehand was weak. That was something else he could help her with. He made some passes with an imaginary racquet and then thought of his own racquet in the garage. Could he roll up the garage door without making too much noise? He could get his racquet and some balls and practice a little while he was keeping watch.

Back at the house once more, he began working the garage

door up inch by inch. He got it up several feet without making any noise. Then he squirmed under it into the darkness of the garage. Once inside, however, he lost interest in the idea of getting his racquet. Soon he was making his way silently toward Rosalind's bedroom. This was very dangerous, he knew, but guards had to face dangers. He still saw himself as Rosalind's guardian, coming now to take a closer look at her. A stair squeaked, and he halted motionless for a full minute until he felt reassured that everyone was still peacefully asleep.

He turned the knob of her door millimeter by millimeter until he felt the catch give. Then he slipped inside and shut the door as carefully as he had opened it. He stood beside her bed, looking down at her. Having come this far, it seemed to him now that he should wake her up to reassure her that everything was all right. He knelt beside the bed and reached out to touch her hair. He meant to awaken her so gently that she would not be startled by his presence, but either he was not gentle and patient enough, or else it was intrinsically hard to prepare a girl for the experience of waking up and finding someone hovering beside the bed. Rosalind screamed. "Sssh! It's me," he said. She stifled her second scream just as it began.

For the second time that night he felt terrified. What if she'd awakened her father with that scream? "It's just me," he whispered, as she thrashed upright in her bed. He could see now that he had made a big mistake in waking her up, probably in coming into the house at all. "I just wanted to be sure you were all right," he said. He had his hand on her arm. "Be quiet," he urged her. He got up to listen at her door for sounds of stirring down the corridor. He could hear her gasping in the dark. He moved back to the bed. "It's all right, I think," he said. "Get out of here, Jerry," she said. "You've got to get out of here." "I know," he said, "I'm going. I just wanted to . . . " "What are you doing here?" she said. She was pushing at him as he knelt beside her bed, touching her shoulder in what he meant to be a reassuring way. "Get out!" she whispered. "You'll wake them," he warned her.

That quieted her a little, but she kept pushing at him. "I'll go out the window," he decided aloud. "Can you let me down with something?" It seemed to him safer than to creep back through the hall. "What about your sheet?" he asked. Rosalind moaned. She was near tears. "You've scared me to death," she said. "What are you doing here?" "I just came to see you," he said. She went on half moaning and half crying. He felt he should calm her down before he left. With that in mind he sat on the edge of her bed and reached for her. This made her slither out on the other side. "Ssssh!" he said again. "I'll scream if you don't go," she told him. "I'm going," he protested. "I just don't want you to be upset."

Then they both heard the sounds he had been fearing all along. A door opened at the far end of the corridor, a light came on in the hall, and footsteps approached Rosalind's door. In a rush Jerry bolted into Rosalind's closet and Rosalind hopped back into her bed. There was silence outside her door; then Mr. Ingleside spoke. "Rosalind?" he said. Rosalind kept quiet. "Is everything all right?" Mr. Ingleside asked. Then, in a shaken voice, Rosalind said, "I was having a nightmare." Jerry heard the door open as Mr. Ingleside looked into the room. "Are you all right?" he said, his voice much clearer now. "I'm all right, Daddy," Rosalind said. Then Mr. Ingleside apparently came into the room for Jerry could hear the sound of someone settling on the edge of the bed. "What's scared my baby?" Mr. Ingleside asked. "It's all right now," Rosalind said. "You're trembling," Mr. Ingleside said. "It was just a nightmare," said Rosalind.

Her father remained for what seemed like ten minutes. He offered to get her warm milk. At one point Jerry heard Mrs. Ingleside's voice calling out, "What is it?" Mr. Ingleside went back to his room to report to his wife. Then he visited Rosalind again. "Sure you're all right now?" he said. "I'm fine, Daddy," Rosalind said. Jerry heard the door close. He moved his bare foot off a sandal he had been standing on, and closed his eyes in relief. Then he waited patiently in the closet for things to settle down before he came out. It was Rosalind who eventually opened the closet door. "You can come out now," she said. She sounded angry, but at least she had collected her wits. "How did you get in?" she asked. "Through the garage," he said. "You can't leave that way," she said. "I know. I'll go out the window," he said.

They knotted her sheets together and twisted them into a rope which she held while Jerry let himself down from her window. He was afraid she would let go of the rope, which would leave him with the problem of how to get the sheets back up to her, so when he was still quite far from the ground he let go and dropped heavily into some peonies. Then he limped away from the house and waved to Rosalind to indicate that everything was all right. He saw her withdraw the sheets and close the screen. Feeling he had done enough for one night, he went home. He had to move slowly. He had hurt his foot in the peonies.

The next day her reaction was pretty much what he expected it to be. He telephoned at ten o'clock to let her know he was coming over. She met him on the road a quarter of a mile from her house. He leaned his bicycle against a tree and they walked off into the woods to have it out. Gentians the color of Rosalind's eyes were in bloom everywhere, but he had little time for them.

She was angrier than he had ever seen her. Probably she was as angry as she could get. She looked at him and spoke to him as if he were a stranger. It was all over, she said. He had scared her to death. They had almost been caught. It was just impossible to go on. "You're too irresponsible," she told him. He had no defense other than to say that he loved her so much he just had to see her the night before. She stared at him. "You're just not the same," she said. "I don't know you anymore." He felt she was the one who was not the same. He was the same as he always had been, only more so, whereas it was very unlike her to be angry and severe and cold. "You're different," he told her. "I've never heard you like this." "Well, how do you expect me to be after what you did last night?" He promised he would never do it again, but that was not good enough. "Jerry," she said, "I can't go on this way." She paused to put her hand on an oak tree as if to get strength from it. "I'm still terrified when I think of waking up with you there." "I know I shouldn't have done it," he admitted. "Why did you?" she exclaimed. She sounded tearful. "Don't you ever feel like doing crazy things?" he asked. "Not like that!" she said. She frowned at him. "You mean you were doing it just for fun?"

He had no answer. Though he had been severely frightened at times, the experience had been fun, but it didn't seem to him he had done it for fun. The best explanation he could give her was to repeat that he loved her so much he just had to go in and see her. "I was sitting outside," he explained, "and then I thought of getting my tennis racquet, and once I was inside I just had to go up to see you." She looked at him with incredulity. "Your tennis racquet?" He nodded. Her eyes crinkled with pain, her forehead was furrowed. "Oh, Jerry, what were you doing around the house looking for your tennis racquet at that hour?" "I wasn't looking for it," he said. He tried to make things clearer to her. He had been sitting outside the house sort of keeping watch. Then the mosquitoes were bothering him so he began to move around, and when he got to the tennis court it occurred to him to get his racquet and maybe do some practicing. "I was thinking of you," he said. "I was thinking of the way you don't get down enough on your returns." A helpless look came over Rosalind's face. He was almost sorry for her. She was losing her anger, and in another few minutes she would be turning to him for comfort. Deliberately he didn't tell her that he had been thinking of giving her tennis lessons. He faced her in silence. "I know how you feel," he said at last. That made her close her eyes and sink to the ground with her back to the oak against which she had been leaning. When she looked up at him it was with recognition mixed with resignation. He felt that if he tried he could probably make love to her there in the woods, but he didn't try.

This episode gave him the sensation that he and Rosalind were members of two different but closely related species. She approached him with the assumption of familiarity, scented some mystifying difference, grew confused in her search for familiar signs, and then, with luck, discovered something that reassured her about him. What he should do, he thought, was to give her a sign, some sort of familiar, visible token of his love. Something she could hang onto when he began to seem strange. He should buy her a ring, he decided. Her birthday was coming. He should go in town and get her a ring and then take her out to dinner at the Spa and give it to her. She could wear it on her right hand if she wanted. It didn't have to be an engagement ring. Probably it would be better if it wasn't an engagement ring. Her parents and his would both have lots to say if she started wearing his ring on her left hand.

He didn't tell Rosalind what he was going to do. He didn't even tell his mother. He just announced one morning after breakfast that he was going into Chicago. "What on earth for?" his mother asked. He said he wanted to see Ernie. "Ask him out here," his mother replied. "He's coming out for the picnic in a couple of days," Jerry said. "Then why do you have to see him today?" his mother wanted to know. "I just feel like seeing him," said Jerry. His mother shook her head. She was suspicious these days. Rosalind was not the only person who thought she and Jerry were spending too much time together. Mrs. Engels agreed, but since this Chicago trip didn't seem to have anything to do with Rosalind, Mrs. Engels finally acquiesced and even drove Jerry to the South Shore station. "When will you be back?" she asked. He wasn't sure, he said. He would get a ride with someone, or else walk. "Don't worry about me," he added. Then, under her still watchful eyes, he climbed aboard the single orange car of the ten o'clock train and waved to her from the back platform.

He got off at 55th Street, walked over to the Hills' apartment, and stooged around with Ernie until lunch. After lunch he went to the Loop. He walked over to Peacock's on State Street where he knew people went to buy good silver and jewels. "What does your cheapest ring cost?" he asked the clerk. He was given a reproving look. This was not how you shopped at Peacock. Nevertheless the clerk did bring out a tray of turquoise rings. Jerry looked them over, not sure what he was getting himself into. None of the rings had price tags. Finally he chose one with Indian-looking chasing on it. He asked its price. The clerk told him, and Jerry felt relieved. He could afford thirty-five dollars for Rosalind. He'd made fifty dollars selling blueberries. He had the box gift-wrapped, and then wandered around the Loop for a while, liking the urban noise and smells and animation. After weeks at the Shores, barefoot most of the time, it was exciting just to be in shoes and walking on pavement again. He window-shopped. He looked at girls. He saw girls looking at him. This stimulated him even more. Finally he wandered out into Grant Park and sat for a while on a bench facing Buckingham Fountain. It was a hot day and the fountain looked refreshing. Occasionally a gust of wind would blow some spray, and water would ring like coins on the pavement around the fountain. He found himself smiling happily at a couple of secretary-looking girls who were sitting on a bench near him. With Rosalind's ring in his pocket he felt somehow anchored to her and yet free to float off into an erotic fantasy involving the girls on the next bench. He thought one of them might be his old friend Mischievous Mabel; the other was Doris. He was very sure about Doris' name. Mabel might turn out to be someone else, but Doris was Doris. And the two of them were talking about him. Only it was not exactly him. It was another version of himself, this one not dressed for town but undressed for the fountain. He was standing naked in the pool below the fountain, the spray falling on his head and shoulders and cooling his flushed face. "Isn't he cute?" Doris kept saying. She was the sort of girl who thought everything was cute. Mabel was more sophisticated. She said, "That's quite a wang he's got."

Then a tourist bus drew up, and the guide began to tell everyone when the fountain was built and who designed it and how many gallons of water it used per hour. Nobody on the tour seemed surprised to see Jerry standing naked in the fountain. The guide even concluded his remarks by saying, "And that young man in the fountain is Jerry Engels." He was accepted as one of the sights in Chicago—like the stockyards or the Water Tower. "Hey, fellow," a man from Texas called out to him, "why don't you hold it in your hand?" The Texan had a camera and wanted a picture of Jerry holding himself, but that seemed a little vulgar, so Jerry ignored the suggestion. He merely smiled as the Texan and several other tourists took his picture. Then the bus drove off and Doris said, "I think it's terrible the way they keep him standing around in there all day and nobody ever does anything for him." "Well, go do it, then," Mabel said. "You think I should?" Doris asked. "I don't see why not," said Mabel.

Doris giggled as she took off her shoes and stockings. Then she waded out into the pool until she was facing Jerry. "I just want to help," she said, as if asking for his permission. He nodded understandingly, and she began to help him. Just then a double file of girls in uniform came by, led by two nuns. They were coming from the direction of the Art Institute and seemed to be heading toward the Field Muscum. The nuns halted the column in front of the fountain and told the girls to admire its design. "It's the most beautiful fountain in the world," one nun said. "Except for Rome," she remembered to add. Some of the little girls began to giggle. "Mary Catherine, Mary Theresa, what are you laughing at?" the other nun said. Then she saw Jerry and Doris who were half hidden by the water pouring down over them. "That is nothing to laugh about!" she said in an angry voice. "That young man has had a long hard day standing in the fountain, and somebody has to take care of him. You'll understand this when you're grown-up and married." She led the girls off toward the Field Museum, and then Doris disappeared, and a gust of wind blew some ringing spray onto the pavement, and Jerry got to his feet and headed for the Monroe Street Station to catch the three o'clock South Shore train.

His mind just seemed to open up to fantasies like that. He didn't make them up; they happened inside his head. He had to be in the right mood, of course, but once he was in that mood, everything and anything could set a fantasy going. He had another on his way back to the Shores. At the 12th Street station a black woman got onto the train. She had been traveling. She had two suitcases plus a shopping bag full of things and an umbrella. She took the first vacant seat she could find, which happened to be beside Jerry. She left her suitcases in the aisle for people to trip over, and put the shopping bag and the umbrella in the rack overhead. The umbrella promptly fell through the bars of the rack and hit Jerry on the head. He handed it back to her saying, "It didn't hurt," though in fact it had. She took the umbrella without a word and promptly put it back on the rack. This time it didn't fall through. Jerry looked up to see if he was safe, and then looked at the woman next to him. She had seated herself and was staring straight ahead. Either she didn't know enough to apologize, or she disliked white people so much she really wanted to hit them with her umbrella. Her presence, her fierce expression, and the crack of the umbrella ferrule on his head combined to produce a long and somewhat involved fantasy that lasted most of the way home.

The woman beside him was Melissa. She was a prostitute, but there was a man who loved her. His name was Sam. He worked at the Shores. He was a sort of general factotum for Mr. Brotherton who lived in a big, modern glassy house built

238

just above the lake in the West End. Jerry could see the site. It was not far from the White Throne, and Mr. Brotherton lived there with Sam and with a cook whose name was Mrs. Underwood. And from time to time Melissa came storming out to the house, mad as a hornet because Sam had not married her. She worked in Gary.

On days when Melissa was at the house, Mr. Brotherton looked harrassed and anxious. Normally he was a rather suave figure, a little blasé and worldly. He had been everywhere and done everything, and now he had retired to the Shores where he kept open house for young men like Jerry. He had lots of "nieces." Parties sometimes got sort of orgiastic at his house, but on days when Melissa was out there Mr. Brotherton was frankly at his wit's end. When Jerry knocked, Mr. Brotherton would throw open the door as if in desperation and then cheer up a little at the sight of Jerry. "Ah, maybe you can help! Maybe you can calm her down. She's in such a state today I almost hate to leave her alone with Sam." He never had to explain to Jerry who "she" was.

Then they would be in the house, which was all open inside like a gymnasium, and Jerry would see Melissa dressed only in boots, a black bra, and panties. She would be stamping around with a whip in her hand while Sam pleaded with her. "Melissa, honey, I loves you," he was always saying. "See what you can do," Mr. Brotherton would say, pushing Jerry forward in his red bathing suit. It was like waving a red flag in front of a bull. "Here's Jerry, Melissa," Mr. Brotherton would call out, and Melissa would turn away from Sam and advance threateningly toward Jerry. "Who cares about him?" she would mutter. "I'll tan his white ass for him, that's what I'll do."

Then she chased Jerry around the gymnasium, cracking her whip and shouting threats while Jerry tried to placate her with smiles and Sam and Mr. Brotherton called out, "Don't hit Jerry. He likes you." Melissa never actually hit him. His role was to absorb her anger until suddenly there was a great reversal of feeling. Melissa would drop her whip and wail, "Can't nobody love me 'cause I'm bad, I'm bad!" Sam would then take over, crying out, "I loves you, Melissa honey baby." At that point Mr. Brotherton would take Jerry's arm. "Let us leave them alone together, consoling one another for the pains and indignities of life." He would guide Jerry from the gymnasium place to another part of the house. Jerry's last sight of Melissa and Sam was of the two of them sinking together onto a kind of wrestling mat. Next he was being fussed over by Mrs. Underwood. "How are they?" she would ask. "We left them in the process of reconciliation," Mr. Brotherton would say. "But my goodness, this boy has been tuckered out by it all," Mrs. Underwood would exclaim. "You just come along, Jerry," and she would lead him off to her room. "Hop out of that wet bathing suit," she would say, "and lie down on my bed while I get something for you." She would reappear with a bowl of crème caramel or chocolate pudding, and then Jerry would find himself lying on his back being spoon-fed by Mrs. Underwood as she crouched above him, her knees spread. "That's better, isn't it?" she kept saying as she rocked up and down over him, feeding him pudding all the time.

Probably a guy with a mind like his had no business even associating with a girl like Rosalind. But he took her out to dinner at the Spa, and in the middle of the meal, with lamb chop bones still on their plates, he produced the box that contained the ring he had bought. "Here," he said. "I'm giving you your birthday present early." He had the box concealed in the pocket of his jacket.

Rosalind looked at the present he was offering her. There couldn't be much doubt what was inside a box shaped like that, and she seemed hesitant about accepting it. "Don't you want it?" he asked her. Finally she took the box and opened it. "Does it fit?" Jerry asked her. "You shouldn't have bought me a ring," Rosalind said. "Put it on and see if it fits," he said. Then he reached across the table to take the ring from its box and put it on her finger. At that point the waiter appeared to clear away the plates and take their order for dessert. "Getting engaged?" he said with tolerant good humor. Jerry smiled up at him. "It's her right hand," he pointed out, fitting the ring on her finger. It seemed to be a good fit. Rosalind made a fist as she looked at it; then she folded her hands in front of her, hiding the ring with her left hand. When the waiter had gone, she said, "You shouldn't have, Jerry." "I wanted to," he said. "Don't you like it?" He handed her the box. "I got it at Peacock's," he explained, pointing to the label. "Thank you," Rosalind said.

Throughout dessert she seemed subdued. Since his visit to her bedroom, they were still not back to normal, though what was normal now? Almost every day was different. Jerry felt himself changing all the time. Fresh images surfaced in his mind, new thoughts flashed through it, colossal fantasies unrolled within it, and behind all this, sustaining and feeding it all, he could feel that strange sense of power and certainty that had come over him with the first tentative beginnings of their affair. He was not daunted by Rosalind's mood. If she felt depressed about something, then he would cheer her up.

He took her for a drive after dinner. He had the car for the evening and there was no reason not to use it. He headed east along Route 20, driving fast but with both hands on the wheel because Rosalind was sitting a distance away from him. "You don't really want the ring, do you?" he said. "You spent all your money on it," Rosalind said. "So what?" he answered her. "You can keep it in a box if you want. You don't have to wear it. I just thought you would like it." Silently Rosalind began to weep. He slowed down to attend to this. "Sit next to me," he urged her. "Only if you keep both hands on the wheel," she said. He promised, and she slid next to him. "I'm sorry, Jerry," she said. "I shouldn't cry, but you're so nice to me tonight, and my parents are so nice to me, and I just feel terrible." "Because of me," said Jerry. "Because of us," said Rosalind. "You always blame yourself, but it's my fault as much as yours." "I don't think either of us is to blame," he said. "I think it just happened." "And what's going to happen now?" Rosalind asked.

He had speeded up after she moved next to him. Now the needle hovered between eighty-five and ninety as they zoomed past Chesterton. "You're going too fast," Rosalind said. Jerry waved a reassuring hand. "I've gone over one ten in this car." He did slow down, however, because he was approaching a State Police barracks near the junction of routes 20 and 49. This evening he did not need flashing red lights in pursuit of him. That was for other evenings when he and Alec and Phil were out in Alec's jalopy. Then it was fun to get chased around and to hang on tight while Alec skidded around corners and charged up country lanes with branches occasionally scraping the paint. Alec was never caught. He knew every byway in the country. Jerry didn't. Anyway, he couldn't risk his father's Oldsmobile along some of the tracks Alec took to evade the police. And besides, he had important matters to discuss with Rosalind.

"Would you be happier if we just saw each other from now on and didn't meet secretly anymore?" he asked. "We tried that," she said. He hadn't tried very hard, but he didn't tell her so. "We could try again. Anyway, in Chicago there will be no place for us to go." Rosalind thought it over. "Do you mean that?" "If it would make you happier," he said. He felt her kiss his cheek. "Do you think we could?" "We'll do what you want," he said. He felt he was being noble. "Whatever you want." "Jerry, you're sweet." Again she kissed his cheek. "It is what you want, isn't it?" He was not surprised. He was not even disappointed. His power was not broken; it was just going to be exercised in a new way. "All right," he said, "that's the way it will be." He put an arm around her shoulders to hold her closer. He fingered the material of her dress. It was the orange dress he had found in her closet in June. "I like you in that," he murmured. "That truck!" she said.

He swerved to avoid it. There was a reproving blast of the

242

truck's windhorn. The sound diminished in the night, and they were alone with the rush of summer air, the song of tires on concrete, and the whisper of music on the car radio. Beside him he felt Rosalind relax. "I love it when we're this way," she said. She held up her hand to look at the ring he had given her. "Oh, Jerry, I love you, I really do." He nodded gravely. "That's all I need," he told her.

His mother was waiting for him when he got back to the cabin. She was sitting up with a novel. Light fell on her dark hair and on the pages of the book. He caught the glint of light from her diamond ring. As he came in through the screen door she checked her watch. It was not very late. "Everything go well?" she asked. "Sure," he said. "Jerry," she said, "I don't want to upset you, but your father and I have discussed it and we both think that it's inappropriate for you to give Rosalind a ring." He had told her what he had bought for Rosalind. "She's wearing it on her right hand," he said. "Even so . . . " His mother patted the couch beside her. "Let's talk," she said. Rather unwillingly, he sat down.

Rosalind was very nice, his mother said, but she was going to be very rich. "You've been brought up differently," his mother pointed out. "You'll have to work." "I know that," he told her. "Your father has always worked hard for everything we have. And everyone in my family has worked. When Uncle Charles lost his business he went right back to work." Uncle Charles was Polly's father. "It's something I believe in," his mother said. "Your father and I both believe in it. I think it's very bad for people to get things they haven't worked for." "Why are you saying this?" Jerry asked. "Well, I'm afraid you're thinking of marrying Rosalind," his mother said. "I'm not!" he said. "I just gave her a ring. Can't I give her things?" This was too much, he thought. First Rosalind, now his mother. How self-denying was he supposed to be? He stirred resentfully as his mother patted him. "I want you to be happy," his mother said.

So did Rosalind. So did everyone. He had no enemies,

though he was beginning to feel threatened from all sides. "I don't know what you're worried about," he told his mother. "It's just a turquoise ring." He looked at her diamond. "It's nothing like that," he said. He couldn't afford a diamond. "It's what it means," his mother said. "I hope you're not trying to tie Rosalind to you. Do you understand?" This—on the night he had half given her up! "Gee, Mama," he said, "I'm not trying to tie her up." Again his mother patted him. "I'm glad," she said.

The conversation sent him to bed feeling cheated out of something-or-other. They thought your love should be self-less, only it wasn't. For the first time in weeks he had trouble controlling himself in bed. His hands wandered over his own body. He felt his own shoulder, he felt his biceps, he felt his chest. Was he admiring his own muscles, or was he searching for something that wasn't there, something that was missing? A sense of emptiness came over him. The wall next to his bunk was formed by the back of the living room fireplace. He pressed himself against the hard limestone. He felt like crying. He couldn't even give Rosalind a ring without getting into trouble! He could give her nothing. He had nothing to give. Everything was going wrong. He had scared her and now the only way to reassure her was to pretend to be satisfied with nothing. With a kiss. He saw himself slipping back into childhood, kissing and holding hands and driving around the countryside at top speed because he couldn't do what he really wanted to do.

The keys of the car were still in his suit pocket. He could slip out of the cabin and take a drive alone without Rosalind to slow him down. It would be better than this, at least, better than lying half aroused and helpless against the hard stone of the fireplace. Then, suddenly, the idea came to him that he could go to Michigan City and see Elaine again. She had told him to come back. She would understand. Or if she were not there, someone else would be there. They probably worked till all hours of the night. He could be there by one. That was not too late, but after taking Rosalind to the Spa and buying her a ring did he have enough money? He hopped out of his bunk and looked into his wallet. Seven dollars. Frustration overcame him and he felt almost like weeping. Then it occurred to him that he could wake up Phil and they could go together and he could borrow what he needed from Phil. Only he knew that wouldn't work. Phil would turn him down. Even Phil would not understand the urgency. He stood for a moment in the dark, holding his wallet in his hand. All right, he thought, he would have to steal the money out of his mother's purse. He had seen her purse sitting beside the telephone on the desk in the living room. Life was just making him into a criminal, he thought. It was too bad, but that was the way it was. He got dressed, crept out of his bedroom, rifled his mother's purse, and slipped out of the cabin. Down in the road, he released the parking brake of the Oldsmobile, let in the clutch, and waited for the car to drift downhill and around a bend before he started the motor. A few minutes later he was on the highway, following the widening cone of his headlights toward Michigan City.

The new, criminal Jerry Engels awoke late the following morning still dumbfounded by his own audacity. He lay for a while in bed trying to reconcile himself to this turn of events. He felt like an imposter inhabiting his own body, lying in his own bed, and then slowly rising and putting on his own clothes. It was useless to pretend anymore, even to himself, that he was good. He kissed his mother tenderly when they encountered each other in the hall. He felt sorry for her that she had such a son. In her innocence and unawareness, she hugged him, and his sorrow deepened. He went out to the porch, burdened with self-knowledge that he could not pass on to anyone, except perhaps Anne. For the first time since the wedding he missed Anne acutely. With his mother, with Joanne, with Verlene, he had to play the game of being the same old Jerry Engels who just happened to have overslept that morning. With Anne it might have been different. He could imagine himself telling her, "I stole some money from mother's purse last night and spent it on a prostitute in Michigan City." "Jerry!" Anne would say, and he would nod sadly. They would discuss his problem, and Anne would come up with a solution. "You should get married," she might say. Marriage seemed to him the only way out. His character was going to get ruined otherwise. Only who would marry him? He was no bargain. He hadn't even finished high school and his financial prospects were not glittering. He was not a Michael. He hadn't fought in the war, and he wasn't admitted to law school, and no one, least of all himself, thought he was good or wise. Spooning up corn flakes and sliced bananas, he shook his head over his case. It could get you down, he thought.

Rosalind's mood, he was glad to find, was still up as a result of their date of the night before. She was wearing his ring when he turned up at her house that afternoon. She let him see it on her finger, and she played with it, twisting it back and forth as they walked together on the beach. After a while, however, she seemed to notice his lack of animation. "What's the matter?" she asked him. It was the weather, he said. It was a very heavy day. Storms were predicted. A new weather front was supposed to be moving in. Dark clouds were piling up in the west. He thought of his blanket tucked under the pine tree. If they had a real storm it would get soaked, but what difference did that make now? He glanced up at the White Throne as they walked past it, but said nothing. Rosalind noticed, however, and asked him if he felt sorry about what they had decided the night before. "No," he said. "You mean that?" she asked. "Yes," he said. It was some relief to him to feel that he would not be dragging Rosalind down with him. She, at least, would escape. He smiled at her. She took his arm and said she was glad. She'd felt better ever since they had made their decision.

"I'm glad," he said. It was nice to feel he was making others happier even if he couldn't make himself happy.

They walked a long way beyond the White Throne. They passed the slanting signboard that marked the boundary of Indiana Shores. Ahead of them was a kind of no-man's-land. Once there had been a boys' camp in this area. It had failed early in the Depression. Now people came down from Miller and Burns Ditch to picnic on this deserted stretch of beach. They generally came by boat, because the roads into this part of the dunes were nothing but sand tracks. Half a mile ahead of them they could see a cabin cruiser anchored in the lake and a party of people on the beach. Nearer to them they could see a single man, standing in the water. As they approached he moved out of the lake and crossed the beach in front of them. He was naked. Nudists sometimes used this part of the beach. Perhaps a nature club owned some land here because you almost always saw the nudists in the same place. There was even a shack in the dunes that they seemed to use.

This nudist was a fat middle-aged man who sat down on the beach while Jerry and Rosalind passed him. "Boy, if I looked like that I wouldn't take off my clothes," Jerry said. Rosalind's eyes crinkled. "He just likes the sun." "Just the same . . . " Jerry said. After all you had a responsibility not to go around looking like that. "He doesn't expect to be looked at," Rosalind said. Jerry wasn't convinced. You couldn't expect not to be looked at, he said. Anyway, people just shouldn't let themselves get fat and ugly. It was irresponsible, he said. "You're a fine one to talk," said Rosalind. "I don't look bad," Jerry said. He might not be good, but he looked good. "Anyway," he asked Rosalind, "how am I so irresponsible?" "I'm sorry," she said. She slipped her arm around his waist. "I shouldn't have said that." "You shouldn't have," he agreed. Memory of what he had done the night before was still heavy upon him, but Rosalind didn't know about that. All she knew was that he had agreed with her that they would be good from now on. "You *are* depressed," she said to him. He shook his head at this. It was just the day, he said.

Ahead of them in the west they could see the beginnings of a summer storm. A far off mutter of thunder came to them. They kept on walking. The picnickers were gathering up their things and preparing to board their cabin cruiser. The father was wading out to the boat with a child in his arms. The mother was folding up a cloth and putting it into a wicker basket. "We should start back," Rosalind said. In the distance the mutter of thunder grew louder. They strolled on for another hundred yards. Behind them they heard the cabin cruiser start up. It passed them, probably heading for shelter in Burns Ditch. "Maybe we should go back," Jerry said. These summer storms could come very quickly. Already the thunder in the west sounded much nearer. It was no longer a distant mutter along the horizon.

They turned and started back. They could see the nudist again, standing now as he, too, prepared to leave the beach before the storm broke. Behind them they heard the first distinct clap of thunder. It was moving in very fast, "We're going to get caught," he told Rosalind. They began to hurry. The air was still; the lake was almost without a ripple, but you could feel the wind coming, and when you looked back, you could see dark clouds piling higher and higher in the sky. "It's going to be a real storm," Jerry predicted, rather looking forward to the prospect. They hadn't had a good storm in weeks. "We should really get off the beach," Rosalind said. Then behind them they heard the zip-crash of lightning and thunder, and against their backs they could feel the first faint touch of wind. The beach grass swayed, and the surface of the lake smoothed itself out still more. "It's really close," said Jerry.

Now the smooth surface of the lake began to wrinkle, the grass bent in the rising wind, and both Jerry and Rosalind could feel the temperature dropping. It was getting cool for the first time in weeks. "We have to get off the beach," Rosalind said. They were trotting now. "I don't think so," said Jerry. He had never believed it was really dangerous to be on the beach in a storm. They trotted on for another few minutes, occasionally looking over their shoulders at the storm that was now almost upon them. Thunder echoed all along the western sky. The surface of the lake was growing dark, waves were already beginning to break along the shore, and the beach grass was really waving now. Then the storm burst with a colossal crash just overhead, and Rosalind abruptly headed off the beach into the dunes. "We'll get rained on here," Jerry said. "I don't care." She sat down and bowed her head over her knees as if to avert lighting. Rain began to fall.

Jerry looked down with amusement. Her fear of the storm seemed charming to him. He liked the feel of the wind blowing his hair and cooling his body. The rolling thunder was fun. "I'll get our blanket," he said, and went dashing off for the White Throne which was just ahead. He climbed so rapidly that he was sweating in the rain when he reached the top. He seized the blanket, started back to Rosalind, and then stopped. Hurriedly he dug up his Sucret box. No point in leaving it there. Then he ran down the dune in giant strides, hardly able to keep his feet under him he was going so fast. When he rejoined Rosalind he opened out the blanket and spread it over their heads.

Huddled under the blanket like orphans in a storm, they watched the white sand around them grow rain pitted and then turn solidly beige as the rain began to pour down. Soon the blanket was soaked and heavy. Every time a sizzling bolt of lightning struck home somewhere near, he felt Rosalind quiver. He sniffed the ozone in the rain-freshened air and wished she could enjoy this as much as he did. Finally he tossed aside the blanket. "It's worse than nothing," he said, watching her blond hair darken in the rain. Then he kissed her rain-sweet shoulder. "Lightning can't strike us here," he told her. There was a crash just above them. Rosalind clutched his arm in fright. He clutched her in response. Fright turned to passion, passion to love, and before the storm front had moved off over Horton's Dock, Jerry and Rosalind were making love on the sand.

The next day had been chosen for the picnic which they were giving for their U-High friends. Jerry had little chance to be alone with Rosalind. Carolyn Webster arrived before noon, coming by bus and train from her family's summer place up in Michigan. Early in the afternoon two carloads of kids arrived from Chicago.

The lake was still rough and the water sand-clouded from the storm the day before. It was a good day for bodysurfing and for beach games. And it was a good, clear night for a picnic. They roasted hot dogs, they ate potato salad and baked beans. Everything tasted of sand just as it ought to at a beach picnic, but everything was not all right between Rosalind and Jerry. It seemed to him that she avoided him. When they lay around the fire, she would not let him lie with his head in her lap. He saw Ernie Hill stretched out with his head in Carolyn's lap. He saw Carolyn dropping grapes into Ernie's mouth. He envied them. He envied Phil and Rachel, sitting with their arms around each other's shoulders. He even envied Shirley and John Williams, who seemed to be flirting with each other.

Only at the end of the picnic when they were cleaning up the beach did he have a chance to be alone with Rosalind. "We have to talk," he told her. She picked up a Coke bottle half buried in the sand. "Rosalind," he said. "I heard you," she told him. "Please, Rosalind." She looked at him almost without expression. "Please what?" "Please don't be like this." She dropped the Coke bottle into a trash bag. "I feel terrible," he told her. She didn't answer him. "Rosalind," he said again. "Jerry, I just can't talk about it tonight." "But I'm leaving tomorrow for Red Crown," he told her. Maybe he could stay behind, he thought. He could move in with

250

the Forsons while his family was gone. "I'll stay," he said. Then others came back from the cars to collect the trash and he had to pretend to be cheerful.

He cornered her again half an hour later when they had said goodbye to their friends who were driving back to Chicago. "Listen," he said, "I'll come over to your house later on. Meet me on the beach." "No," she said. He could see her point. "All right, but walk with me a little now. I have to talk to you." He walked her down the road away from the Hyatts'. "It hasn't changed," he asserted. What had happened the day before was exceptional. Their new relationship was a steady one. A storm couldn't upset it. She had to believe that. "I don't know what to believe," she said. "Look, I'll tell my parents I just can't go to Red Crown with them," Jerry said. He couldn't leave Rosalind in this state of mind. "No. You should go," she said. "Will you be all right?" "I guess so," she said. "I'll write you," he said. "We'll be gone only five days. I'll telephone you. I'll telephone on your birthday." "All right," she said. He turned to her. "Rosalind, you will be all right, won't you?" She didn't answer. Then she said, "It just seems as if that always happens when we're together." She put her hand on Jerry's chest. "Don't push me away," he said. "I'm not, Jerry, I'm just so confused . . . " She smiled forlornly. "Maybe when you get back I'll be better."

The next morning he left for Red Crown with his family. They stopped in Chicago to put Joanne on the train to Lexington. "Now you promised to answer my letters," she said to Jerry. "I will," he said. He had ignored her so much during the last few weeks that neither of them really believed this. "I bet you won't," she said. He hugged her tightly. "I will," he asserted. "I bet!" she said. Then she climbed aboard the train and waved at them all, and as soon as she was gone he found himself right back in the middle of his thoughts about Rosalind. They kept him preoccupied all during the drive up to Trout Lake. He could kick himself for losing control during the storm. He kept seeing Rosalind's expression the night before. He visualized the slump of her shoulders as she dropped the Coke bottle into the trash bag, and the tone of her voice when she said *that always happens when we're together.* For her they were not treasured experiences. They were *that.* He felt awful as he focused on her plight. She did respond to him, and yet she felt she shouldn't —at least not in *that* way.

He wrote her that evening after dinner at Red Crown. Among other things he told her he wasn't going to enjoy himself worrying about her as he was. Yet, once the letter was finished and he had climbed into bed, he found himself responding to the unfamiliar pine-scented air and luxuriating in the feel of the sheets and pillows and mattresses. Red Crown Lodge was a rustic place but luxurious. The bath towels were bigger and thicker than bath towels anywhere else, the sheets were finer, and the steaks and lamb chops juicier. Even the servants were nicer than at any hotel. They knew your name instantly and changed your towels all the time and turned down your bed for you at night. He realized it was going to be hard to worry intensely when he felt so comfortable and well taken care of.

The Clarks were at Red Crown. They were old family friends who used to visit at the Shores in the summer and have Thanksgiving meals with the Forsons and the Hyatts and the Engels. Then Mr. Clark had been offered a big job at the Mandan refinery and had left the Research Department to make his career in Management. Jerry had stopped seeing the Clarks, so for him it was a real reunion. Also, it was good to have a couple of guys his age to hang around with, though in general life at Red Crown was like a family party. The generations did not separate. On Sunday morning Jerry played golf with his father and Mr. Clark and Ralph. On Sunday evening he sat down to play bridge with his mother and the Larsens. On the porch, other members of the party sang.

Jerry could hear Mr. Garve, a member of the Board, doing his famous rendition of "Old Man River." Then he heard Mrs. Garve say, "Henderson, give us 'Blue Tail Fly,' " and presently Jerry could hear his father singing. His mother raised her head from her cards and looked toward the porch with the expression she got when she was afraid Jerry's father was getting high.

His father did drink more at Red Crown than at home, but so far as Jerry could see no one at Red Crown got really high. People just relaxed and enjoyed themselves on the golf course and at the card tables and on the porch in the evening. When they talked about their work, it was always about events in the past when they had first come to the company. None of the people at Red Crown lived in Whiting anymore, but they had all spent some time there. They talked about life in Whiting back in the 1920s and even earlier. They told anecdotes about the flamboyant Colonel Stewart, who had been ousted as Chairman of the Board at a famous stockholders' meeting at the Whiting Community Center. They talked about Charlie Wagner who had succeeded Stewart and had only recently retired after a long reign. He could no longer use Red Crown, a place he loved. Now he spent vacations at a resort nearby and hung around the Red Crown golf course, hoping someone would ask him to play or invite him back to the lodge for a drink. He was exiled by his own ruling that retired employees could not eat or stay at Red Crown. It was all a little sad and a little funny. He was bored to death in retirement. "I won't be," Mr. Garve said loudly. "We're going to travel." He was planning to take Mrs. Garve around the world. They were going to see everything from Trinidad to Tasmania. Mrs. Garve seemed faintly appalled by the prospect.

When Jerry telephoned Rosalind on Monday she sounded fairly normal. He hung up with the feeling that she was all right, and so he went off with Ralph Clark on a canoe trip they had planned. They portaged into the next lake and only got back to Red Crown at dusk. As they paddled in toward the lodge they could hear the party sitting down to dinner. The sound of the Standard Oil song came floating out across the water:

> Standard Oil! Standard Oil!
> Turns the darkness into light,
> Makes the customer feel all right,
> Standard Oil! Standard Oil!
> Curse it, darn it, can't do without it,
> Stannnnnnnnnndard Oil!

It was an old song that went back to the days when kerosene for lanterns was one of the principal company products. It was a song that went back into his childhood as well. They used to sing it at beach picnics. Hearing it at dusk as he paddled his way back, tired and hungry, made him feel good and happy and peaceful and secure. He knew that although he and Ralph were going to be late for dinner there would be a tremendous amount of chicken or roast beef left for them.

Yet, as soon as he left Red Crown it was as if the excursion had never taken place. Once more he was obsessed with thoughts about Rosalind. All the way home he planned what he would say to her. He had to make her feel secure with him. He had to show her that it would be all right. "All I want is for you to be happy," he would say. "I just want you to be happy. That's all that matters. Just so you're happy." He saw himself gripping her by her shoulders, almost shaking her as he said it. "If you feel guilty, then you're not happy, so we'll never do anything that makes you feel guilty." He had it all in his mind. It would come out sounding right, and she would believe him and stop worrying about herself and about him. Then she would be happy, and he would love her ten times more than he already did because he would have given up something for her.

He was driving. He kept gripping the steering wheel as if

it were Rosalind, and pressing down on the gas pedal to get to her. Several times his father slowed him, but after each interval of tame driving, he gradually speeded up again until his father said, "Is this how you usually drive?"

Then, when they reached the Shores, he found a letter for him from Rosalind. It was very short.

> Dear Jerry,
>   Mother and I have decided to go to New York earlier than we planned. We're leaving tomorrow. If you want to write me, we'll be at the St. Regis hotel. I'm going to tell Mother everything.
>
> Love,
Rosalind.

At first he was just puzzled. When had she written this? What was it all about? He studied the postmark on the envelope. The letter had apparently been mailed in Chesterton on the seventh, the day after he'd talked to her on her birthday. But she'd said nothing about going to New York. Then as the point of her message sank in—*I'm going to tell Mother everything*—he felt shocked. "What's the matter?" his mother asked him. He stared at her dumbly. "Rosalind's gone to New York," he said. "Well, you'll see her when school begins." It seemed to him a very unfeeling response. He went back to his room to think things over.

Rosalind was very close to her parents, of course, particularly to her mother. But still, was it wise to tell Mrs. Ingleside everything? Did Rosalind think her mother was going to be sympathetic about the fact that she was having an affair with Jerry? It seemed very doubtful. Mrs. Ingleside was likely to take a dim view of it. She would probably try to persuade Rosalind to end the affair. She would urge Rosalind to stop seeing Jerry. Maybe she would even forbid Jerry to come to the house. This seemed so probable to Jerry that he could not understand why Rosalind hadn't foreseen it. Then it occurred to him that she had foreseen it. She was turning to her mother for help in disentangling herself from him. She *wanted* her mother to interfere. She felt weak and so she was borrowing strength from her mother.

He sat for a while wondering what he could do now. He had a sense of things falling apart. He couldn't turn Mrs. Ingleside around, and she would probably tell Mr. Ingleside. Where would that lead? He shook his head. He felt strong forces were suddenly at work threatening to separate him from Rosalind. But did she really want that? He couldn't believe it. She wanted to be strengthened, but did she want to be overwhelmed by her parents? Again he shook his head. She had just not been thinking clearly when she decided to tell her mother. It had been a purely emotional decision. One should not make purely emotional decisions. One should think things out ahead of time.

He reread Rosalind's letter. *I'm going to tell Mother . . .* She hadn't yet told her mother when she wrote that, and maybe she still hadn't. Maybe there was still time. He seized pen and paper and began to write:

Dear Rosalind,
Please listen to me. Please don't tell your mother. You don't realize what will happen if you tell her. If you tell her she'll tell your father. I won't be able to see you at all. It will be the end of everything. They won't understand that it's going to be different between us. We agreed about that. They'll persuade you not to see me at all. You don't want that to happen. Please think this over. Please pay attention to what I'm telling you. You have to believe that I'll be different. We'll both be different. You have nothing to be afraid of. I just love you. I don't want anything, but I have to see you. Please believe me, please listen to this. It's wrong to tell your mother. It will just upset her. It won't help, it will just break things up. It won't make you feel stronger or better. I know it won't. Please believe me. You have to listen to me. You should have talked to me before you

thought about doing this. I could have helped you. I still can. You have to wait to talk to me before you tell your parents. Please believe this.

Love,

Jerry.

He reread his letter, decided he could not improve on it, and slipped it into an envelope. His parents were surprised when he said he was driving over to Chesterton to mail a letter, but they didn't stop him. On the way to Chesterton it occurred to him that this letter would take two or three days to get to New York. Speed was essential. He should send Rosalind a telegram, so after mailing the letter he sent a telegram: WAIT UNTIL MY LETTER ARRIVES STOP LOVE JERRY. Then after sending his telegram it occurred to him that the simplest thing to do would be to telephone. Why hadn't he thought of that in the first place? He was already in the car heading back to the Shores when the idea came to him. He turned around and drove back to Chesterton, got some change at the counter of a drugstore, and went to the booth in the back. He emerged twenty minutes later rather frustrated. Rosalind was out. He had left her a message saying that a telegram and a letter were on their way.

The next day he asked Shirley what Rosalind had said before she left. Shirley shrugged. Rosalind had said nothing in particular. He asked Phil the same question. "Are you two having trouble?" Phil asked. "She was thinking of telling her mother," Jerry admitted. Phil whistled. "Why?" "She's upset," Jerry explained. Still, as he thought about it, he came to the conclusion that he had a chance. Probably Rosalind had planned to tell her mother once they were in New York, but in New York she would certainly feel differently about herself. Even the trip to New York would make her feel different. A stateroom on the 20th Century Limited, porters, waiters, taxicabs . . . She'd feel taken care of and insulated. And in New York she would be visiting dress shops and museums and going to plays. What had been happening to her at the Shores during the summer would begin to seem less real. She'd come to the conclusion that she didn't need her mother's help. She'd see that in Chicago once school began, she and Jerry could handle things.

He wrote her again, repeating most of his points. Her mother would just be upset, and there was no point in upsetting her when, from now on, things were going to be okay. Then he went on to describe the succession of autumn storms which were cooling the lake and cutting away at the beach dunes. Some houses in Horton's Dock were threatened, he wrote, and people at the Shores were putting in steel pilings. Nancy had left for Wheaton. Alec Walker was in school. He was seeing just Phil and Shirley these days. He missed her. Summer was ending as it had begun.

Then he got a letter from her. It was as short as her previous one. She had told her mother and now she felt better about things. Her mother had taken it well. "We still haven't decided what I will do. I'll let you know as soon as anything is decided." Again she signed it, *Love, Rosalind.*

Now that the worst had happened, he decided it could not be as bad as he had imagined. Her mother had taken it well. Maybe even her father would take it well. Jerry imagined himself facing Mr. Ingleside and apologizing for what he had done. Mr. Ingleside would be stern, but underneath the talk there would be a man-to-man atmosphere. "I love her," Jerry would say, and Mr. Ingleside would show he understood by saying that these things happened. He would lay down the law, however, saying that Jerry could not be alone with Rosalind anymore. Jerry would accept this. He had no alternatives, after all. He would promise to be on his best behavior with Rosalind. They would see each other at school. He would walk her to within a block of her house. He would not be allowed to telephone her, at first, but gradually her parents would relent, especially if Rosalind began to argue for a limited amount of freedom to see Jerry socially.

They would be permitted to date. He would get her home at ten-thirty or eleven or whatever hour Mr. Ingleside decreed. Then he would be given the right to telephone her for ten minutes every evening. Next they would be allowed to see each other at her house. It would be humiliating in many ways, but he could accept that. He was not proud. He would accept whatever conditions the Inglesides imposed, and gradually as they saw he was really chastened, they would begin to trust him again. Things would get back to normal. He could not imagine things otherwise.

Autumn was in the air. Houses were being closed. Boats were disappearing from the beach. Jerry went to sleep at night to the sound of the wind in the trees and the roar of the lake. He awoke to the same sounds. Leaves on the blueberry bushes were beginning to pinken. The sumacs and gums were turning. Clusters of sour blue grapes hung from the vines. He began to try on clothes he had not worn all summer. He found he had filled out. "This is tight," he said, showing his mother that the jacket of his old tweed suit no longer fit him. His mother authorized him to buy a new suit for school, so he went in town one windy day to do some shopping at Fields. He was looking forward to school, and to Rosalind.

Mrs. Kelly was the only other person waiting for the ten-thirty train. She looked strange and out of season in a mink coat. She was going in town, she explained, because she could not stand the sound of the lake which was practically in her living room. Her house was threatened and Bob Meier and his men were at work that day putting in pilings to try to save the house. "I just had to leave," Mrs. Kelly said. "I decided to go in town and spend some money." She was going to buy herself a set of Wedgwood. She had always wanted Wedgwood. She might not have a house when she came home, but she'd have her Wedgwood. "Now isn't that dumb?" she asked Jerry. He didn't think so. "I didn't try to save anything out of the house," Mrs. Kelly said. She had just thrown on her new mink coat and gone off to town. "We may not even have toothbrushes tonight. Jim will bawl me out if everything's washed away." "Bob will save the house," Jerry predicted. Mrs. Kelly patted his arm. "Well, you're sure a help," she said, "listening to me all the way to town and telling me I'm not dumb to be buying dishes when my house may wash away." At the Randolph Street station she said, "Come on! I'll buy you lunch anywhere you want."

She took him to the Pump Room where they ordered smoked salmon. Mrs. Kelly called for the wine list and ordered a bottle of Montrachet. "I don't know anything about wine," she explained to Jerry, "but that's the most expensive white wine they have so I guess it should be good." The sommelier offered Jerry a sip before he filled the glasses. Jerry sipped and approved of the wine, which tasted like autumn sunshine over cold stone. "Why, it is good!" said Mrs. Kelly when she had tasted. They saluted each other. It was turning into an adventure, Jerry thought.

He was a little high when the meal was finished. Out on the sidewalk in front of the Drake, Mrs. Kelly, who seemed a little high herself, climbed into a cab. "Where you going?" she said, looking back at Jerry over her own fur-clad rump. "Fields," he said. "Come on!" she said, "I'll drop you there." He climbed in after her. "Jerry," she said, "that's just what we both needed—a good lunch." He agreed, though as he tried on suit after suit at Fields he found it hard to make up his mind. Nothing seemed quite right. Nothing seemed good enough. Finally the clerk brought out a pale beige lambswool suit. "Feel this," he said. Jerry felt the cloth. "You'll look nice in it," the clerk suggested. Jerry tried it on. He looked at himself in the triple mirror. The clerk smoothed out a wrinkle across his back. "The jacket fits you perfectly," he said. "But it's 175 dollars," Jerry pointed out. "It's a good suit," the clerk said. "All right, I'll try on the pants," Jerry said. It was twice or three times as much as he was supposed to spend, and it wasn't practical. It wasn't a school suit. His mother would be annoyed when she saw it, but there were just times when you needed to splurge.

He started back to the Shores feeling more hopeful and confident than he had for weeks. He saw himself in his new lambswool suit, escorting Rosalind to a dance. He saw himself proposing to her. Her parents and his would both be opposed, but steadily, calmly, he would whittle away at their opposition. He and Rosalind were in love. They wanted to be married and live together for their whole lives. They would wait until their education was over, but they were engaged right now. They considered themselves engaged. No one could stop them from feeling engaged. And engaged couples had to be allowed some liberty. Even Rosalind would feel this. She would say to her mother, "It's different now, Mother, he's really my husband." Husband. It was a sweet word, Jerry thought. He grew fonder and fonder of it. Husband. He would be a husband to Rosalind. That was what she wanted, a man who was a husband. She was made for that kind of relationship. She would be a wonderful wife. All her tenderness and generosity and niceness would flourish when she knew she was his wife. She would no longer feel guilty or alarmed.

He imagined them meeting for tea at Mr. Brotherton's house, only now Mr. Brotherton lived in Chicago, and Sam and Melissa and even Mrs. Underwood were no longer around. Mr. Brotherton lived in a quiet mansion somewhere along Greenwood or University and entertained young couples like Rosalind and Jerry. He had them to tea and played music and talked about his art collection. Rosalind fitted right into the surroundings. She loved art. And when Mr. Brotherton was called out of the room by some emergency she would get up from the sofa where she was sitting and move to the wall to look at a picture. Jerry would join her. Rosalind would explain the picture as well as Mr. Brotherton could explain it. Then they would drift around the house looking at the things in it, until finally they would come to the threshold of a bedroom. "I wonder what's in here?" Rosalind would say. She would enter of her own free will. Jerry would follow and close the door silently behind him. Then they would be alone in a quiet bedroom with a view of trees in the garden outside, and Rosalind would sit on the bed looking out the window until, almost absent-mindedly, she would turn to Jerry beside her and say, "It's so beautiful and quiet here."

He did not let the fantasy run on beyond that point. It was a law of his fantasies that he could not involve Rosalind in them, except in a sort of preliminary way. She was sacred, at least in his imagination. He adored her, he respected her, he would never frighten her again. From now on his love would be what she wanted it to be. He could not wait to see her in order to make this perfectly clear.

His last week at the Shores was like the first week. He ran, he swam, he sailed when it was calm enough, and while he didn't write to Rosalind as he had in June, he thought of her even more intently. She was a gentle person. He loved her for that, and so from now on his love would be gentle.

On the twenty-fifth he drove into town with his mother, the car piled high as usual, with Jill fitted into a sort of cave in the back seat. His mother took the opportunity to talk to him about Rosalind as they drove together. "You seem happier," she said. "I am," he told her. "Your tiff with Rosalind is over?" "It wasn't that," he said. "We didn't fight." "Then what was all the drama about?" his mother asked. "I was just upset that she went to New York without saying goodbye to me," Jerry explained. His mother fell silent. He knew she didn't quite believe him, but there was nothing he could tell her. Then on the twenty-seventh the blow fell.

He was standing in the Language Corridor of Belfield talking to Ernie and Jim Kaplan when Shirley rounded the corner and came right up and broke into their conversation without any preamble. "Have you heard Rosalind isn't coming back?" she said. It was a phrase he had heard before at the beginning of every school year when some classmate failed to reappear. He could remember his feelings at the beginning of ninth grade when someone told him Gloria wasn't coming back, but then he no longer loved Gloria. Now, looking at Shirley's face and hearing both Ernie and Jim exclaim, "Rosalind!" he felt as if he were going to faint. "Rosalind's not coming back?" Ernie said. In a class as small and close together as theirs had become the disappearance of someone like Rosalind was like a natural disaster, an earthquake. "Gee, Rosalind!" Kaplan said. He and Rosalind had been going to school together since kindergarten. "Did you know this?" Shirley demanded, looking straight at Jerry. He shook his head dumbly. "But why?" Ernie asked. "Where is she going?" Kaplan said.

Her parents had put her into Miss Chapin's school in New York, Shirley said. Shirley had been trying to talk to her for the last few days, but every time she called she had been told that Rosalind wasn't there. This morning, not finding Rosalind at registration, she had called again, and Mrs. Ingleside had finally come to the phone and explained that Rosalind had changed schools. "Wow!" said Ernie. He, too, had been a classmate of Rosalind's since kindergarten. "Wow!" he repeated. Then he turned to Jerry. "What's the deal, Engels?" "I don't know," Jerry said. His hands were full of new gym clothes he'd just bought in Sunny Gym. He dumped them onto the leather couch in the Language Corridor and walked out the door into Scammons Gardens, leaving Shirley and Ernie and Kaplan staring after him.

In the Gardens he began to cry. This was it; it was final. He felt all collapsed inside. He just knew he could do nothing about what had happened. His power was gone. This was just not a situation he could handle. He had come up against something that would not respond to him. Miss Chapin's. What was that? He thought of his cousin Joanne in Ashley Hall. He thought of walls, of bells, of rules. Now they had Rosalind, he thought. He saw her locked into her room at

263

night. But no, Miss Chapin's couldn't be like that. Her parents wouldn't do that to her, and anyway Rosalind had decided it for herself. That was what she meant when she had written that she would write agan when she and her mother had decided what she would do. Only she hadn't written. She had not even bothered to let him know that she would never be back. He had lost all power over her. Those little letters she had written . . . they were like gestures, small waves of the hand as she disappeared from his life.

After a while he became afraid someone would see him crying in Scammons Gardens, so he left by the gate onto Kimbark Avenue. Half an hour later he was in front of the Ingleside house, where he saw cars parked along the curb and other cars in the driveway. Mrs. Ingleside was apparently having a luncheon. He walked slowly up the front path and knocked at the door. Mrs. Moxon answered. He asked for Mr. Ingleside. He was at the University, Mrs. Moxon said. She left Jerry standing in the hall while she went to tell Mrs. Ingleside that he was there. From the direction of the Garden Room Jerry could hear a high, lovely chorus of women's voices. Then Mrs. Ingleside came swiftly into the hall. He flushed as he saw her. "In here," she said, steering him into a little room he had never seen the family use. She closed the door into the hall and then stood with her hands behind her, holding the doorknob. "Oh dear," she said. She was looking elegant in a gray suit with a white frilly blouse. "What do you want, Jerry?" she asked. "I just heard Rosalind isn't coming back," he said. "You got her letter?" said Mrs. Ingleside. "Shirley told me." Mrs. Ingleside heaved a sigh. "You should have had Rosalind's letter by now. . . . Well?" "She shouldn't have to go away," said Jerry. "It's my fault." "I blame myself, too," said Mrs. Ingleside. "I just didn't dream . . . you looked so sweet together." She frowned. She let go of the doorknob and put a hand on Jerry's arm. "It was just wrong, Jerry." There was a coaxing, almost cajoling tone in her voice. "But she shouldn't have to leave

U-High because of it," Jerry said. "I'll leave." It took Mrs. Ingleside a moment to focus on what he was saying. Then she shook her head. "She doesn't really want to come back, and frankly we don't want her to." "But I won't be here," said Jerry. Mrs. Ingleside patted his arm. "It's better this way, Jerry. I'm even glad we could get her into Miss Chapin's at the last moment. Jack isn't, of course. He thinks no one can be educated except at the University of Chicago, but . . . " "She'll miss a lot, being in a new school her senior year." "Well, you'll miss something, too, if you leave U-High." "But I'm the one who should go," said Jerry. "I'm going. She can come back." Mrs. Ingleside shook her head again. "Is that what you wanted to tell me?" she said. Their eyes met. "And that I'm sorry," Jerry said. "I'm sure you are," said Mrs. Ingleside.

She was being nice, but she wanted him to go. In the hall he tried to tell her again that it would be safe for Rosalind to return to U-High. "I won't be here," he said. "It just isn't worth discussing," said Mrs. Ingleside. She opened the front door herself. He hesitated, wanting to shake her hand or do something, but he could tell by her expression that she wanted him out of the house. It wasn't so much that she was angry with him or that she disliked him now. It was just that he was something she wanted out of sight. He wouldn't be welcome there ever again. "Goodbye," he said. "Goodbye, Jerry," said Mrs. Ingleside.

On the train to the Shores he sat by a window, hardly conscious of what he was seeing. Between East Chicago and Gary there were patches of rippled gray water where cattails bent in the wind. In Gary the plumes of smoke from the mills were bent almost flat. In the streets he could see newspapers blowing around. He saw all this, but it seemed remote, as if it were all happening in the past. Those blowing papers could be the same papers he used to see in the streets of Gary during the Depression when everything looked shabby and littered, and he had been driven out to the Shores past long lines of men waiting patiently for something or other: a job, a handout, a bowl of soup. In the old days as he'd watched those out-of-work men he had not been able to imagine what they felt like. Now he knew. They felt beaten, the way he felt beaten.

He was the only person to descend from the train at Indiana Shores. He swung down and as his feet hit the ground he heard the conductor signal the motorman. The train began to pick up speed before it had come to a full stop. Then he was facing the wind as he walked the straight road across the swamp. The ditches were still colorful with blackeyed susans and asters and Queen Anne's lace. When he was in the woods, out of the wind, he saw butterflies. September was butterfly month at the Shores. He saw fritillaries, monarchs, red admirals. Overhead the wind was loosening leaves that came drifting and blowing down.

At the foot of Club House hill he went through the mail. His letter from Rosalind was there. He stuffed it in the pocket of his jacket and turned west toward her house. It looked as it had looked in June when he and Phil had first started coming over to get the court ready for play. Already leaves were piled up against the backstops. The lawn looked untended once more. When he circled the house the wind met him again, and now he could look out at the lake. It was all colors from milky blue to lead gray. It was wild. The roar of waves drowned out even the sound of wind in the trees.

He descended the steps to the beach and walked slowly above the wave line until he found the spot he wanted. There he sat down on the hard sand and opened the letter in his pocket. Rosalind had written that she would not be coming back to U-High. She was returning his ring. which she had taped to the letter. She was very sorry. She hoped he would forgive her. She felt better now that she had told her mother. She knew how he would feel, but she was sure he would feel better eventually. She signed it with her love.

266

He had to hold the flimsy paper in both hands to read it, and even so the wind tore at the paper and made the lines waver as he read them. When he had finished reading, he detached the ring from below Rosalind's signature. Then he put the letter away and lay back with his head on the sand, the ring in his hand. Some clouds were moving rapidly south like the smoke from the mills in Gary. They were torn clouds in a high September sky. He watched them being driven south. He felt almost calm now as he thought of Rosalind. She had never needed him as he needed her.

Then why had she let it begin? He lay for a while looking up at the clouds, the question revolving through his mind. Probably it had been curiosity more than anything else. All boys have a good idea of what it is going to be like. They have visited women like Elaine, but a nice girl has no idea. It had been curiosity, he thought, which led Rosalind to lie back that night in July, moved by his kisses and the warm night and the sound of Malcolm's flute Probably she had felt a slightly detached wonder at what was going to happen, just like the wonder he now felt about what was going to happen to him.

What would it be like to drown? He could hear the lake roaring close by him like a loud, boisterous friend. Would it be painful, he wondered. He had never even felt close to it before. Now he was very close, only for the moment the clouds overhead still interested him, and the feel of the hard beach delayed him, and the ring in his hand seemed like a final link with life. He would have to dispose of it.

He got up and climbed off the beach. He found the place where he and Rosalind had first made love, and then knelt to bury the ring. He patted the sand. Then he stood up. He could feel the full force of the wind, and when he turned to face the lake, he felt almost afraid of what he saw. Breakers for as far out as he could see. He watched them crashing on the bar. Maybe he was such a coward that he could not even bring himself to walk into the water wearing his oxfords and his wool suit? Yet what was there to be afraid of? It was the lake. It had never hurt him, and drowning was supposed to be painless, wasn't it? He would walk out into the lake and begin to swim and the waves would crash down on him and toss him around and his clothes would weigh him down and he would struggle for a while and then just sink. After that he would drift with the currents, sinking deeper all the time until he settled to the bottom out of all that turbulence. It would be easy, he thought. He should do it now.

Rosalind seemed very far away from him. He had never deserved her, and shouldn't have had her, and so now it was right for him to have lost her. It was right. He was doing what was right, and that was all he wanted to do now: what was right. It was right to walk into the lake. Then he felt water surging around his legs, tugging at his pants, as he slogged his way forward. Instantly his trousers were waterlogged, and his shoes filled, and walking began to be difficult. He was floundering just in the wash of the waves, which wasn't right. Then he let himself be swept out as a wave drained down the beach.

He tried to swim forward, ducking under a fresh wave that rolled toward him. His soaked clothes made swimming impossible, however, and he felt himself being swept back toward the beach. It was as if he were a child again in the days when he had been unable to force his way out to the sandbar where the others were holding hands and jumping the waves. It was frustrating. He lowered his feet to get some purchase on the bottom. He would walk forward, or dive forward, until he got to the sandbar. But when he felt for the bottom it wasn't there. The lake was so rough it had dug out the channel between the bar and the beach until he was actually over his head only a few feet from shore. It happened like this sometimes.

So he would have to swim through these foaming waves that rolled over him one after another until he was feeling breathless. He seemed to be underwater most of the time.

Then it occurred to him that he was probably drowning already, right at the shore. It was a shock. How could he drown so soon and so easily! He was such a good swimmer that even with his clothes on he had thought it would take a long time. Now it seemed to be happening almost at once. He was like some waterlogged piece of flotsam, barely able to keep himself afloat. He was drowning like someone who barely knew how to swim. This was a humiliation for which he was not prepared. Ducking as a fresh wave foamed toward him, he undid his shoelaces and got rid of his oxfords.

He could feel the improvement at once. Now he could kick a little. And with his jacket off he could begin to use his arms. And when he had shed his pants, he felt buoyant again. He could swim at last. He was still going to drown, but now he could swim out to meet his fate. He would go down as a swimmer should, far out in the lake, all alone with only the waves and the wind for company. He felt the sandbar underfoot. Good. He was making progress. He dolphined forward, diving under the waves until he was over his head again. Then he began to swim in earnest, and the waves which had overwhelmed him inshore now seemed manageable. In fact he was enjoying his rough, cold struggle with the lake. There was something comradely about it. He thought of Phil, but Phil was not cold. He thought of David Ingleside and Eric and his Uncle Jeremy. They were dead; they were cold; they were the companions for a swim like this. Maybe they were with him in a way. The idea came to him that the dead appeared to convoy a new arrival. He was swimming with them, or maybe toward them. Yes, toward them. It gave him a goal. He would swim out to where they had gone down. Already he felt he was past Eric, who had gone down in the shallows while just a boy. His Uncle Jeremy and David were much farther out. They had been men. He would swim toward them.

Only now his cotton shirt was hampering his movement. He paused to shed it, and then he got rid of his undershirt

and underpants and socks. Why bother with clothes anymore? He wouldn't need them where he was going. The
thought excited him. He saw his naked body growing cold
and numb. He would grow weary at last, and while David
and Jeremy still called to him to come out farther he would
just shake his head in their direction. He would have reached
his spot, not as far out as theirs. He would sink at seventeen
and his body would drift downward into cold, calm water. He
would lie on the clean bottom and little fish would come to
nibble at him. It was another reason for being naked. Clothes
meant nothing anymore . . . only that made him think of the
lambswool suit he had bought at Fields. The pants were
being altered for him now. Abruptly he stopped swimming.

As he thought of his suit the whole world came back to
him. His mother. His father. Anne. A feeling of absolute
despair came over him. He couldn't even drown himself!
They wouldn't let him. And it wasn't just them. It was Phil
and Shirley. It was Rosalind herself. It was his whole family.
Polly. Joanne. Rufus. His grandmother. His uncles and
aunts. They just wouldn't let him do this. He couldn't swim
out and drown as he wanted to drown. He had to go back.

He was treading water, rising and falling with these waves
which were ready to bear him back to the shore if only he
wanted to ride them. From the top of each wave he could
see a host of waves crowding in toward him. He could feel
the wind blowing in his face. Waves and wind and family
all seemed to urge him away from his death. He felt completely helpless. Not being able to die was worse than dying.
In fact dying would be a relief, only the shoreward tug of
his family was too strong, as strong as the waves themselves.
He felt almost angry about it. He had to go on living, even
when he didn't want to live. He looked longingly toward
the wave-shaped horizon. If only he could get out there, but
he couldn't.

He was letting the waves nudge him toward the shore. He
felt no relief at all. Each yard toward the shore took him
farther from what seemed his destiny. He didn't want to go

back. Nothing made him want to go back, except perhaps the waves themselves on which he was now beginning to get rides. He cooperated with them, kicking as they rolled toward him, digging in and riding them for a few yards, and then letting them roll on, leaving him a trough with a fresh wave coming up to carry him further in.

He was standing on the sandbar waiting for the right wave to carry him clear into the beach when he saw two women waving to him from the shore: Miss Smith with her gray curls blowing in the wind, and Miss Jones with her Trilby hat tied down by a scarf. They had spotted him in the water and were waving to him. He did not feel like waving back, but he raised his arm and waggled his fingers. It seemed to redouble their waving, and it occurred to him that they might think he was in trouble in the water. Then the wave he had been waiting for began to crest at the right distance from him. He crouched, shoved himself upward, and felt the wave seize him. He flung out his right hand to break the water ahead of him, and went shooting toward the beach as if the lake itself were flinging him onto the shore.

Then he was standing waist deep at the very edge of the beach and Miss Jones, risking her sensible walking shoes, was following a receding wave across the glistening sand, her hand held out toward him. The wave receded still farther and she saw he was naked. A strange look came over her face. Abruptly she backed up the beach where she stood beside Miss Smith. The two old ladies looked at each other. He looked at them. "Come out!" they called to him above the crash of a new wave. He felt himself thrust forward. Gravel was underfoot, and then the fine sand of the beach itself. Water surged around his thighs. He walked out of the lake, and Miss Smith and Miss Jones turned their backs. He could see Miss Smith getting out of her windbreaker. "Here," she said, over her shoulder. "Tie it around you." He took it from her hands and fashioned himself a clumsy loincloth. The ladies turned around.

"Goodness gracious!" said Miss Smith, "whatever were

you doing all alone in the lake on a day like this?" In a sterner voice, Miss Jones asked, "Where are your clothes?"

He could think of no simple answer to either question, so he just shook his head at the ladies. The brisk wind was drying and freezing his wet body. He began to tremble. "Jerry!" said Miss Smith, "you're turning blue." It did not surprise him. "Where are your clothes?" Miss Jones asked again. "I took them off," he replied. "Where?" She looked both directions along the beach. "Out in the lake," Jerry said. The ladies stared at him. "Out in the lake?" Miss Smith exclaimed. "You went in the lake with your clothes on?" Miss Jones said. He nodded. "Jerry . . . " Miss Jones began, but she was interrupted by Miss Smith. "He's freezing. We can't keep him here talking." She put her hand on Jerry's cold shoulder. "Run down to our house. The door's unlocked. Go in and take a hot shower. We'll follow. Now run!" She gave him a push, and he took off.

His loincloth banged unmercifully as he ran, so after a hundred yards he removed Miss Smith's jacket from around his waist and ran with it over his shoulders. He met no one on the wave-swept beach.

The living room of Miss Smith's and Miss Jones' house was filled with plants. There were African violets, cactuses, succulents, and a Boston fern. There were also vases of dried flowers and cattails and tall grasses. On the mantlepiece and on windowsills he could see odd-shaped bits of driftwood that the ladies had picked up on their walks and brought home for decoration. On the hearth there were less interesting bits of driftwood which they evidently intended to burn. His run had warmed him, but he did as Miss Smith had told him to do. He went into the bathroom and got into the shower stall and let the hot water run. The terrible thing was that it felt good.

He was still showering when he heard Miss Smith's voice raised above the drum of hot water. "Jerry," she called out, "I'm leaving you a towel and a bathrobe." He did not answer, but when he peeked out from behind the shower curtain a minute later he saw she had withdrawn and the door was closed. He turned off the water and stepped out into the steamy bathroom. His fingers were puckered, and his whole body felt soft and tender. He wiped steam from the mirror above the sink and looked at himself for a moment. How was he going to get out of this, he wondered, and was he glad to be alive? Then he dried himself, put on the robe, and went out to face the ladies.

They had lit a fire in the fireplace and made him sit beside it as if he were an invalid. Miss Smith sat down across from him. Miss Jones stood over him. "We just don't understand this," Miss Smith said. "You went in with your clothes on and then took them off in the water?" "Yes," he said. "Then they're lost!" said Miss Jones. "Yes," he said. Miss Smith's face got even more serious. "Now Jerry, you wouldn't have done that just for fun." "No," he agreed. "You might have drowned." "I know." The ladies looked at each other. "Jerry," Miss Smith said, "were you trying to drown yourself?" "Yes," he said. She seemed to collapse at that news. "Oh, we've been so afraid of this! It's what we talked about all the way down the beach. What is it, dear, what is the matter?" He didn't answer her. "Is it Anne?" He didn't understand. "Anne?" "Then it's your mother or father!" Miss Smith cried, "and we saw them only a few days ago." She seemed on the point of tears herself. "What's happened to them?" "Nothing," said Jerry. Miss Jones now intervened. "Jerry, why were you trying to drown yourself?" Miss Smith said, "You mean your family is all right?" "They're fine," said Jerry. Miss Smith heaved a great sigh of relief. Then she focused on Miss Jones' question, which Jerry had not answered. "But if your family is all right, what could possibly be so bad that you'd want to kill yourself?" He couldn't answer her. He couldn't tell her about Rosalind. She had been Rosalind's first grade teacher.

Miss Jones said, "Now, Jerry, you've got to tell someone

about this. You can't keep it a secret." "She's right," said Miss Smith. "Do your parents know what it's about?" "No," he said. "Well, you have to tell them." She reached out to touch his knee. "Jerry, this is very serious. You can't just do a thing like that and keep it a secret from your mother and father. It's too serious. They have to know. They want to help you." "I know." Miss Jones asked, "Have you done something very bad, Jerry?" He hesitated. Miss Smith saved him from answering that by asking him what he was doing at the Shores. His family had moved into town. When had he come out? "I don't remember," he said. He had no idea what time of day it was.

That astonished them. They discovered he had had no lunch. This gave them something to do. They fixed him soup and gave him a ham sandwich which he ate with appetite. Then they discussed what to do about his clothes. They decided they would telephone Eric Anderson and ask him to open up the Engels' cabin. Jerry could get summer clothes there. They would not tell Eric how Jerry had lost his clothes. It took them some time to decide what story they would tell Eric. All the time they were fixing him food and telephoning Eric, they kept coming back to where he was sitting beside the fire. "Jerry," said Miss Smith suddenly, "is it Rosalind? Is that what's the matter?" *She knows*, Jerry thought. "Is it something wrong with Rosalind?" "Rosalind's all right," he answered her, but as he spoke Rosalind's name he began to cry. "Oh, dear!" Miss Smith said.

He could see her through his tears, her kind face blurred and worried looking. "Oh dear," she said again. He struggled to control himself. "Rosalind's really all right," he said, but that only made him cry harder. Miss Smith patted his shoulder. "I understand," she said. Did she, he wondered. Could she know how it felt to lose everything, to feel yourself broken and powerless and lost? "Here," she said, "blow your nose." She put a handkerchief in his hand. When he had dried his eyes and blown his nose he could see both

274

ladies looking down at him with very sorrowful expressions. "I'm just so sorry," Miss Smith said. He nodded over the empty soup bowl in his lap. He felt small. He was not behaving like a man, he thought. "I shouldn't have done it," he told Miss Smith and Miss Jones, not sure whether he was talking about his affair with Rosalind or his attempt to kill himself. "You certainly shouldn't have," said Miss Jones. "You must never do it again," said Miss Smith, and he was not sure what they were talking about either. Yet he felt they understood each other well enough. "You've been nice to me," he said. "Well, remember how nice you were to us when we built this house?" Miss Smith replied. "You helped us put railway ties on the bank and plant things to stabilize the sand . . . Why Jerry, it would break our hearts if anything bad happened to you." "That's why we're so worried now," Miss Jones said. "We want to help if we can," said Miss Smith. "You've helped a lot," he told them, feeling somehow sorry for them as well as for himself. If they didn't know what it was like to lose everything, they'd find out one of these days. Miss Smith or Miss Jones would die, and then the one who had gone on living would take a walk some afternoon, a walk like the one they'd been taking together when they saw him in the lake, and maybe she would stoop down to pick up an interesting piece of driftwood and turn to show it to her companion, and realize she was alone and that she'd lost the person she loved most. Fresh tears came to his eyes as he thought of it. You lost; everyone lost. You had everything, and then you lost it, and it was all so painful that nothing could really ease the pain. Nothing. Nothing.

Epilogue

It was October and the Hard Core was deeply involved in the approaching presidential election. Phil was for Dewey, Stan Wengrowitz for Truman, and Ernie Hill for Wallace. The others argued for the sake of argument. Everyone was convinced that Dewey would win, but they found it an interesting election all the same. Only Jerry Engels had nothing to say about it. When asked, he announced he was for Norman Thomas, but since he had no reasons for his choice, no one tried to argue him out of it. He was left alone to brood over whatever he was thinking about these days. The members of the Hard Core treated him with the consideration due to one whose heart was known to be broken. They let him teeter on the edge of the old sandbox, eat his sandwiches in silence, and stare around at the ruined garden.

Scammons had been laid waste by the hard frosts of October. Some marigold stalks still supported faded blooms. The lilac bushes were acquiring that mildewy look that came over them every fall. The grass was covered with dead cottonwood leaves, and the oak leaves had already lost the faint glow of city foliage. The garden was dead. And in that other garden, the garden of his mind? Were all the birds and the flowers and the girls gone from it?

He wasn't sure. Sometimes, now, a whole morning would pass when he didn't think of his loss of Rosalind, when life seemed almost normal to him. He would wonder why he was feeling so good, and realize he had temporarily forgotten her. Then the very process of examining his happiness would plunge him back into unhappiness. When he remembered her, he felt his life was really over. She was gone, he was crushed, and he had no hope that he would ever win her back. When he remembered her, she usually appeared before him with the outlines of her figure distorted by a sort of heat haze of pain. He did not see her clearly or think about her rationally. She was just there within the haze, separated from him by shimmering grief. It was over, dead, and from now on he would have to drag along half alive.

What helped him was the sympathetic attitude of his classmates, particularly the girls, particularly Shirley. Shirley mourned Rosalind almost as much as he did. He and Shirley had gone to a movie one Friday night and then to the T-Hut where Shirley said, "I really miss her." Jerry squeezed Shirley's hand to show that he echoed the sentiment but felt it too deeply even to say that much. He couldn't really talk about her, but he listened gratefully while Shirley told him about a letter Rosalind had written. He felt that letter was partly meant for him, because in it Rosalind emphasized the fact that, though she missed her U-High friends, she was enjoying Miss Chapin's. She said it was wonderful to be in New York with the ballet and the opera and concerts and art galleries. Jerry felt she was telling him she had found consolation, just as he was finding consolation from listening to Shirley and from feeling that Shirley was no longer critical of him. She had forgiven him his manifold flaws, his lounging around, his taste for low company like Alec Walker. He wasn't sure why he was forgiven, but he thought it was probably because Shirley recognized that, in spite of everything, he had really loved Rosalind. She was being nice to him, anyway, and he felt very grateful. At last they had reached the kind of intimate, brother-and-sister friendliness for which they were destined. When he walked her back to the Forsons that Friday night, he hugged her on the doorstep and felt her hugging him in response. "Thanks," he said when they parted, and she nodded tenderly before going inside. He walked home feeling better than he'd felt all fall.

He didn't think he could ever fall in love again. What he looked forward to now was simply a tender, affectionate, brotherly relationship with girls like Shirley. He would have sisters, spiritual sisters, for the rest of his life. He envisioned a series of kind, intelligent, attractive girls he would get to know so well that eventually he could reveal the great sorrow of his life. He would tell them about Rosalind, and they would understand that his heart was broken, but he needed feminine company. They would grow to love him as a brother, and he would be able to tell them everything about himself. The prospect cheered him up and helped him in those black moments when he suddenly remembered his loss of Rosalind and felt his whole inner world collapse.

These were terrible moments when the ground gave way. It was like stepping into wave-dug holes on the sandbar and feeling a towering breaker about to collapse on top of him. He cowered at such moments, feeling he couldn't take anymore of this, but then the fresh breaker of grief deluged him and he surfaced once more, roughed up by the experience but not really harmed. He thought maybe he was a shallow person whose feelings were not deep enough to cause permanent harm. He had evidence for this. He felt he had loved Rosalind as deeply as he could and that his heart was broken by his loss of her, but somehow he was not really harmed by his broken heart. Evidently it was just not a very deep heart. It could break without destroying him. He had survived, a little bruised here and there but capable of being comforted, and not just by Shirley.

He drew comfort from all the girls in class. They knew his loss of Rosalind was too fresh to make him want to go out on dates, but he felt they were waiting, and when he was finished with his despair he could turn to them and they would accept his invitations. He would take one girl to a movie and another to a dance and a third to a party at Carolyn's, and gradually he would be reintegrated into life. It was just a question of time. Already he was noticing the girls more keenly as they went about their daily affairs, and what he noticed confirmed his most basic feeling about life, which was that girls were much nicer than boys. He liked boys, but when he heard Phil and Ernie and Stan arguing about the election he couldn't help but feel that boys or men (or whatever they were at this age) were rather boring compared to women. It was nice, of course, that someone cared who was elected President, but he was tired of hearing the matter discussed. It was not so much his broken heart that kept him from participating in these discussions as his absolute lack of interest in the outcome of the election.

If he had learned anything from all that had happened to him during the summer, he had learned that he was probably not like most boys. He didn't care about politics, he didn't care about making money, he didn't care about learning things or finding out how to do things, he hardly even cared about cars or winning races. He felt surprised and even a little shocked by this sweeping lack of interest, but he couldn't pretend it was otherwise. He was bored by most of the things that interested other guys. The one point he had in common with them was that he cared about girls, but now he was not even sure he cared about them in the same way that other guys did.

He thought of girls as a kind of blessing. When he saw a girl like Betty Lomax walking through Belfield Hall with a fresh flower tucked into her hair, he felt like kissing her out of gratitude for having bought that flower and put it in her hair. It seemed to him such a nice thing to do, and only girls did such things. They wore flowers, they changed the color of their lipstick, they put on new skirts, and bought big safety pins which they pinned to their skirts because it was fashionable now. Every time he saw a decorative safety pin, or a new locket, or a fresh shade of nail polish, he felt how wonderful girls were. And they did such things not just to attract boys but because they liked flowers and bright clothes and ingenious pins and lockets and bracelets. They enjoyed their own beauty and took pleasure in sort of passing it on with a flower added to their hair and a fresh color added to their fingernails.

Boys were not like that. The best-looking boys had mixed feelings about their own looks. He did, and he was sure John Williams felt the same way. Boys just did not welcome beauty the way girls did and add a flower to it and pass it along. Boys tended to mess things up, the way he had messed up Rosalind and had dreamed of messing her up even more. Boys argued, boys fought, boys were always trying to assert themselves and make out with girls. He was finished with that. He was putting sex behind him. When he started to date again, the first thing he would make clear to the girl was that she need have no fear. He would show her that he liked her for herself alone and not for anything that he could get from her. He would hug her as he had hugged Shirley, tenderly and chastely, and if she got a little carried away with the experience, he would kiss her a bit. He was not going to be prudish or standoffish, but he would certainly not try to take advantage of anyone. He would behave himself from now on. He would just be friendly.

Friendliness would be his chief emotion. It already was. He felt friendly toward everyone. Being brokenhearted much of the time had widened his sympathy, and he now paid much more attention than before to classmates like Betty Lomax who had never been popular or well liked. She had beautiful hair, but she was a little overweight, and her skin was a bit sallow, and she was not particularly witty or bright. Yet he felt she was a sweet and lovable person, and he smiled at her in the hall and talked to her when he had the chance.

281

He felt he was brightening her life, just as the sight of that white flower in her hair brightened his life. That was how it should be. People ought to brighten each other's lives without trying to get something in return.

At home he had reached a new level of intimacy and tenderness with both his father and mother. He had had to tell them how he lost his suit and his practically new oxfords. Miss Smith had insisted he tell his family. She had even telephoned after driving him to the South Shore, so that when he arrived home his mother knew most of what had happened. He had never felt her so passionate and emotional as when she had let him into the apartment—he had lost his key, of course, and had had to ring the buzzer in the lobby. "Jerry," his mother had said when she saw him at the door in his cotton trousers and a sweater. "Oh Jerry!" She had wept, and so had he. They were still weeping when his father came home from work.

He would never forget the look that came over his father's face when his father learned what he had tried to do. There was consternation, horror, shame . . . everything. Uncontrolled, purely emotional actions simply wiped out everything that Mr. Engels believed in, and for a moment Jerry felt he had come closer to killing his father than to killing himself. He had tried to reassure his father. "I was never close to it," he said. "I was never in real danger." His father, still holding his briefcase full of papers, simply crumpled up. "Oh my God," he said, tears starting to his own eyes, and to Jerry it sounded like a deeper and more solemn echo of what his father had said when Anne came home that Christmas with a nickel in her pocket. When either of his children did something he simply could not understand, he fell back almost helplessly, calling on a God he didn't believe in.

That night he had come into Jerry's room when Jerry was already in bed with the lights out. Mr. Engels was in his pajamas, smelling strongly of the cigarettes he had been smoking all evening and the bourbon highball or highballs he had had after dinner. He sat on the edge of the bed and sought for Jerry's face with his hand. "I couldn't bear to lose you," he said. "You haven't," said Jerry, "and it won't ever happen again." His father patted his cheek. He sat heavily on the bed, still desolated that this should happen in his family, and that his son should have so misbehaved with a girl like Rosalind. "I couldn't bear to lose you," he said again, still patting Jerry. Then he had gotten up. He couldn't tear himself away, however, and he had stood over Jerry for a minute or more trying to say something. "Maybe I brought you up wrong," he said at last. Then he sat down on the bed again. "I didn't have a father myself," he said. "Maybe I haven't known how to bring up a son."

It had made Jerry feel, for once in his life, older than his father. "What I've done isn't your fault," he said. "You brought me up differently. I just   ." He was going to say that he just couldn't control himself, but it seemed so untrue he had to stop. He felt very controlled at the moment, though it was not self-control but the kind of control he had felt at times during his affair with Rosalind. It was the control that came from feeling powerful. It surprised him. He thought his power was gone but somehow it was there, although it felt different now because he was so sad and sorry for his father and mother and Rosalind and the Inglesides and himself. "I'll be all right," he told his father at last. Rosalind might not be all right, and his father might not be all right, and the Inglesides might not be all right, but he would be. He didn't think it was much comfort to offer his father, but it seemed true, and when he said it his father responded by kissing him.

Since then he and his father had been close without talking very much, whereas he and his mother talked a great deal. Gradually he told her most of what he had done during the summer. She was disapproving but curious. She had what he had begun to think of as a fundamental feminine trait, an emotional curiosity about what was going on inside people. She wanted to know more, and so he told her more and more about his feelings for Rosalind and even incidents in their affair. He told her when it had begun and how Rosalind had reacted and how he had reacted. She shook her head. "She's such a nice girl," she said. "She is!" Jerry agreed. "She's the nicest girl I'll ever know." He and his mother looked at each other almost tragically. "There'll never be a better girl than Rosalind," he said.

This was just true. When he thought of girls now, he accepted the fact that he had lost the best one. He thought probably his new interest in slightly plain and unpopular girls stemmed from the fact he wanted to avoid close comparisons with Rosalind. The prettier the girl the more he would be reminded of how beautiful Rosalind was, and he didn't want that. Also, it had occurred to him that if he fell for a plain girl, it would be easier to control himself with her than with Rosalind. She would not be so tempting.

Though he accepted the fact that he would never fall deeply in love again, by late October he had begun to think he might fall somewhat in love. He seemed to be the sort of person who fell in love, and if he fell for another girl his life might begin to be normal and almost happy once more. He would be admitted to one or another of the state universities he was going to apply to. He would go on. Life was not completely over. Yet he was sure he would never forget Rosalind, and though his memories of her might grow more peaceful and happy, they would never be painless. Still, maybe even that would happen. Maybe the ache and pain would disappear. Already some sharp images had begun to emerge from the heat haze of pain in which he generally saw her. Now he could remember a fading palmprint on a cold window pane, a pair of smooth legs striking sparks in the water, and a turquoise ring buried in the sand. It was all a little sad, but it was beautiful. It was a pleasure to remember it, just as it was almost a pleasure to feel the hot surge of despair on these crisp autumn days.